# POISON IN THEIR HEARTS

# Books by Laura Sebastian

*For Young Adults*

### THE ASH PRINCESS SERIES

*Ash Princess*

*Lady Smoke*

*Ember Queen*

### THE CASTLES IN THEIR BONES SERIES

*Castles in Their Bones*

*Stardust in Their Veins*

*Poison in Their Hearts*

*For Middle-Grade Readers*
*Into the Glades*

*For Adults*
*Half Sick of Shadows*

# POISON IN THEIR HEARTS

## LAURA SEBASTIAN

DELACORTE PRESS

This is a work of fiction. Names, characters, places, and incidents either are the product of the author's imagination or are used fictitiously. Any resemblance to actual persons, living or dead, events, or locales is entirely coincidental.

Text copyright © 2024 by Laura Sebastian
Jacket art copyright © 2024 by Lillian Liu
Jacket frame used under license from Venimo/Shutterstock.com
Map art copyright © 2023 by Virginia Allyn

All rights reserved. Published in the United States by Delacorte Press, an imprint of Random House Children's Books, a division of Penguin Random House LLC, New York.

Delacorte Press is a registered trademark and the colophon is a trademark of Penguin Random House LLC.

Visit us on the Web! GetUnderlined.com
Educators and librarians, for a variety of teaching tools, visit us at RHTeachersLibrarians.com

*Library of Congress Cataloging-in-Publication Data*
Names: Sebastian, Laura, author.
Title: Poison in their hearts / Laura Sebastian.
Description: New York : Delacorte Press, 2024. | Series: Castles in their bones ; book 3 | Audience: Ages 14+ | Summary: In a final stand against their mother, the princesses Daphne and Beatriz join forces with allies across Vesteria and use the magic of the stars, while battling ancient prophecies and secrets from their past.
Identifiers: LCCN 2023027349 (print) | LCCN 2023027350 (ebook) | ISBN 978-0-593-11824-5 (hardcover) | ISBN 978-0-593-11825-2 (library binding) | ISBN 978-0-593-11826-9 (ebook) | ISBN 978-0-593-81522-9 (international ed.)
Subjects: CYAC: Princesses—Fiction. | Sisters—Fiction. | Kings, queens, rulers, etc.—Fiction. | Prophecies—Fiction. | Fantasy. | LCGFT: Fantasy fiction. | Novels.
Classification: LCC PZ7.1.S33693 Po 2024 (print) | LCC PZ7.1.S33693 (ebook) | DDC [Fic]—dc23

The text of this book is set in 11.6-point Sabon MT Pro.
Interior design by Megan Shortt

Printed in the United States of America
10 9 8 7 6 5 4 3 2 1
First Edition

Random House Children's Books supports the First Amendment and celebrates the right to read.

Penguin Random House LLC supports copyright. Copyright fuels creativity, encourages diverse voices, promotes free speech, and creates a vibrant culture. Thank you for buying an authorized edition of this book and for complying with copyright laws by not reproducing, scanning, or distributing any part in any form without permission. You are supporting writers and allowing Penguin Random House to publish books for every reader.

For Krista Marino,
who helped me spin an idea into a story

# The Royal Families of Vesteria

## Bessemia
### House of Soluné

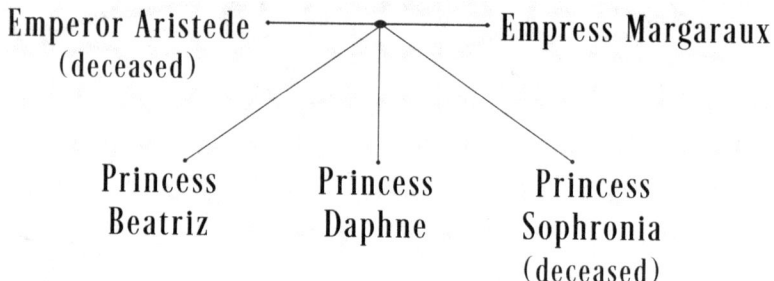

## Friv
### House of Deasún

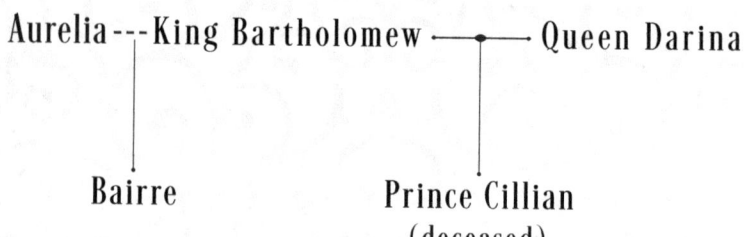

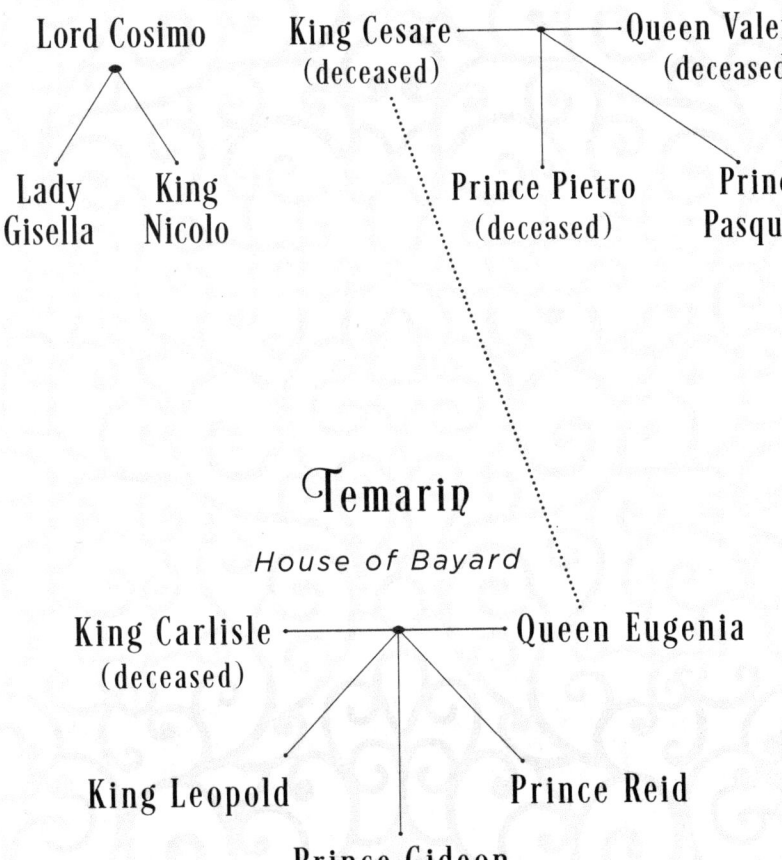

# Daphne

From where Daphne sits in the little-used parlor in the north part of Eldevale Castle, she has a perfect view of the main gate. All morning while she sips her tea, people have come and gone. A mail carriage, a produce wagon, several dozen courtiers on horseback off to shop on Wallfrost Street or hunt in the woods. Each time anyone approaches the gate, Daphne sits up straighter, but each time she slumps back again, disappointed.

"Something's wrong," she says aloud, stirring her tea and tearing her gaze away from the gate just long enough to glance at Cliona and Violie. The three of them have been sitting around the small table by the window since breakfast, Cliona and Violie chatting and Daphne pretending to listen. If she were less distracted, she might find herself bemused at what fast friends Cliona and Violie have become despite how different they are—Cliona the privileged Frivian lady secretly working for the rebellion her father is the head of, Violie a common-born Bessemian maid who'd been secretly working as a spy for Daphne's mother until her allegiances changed. If Daphne were less distracted, she might even be unnerved by their friendship. After all, not long ago, Daphne considered both girls her enemies.

Not anymore, but Daphne is far more accustomed to having enemies than friends, so the adjustment is taking some time.

"That's what I've been saying," Cliona answers with a sigh. "But something tells me *you* aren't talking about King Bartholomew's plan to move the court to Notch Castle a month ahead of schedule."

That distracts Daphne for only a second before she shakes her head. "The winter has been unseasonably warm, as I understand it. Perhaps he means to enjoy the weather better."

She looks out the window again as two armored guards ride through the gates. Alone.

"Beatriz should have been here by now. She should have been here two days ago," Daphne says.

It's been a week since Daphne used stardust to speak with her sister in Bessemia, and Beatriz said she was on her way to Friv. She was taking a more circuitous path than Daphne followed when she left home to come to Friv—Beatriz had to in order to avoid their mother, who would surely be looking for her—but even allowing for delays, she should be in Friv by now.

"Any number of things could have delayed her," Violie says, setting her teacup down. *No,* Daphne thinks. *Not Violie.* Even in her own thoughts, Daphne should think of her by the alias she's living under, and as far as most of Friv knows, the girl sitting across from her isn't Violie, she's Sophronia—Daphne's other sister, who was murdered by a mob in Temarin. Daphne needs to get used to calling her by her new name—or at least Ace, the nickname Violie had as a child that they agreed Daphne could call her to avoid suspicion—but it's more difficult than she thought it would be. The idea of the ruse still sours Daphne's stomach when she thinks about it, about someone else living Sophronia's life, but it was the only way to keep Violie from being executed for attempting to murder Queen Eugenia—a murder Daphne herself ended up committing.

Daphne shakes her head. "No, I just . . . I feel it. Something is wrong."

"Are you thinking to use stardust again to talk to her?" Cliona asks, frowning. "I can ask my father for another vial, but I think he's getting suspicious."

Daphne considers it for a moment. "No," she says finally. "It'll be the same as it's been the last few days, and I'm not keen on facing the repercussions again."

Every time Daphne has tried to talk to her sister via stardust, all she's heard is an empty silence that makes her head ache like one too many glasses of ale.

Though she tries not to, Daphne can't help but wonder if that's what would happen if she tried to speak with Sophronia. If Beatriz has joined their sister now. The thought makes her sick.

*No. Beatriz isn't dead. She can't be. Daphne would know if she were.*

*Wouldn't she?*

Daphne pushes the thought from her mind. Beatriz has always managed to take care of herself—wherever she is, whyever she's delayed, she can handle it. In fact, Daphne thinks, she pities anyone foolish enough to try to stand in her sister's way. She forces her gaze from the window and focuses on Cliona.

"Why would it be troubling that the court is moving to Notch Castle early?" she asks, grasping onto the distraction offered.

"Because," Cliona says, adding another spoonful of sugar to her tea, "in the centuries-long history of the Clan Wars, Notch Castle alone remained impenetrable. Its location, in the mountains, makes for a natural defense, and everything about the castle amplifies that. If Bartholomew was anticipating an attack, that would be the smart place to be."

Daphne considers this. Bartholomew would be right to anticipate an attack, either one of her mother's making or one designed by Cliona's father and his rebels. Daphne suspects the former, but she knows Cliona is more concerned by the latter. Friends they may be, but Daphne knows Cliona doesn't tell her everything the rebels are planning. This, though, Daphne can guess at herself. With Daphne and Bairre married and public support high in their favor, the rebels have every reason to remove King Bartholomew from power, paving the way for Daphne and Bairre to eliminate the monarchy altogether from their new thrones.

"If my mother realizes I've turned against her," Daphne says slowly, "there will be far worse places to be than Notch Castle."

Cliona's jaw tightens, and Daphne sees her mind turn. "The rebellion believes Friv is facing bigger threats than a power-hungry upstart empress," she says finally.

"You mean your father believes that," Daphne infers.

Cliona's father, Lord Panlington, is King Bartholomew's closest friend, but he's also been working to dethrone him for the last two decades. When Cliona doesn't protest, Daphne looks to Violie for support—after all, few people know what the empress is capable of better than Violie, who worked as one of her spies until recently—but Violie is distracted, gazing out the window with a furrowed brow.

Heart leaping, Daphne follows her gaze, but just as quickly her heart sinks again, leaving dread in its wake.

A single rider on a pure white horse pulls to a stop at the gate, but it's his livery that gives Daphne pause. He's dressed head to toe in Bessemian blue.

"Your mother's sent a letter?" Violie asks.

"A letter would come in the post," Daphne says, setting her teacup down and getting to her feet. She can think of very few things that would entice her mother to send her personal messenger to Friv, and none of them are good.

Daphne and Cliona make their way to the entry hall without Violie in case the messenger is someone who might have seen Sophronia before and recognize that Violie isn't her. As soon as they reach the castle's ground floor, they meet Bairre, flanked by two guards, coming from the entry hall. When his eyes meet Daphne's, she knows that whatever he has to say is bad.

"My mother sent a messenger," she says, so he doesn't have to. "We saw him come through the gates."

Bairre nods. "He said he would only speak to you and Sophronia," he tells her.

Daphne's stomach sinks and she spares a glance at the guards accompanying him. "I'll speak to him, but my sister is feeling indisposed. I'd rather not disturb her."

Bairre nods, understanding her meaning. As he leads her through the hall to the entry, she glances sideways at him.

It's been a week since they were married, but she still has difficulty thinking of him as her husband, difficulty thinking of herself as someone's wife. Perhaps that is, at least in part, because the marriage hasn't been consummated.

It was an agreement they came to on their wedding night, a protective measure to use to dissolve their marriage if the empress tries to turn it into a weapon against them.

"If she's received word Sophronia is alive, she'll want to verify that," Daphne says. "Of course, we expected as much, didn't we?"

Bairre gives a terse nod, but neither of them says that so much of their plan hinges on chance. And it will be a lot easier if the messenger is one Daphne doesn't recognize, one who is unlikely to recognize that Violie isn't, in fact, Sophronia.

Any hope of that, though, is dashed as soon as Daphne steps into the entry hall, finding herself face to face with Bertrand, a man who has been in her mother's service for as long as Daphne can remember.

"Your Highness," Bertrand says, bowing deeply.

"Bertrand," Daphne replies with a smile, leaving Bairre's side to step toward him, extending her hands to take his, like she's greeting an old friend. "How good to see you again."

"And you as well, Princess Daphne," Bertrand says, squeezing her hands before releasing them. He glances over her shoulder, but when he sees only Bairre, Cliona, and the guards accompanying her, he frowns. "Is Princess Sophronia not with you?" he asks.

"*Queen* Sophronia isn't feeling well," Daphne says. "I'm sure she'll be terribly disappointed to miss you, but the . . . trauma of escaping Temarin and all that passed since has taken its toll on her, I'm afraid. I'm loath to interrupt her rest for any reason. You understand, I'm sure."

Daphne punctuates those last words with another squeeze of his hands, this time pricking his skin with her poison ring.

"Oh," Bertrand says, jumping and pulling his hands out of Daphne's. She frowns.

"Are you all right, Bertrand?" she asks, all wide-eyed worry. "You look exhausted—unsurprising, since you've had quite a journey."

Bertrand shakes his head, like he's trying to clear it. When he looks back at Daphne, his eyes have gone glassy and unfocused. "Exhausted," he echoes. "Quite a journey."

Aetherleaf powder leaves its victims drowsy and suggestible, precisely how Daphne needs him for her plan to work.

"I thought as much," Daphne says with a sympathetic smile. "Why don't you rest up for a bit? Perhaps Sophronia will be well enough to say hello at supper."

"Supper," Bertrand says.

"Yes, exactly," Daphne says, glancing up at Bairre and giving him a small, triumphant smile. "Come, I'll show you to a guest room."

As Daphne escorts Bertrand down the hall, giving no outward indication of exactly how much weight he is putting on her arm, she monitors his steps, the rate of his breathing, and the speed of his motions. When she's satisfied the drug has fully taken hold of him, she glances over her shoulder to ensure that Bairre and Cliona are keeping the guards at a safe distance. Satisfied, she begins to speak in Bertrand's ear, her voice low and soft.

"You enjoyed a lovely dinner with Queen Sophronia and me. Didn't you think she looked well?"

"She looked well," Bertrand echoes, nodding his head.

"She was so thrilled to see you, Bertrand. She asked after your wife and son back in Bessemia and you had a lovely conversation about them. Sophronia is always so thoughtful that way, isn't she?"

"Thoughtful, yes," he says.

"But you had far too much to drink at dinner. It's a bit embarrassing how in your cups you became—when you wake up in the morning you'll be anxious to leave the castle at once to return to the empress."

"Return to the empress."

"And when you see her, you'll tell her how you saw Sophronia, how well she looked, how you spoke with her and she was just as you remembered her. Can you do that?"

"Can do that."

"Tell me, then," Daphne says. "What will you tell my mother?"

"I saw Queen Sophronia," he says, his voice drowsy but the words clear. "She looked well, we spoke and she was just as I remembered her."

"Very good, Bertrand," Daphne says.

He is leaning too heavily on her now, all but dragging her to the stone floor.

"Guards," Daphne says over her shoulder. "I fear Bertrand had a bit too much to drink on his journey. Will you help him to bed before he hurts himself?"

"Of course, Princess," one guard says, sweeping forward to relieve her of her burden.

# Beatriz

The first thing Beatriz becomes aware of is the scent of sea air—Cellarian air, she knows right away. She resists the urge to open her eyes and alert anyone around her to the fact that she's awake, instead taking an inventory of her body and surroundings. Distantly, she remembers coming to consciousness several times before, brief stabs of awareness—a rocking carriage, Gisella's intent face, trying and failing to speak before the darkness dragged her back under.

Now everything is still. She is no longer in a carriage but in a room. Listening closely, she hears birdsong telling her it's daytime, and the faint crashing of waves against the shore. Her head feels like it is stuffed with cotton, but slowly events trickle back to her. She remembers standing in her mother's bedchamber as the empress told her she'd be leaving for Cellaria to marry Nicolo. She remembers escaping the Bessemian palace through a secret tunnel with Pasquale, Ambrose, and Gisella in tow. She remembers Daphne using stardust to communicate with her and Beatriz promising her they'd be reunited in Friv soon.

But she isn't in Friv—she's in Cellaria. She sifts through

more hazy memories—staying the night at an inn and sharing a room with Gisella, the world turning fuzzy and the dim sound of Gisella's voice: *For what it's worth, I am sorry.*

Beatriz can draw constellations from those dots—Gisella was working with the empress; she poisoned Beatriz and brought her back to Cellaria on the empress's orders. Once again, Gisella betrayed Beatriz because *of course she did.* Beatriz had been a fool to expect any different.

Without opening her eyes, Beatriz knows exactly where she is—back in the Cellarian palace, just as her mother told her she would be, though her mother didn't tell her the whole truth of the reason she needs Beatriz here. Her mother's empyrea, Nigellus, did, though. When he started training her to use the magic that made her an empyrea as well, he let slip the truth of the wish her mother made before she and her sisters were born, and the condition placed upon it. In order for the empress to take control of all of Vesteria, her daughters would need to die on the soil of the lands she wished to conquer, by the hand of someone who called that land home.

Sophronia was killed by Temarinian hands on Temarinian soil.

Daphne would need to be killed by Frivian hands, in Friv.

And Beatriz... she needed to die here, in Cellaria, at the hands of any number of people who must want her dead.

But there is a piece of the empress's plan missing, and when Beatriz realizes what it is, her stomach drops. *Pasquale.* Pasquale already is Beatriz's husband, even if in name only, and if her mother intends for her to marry Nicolo, she'll need Pasquale dead. The last time Beatriz saw him, he and his paramour, Ambrose, were disappearing into a second room at the inn, but if Gisella poisoned her on the empress's orders, she must have gone to their room next and . . . the thought makes Beatriz's stomach lurch. No, even for Gisella, that is too far. Pasquale is her cousin and Beatriz knows she loves him, even if she did betray him, too, turning both Pasquale and Beatriz in to Pasquale's father, the late King Cesare, so that Nicolo, Gisella's twin brother, could be named Cesare's heir in Pasquale's stead. But stealing a throne is different from stealing a life, isn't it? Surely there is a line even Gisella won't cross? Even as she thinks it, though, Beatriz fears she's wrong and that she is, once again, giving Gisella far more credit than she deserves.

"I know you're awake."

The voice cuts through the lingering fog of Beatriz's mind and she opens her eyes, staring at the white canopy hanging over her bed, then taking in the room around her—ornately decorated with carved oak furniture, polished to a gleam, red-and-gold brocade textiles, and gold-framed paintings of the Cellarian seaside adorning the walls. Only after taking in each detail of the room does she allow herself to look at Nicolo.

He's slouched in a chair near the door, blond head propped up on an elbow and dark brown eyes resting heavily on her. He appears to be more sober than the last time she saw him, when she spoke to him after wishing on a star in Bessemia, but otherwise he looks much the same. Still handsome, still haughty, still looking at her like he knows exactly what she's thinking.

He doesn't, of course, but Beatriz knows it's better to let him assume as much.

"Barely," she says, blinking around the room and letting uncertainty flicker over her face. "Where am I?" she asks. She might know, but the less capable he believes her to be, the easier it will be to escape. She needs to get out of Cellaria, she needs to find Pasquale and Ambrose—because they *cannot* be dead—and she needs to get to Daphne in Friv.

"Come, Beatriz," Nicolo says with a knowing smile. "Do you think I didn't see you take in your surroundings, even before you opened your eyes? You know exactly where you are."

It's true. Even if Beatriz hasn't been in this room before, she can guess where it is and what it's for. *Who* it's for.

"The queen's chambers in the Cellarian palace," Beatriz says, sitting up. Very well, if playing the oblivious fool doesn't suit her, perhaps she can bluster her way through. "Have you surrendered, then? Is Pasquale fast asleep in the king's chambers, as he should be?"

A small, amused smile flickers at Nicolo's mouth. "Unfortunately not," he said. "Cellaria has reached an . . . agreement with Bessemia."

Beatriz raises her eyebrows. "My mother intimated as much the last time I spoke to her," she admits. "But I didn't think you foolish enough to believe I'm content to be traded like a rare coin."

"Your contentment hardly matters," Nicolo says with a shrug.

Beatriz tightens her jaw and looks at him, the clever boy

she thought herself falling for turned ruthless king who's kidnapped her, who intends to marry her against her will. If he won't hear no as an answer now, what will happen when she's forced into their marriage bed? That isn't the Nicolo she knew. Many things about him might have been proven a lie, but that?

"And you?" she asks, lifting her chin. "You once risked your own safety to save me from your uncle's forced attentions. I thought that noble of you, but perhaps you're more like him than I realized."

That gets a reaction. Nicolo's hands grip the armrests of his chair and his eyes flash. "You know better than that, Beatriz," he says, his voice low.

"Do I?" she asks, letting out a harsh laugh, though inside she's taking note of what, exactly, Nicolo's triggers are so that she can use them against him. "All I know, Nicolo, is that you're kidnapping me and forcing me into a marriage I do not want."

His eyes flash again, but after a second he takes a breath and gets to his feet, reclaiming his cool facade. "It won't be the first time you married someone because you had to," he points out. "That one was unconsummated as well, just as ours will be until you choose otherwise."

"Oh, how magnanimous of you," Beatriz snaps. "Allow me to extend a courtesy of my own—my mother is not your ally; whatever agreements she's made with you were broken before she finished uttering them. And if I didn't find myself thrust into the middle of it, I would relish seeing her destroy you and your snake of a sister."

Nicolo only laughs, making his way out of the bedroom and into what Beatriz sees is a sitting room. She cranes her neck to watch him open the door that must lead to the hallway, giving her a glimpse of the guards standing outside. "You're still underestimating me, Beatriz," Nicolo says. "You really ought to know better by now."

Beatriz is not a stranger to being under house arrest in the Cellarian castle, though this time the decree isn't official. When she tried to leave the room shortly after Nicolo, they told her that the king had instructed she remain inside *for her safety*. She isn't sure whether they truly believe that or not, but she knows she can't get past them by force.

Luckily, she doesn't need to.

She paces the suite of rooms, inspecting the bedroom, the sitting room furnished with two brocade sofas, a low-burning fireplace, and a writing desk, and the adjoining dining room intimately decorated with a small, round table and two high-backed chairs.

While the décor is lavish, it strikes Beatriz as a blank slate, lacking any personal touches. Unsurprising, she supposes, since it's very likely no one has resided here since Pasquale's mother's death nearly a decade ago, but after a mere half hour of exploring, she has nothing else to do. No books to read, no letters to write—even needlepoint would be welcome to keep her from going mad waiting for the sun to go down and the stars to rise.

But after what feels like several lifetimes, they do, and

Beatriz looks out her window, at the sprawling city of Vallon below, at the ink-dark sea stretching out beyond that, and the sky above it all, littered with stars.

As she searches the constellations, she thinks of Nigellus, her mother's trusted empyrea, who had the rare gift of pulling down stars from the sky to bring wishes to fruition. A gift Beatriz herself has, even if the lessons he gave her were cut short before they really ever started. He was adamant that it was a gift that should be used only under the most dire of circumstances to preserve the stars that remained in the sky— a finite resource that had already been drained in the millennia before either of them was born. If Nigellus could see her now, ready to wish on another star regardless of the consequences, would he support her? After all, Beatriz's magic works differently from his and differently from every other empyrea's—when Beatriz wishes upon a star, it reappears in the sky within a night or two like nothing happened at all.

As soon as she begins to think about Nigellus, memories sharpen into focus of the last time she saw him. He told her that he believed her magic was killing her each time she used it, and when she told him she didn't care, that she would still use it to defeat her mother and protect her sister and the rest of Vesteria from her plots, Nigellus grew angry. She remembers him at his telescope, wishing upon a star to take her magic away by force because, as he said, she couldn't be trusted to wield it. Beatriz tried to stop him, the two of them fighting in his laboratory until, in a burst of desperation, she broke open the vial of poison she'd meant to use on her mother and smeared the paste into his open wound, killing him instantly.

She pushes the image of his lifeless face from her mind and focuses on the constellations moving across the sky, searching for one whose meaning suits her motives tonight.

There's the Hero's Heart, symbolizing bravery, but that doesn't feel right. Wishing her way out of this situation is hardly brave, but Beatriz cares less about that than finding Pasquale and Daphne.

The Tiger's Tail signals revenge, and that is tempting, especially when she thinks of Nicolo's smug face and Gisella's hollow apology, but ultimately, Beatriz decides against using it. Revenge can come later; now she needs safety.

She finds it in the Clouded Sun, the sign for solace.

Remembering how wishes have affected her in the past, she braces her hands on the windowsill, clutching it tightly as she picks out a star from the constellation, focusing on one at the end of a sunray.

"I wish I were with Pasquale, wherever he is," she says aloud, readying for the same pull of magic she felt when wishing to escape the Sororia.

It doesn't come. The words she speaks are only that—words.

Nausea rises up, but it has nothing to do with the side effects of magic she's become so familiar with. If her wish isn't working, does that mean Pasquale is dead? *No,* she can't think of it. Perhaps there is some other explanation, something she can figure out once she's left Cellaria.

She tries again, finding another star, on the edge of a cloud this time.

"I wish I were with Daphne, in Friv," she says, thinking that a more precise location will help the stars grant her wish.

But that, too, fails, and Beatriz finds herself in exactly the same place, still in Cellaria, and still trapped. A queasy feeling sinks into her gut, bringing with it a knowledge Beatriz can't face.

Desperately, she searches out another star—this one in the Glittering Diamond.

"I wish my dress were blue."

It's a shallow wish, one so small that it could be accomplished by stardust, but when Beatriz looks down and finds her dress still Cellarian red, she backs away from the window, her hands shaking, forced to acknowledge the truth.

Her magic is gone.

# Violie

Violie doesn't think she will ever get used to being treated as royalty. Even in Friv, a court that stands on ceremony far less than any other in Vesteria, people still bow and curtsy as she passes. As a child growing up in a brothel and then later as Empress Margaraux's spy masquerading as a servant to keep watch on the empress's daughter Sophronia, she was accustomed to being looked past and ignored. In both roles, being ignored was what kept her safe. But now, no matter where Violie goes, people are always noticing her, even when they pretend not to.

It's somehow both better and worse when she's with Leopold. Even before he became King of Temarin at fifteen, he was the crown prince and attention was his birthright. Now, living in exile from the country he was meant to rule, he draws attention like the sun each time he walks into a room, making it seem especially ridiculous that he managed to play at being a commoner for as long as he did, when he and Violie escaped Temarin after the siege that killed Leopold's wife, Sophronia. Leopold's identity is known by everyone at Eldevale Castle now, though, and when Violie walks beside him, more people than ever are looking in her direction, but fewer seem to be looking directly at her, and that at least is a comfort.

"And so when Bertrand wakes up this morning, he'll think he had dinner last night with Daphne and Sophronia—the Sophronia he remembers, not, you know, *me*," she explains, catching Leopold up on their plan to trick Bertrand into reporting to Empress Margaraux that Sophronia is well and truly alive.

Leopold nods, but Violie notices the furrow in his brow. It's almost always there these days, getting deeper whenever they discuss Sophronia, or how Violie has taken on her identity.

He agreed to the plan Daphne concocted after Violie was arrested for attempted murder, even helped to identify her as Sophronia during her trial, but Violie knows that it bothers him perhaps even more than it bothers her. After all, he was in love with Sophronia, and he has only just begun to mourn her. Calling Violie by her name, treating her in public like his wife, can't be easy.

To say nothing of the fact that the woman Violie attempted to murder was his mother, Queen Eugenia. There was no love lost between the two of them—Eugenia had been largely responsible for the siege that killed Sophronia, and her aim had been to kill Leopold as well—but she was still his mother. He doesn't blame her—or Daphne, who succeeded where Violie fell short in ending Eugenia's life—but Violie knows part of him must mourn her.

And so, no, calling Violie by Sophronia's name, treating her in public as his wife and queen, while knowing who she is and what she is capable of, can't be easy for Leopold.

Even now, his arm feels stiff beneath her gloved hand as they take a turn around the snow-draped garden—one of the few places they can speak privately, assured that anyone who can overhear is too far away to make out their whispered words.

"Then the plan is succeeding," Leopold says. "Does he want to meet with me as well?"

"He didn't say," Violie tells him. "But he'll be gone in a matter of hours, and as long as you keep your distance until then, you won't have to worry about keeping up the pretense."

"I like to think I'm getting good at the pretense," Leopold says. "I'm certainly getting enough practice."

They pass another couple on the garden path, a middle-aged man and woman Violie recognizes as Lord and Lady Kilburrow, who stop to bow and curtsy and exchange small talk for a moment before continuing on their way. When they're out of earshot, Violie looks at Leopold.

"You are getting to be a better liar," she admits, unsure why paying that compliment digs beneath her skin. It's the truth, but that makes it worse. Until recently, Leopold lacked the guile to convincingly lie about liking someone's haircut, let alone commit to holding up the delicate tower of lies keeping them, and more specifically her, safe. She hates that she's done that to him, dragged him into a web of deceit he has no business being in, but as soon as she thinks it, she corrects herself.

*She* didn't drag him into this, and in fact she's given him every opportunity to run. The empress laid ruin to everything he knew. She took his country, his wife, and even in some ways his mother. The empress is responsible for destroying the spoiled boy king he was, and Leopold himself is responsible for the man who has risen in his place.

It isn't a tragedy, she tells herself, looking at him again. Rogue snowflakes stick in his burnished bronze hair, and there is a sharpness to his regal features that she still isn't quite used to seeing there, but it suits him.

*Oh, if Sophronia could see you now,* she thinks, with an echoing stab of guilt.

When a servant finds Violie in the rooms she shares with Leopold to tell her that Bertrand has woken up, she hurries to his room, meeting Daphne just outside the door. Daphne gives her a tight smile, but her gaze quickly goes to the guards around them.

This is a delicate balancing act to pull off—the guards will need to see Violie go into Bertrand's room as Queen Sophronia, so that they don't find it strange that she never saw the man while he was here, but Bertrand must not see Violie as anything more than a servant.

The key, Daphne and Violie have worked out beforehand, is in the clothing. Because it's winter and even the halls of Friv's castle are freezing, Violie is wearing an elaborately embroidered ermine-lined velvet cloak—part of the wardrobe King Bartholomew gifted her with when she first claimed to be Sophronia. But beneath the ornate cloak, she's wearing a plain gray wool dress, not unlike the ones the castle servants wear beneath their far less ornate cloaks.

Daphne enters the room first and Violie follows, shrugging off the cloak as she steps inside and folding it over her arm. Daphne shrugs her cloak off as well, revealing a violet velvet gown whose bodice is embroidered with silver flowers, embellished with crystals—the gown's ornateness serving to highlight just how plain Violie's is by comparison—and passes it to Violie as soon as the door closes, allowing Violie to hide her own cloak beneath Daphne's.

Now, alone in the room with Bertrand, whose glassy eyes and sallow skin do make him look like he indulged in far too many pints of ale the night before, it's easy for Violie in her plain dress to melt into Daphne's shadow, a lady's maid accompanying her princess.

It isn't only the clothes that accomplish the transformation; Violie's posture shifts as well, going from upright and regal to ever so slightly slouched. Instead of keeping her chin lifted and boldly meeting the gaze of everyone around her, Violie keeps her eyes on the floor. Her steps become timid. Even her breathing shifts. Once again, she lets herself fade into the background, into a role she's missed, where all she needs to do is avoid notice and pay attention.

Bertrand bows when he sees Daphne but doesn't spare Violie more than a passing glance. She's careful not to stare outright, but she manages to look him over out of the corner of her eye, noting not just the queasy green tinge to his skin but the flustered expression and the way he wrings his hands in front of him.

"I'm afraid I lost my head last night, Your Highness," he tells Daphne, eyes downcast.

Daphne smiles benevolently. "Oh, you're hardly the first foreigner to fall prey to Frivian ale—it's dreadfully strong stuff, I'm afraid," she says, waving a hand. "Queen Sophronia couldn't join me to see you off since she and King Leopold had a prior engagement in town, but she sent along her wishes for a safe journey."

Bertrand's face grows redder. "It was very good to see your sister again, Princess—and you as well, of course, but after the news from Temarin, we all believed she was . . . well, the stars have truly given us a miracle, haven't they?"

Violie internally lets out a sigh of relief, though she keeps her features placid.

"Indeed they have," Daphne says, relief practically rolling off her as well. "Sophronia also has a letter she hoped you would pass along to our mother, when you see her. I do hope we can trust you to keep it safe."

Daphne pulls a rolled letter from her pocket—one she and Violie labored over the night before, arguing about the details of Sophronia's handwriting and word choice until it was perfect.

But Bertrand doesn't move to take it, his brow creasing as he drags his gaze from the floor and looks at Daphne. "I'm not certain I understand, Princess," he says slowly, eyeing Daphne with a wariness that raises alarm bells in Violie's mind.

Daphne, however, doesn't lose her smile. "Well, as you said, my sister's being found alive and well is nothing short of a miracle. I know the empress trusts you, Bertrand, but surely she will want to hear from Sophronia herself?"

"Well, of course, Princess Daphne," Bertrand says,

stumbling over the words. "It's just . . . would Princess Sophronia not prefer to give her mother this message in person?"

Ice trickles down Violie's spine, and Daphne's shoulders go rigid.

"Forgive me, but your mother is only a day away now, she should be here tomorrow morning. Is this message something that cannot wait until then?"

"My mother is coming here," Daphne says slowly. "To Friv."

Daphne can't hide the shock in her voice, and Violie can't blame her. Leopold raised the possibility when they concocted this plan, but Daphne was adamant—the empress had never in her life left Bessemia. She rarely even left the capital city of Hapantoile, convinced that if she was gone from court for any stretch of time, she would find herself at the center of a coup that had threatened since she ascended to a throne she had no true claim to sixteen years before. Traveling to another country seemed less likely than the stars going dark.

"Yes," Bertrand says slowly. "Surely we discussed it last night, Your Highness?"

Daphne, for her part, recovers quickly, regaining her smile. "Oh, I'm sure you must have, Bertrand, but I suppose I'm not quite accustomed to Frivian ale myself. It must have slipped my mind."

"Of course, Your Highness. Your mother is looking forward to seeing both you *and* your sister. I was sent ahead to announce her arrival and see that there was a room prepared for her at the castle. She should arrive tomorrow."

"Tomorrow," Daphne says, the word barely making it out through her clenched teeth.

"Yes, Your Highness."

"Well, that is . . ." Daphne swallows down what Violie suspects are any number of very unpleasant adjectives before bracing herself for a lie. "*Wonderful*. I look forward to receiving her. *We* look forward to receiving her."

Without waiting for an answer, Daphne sweeps from the room, and Violie trails after her, struggling to keep from breaking into a run.

# Daphne

Daphne doesn't stop walking down the castle hallway, even when Violie shouts after her.

Tomorrow, she will see her mother again.

Just weeks ago, the news would have been welcome. Daphne wanted nothing more than to run into her mother's arms, desperate to fulfill the conditions the empress placed on her love, desperate to be exactly the person her mother wanted her to be, desperate for her approval and the pride the empress dangled like a carrot, always just out of Daphne's reach.

Now, though, the thought of seeing Empress Margaraux—of being seen *by* her mother—fills Daphne with dread. She knows that the empress will take one look at her and see all of her betrayals and her failures as clearly as if they were spelled over her skin.

Daphne was meant to be driving Friv to a civil war that would weaken it so the empress could conquer the country with ease. She was meant to kill Leopold as soon as she discovered him, and his younger brothers, Gideon and Reid, along with him. She was meant to be her mother's most loyal spy and saboteur, helping her take over the continent of Vesteria and return the Bessemian Empire to its former glory. She was meant to be proving herself a worthy heir to that empire.

Instead, Daphne found herself working with the Frivian rebels *and* King Bartholomew to make Friv stronger. She not only let Leopold live but helped to keep his brothers safe and out of her mother's grasp. Daphne turned against her mother and joined with the people who were supposed to be her enemies, and her mother will never forgive her for it. Daphne knew this—she was aware of her actions and the cost and she does not regret anything, but the thought of being in her mother's presence again causes a thorned vine to tighten around her heart.

A hand comes down on her shoulder and Daphne whirls around, fist clenched, prepared to strike, but when she sees Violie's concerned face, Daphne shakes her head, focusing on the most pressing issue at hand.

"You and Leopold will leave as quickly as we can manage it," she says, shrugging Violie's hand off and turning to start walking again, this time with a purpose. She takes a left down the corridor that leads to the guest wing where Violie and Leopold's room is.

"We're expected to run?" Violie asks with a harsh laugh, falling into step beside her. "You can't be serious."

Daphne grits her teeth. "What is it you imagine will happen if my mother arrives to find you here, pretending to be Sophronia?" she asks, her voice dripping with derision. She isn't angry with Violie, not really, but Violie makes a perfect target for the panic roiling through her, and for her part, Violie takes Daphne's temper in stride. "Do you think she'll call you her daughter, go along with this charade that you're truly Sophie?"

"Honestly?" Violie asks. "Yes, I believe that is exactly what she will do."

Daphne stops short, turning to look at Violie in shock.

"What is the alternative?" Violie presses on. "That she calls you a liar? Accuses you of supporting a person who, in her version of events, was responsible for the coup that killed the real Sophie?"

When she says it outright, Daphne recognizes that she has a point.

Violie continues. "She can't say any of that without implicating you, and right now, she needs you to take Friv."

Daphne nods slowly. "I finally married Bairre," she says, less to answer Violie and more to give voice to her thoughts. "She's one step closer to getting what she wants, but she still needs me until Friv is hers for the taking."

"Exactly," Violie says. "And she isn't coming here to destroy either of us, not yet. She's coming here because she knows that whether or not Sophronia is truly alive, she has lost your allegiance. She's coming here to get it back."

The idea knocks Daphne off-kilter. For as long as Daphne can remember, her mother has held all the power—something Daphne didn't mind, unlike Beatriz. Daphne was always content to follow her mother's orders and dance to any tune she decided to sing for the chance of some slim scrap of approval, and the secondhand power that came along with it. The thought of her mother arriving on her doorstep to woo Daphne back to her side is as ludicrous as it is terrifying.

After all, it's one thing to stand against the empress from hundreds of miles away, through underhanded plots and secret alliances. It is going to be another thing entirely to stand in her mother's presence and disobey her. Daphne feels sick.

Violie must see it in her expression, because she looks at Daphne half with annoyance and half with pity—Daphne isn't sure which is worse.

"We'll have to proceed carefully, then," Daphne says, straightening her spine and fixing her gaze straight ahead. "And we can be assured that she isn't coming alone—she'll have her spies and her assassins with her, and I think we know better than to underestimate what she's capable of."

"We'll need to meet with Lord Panlington," Violie says, as if reading Daphne's mind. Lord Panlington, Cliona's father, is the head of Friv's rebel faction, which has been working to dethrone King Bartholomew and do away with Friv's monarchy altogether, returning the country's rule to the individual clans who governed two decades before. Though until recently, Daphne considered the rebels her enemies, who could occasionally be useful, she and Lord Panlington not long ago made an alliance that Daphne still doesn't understand the depth of.

But even if she doesn't trust Lord Panlington, she knows they have a common enemy in her mother.

"And you," Daphne says to Violie, "will need to leave, with Leo."

Violie scoffs. "I just told you—"

"My mother may not reveal your ruse in front of everyone, but she is still claiming, at least publicly, to be ruling Temarin only temporarily until Leo or his brothers are found.

She ordered me to kill all three of them already, and just because I failed in that doesn't mean she'll have simply given up. And as for you—suffice to say my mother has done away with enemies who have made themselves far less of a nuisance to her than you have."

"I can handle anything your mother sends my way," Violie replies coolly.

Daphne shakes her head. "And can Leo?" she asks.

Violie is quiet for a second. "He's been training in sword fighting with Bairre and he is improving." She sounds like she's trying to convince herself as much as Daphne. They both know that the only fighting Leopold was meant to do in his life was with blunted swords and opponents eager to let him win, and it will take more than a couple of weeks to improve that. When Daphne doesn't reply, Violie sighs. "Fine, yes, you're right," she snaps.

Daphne pauses, her mind turning. "It would be very suspicious if you fled now, after you've received word that your beloved mother is coming to see the daughter she believed dead," she says. "My mother loves a good spectacle. She'll want a public reunion, with tears and embraces."

Violie shudders but then nods. "I can do that."

"Knowing my mother, she'll doubtless whisper some warning in your ear during the performance," Daphne says before pausing and glancing sideways at Violie. "She knows your own mother is a weak spot; I don't doubt she'll use that against you."

Violie nods, but her jaw is tight. Daphne knows that Violie's mother is ill—so ill that the hope of healing her was what led Violie to become the empress's spy in the first place—but beyond having told her that, Violie doesn't speak of her mother.

"You and Leo can stay a day, maybe two, before you leave. In secret to ensure that you aren't followed. I'll come up with a story to explain your absence."

"And where would you have us go?" Violie asks, resigned.

Daphne doesn't speak for a moment. "Something is wrong with Beatriz, I know it," she says. "And I also know that my mother's behind it. Stay long enough to see if she tips her hand and gives us some idea of where Beatriz has gone. If anyone can find her, I trust it's you."

# Violie

"The empress is coming here?" Leopold asks slowly, looking between Violie and Daphne with a furrow in his brow.

"Tomorrow," Daphne confirms. She paces the length of the sitting room in the quarters she and Bairre now share, which also contain two separate bedrooms and studies, plus a dining room. The rooms are fit for the new crown prince and princess of Friv, sumptuously decorated with heavy oak furniture upholstered in intricately woven brocade, but there is no trace of Daphne in the stark Frivian designs, and Bairre likely sees the renovated space as a waste of money. He certainly looks uncomfortable, even as he lounges on the plush velvet chaise near the fireplace, eyes locked on Daphne as she paces.

"So then why aren't we panicking?" Leopold asks. He's standing near the fire, hands clasped behind his back, and Violie knows he's resisting the urge to fidget.

"Oh, we are," Daphne mutters with a strangled laugh.

"Panicking while we do nothing, though," Leopold says. "We aren't running?"

"We aren't running," Violie confirms before repeating

her earlier conversation with Daphne. "Empress Margaraux is a stranger here, and Friv doesn't like strangers. We can use that against her," she finishes.

"*We* can use that against her," Daphne corrects, gesturing between herself and Bairre. "*You*," she adds, gesturing to Violie and Leopold, "can knock her off-balance and then go to find Beatriz."

Violie resists the urge to roll her eyes. She knows Daphne has a point about their leaving Friv. The empress may be a stranger in a strange land, but she'll have an entourage of devotees at her back—several of whom Violie would wager are assassins. The longer Violie and Leopold stay in Friv, the more danger they're in. But they aren't the only ones.

"She'll want to kill you, too," she tells Daphne and Bairre. "Both of you."

"I can handle my mother," Daphne snaps.

"Can you?" Violie volleys back, almost regretting the words when Daphne winces. But she knows she's right—Daphne's loyalty has only just shifted, and Violie doesn't trust that it won't shift back as soon as the empress gives Daphne just a bit of that approval she's always craved. By the look on Daphne's face, she doesn't trust herself, either.

Bairre clears his throat, breaking the silence. "I don't pretend to know much about what the empress is capable of, but from my understanding, she isn't a fool. It would be foolish to begin a siege of Friv while she's in its capital, without an army to support her."

"Are we certain she doesn't have an army?" Leopold asks. "She very well may have one following, lying in wait until she gives them a signal."

"I discussed that possibility with Cliona," Daphne says. "She's speaking to her father now about sending a scouting party to ensure that my mother and her entourage are alone." She glances at Bairre. "I assumed that would be better than getting your father up to speed on things. As far as he's concerned, there's little reason to view my mother as anything but that."

Bairre shakes his head. "My father may be a lot of things, but he isn't oblivious. And he didn't become King of Friv by underestimating his enemies."

"He became King of Friv because a powerful empyrea made a pawn of him," Daphne replies. "And speaking of your mother, have you spoken to her about this development?"

"My mother still hasn't returned from Lake Olveen," Bairre says. "But I'll add this to the long list of things I need to discuss with her."

At the top of that list, Violie imagines, is the fact that Bairre's mother, the empyrea Aurelia, arranged to have Leopold's younger brothers kidnapped, and, after Daphne and Leopold rescued them, she gave Cliona instructions to kidnap them again. To what end, no one seemed to know.

"The point I'm trying to make," Daphne says with a sigh, "is that your father tends to be far too compassionate, at the expense of common sense. I say that as someone who has used that compassion against him several times now, as did Queen Eugenia, not to mention Cliona's father, who Bartholomew considers his closest friend despite the fact that the man is the head of the rebels looking to overthrow him."

Bairre opens his mouth to argue but quickly closes it

again, which is just as well. Violie doesn't think he can argue against anything Daphne just said, which Bairre should know better than anyone, considering he himself joined the rebellion against his father.

"Fine," Bairre says. "We'll leave my father out of this. For now."

Daphne continues to pace, her steps growing more agitated. "And once Violie and Leopold leave, they can search for Beatriz."

"Are we sure that's wise?" Leopold asks.

Daphne stops short, whirling to face him with blazing eyes. "You think Beatriz is dead?" she asks, her voice suddenly dangerously low.

"I didn't—"

"You're wrong," Daphne snaps. "If Beatriz were dead, I would know it. I would feel it, like I felt Sophie."

Violie doesn't bother to point out that Daphne was magically connected to Sophronia when she was killed. Logical as it is, it won't accomplish anything. And Violie doesn't know that Beatriz is dead, or that she isn't perfectly safe and simply delayed by a spot of bad weather, but if her dealings with the empress have taught her anything, it's to assume that the empress is always one step ahead of everyone else.

"I only meant that we don't know where to look," Leopold says carefully, the way someone might speak to a ravenous wolf.

"I think," Violie interjects before Leopold can get himself into deeper trouble with Daphne, "that your mother wouldn't be coming to Friv if she didn't have reason to believe she had

Beatriz and therefore Cellaria secured. Cellaria is as good a place to start looking as any."

Daphne holds her gaze a moment longer, her jaw tightening, before she gives a sharp nod.

"When Violie and Leopold leave, you should go with them," Bairre says to Daphne, who gives a snort of laughter. "I don't see what's funny about the suggestion. Your mother wants you dead, you know that. And even if she doesn't accomplish it here, in person, it's imminent. I know you want to save Beatriz and avenge Sophronia, but perhaps the best thing to do is—"

"Run?" Daphne interrupts with a scoff, turning to glower at him. "And tell me, Bairre, would you be running with me? After all, my mother will need you dead as well, in order to take Friv."

Bairre doesn't answer, instead looking away, toward the fire in the hearth.

"No," Daphne infers. "You won't run, because you aren't a coward and neither am I."

"I won't run because Friv is my home," he corrects.

"And it's mine, too," Daphne says, before she snaps her mouth shut, both she and Bairre surprised at the proclamation. She hesitates a second. "Friv is my home now too," she says, more firmly this time. "Even if there is no hope for my sister, even if it means putting myself in danger, I won't let my mother take Friv as well."

For a moment, Bairre doesn't speak, but finally he pushes to his feet and closes the distance between him and Daphne in two long strides, wrapping his arms around her just as

Daphne presses her face into his chest. Violie glances away, meeting Leopold's awkward gaze. Leopold clears his throat.

"We should get some sleep—I'm sure we'll need it to face tomorrow," he says, standing up.

Violie follows him out the door, glancing back at Bairre and Daphne, still caught up in their embrace, Bairre's hand tracing gentle circles on Daphne's back.

The sight of them sends a pang through her that Violie can't quite place, even as she closes the door and steps out into the hallway.

# Beatriz

Beatriz spends the next day shut away in her room, with breakfast and lunch delivered on trays by servants who don't meet her gaze, let alone speak to her. It reminds her of the last time she was under house arrest in Cellaria, but then she had Pasquale at her side to bolster her and keep her sane and strong. Now, though, she's entirely alone with nothing but her very loud thoughts to dwell on.

Her magic is gone—why, she doesn't know, but she has a feeling it's to do with Nigellus, since she hasn't made any wishes since he died. Was it possible that one of his wishes to strip her of her magic actually worked, even if he never fully got the words out before he died? Or perhaps this is the stars' way of punishing her for killing him. Perhaps they've seen fit to finish what Nigellus began.

But even the stars themselves aren't strong enough to keep Beatriz in Cellaria. If they've taken her magic, Beatriz needs to take it back. And in order to do that, she first needs to find a way out of this room.

The sun outside her window goes down, and not long after, a knock sounds at the door—her dinner, she assumes, but she doesn't respond and the servant doesn't wait for her to. But the door opens, and instead of a single servant carrying a dinner tray, five servants file in one after another, heading toward the dining room attached to her quarters with table linens, wine goblets, fine china and silverware, and a feast fit for an army. Beatriz watches them set up, dread growing. After a day spent trapped in a loop of her own thoughts, she doesn't have the strength to engage in another mental game of chess masked as conversation with Nicolo, but perhaps she can convince him that she'll behave herself enough to be allowed out of this room. It seems a fool's errand, though—Nicolo has always had an uncanny way of seeing straight through her.

But when the servants file back out of her rooms and another figure appears in the doorway, it isn't Nicolo but Gisella, no longer in the dirty shift dress she wore the last time Beatriz saw her, but clad in an elegant brocade gown, fit for a princess. Officially, Gisella isn't that, but it seems to be the role she's claimed for herself in Nicolo's court—the last time Beatriz was in this palace under house arrest, after Nicolo claimed the throne that should have been Pasquale's, Gisella even came to gloat wearing a tiara.

"I thought I'd join you for dinner," Gisella tells her with a breezy smile, as if she didn't poison and kidnap her days before.

"Oh, are we moving on from imprisonment to torture, then?" Beatriz asks. She looks at the girl standing in front of her—suntanned skin clean and gleaming, pale blond hair braided in an elaborate style without a strand out of place, a smile curling at her lips that Beatriz desperately wants to smack off. But Beatriz tries to tamp that impulse down, searching beneath the facade and looking for the Gisella she met when she first arrived in Cellaria, the one she considered a friend and the cousin Pasquale loved. *Did she kill him and Ambrose?* Beatriz wonders, looking at her now. Beatriz isn't sure, but she's learned what a mistake it is to underestimate Gisella, and it isn't a mistake she will make again.

Gisella's smile widens. "Perhaps I should remind you which of us has a habit of poisoning the other when we sit down for meals," she replies.

"Next time, I'll make sure to double the dosage, since it clearly didn't suffice," Beatriz says, taking a seat, watching as Gisella follows suit, reaching for the carafe and pouring both herself and Beatriz a glass of red wine.

"Oh, you could have given me the whole bottle and it wouldn't have had any effect. Salt water often doesn't," Gisella said. When Beatriz doesn't respond, she shrugs. "Your mother had a servant go through your belongings and switch out all of your poisons."

Beatriz purses her lips. "You're a fool to trust her," she says.

Gisella laughs. "I assure you I'm not and I don't."

"And Pasquale and Ambrose?" Beatriz asks, the question she's been dreading the answer to. "I assume my mother told you to kill them."

For a moment, Gisella doesn't respond. She swirls her glass of wine, eyes focused on the red liquid inside as if she's scrying, before she takes a long sip.

"She did," Gisella says slowly, setting the glass back down. "She also told me to ensure that the poison I told you to make wasn't *actually* lethal, since she didn't want to end up dead by mistake."

Beatriz blinks, struggling to hide her surprise. She used that poison on Nigellus, and it certainly did its job. "You were playing both sides," she realizes.

"Up until you failed to kill the empress like you were supposed to. You had your chance and you didn't take it," Gisella says. "You became the losing side."

"So it wasn't personal," Beatriz says, her voice scathing. "Just like betraying Pas and me the first time wasn't personal. Do you truly believe that absolves you of guilt? Pasquale and Ambrose are *dead* by your hand."

Beatriz expects the accusation to land—Gisella did love her cousin, even if she's proved she loves herself and her power far more—but Gisella doesn't flinch. Some stray bit of hope sparks in Beatriz's chest, catching fire.

"You didn't kill them," she says quietly.

For an eternity of a moment, Gisella doesn't speak. Finally, she leans back in her chair.

"I didn't kill them," she admits. "You and I are the only ones who know that—though I daresay your mother figured it out when her men didn't find their bodies in the inn where they expected to."

"You didn't tell Nicolo?" Beatriz asks, surprised again.

"He's set to marry you—it didn't seem prudent to give him any reason to believe the union won't be legally binding because your husband is still alive," Gisella says, shrugging.

"Then why are you telling me?"

Gisella surveys Beatriz over her glass of wine, taking a sip. "Because you're a smart girl," she says, her voice cool. "And you know that if the rest of the world—my brother included—knows that Pas is alive, he will have a target on his back and a price on his head. I'm sure your mother already has people hunting him—would you add to those numbers?"

The hope in Beatriz fizzles slightly. "Of course I wouldn't," she says softly.

"Then I expect," Gisella says, drawing each word out, "that you won't cause any trouble. That you'll marry Nicolo without any hysterics and stop acting like being Queen of Cellaria isn't *exactly* what you were born and raised to do."

*Your mother raised you to die.*

Nigellus's words come back to her like a bolt of lightning. That is what Gisella is telling her, even if she doesn't realize it. In order to keep Pasquale safe, Beatriz has to go along with her mother's plans, sacrificing herself and Cellaria in the process. If Beatriz were in the mood to be amused, she might find it funny that Gisella is blackmailing her into going along with a plot that will see her and Nicolo dead too.

"Very well," Beatriz says after pretending to think over Gisella's terms for a moment, when in fact it's the easiest lie she's ever told and one she feels no guilt over. "I take it that means I get to leave these stars-forsaken rooms, then?"

"But of course," Gisella says, not even trying to hide the triumph in her smile. Beatriz wants to launch herself over the table and slap her former friend across the face. "The Cellarian people will be anxious to reacquaint themselves with their lost princess."

The way Gisella says those words sounds like a threat, but as they begin to eat their supper in silence, Beatriz's thoughts are spinning madly. She has no intention of keeping her promise not to cause trouble—she just needs to do it wisely if she's going to have any chance of seeing Pasquale, Ambrose, and Daphne again.

Beatriz isn't sure how Gisella convinces Nicolo that it's safe to release Beatriz from house arrest without telling him about using Pasquale's safety as leverage, but she must have figured out a way, because the next morning, Beatriz is awoken with an invitation to join Nicolo and his advisors for lunch, and a legion of handmaidens follow the missive, arranging her hair, painting her face, and lacing her into an ornate ivy-green brocade gown.

The five girls chatter in rapid Cellarian as they get her ready, but they don't speak to Beatriz at all—not that she minds. The sound of their voices serves as the background to her thoughts.

Star magic, and stardust, are illegal in Cellaria, but Beatriz knows that doesn't mean they've been eradicated completely. And with the overzealous King Cesare dead, it's possible proprietors of stardust are beginning to make their way out of the shadows, now that the threat of execution by burning doesn't loom quite so large. Beatriz only needs to be smart and patient—the latter far more difficult for her than the first.

She's so lost in her thoughts she almost doesn't hear the girl combing her hair mention her eyes.

"Have they always been silver?" she whispers to the girl holding a small brush and a pot of cream that matches

Beatriz's skin, dabbing lightly at a pimple that appeared on her chin at some point since she left Bessemia.

Beatriz's stomach sinks. *Her eyes.* The last time she was in Cellaria, she had eye drops from her mother's apothecary, specially brewed to turn her star-touched silver eyes green. In Cellaria, star-touched eyes can get a person arrested or killed—at least, that was the case in King Cesare's Cellaria. She doubts that so much has changed in the few weeks that Nicolo has been king.

"My sister saw her once—she swore the princess had green eyes," the girl applying Beatriz's cosmetics whispers back in quick, rushed Cellarian that Beatriz nearly misses. The girl lacing Beatriz's dress sees her understand their conversation, though, and hushes the other girls.

"When the traitor prince attempted to use magic to take King Nicolo's throne by force, Princess Beatriz risked her own life to stop him," the girl fastening Beatriz's dress tells them, though her gaze remains locked on Beatriz's. "The stars struck Prince Pasquale down where he stood, but showed their blessing for the princess by touching her eyes, and returning her to Cellaria as our queen-to-be. Is that not right, Princess?"

It's a ridiculous story—concocted by Nicolo and Gisella, no doubt—but Beatriz supposes the truth of what's transpired since she left Cellaria would sound even more ridiculous. Still, the handmaiden's words sound almost like a challenge, like she's daring Beatriz to contradict her.

"Yes, that's correct," Beatriz says slowly, already thinking of all the ways she can use this story to her advantage.

The story has been designed to explain Beatriz's return, to ensure that Cellaria believes Beatriz innocent of Pasquale's supposed treason and is therefore the ideal bride for Nicolo to take. It's designed to add to the mythos of Nicolo's reign, by giving him a queen blessed by the stars themselves. But it also makes Beatriz herself a saint, and that comes with power Beatriz can use against them.

# Daphne

Daphne stands in front of Eldevale Castle's main entrance, alongside King Bartholomew, Bairre, Leopold, Violie, and a dozen courtiers, including Cliona and her father, waiting for the empress's imminent arrival. The frigid winter air whips through Daphne's black hair, mussing the elegant updo she asked her servant to arrange it into, and Daphne clenches her hands into fists to fight the urge to smooth it down again, knowing it will be a losing fight and she isn't sure how many of those she can survive today.

A messenger appeared while they were eating breakfast to announce that the empress would arrive in the next fifteen minutes, and Daphne forced herself to take five more bites of her porridge before getting to her feet, even as the food curdled in her stomach. She refused to show how much her mother's arrival unnerved her, not to anyone, not even Bairre, who watched her closely throughout breakfast and even now keeps glancing at her sideways as if she is an equation he's anxious to solve. But that would mean letting him see the dark and desperate girl who both loved and hated her mother, who was determined to destroy her and yet, mortifyingly, still craved her approval like drought-stricken earth craves rain, and Daphne couldn't stomach that.

So she doesn't meet his gaze and instead keeps her eyes trained on the open gate.

She hears the sound of approaching hoofbeats before she sees the horses that make them. Ten guards on proud white horses, decorated in Bessemian blue regalia, enter first, followed by two blue enamel carriages pulled by more white horses; then, finally, the large gold carriage Daphne knows contains her mother. Another ten guards trail behind, the gate closing at their backs.

Daphne keeps her eye on her mother's carriage as it reaches the steps to the palace, pulling to a stop. A footman Daphne vaguely recognizes jumps down from his perch beside the driver and opens the door.

A dainty gloved hand reaches out of the shadowy carriage, each finger ringed with jewels, taking hold of the footman's proffered hand before Empress Margaraux steps out into the pale gray winter light.

For a moment, Daphne feels as if she is looking at a stranger—her mother is taller than this woman, isn't she? She looms larger, an immortal figure who has the power to destroy with a single look. But the woman who stands before her now doesn't stand quite so tall, and in the stark light, Daphne can see the wrinkles creasing the skin around her eyes and mouth. Most surprising of all, when her eyes meet Daphne's and that unmasked fury briefly flashes through them, Daphne finds herself wholly undestroyed.

The woman before her isn't an infallible goddess with the power to damn and absolve, she's just a woman—a powerful one, certainly, but Daphne supposes that since the last time they were face to face, she herself has come into power of her own. They are meeting here and now as equals, and if the empress doesn't know that yet, she will.

Daphne makes her way down the steps, holding the hem of her silver velvet gown up to avoid tripping and summoning a bright smile. "Mother," she says, pitching her voice loud enough to be heard by the gathered audience of Frivian courtiers and the entourage her mother brought, who Daphne knows are watching from the windows of the two smaller carriages. Violie is following a step behind her, and if she's nervous about the ruse and how the empress will respond to it, it doesn't show. "It's so good to see your face again," Daphne says, coming to stand before the empress and taking hold of her cool hands.

The empress surveys Daphne, looking at her like she's seeing a stranger—and not one she likes—before glancing over her shoulder to Violie and narrowing her eyes slightly. For a moment, Daphne holds her breath. Logically, she knows her mother has more to lose than anyone by proclaiming Violie a fraud, but what if she and Violie miscalculated? What if—

"Oh, my darling girls," the empress says, suddenly squeezing Daphne's hand with one of hers and reaching toward Violie with the other. "I feared I might never see you again."

She releases Daphne entirely, turning fully toward Violie and reaching a gloved hand up to lay her palm against Violie's cheek. Daphne sees the flash of horror cross Violie's face the second the empress touches her, but it's gone so quickly she doubts anyone else does—at least apart from the empress herself.

"Sophronia, they told me you died—I thought—"

"Oh, Mama," Violie says, her voice coming out loud enough to be heard by all. "I thought for sure I wouldn't survive, but . . . oh, it is such a story, and you've had quite a journey. Come inside, King Bartholomew has had a room prepared for you."

Violie gestures to where King Bartholomew is waiting at the top of the stairs, Bairre and Leopold standing on either side of him. As Empress Margaraux approaches, all three bow deeply.

"Your Majesty," King Bartholomew says, taking the empress's hand and bowing low over it, brushing a polite kiss over the back of her hand. "Welcome to Friv."

"Thank you, Your Majesty," the empress replies, dropping into a deep curtsy. It occurs to Daphne that she's never actually seen her mother curtsy, has only seen her be curtsied to. "And thank you as well for keeping my daughters safe in these troubled times."

"Both Daphne and Sophronia are credits to you," Bartholomew tells her, earnest and oblivious to the performances being enacted around him.

"Are they?" the empress drawls, eyes moving between Daphne and Violie. "How nice to hear. I would like the opportunity to catch up with my daughters—somewhere warm, perhaps," she adds, pulling her ermine cloak closer.

"Of course," Bartholomew says, bowing his head again. If he's offended that the invitation wasn't extended to him, he gives no sign. "I'm sure there is much for you to discuss, given all that's happened. I'll have refreshments set up in the library—it is the warmest room in the castle, and I'm sure after your journey, that's precisely what you need."

"Very thoughtful, King Bartholomew," the empress says with what Daphne recognizes as her demure smile—chin tucked down, looking up at him from beneath her eyelashes, a small curve to her lips. Daphne has seen that smile wrap council members and ambassadors around her finger—she's sure that her mother once used that smile against her father, too, that it's at least one small part of why she is now empress.

King Bartholomew isn't immune to it either. His cheeks turn faintly pink as he bows again, ushering the empress inside.

A round table has been set up in the library, just in front of the roaring fireplace, and set for three people, with a teapot and a plate of small, frosted cakes in the center. The three chairs surrounding it are typically Frivian in their sparseness, and Daphne knows even before the empress lowers herself into one that she'll find them wanting.

"I think I'd rather be back in a stars-forsaken carriage," the empress mutters as Daphne and Violie join her. "Now," she says, her voice snapping as Daphne reaches for the teapot and begins to pour for everyone. "Tell me what, exactly, is going on here. Who else knows she's a fake? I suppose Leopold must—I'd heard he was dimwitted, but even *he* would notice if his wife were replaced with a servant," she adds, motioning toward Daphne and Violie. "Does King Bartholomew? Prince Bairre?"

"The king doesn't, but Bairre does," Daphne says with a broad smile as she pours tea. "He was quite instrumental in pulling off this charade—you ought to thank him, Mother."

The empress's penetrative gaze moves to Daphne and lingers. It's always been difficult to see much of anything beneath the placid exterior her mother puts up, but Daphne thinks she might see a flicker of uncertainty.

"Explain," she says—or rather, commands.

"Queen Eugenia betrayed us," Daphne says, launching into the story she and Violie concocted late last night with some help from Bairre and Leopold. A story her mother will likely not believe, but one solid enough that she won't be able to call it a lie outright—not without revealing truths she would rather keep hidden. "She was responsible for Sophronia's death—Violie witnessed her pulling a pistol on Sophie before turning her in to the rebels she was working with."

"So she claims," Margaraux says, eyebrows arching and gaze darting back to Violie, who, for her part, meets her stare unflinchingly. "Eugenia wrote to me with a similar story about you, claiming you were the one who betrayed Sophronia," she adds, motioning to Violie with her free hand while taking a sip of tea with the other. "Convenient that Eugenia is now dead and unable to defend herself."

Violie opens her mouth, and Daphne has learned enough about her over the last weeks to know she is about to say something brash—a temperamental slipup the empress is no doubt trying to instigate. "I had my doubts too, when Violie first approached me with this story," Daphne admits, drawing her mother's attention back to her. "But Violie didn't try to kill me. Eugenia did."

This time, there is no mistaking the flicker of surprise in the empress's face as she sets her teacup down in the saucer with a clatter.

"I'm fine," Daphne assures her, reaching out to lay her hand over her mother's, intentionally misreading her surprise as maternal concern. "I told you about the attempts that were made on my life. Another was made, and this time the assailant was kept alive long enough to point the finger at Eugenia."

"Confessions under torture—" the empress begins, withdrawing her hand from Daphne's.

"—aren't to be believed," Daphne finishes with a knowing smile. "Yes, Mother, you taught me well in that. But this particular confession pointed me in the right direction, and after some . . . snooping, I discovered letters between Eugenia and a man named Ansel, who Violie remembered as the head of the Temarinian mob that killed Sophie."

"Letters can be—"

"Forged, I know," Daphne interrupts again. "But I trust my ability to tell a forgery from the genuine article, and you should too, given the education you provided me. I know I'm no Sophronia in that area, but I'm more than competent."

The empress's mouth tightens, but she inclines her head in a nod.

"There were other letters," Daphne continues. "But unfortunately, they were written on verbank paper and crumbled in my hands."

Daphne watches her mother's face carefully, but she gives no reaction. Daphne doesn't need one to confirm what she knows, though. Violie saw enough of those letters in Eugenia's things to know they'd been sent by the empress. It was proof that the empress and Eugenia were working together, even if they crumbled before she could read more than a few words. But the empress knows exactly what those letters said, since she wrote them, and Daphne and Violie have planned a way to use that knowledge against her.

"That is the troubling bit, I confess," Daphne says with a sigh. "While most of the letter crumbled, I did see the address, or rather, part of it."

"Oh?" her mother asks, still not troubled. She has no reason to be—according to Violie, she used an alias.

"The letters came from Bessemia," Daphne says. "It seems someone there is working against you, Mother. Conspiring with Eugenia to kill Sophronia, and trying to kill me as well. For all we know, they're targeting Beatriz next—I'd hoped she would be joining you so we could see that she's safe. She is in Bessemia, is she not?"

The empress's lips purse. "She is not," she says slowly. "I finished negotiations with the boy currently on the Cellarian throne and we reached an agreement. Beatriz will be crowned queen there before the end of the week."

Daphne fights not to look at Violie, even as the information wedges beneath her skin. Daphne hears what her mother doesn't say, how she makes no mention of Prince

Pasquale, doesn't even pretend that Beatriz went to Cellaria of her own volition. Perhaps she worries that Daphne or Violie will see through the lies, or perhaps she simply doesn't care enough to construct convincing ones.

"How wonderful," Daphne says, forcing a smile she hopes looks real. "Though if I'm right, she is in grave danger there—"

"*If* you're right," the empress says coolly. "And you still haven't explained this charade," she adds, waving toward Violie, who seems content to sip her tea and let Daphne steer the conversation. Which is just as well, Daphne supposes. She likes Violie, and trusts her, but at the end of the day there is no one whose abilities she believes in more than her own.

"Violie saved my life," Daphne says, launching into the lie she and Violie crafted—one that hews as close as she dares to the truth of Eugenia's death. "She uncovered a plot that Eugenia and her maid were planning to kill me with septin mist—I was on my way back from Lake Olveen at the time, but they were ready to put the plan into motion as soon as I returned. Violie snuck into Eugenia's rooms one night to recover the poison, and Eugenia woke up and called for her maid, who attacked Violie, causing her to spill the septin mist and . . . well . . . you know how septin mist works."

"The maid died on the spot," Violie clarifies, which is true, but it was Violie wielding the septin mist, intent on using it to assassinate Queen Eugenia. She'd been in Eugenia's bedchamber, the mist container open, when the maid entered suddenly, startling Violie, waking Eugenia, and ruining everything. "Eugenia and I both inhaled less, leaving me unconscious for a day or so and Eugenia awake but bedbound. I was, of course, arrested."

The empress's dark brown eyes cut between them, skeptical but silent.

Daphne jumps in to finish the story. "When I returned and realized what had happened, the truth seemed . . . imprudent to divulge, but when Leopold came to me, confessing his true identity and begging me to save the girl who had saved his life and now mine, I was powerless to refuse."

"Did you try?" the empress asks dryly.

Daphne falters for an instant, some deeply buried part of her shriveling at the derision in her mother's voice.

"You instructed me to find Leopold, Mama," Daphne says pointedly. "If I had refused his wish, he would have fled. Saving Violie kept him here. I sent word to you, but I assume you and the messenger crossed paths on your way here."

"Hmm," the empress says, taking another sip of her tea. "And you?" she asks Violie. "What did you tell her?"

Violie offers the empress a bland smile. "Everything, of course," she says, and there is a brief flash of uncertainty in the empress's eyes about what *everything* entails. But those are cards Daphne and Violie are keeping close to their chests for now, and they decided it's best if the empress believes that Violie is still loyal to the empress. So Violie settles for half-truths. "That you worried for Sophronia's sake, that you feared she was too vulnerable to survive in the Temarinian court alone and sent me to watch her. That I failed in that, and did my duty in bringing Leopold to Friv."

The empress's brow furrows just slightly, but Daphne knows she can't question Violie's story in front of Daphne, not without revealing that Violie's true mission was quite the opposite—to ensure that Sophronia did the empress's bidding even when her conscience objected, or else do it for her. But the goal is for the empress to believe that Violie is on her side, and that she is keeping Daphne on her side as well.

No doubt the empress will seek Violie out for a few words alone, to find out why Leopold is alive at all and why Violie has brought him to Friv rather than Temarin. But one matter at a time.

"I'd heard you were having trouble maintaining your hold on Temarin," Daphne tells the empress—a bluff, but an educated one. The empress herself has always said that taking a country is easy, holding it is harder. And Daphne sees the words find their mark in the way the empress's mouth tightens. "Now I've given you Sophronia back and both of us have earned Leopold's loyalty. As you said, he isn't the sharpest sword in the cupboard—it will be easy enough to convince him to officially cede control of Temarin to you and then escape to some far-off island to live the rest of his days in exile, so that your reign can go on, unchallenged."

The empress is quiet for a moment, but Daphne can practically hear her turning every facet of the story she and Violie have spun over, searching it for flaws, noting how they fit together. After what feels like a lifetime, she smiles the sort of smile Daphne has never seen from her before, a broad, beaming grin that reaches her eyes, almost making her glow. Daphne feels as if she could bask in the warmth of it forever. "It seems you've thought of everything, my dove," she says, the sort of words Daphne would literally have killed to hear her mother say to her. The empress leans across the table and lays her hand on Daphne's cheek, her touch cool and dry. "I am so proud of you."

As Daphne smiles back demurely, it occurs to her that the words she's dreamt of hearing from her mother for so long sound more like a threat than a compliment.

# Beatriz

Lunch is held on the South Terrace of the Cellarian palace—a small but sumptuous setup of a single long oak table brought out from indoors, along with eight matching chairs, a white silk tablecloth embroidered in gold thread, heavy gold goblets filled with red wine, and porcelain platters piled high with fresh fruit, cheese, toasted bread, and sliced cured meats.

As Beatriz steps out onto the terrace, she's struck by how different the weather is here than it was in Bessemia, where there was a chill in the air as winter settled in. But winter hasn't touched Cellaria—the weather doesn't seem to have changed at all since the first time she came here in late summer. The air is hot, humid, and heavy on her skin, with a gentle breeze rolling in off the sea just below. A bright red canopy has been erected to block out the worst of the sun, and it has the added effect of casting the entire terrace in a garish light.

Beatriz is the last to arrive, and as she approaches the table, everyone else rises to their feet, with the exception of Gisella, who remains seated to Nicolo's left, leaving the seat at his right open for Beatriz, who takes it. As she lowers herself, she takes in the other five men at the table. She vaguely recognizes the man on Gisella's other side as Gisella and Nicolo's father and Pasquale's uncle, the Duke of Bellario; the others she can't put a name to, yet she feels certain she saw three of them around the palace during her last stay. None of them was part of King Cesare's inner circle, though, and Nicolo is either smart for ensuring the loyalty of those he surrounds himself with, or else he's a fool for alienating a group of people who were accustomed to power.

It's no concern of Beatriz's whether he's being smart or a fool, she reminds herself. She'll be long gone from Cellaria before any rewards or repercussions can find him.

"Princess Beatriz," the duke says, bowing low at the waist, followed a beat later by the others. "It is wonderful to see you safely returned to us. How have you recovered from your ordeal?"

"My ordeal?" Beatriz asks, cutting a glance at Gisella, who responds with a loaded look of her own. The threat she made against Pasquale and Ambrose hangs over Beatriz, so she fixes a smile on her face and turns back to Lord Bellario. "I assure you, Your Grace, I am recovering from my ordeal quite well and I'm happy to be home in Cellaria."

Nicolo clears his throat. "Beatriz, I don't believe you've met Lord Faviel, Lord Gustin, Lord Warrel, or my cousin, the Duke of Ribel."

The last name gives Beatriz pause—during the council meeting she attended in Bessemia, General Urden apprised them of the threats facing Nicolo's reign, and chief among them was the Duke of Ribel, whose claim to the Cellarian throne was just as strong as Nicolo's and who had been amassing his own support among the nobility that was turning on Nicolo. Once again, Beatriz wonders if Nicolo is brilliant or a fool.

"My lords," she says, inclining her head toward the first three men before turning her attention to the Duke of Ribel. "Your Grace."

She takes the opportunity to look him over, surprised at how young he is. She has never heard much about the duke, who preferred to stay at his estate on Cellaria's western coast to avoid becoming the target of the late King Cesare's mercurial temper—a smart decision in Beatriz's eyes, but she'd thought he would be older. Instead, he's close to her own age, with hair such a dark shade of brown it's nearly black and hooded sea-blue eyes. Though his coloring is different from Nicolo, Gisella, and Pasquale's, she sees the family resemblance in the sharpness of his features, the aquiline nose. Her gaze lingers on his mouth, full and curved into a slight but knowing smile that Beatriz feels like a caress.

Beside her, Nicolo clears his throat, and Beatriz tears her gaze away from the duke, looking instead at the boy who is, at least for the moment, her husband-to-be.

"Lord Gustin asked how you're finding being back in Cellaria," Gisella supplies.

"Oh," Beatriz says with a laugh, focusing on Lord Gustin—a tall, wiry man with a balding head and a glorious mustache that reminds Beatriz of illustrations she's seen of walruses. "I believe we were anticipating snow when I left Bessemia—this sun is certainly an improvement."

The table laughs politely. After a few moments during which servants arrive to fill their plates with a little of everything, and everyone begins to eat, Lord Faviel smiles at Beatriz—the sort of smile, she thinks, that looks rehearsed.

"I confess, Princess Beatriz, we have all heard . . . rumors of what transpired between when you left Cellaria and when you returned, but I find myself curious about what actually happened."

Beatriz glances at Gisella uncertainly. She overheard what the servants claimed she'd gone through, but she didn't gather nearly enough information from that brief conversation to be able to spin the tale herself, or to know how much of it is in line with what Gisella wants the story to be. With Pasquale's safety at stake, Beatriz knows she has to follow Gisella's lead, as much as she might hate it.

"The princess is surely exhausted from telling that story so many times already," Gisella says with a bright smile. She claps her hands. "Oh, I have an idea—wouldn't it be fun if *I* told the story, as I've heard it, and you can correct me if I get anything wrong?"

"I'm sure that will be fun," Beatriz says, managing to keep the sarcasm from her voice as she reaches for her goblet of wine and takes a sip.

"So," Gisella begins, sitting up straighter in her chair. "After the traitor prince, Pasquale, forced us all into his depraved plot against his father, you ended up caught in the mess. It was so unfortunate—when Nicolo was crowned, he had every intention of pardoning you, but he feared that if Pasquale believed you'd betrayed him, he would kill you. It was his intention to have you separated at the Sororia and Fraternia and rescue you from there as soon as possible, but Pasquale stole you away before Nicolo had the chance, forcing you to return to Bessemia so he could leverage your safety for your mother's support against Nicolo."

"Hmm," Beatriz says, taking another sip of her wine and pondering the story. It's ludicrous. The "depraved plot" Giselle spoke of—to rescue Lord Savelle from the dungeon before King Cesare could use him to incite war with Temarin—had been Beatriz's idea, and one Gisella and Nicolo had been happy to go along with. And surely no one could believe that Pasquale would hurt anyone, let alone her. But supporting these lies is the only way to keep Pasquale safe. Still, every part of her rebels against saying one word. Eventually, she chokes it out. "Indeed."

"But you never stopped working against Pasquale in the interest of Cellaria," Gisella continues, lifting her wine goblet toward Beatriz in a miniature toast before taking a sip. "You and your mother were trying to figure out how best to sever your marriage to him without endangering you, your reputation, or the alliance between Bessemia and Cellaria. Then I arrived, and Pasquale was absolutely furious. He insisted your mother have me arrested and threatened to publicly proclaim you all manner of indelicate things. A harlot. A traitor. An empyrea. Your mother went along with his threats in order to protect you."

Beatriz struggles not to laugh. If Pasquale—or anyone like him—tried to blackmail the empress, they would meet with a mysterious death within the hour, and she certainly wouldn't so much as lift a finger to protect Beatriz. What's more, Beatriz is sure her mother had no hand in this story Gisella is spreading, one that paints her as a weak and easily manipulated ruler, because if she did, Gisella herself would not be long for this world.

"I fear," Beatriz says, meeting Gisella's gaze, "that my husband had begun to inherit his father's mercurial temper. I would never wish to say a bad word about the late king," she hastens to add, looking around the table with dramatically wide eyes as she bites her lip. "But I believe we all experienced that temper firsthand, did we not? There were shades of that in Pasquale, and they grew worse each passing day."

Gisella clicks her tongue. "You were so brave to withstand that for as long as you did, Princess," she says, her tone so simpering Beatriz is surprised that the others at the table seem oblivious to it, with the exception of Nicolo, who cuts a glare at his sister. Gisella ignores it, keeping her attention on Beatriz. "And luckily, with my help, we were able to convince your mother that it would be in Bessemia's best interests that your marriage to Pasquale be annulled and you marry the true king of Cellaria instead. After all, your marriage was never consummated."

There is no question in Gisella's voice, but Beatriz knows she needs that statement validated. It very well may be the only true part of the story Gisella is spinning, but Beatriz doesn't even want to give her that much. Yet again, she reminds herself it is for Pasquale's own good, to keep him safe.

"No, it wasn't," she says, her voice tight.

The Duke of Bellario clears his throat. "Forgive my indelicacy, Your Highness, but I must ask—a dozen of the late king's closest courtiers witnessed the aftermath of your wedding night."

Beatriz remembers the hasty charade she and Nicolo

orchestrated that morning before King Cesare burst into their bedroom to inspect the bedsheets. It was the first time Beatriz trusted anyone apart from her sisters, and the beginning of her friendship with Pasquale. Thinking about him now causes a pang in her heart.

At least in this, though, Beatriz can simply tell the truth.

"Strawberry juice," Beatriz murmurs, lowering her gaze.

"Our marriage wasn't consummated—that night or any that followed."

"If we required any further proof that my cousin was mad, surely that is it," Nicolo says, reaching out to cover Beatriz's hand with his. It takes all of Beatriz's self-control not to pull away, even as the words churn her stomach. There was a time when she *wanted* to be wanted by Nicolo, but not like this. The words, spoken with an audience, remind Beatriz far more of the skin-crawling comments King Cesare used to make about her than of the tentative flirtation she and Nicolo had shared and painstakingly kept private.

"Indeed," the Duke of Ribel says, leaning back in his chair. Beatriz can feel his eyes on her, but she doesn't let herself meet them. Instead, she looks to Gisella and tries not to think of Nicolo's hand on hers.

"My mother agreed, but Pasquale discovered what we were planning," Beatriz offers, able to surmise where this story is going.

"Yes," Gisella agrees, shaking her head. "While in Bessemia, he'd been seduced by the ideas of a heretical empyrea—a traitor in the midst of your mother's court: Nigellus."

The name gives Beatriz pause. If that is the story Gisella

is telling, Beatriz has to assume her mother found Nigellus's body, that she and Gisella have been in touch since the escape from the palace. Beatriz expects guilt to follow the mention of the man she'd known her entire life, who had, albeit briefly, served as a mentor before Beatriz stabbed him with a shard of glass and rubbed poison into his bleeding wound. But the guilt is fleeting.

"Nigellus promised Pasquale that he could use his gift of exploiting the stars to return Cellaria to his rule, and Pasquale was thrilled to do it. He went up to Nigellus's laboratory late one night to make his wish while Nigellus brought down a star to make it come true, but little did he know that you, sensing he was up to something, followed. When you realized what he was doing, you went out on the laboratory balcony and tried to stop him, but it turned into a fight. In the struggle, you and Pasquale both tumbled off the balcony and fell six stories to the ground—a fall that should have killed you, but the stars saw in you a savior and so they protected you, and when you awoke, your eyes had become star-touched silver. Not a curse, but a blessing."

Beatriz takes another sip of her wine before smiling tightly at Gisella. "I would scarcely believe such a story myself if I hadn't lived it," she says, setting her goblet down again. An idea occurs to her, one she is sure she'll come to regret but is powerless to resist. Her smile widens. "But my dear Gigi, you're selling yourself short—I never would have known what Pasquale and Nigellus were planning if *you* hadn't bravely taken to the sewers to find those incriminating letters between them. I suppose Pasquale thought he'd destroyed them by tearing them up and throwing them into his chamber pot, but you weren't to be deterred, were you?" she asks, noting the shock and horror on Gisella's face, chased by the flush of embarrassment crawling up her neck. Beatriz smiles and looks at the others. "Let it be known that Gisella is a true heroine of our age—tirelessly sifting through sewage—"

"To Lady Gisella," Nicolo interrupts, sparing his red-faced sister a sympathetic look, though Beatriz could swear he's fighting a smile of his own.

"To Lady Gisella," the others echo.

Beatriz ignores Gisella for the rest of lunch, but she feels the other girl's glare throughout the meal and she knows there will be revenge coming.

When lunch is over, Nicolo offers to escort Beatriz back to her rooms, and after the stunt with Gisella, Beatriz decides not to push her luck. When Nicolo offers her his arm, she forces herself to take it, resting her fingers lightly on his brocade sleeve. As they walk inside and begin to navigate the palace halls, Beatriz keeps an eye on her surroundings, searching for anything or anyone that could potentially lead her to finding illegal stardust.

"It'll be in six days," Nicolo says, drawing her out of her thoughts. She realizes he's been talking for a few moments and tries to recall what, exactly, will be in six days. She hazards an educated guess.

"You're really in such a rush to marry me?" she asks, keeping her voice light even as her eyes scan the hall, noting servants carrying trays, courtiers she has idle tidbits of gossip on—could she leverage any of that gossip for stardust? She doubts any of it is *that* salacious.

"I am. Because you're searching for an escape route," Nicolo says, his voice low in her ear. "And I know you well enough to know that you'll find one, sooner rather than later."

Beatriz stops short, but Nicolo urges her to keep walking. It was easy to forget, when she was in Bessemia, just how well Nicolo manages to see through her. Even from the first night they met, when she was thoroughly drunk at her wedding to Pasquale, Nicolo looked at her like he saw who she really was, like he knew every secret she held.

He doesn't, she reminds herself. He can't. But he does know an awful lot more about her than he did when she left Cellaria, and she realizes she can't say the same about him.

"What are the details of your agreement with my mother?" she asks him. "What, exactly, did she offer you?"

Nicolo glances sideways at her, frowning. "I don't see what that has to do with you," he says.

Beatriz considers her next words carefully, hewing as close to the truth as she can to convince him of her honesty. "Of course I'm looking for an escape route, Nico," she says, making the choice to use the nickname she called him by before everything between them changed. She feels his arm flex under her fingers, notes that he likes her calling him that. "I was torn away from Pas—who, yes, might have been my husband in name only, but was my most loyal friend—and shipped back here to marry you like a pawn in a game of chess, with no say whatsoever in my future. Are you telling me that if you were in my place you wouldn't be looking for an escape of your own?"

Nicolo's jaw tightens and he doesn't answer, but Beatriz doesn't need him to. She continues.

"However," she says, "it is possible that the smartest escape route isn't out of Cellaria at all. My mother sought to use me as a pawn to further her own agenda, but to do that she also has to make me her equal—a queen in a country of my own."

"Well," Nicolo says, clearing his throat. "Queen consort."

Beatriz laughs at that. "Please, Nicolo," she says, shaking her head. "You said it yourself—you know me. And you know that if I wanted to wrest power away from you once I have that crown on my head, I could do it. Your hold on it isn't terribly strong at the moment, and *I* am a saint now. I daresay I could be Cellaria's sole ruler by the next full moon."

Nicolo glances around the busy corridor before making a sudden turn down a deserted hallway—a servants' corridor, Beatriz guesses—and dropping her arm. The hallway is narrow, and with no one else around, Nicolo steps close to her, crowding her against the stone wall, though he doesn't touch her. "Are you . . . threatening me?" he asks, sounding more bemused than concerned, though the concern is there as well. Beatriz hears it, lurking beneath the blasé surface. Rather than cower against the wall, Beatriz stands up straight, even though that puts her face inches from Nicolo's, his dark brown eyes nearly black in the dim lighting.

"Mmm," Beatriz says with a casual shrug, lowering her

voice to a murmur. "It sounds awfully messy to me. It would likely involve a lot of blood—including *all* of yours. And, frankly, I don't *want* to be the sole ruler of a country. Can you blame me? *You're* not having fun. It appears you haven't slept in weeks."

Nicolo frowns, looking like he wants to argue that, but Beatriz silences him by placing her palm against his cheek.

"I don't want to rule Cellaria alone," she says softly. "But I won't settle for being a powerless queen consort, either. We'll rule equally, as partners."

"Partners," he says, laughing softly, though he reaches up to catch her hand, holding it fast to the side of his face. His skin is warm, the barest hint of stubble prickling her fingertips.

"Partners," Beatriz says, firmer this time. She tilts her head up toward him, her lips a hair's breadth from his. If the courtesans in Bessemia could see her now, they would be proud, Beatriz thinks. And then she goes in for the kill. "And when we are sitting side by side on our thrones, we will declare war on Bessemia."

Nicolo blinks, shock cutting through the fog of lust in his eyes. He pulls back, dropping her hand. "You want to declare war on your home country? Surely you aren't so angry at your mother that you want to do that. She is acting in your best interests."

Beatriz wants to laugh at that, but she can see the story her mother must have spun him to make him believe that. More than that, Nicolo *wants* to believe it. She searches for an answer that isn't far from the truth. "No matter what her motives are, my mother has betrayed me for the last time," she says. "And I want to see her pay for it. Will you help me make her pay, Nico?"

Nicolo stares at her a moment longer, as if waiting for her to laugh and tell him she's joking. But Nicolo isn't a fool. Beatriz watches his mind work around the scenario, seeing the ways going to war with Bessemia would suit him, too—namely, adding another country to his domain. If he could do that—something his predecessor tried and failed to do with Temarin—his position as king would be far more secure.

"When we struck our deal, your mother promised to keep our former trade agreement and return Gisella unharmed," he says finally. "In return, she would help to ensure that Pasquale was no longer a threat to my place on the throne."

Beatriz pulls back from Nicolo at the mention of killing Pasquale—which, as far as Nicolo knows, is what happened. She knows that if she tried to fake understanding, Nicolo would know she was manipulating him, so she lets her revulsion show on her face. She shoves his shoulder and he steps away from her, a flash of guilt crossing his face, but it's gone just as quickly as it appeared, stowed away behind his placid expression.

"I'll consider your offer," Nicolo tells her, his voice stiff and formal once more.

"You mean you'll run it by Gisella," Beatriz replies, rolling her eyes. "Perhaps I will—surely I'd be better off negotiating with the true power behind the throne anyway."

Beatriz turns away from him, starting back down the hallway he pulled her through, but Nicolo's hand grabs her wrist—firmly, but not so tight that she would have difficulty getting away if she wanted to. For the moment, though, she allows it, turning back to him with raised eyebrows.

"Keep this conversation between us," he says before glancing around the deserted hallway and back to her. He sighs and his voice softens. "Please."

*Interesting*, Beatriz thinks. She's seen signs of a fracture between Nicolo and his sister since Nicolo became king, after he showed up drunk at Beatriz's window to try to convince her to marry him—a reckless move Gisella had no part of. The fracture deepened when Nicolo sent Gisella to Bessemia in person to renegotiate the treaty, leading to her being taken hostage. Beatriz has assumed that now that they've been reunited, whatever disagreements they had would have faded, the way her own conflicts with Daphne faded as soon as she heard her sister's voice in her head, apologizing and coming together for just a few moments, but that doesn't appear to be the case.

"Fine," Beatriz says. "But I want an answer to my proposal before I marry you."

"Or else what, Beatriz?" Nicolo asks, his voice more curious than scathing.

"Or else nothing," Beatriz says. She feels as if she is wearing half a dozen masks, all piled on top of one another, but for a moment she lets one slip, showing a flash of vulnerability. That, too, feels like a mask, though, a way of disarming Nicolo, convincing him she's vulnerable. She bites her lip and looks away from him. "I would simply like marrying you to be something I choose, whatever the reasons behind that choice may be. I thought perhaps you might like that too."

Nicolo doesn't answer, but after a second he loosens his grip on her arm and Beatriz twists away from him, walking down the hall the way they came. In the brief moment before she steps back into the main hall, she allows herself a triumphant smile, feeling as if she's scored a sorely needed point in this game she still doesn't fully understand.

# Violie

Rather than wait for the empress to seek Violie out at what will likely be an inconvenient time, Violie decides to go to her. She excuses herself from dinner early that night, claiming a stomachache, but after the guards King Bartholomew assigned to her leave her in her bedroom, she changes into the servant's dress she keeps hidden in the back of her wardrobe and tucks her blond hair under a scarf.

She slips out the window and carefully walks along the thin ledge that borders the castle, fingers scrabbling to keep a hold on the stone walls. She only has to go two windows over to reach the guest suite the empress is staying in. Violie nearly loses her balance wedging the window open, but she catches herself on the frame, taking a moment to steady her rapidly beating heart before slipping into the empty room.

She looks around, noting that she's in a private dining room, furnished with a small table and four chairs, with a fire blazing in the hearth. After only a few seconds in the room, Violie is already sweating, though she's sure it's

Margaraux's direction to keep her rooms as warm as possible. She closes the window and makes her way out of the dining room and into the sitting room.

Here, there are more signs of the empress in residence—several open, gilded trunks emblazoned with the Bessemian royal seal sit in the center of the room, and Violie notes a distinctly Bessemian-style tea set sitting on a tray on the low table between three overstuffed velvet chairs, as well as bejeweled golden candlesticks on the mantel holding honey-and-lavender-scented candles that Violie has difficulty imagining anyone in Friv buying or selling. A quick peek into the empress's bedroom shows her that Margaraux brought along her own silk bed linens and pillows as well—the perfectly nice but more drab Frivian cotton ones folded neatly on the chair beside the bed.

Though she knows she won't find anything, Violie can't help but snoop anyway, riffling through the desk already filled with Margaraux's fine feather quills and personal stationery, but no letters or papers that strike Violie as important. She looks through the books as well, remembering the ersatz book where Eugenia kept her letters hidden and where Violie discovered the correspondence between Eugenia and the empress, but there is nothing suspicious there. She is just considering digging into the still half-packed trunks when she hears Margaraux's voice in the hall outside the suite, instructing a servant to order her breakfast from the castle's cook.

Violie quickly sits down in one of the overstuffed velvet chairs, crossing her ankles and clasping her hands in her lap.

The doorknob turns and Margaraux pushes inside, her eyes immediately going to Violie and narrowing slightly before she speaks over her shoulder.

"That will be all," she says to the guards and servants accompanying her. "Fabienne will attend to me when she returns from the kitchens."

There is a murmuring of *Yes, Your Majesty*s, but they're cut off when Margaraux closes the door firmly and turns back to Violie.

"Well," she says, voice curt as she makes her way toward Violie, sinking down into the chair opposite her. "What do you want?"

Violie smiles, ignoring the thrum of panic rushing through her. It's always been there when she's been alone with the empress, though that was never a common occurrence. Most of her work as the empress's spy was done through letters, the training she received in Bessemia handled through instructors. The empress oversaw her daughters from a closer vantage point, but was content to monitor Violie's progress through secondhand reports—a fact Violie is grateful for. She isn't sure how Daphne, Sophronia, and Beatriz survived a childhood with the empress. Even now, at seventeen, Violie feels like a fawn in the woods that has just locked eyes with a frothing-at-the-mouth wolf—quickly and quietly weighing the odds of her walking out of this room alive.

"I thought it best we chat without Princess Daphne present," Violie says, smoothing her hands down the rough wool of the servant's dress she is wearing. "I'm sure you'd rather I not answer your questions honestly with her around."

Even without Daphne in the room, Violie feels her presence all the same. She knew it would be necessary to speak with the empress alone, and Daphne is trusting Violie to relay the conversation to her afterward—a meaningful gesture, Violie knows, since trust is not something that comes easily to either of them.

Margaraux seems to believe her lie, though, and huffs out a humorless laugh. She leans back in her chair, surveying Violie with that cold gaze Violie hasn't seen replicated in any of the woman's daughters—not Sophronia when she banished Violie from court after learning of her betrayal, not Beatriz after she punched Violie in the face, not even Daphne when Violie believed she meant to kill Leopold and his brothers. "All right, then," the empress says. "Let's start with why King Leopold is still breathing."

Violie shrugs, the lies flowing from her lips with casual ease. "I suppose it would have been easy enough to do away with him in the woods as soon as I found him. Stab him—quite literally—in the back and leave him to bleed out. I certainly had dozens of chances during our travels. I doubt he'd have put up much of a fight. But his death was meant to be public, was it not? And you've seen how rumors of his being alive have sprouted up, even coming from people who can have no idea of the truth. If I'd killed him quietly, with no witnesses, those rumors would never have died and your grasp on Temarin would never have been secure."

Margaraux's mouth twists, but she doesn't argue. "Then why not bring him directly to me?" she asks.

Another good question, and another answer Violie has at the ready—this time, the truth.

"Because he knows you want him dead," she says. "I could sooner have convinced him to walk into a burning house than to set foot in Bessemia after Sophronia told him of your plans."

"Sophronia," Margaraux says slowly, the name heavy in her mouth, "wasn't supposed to know my plans. She believed Leopold would be exiled, not killed. Unless you told her otherwise?"

Another answer Violie has—this one half lie and half truth. "I didn't," she says, the lie. "Ansel did." The truth. Ansel was another of the empress's spies, this one a Temarinian peasant she'd used to instigate the mob that killed Sophronia. After he captured both Sophronia and Leopold, Ansel told them more of the empress's plans than Violie had even known, including the part where the empress set Sophronia up to be executed. Sophronia's death had always been part of the empress's plan, and Ansel had reveled in telling Sophronia as much. "I hope you'll forgive me for saying so, Your Majesty, but you shouldn't have been so loose-lipped with a boy with such . . . faltering allegiances."

"That," Margaraux says, voice full of ice, "was Nigellus's doing, and suffice to say he's paid the ultimate price for his foolishness."

Violie knows better than to follow that statement up with questions, but they ring through her mind regardless. Is Nigellus dead? At whose hand? The last time Violie saw him, he'd rescued Beatriz and Pasquale from Cellaria and was escorting them back to Bessemia. Beatriz didn't trust him, but she believed they were working toward a common goal.

"I understand that these circumstances are less than ideal," Violie says, focusing on the present issue. "But I have done everything in my power to get Leopold to someone whose loyalty to you was strong, and Princess Daphne seemed the best option."

"And the truth about Eugenia?" Margaraux asks. She must see Violie's blank look, because she gives a tight-lipped smile. "Surely, Leopold would have been thrilled to see his beloved mother."

"Oh, that," Violie says, careful to hide her relief. "Not so beloved, it turns out, not after Ansel also told *him* that he was working with Eugenia as well as you. Not after Sophronia told him that Eugenia tried to kill her. When he learned she was here, he wanted revenge, but I talked him into avoiding her notice until I could ascertain her true allegiances and motives. Once I realized she was double-crossing you, I eliminated her."

"So, the story Daphne told about learning that Eugenia was trying to kill her?" Margaraux asks. "Does she believe that?"

Violie lets herself smile. "Well, Your Majesty, as you yourself like to say, the best lies are close to the truth. I knew Eugenia was responsible for Sophronia's death, and Daphne was mad with grief—it was easy to direct her ire at Eugenia, easy to convince her that her life was in danger too. I was not expecting to get caught planting those letters with Ansel that confirmed the plot against her, but all in all, I'd say it didn't work out too terribly."

"Well, of course you think that," Margaraux says, her voice turning mocking. "Here you are, born the bastard daughter of a courtesan, and now you're a princess of one country and the queen of another."

The words prickle at Violie's skin—she never *wanted* to be a princess or a queen. But a woman like Margaraux will never believe that, and it is so much easier to maintain a facade if Violie simply shows her what she wants to see.

"Yes," she says before tilting her head. "Do you judge me for climbing, Your Majesty, or do you perhaps respect me for it?"

A true smile curls at the corners of Margaraux's mouth as she pushes to her feet. Violie hastens to stand as well.

"You're an impudent little thing, aren't you?" Margaraux asks. "Very well, enjoy your time playing princess. We both know it will come to an end quickly, but if you play your cards wisely, perhaps you won't have to fall *too* far in rank." The empress gathers up her skirts and makes her way to her bedroom, turning to say over her shoulder, "I trust you can leave the way you came in?"

When Violie arrives back in the room she shares with Leopold, he's waiting up for her, sitting on the edge of the large bed, still in the clothes he wore to dinner. When he sees her, his shoulders sag and he lets out a low sigh—he's relieved, she realizes. Relieved she's alive. It shouldn't surprise her, not after everything they've been through together, but it does.

"Did you think she would stab me with her letter opener?" Violie asks, crossing to the trifold screen that divides the room, allowing them to dress and undress with at least a modicum of privacy. Her nightgown is already hanging over the screen, so she makes quick work of the buttons on her servant's dress.

"I may not know as much about the empress as you do, but I'd wager she has far more dangerous weapons at her disposal," he says.

Violie gives a snort of laughter as she pulls the dress over her head and reaches for the nightgown. "I'm sure she does, but she has far more to lose than to gain by killing me now, and she knows it."

Leopold falls silent. Violie frowns and pulls the nightgown on. When she steps out from behind the screen, Leopold clears his throat. "As far as we know," he says. "But you've said it yourself—she's always one step ahead of us. If she knows something we don't—"

"I know," Violie interrupts, coming to sit next to him on the edge of the bed. "That's why we're leaving at dawn. Daphne and Bairre will claim that an emergency came up with your brothers—without disclosing where they are," she adds quickly when Leopold opens his mouth to argue. "But we'll head to Cellaria to find Beatriz."

Leopold groans, flopping back on the bed and throwing an arm over his face.

"There's nothing wrong with that plan," Violie snaps. "Daphne and I have been over everything, and—"

"It isn't that," Leopold says, and when he lowers his arm, Violie realizes he's laughing. "I'm just not excited to be with you on a ship again."

Violie feels her cheeks heat up as she remembers their journey from Cellaria to Friv—the one she primarily spent in their cabin, vomiting.

"Well, we're both in luck," Violie tells him. "Daphne used her connection with Lord Panlington to secure horses. We'll have to ride—if we use one of the royal coaches, Margaraux's men will find us before we're out of the Trevail Forest."

Leopold nods slowly. "Then I suppose we'd better get some rest," he says, pushing himself to his feet. He grabs a nightshirt from where his valet left them on the armchair in the corner and takes it behind the screen.

"Have you heard from your brothers?" Violie asks, getting up and making her way to her side of the bed, pulling back the heavy duvet. The first couple of days they shared the room, Leopold insisted on sleeping in the armchair, but after a servant nearly caught them sleeping separately—which certainly would have raised questions—they have been sharing the bed. An easy thing to do given how large it is. Violie would wager that a family of six could sleep comfortably in it.

"Bairre passed a letter along today," Leopold says. Because any letters to Leopold would certainly be read and the rebels may very well still want Gideon and Reid killed, the man who took them in—Lord Savelle, the former Temarinian ambassador to Cellaria—has been instructed to send letters to Bairre instead. "They say they're doing well, but they're angry that I'm keeping them out of the *fun*, as they put it."

"You'd think getting kidnapped and nearly killed would have cooled their adventurous streaks," Violie says, climbing into bed. Only then does she look toward the screen and freeze. Because of the way the screen is positioned in front of the fire, she can see the outline of Leopold's body as he pulls his shirt over his head, draping it over the screen. Violie's eyes linger on the strong line of his shoulders, the bulk of his biceps as he reaches for the waist of his trousers.

Cheeks burning, she tears her eyes away from the shadow on the screen.

"Lord Savelle will be able to keep them safe, though," she says, staring instead at the dark green velvet duvet.

*Stars*, she thinks. If Sophronia were here to see her ogling Leopold . . .

She pushes the thought from her mind, rolling onto her side so her back is to the screen.

"I'm sure he can," Leopold says.

Violie hears the rustling of clothes as he finishes changing into his nightshirt his footsteps emerging from behind the screen.

"Dawn, then," he says, climbing into bed beside her. She doesn't need to turn around to know that he's in the same position as she is—on his side with his back toward her. It's the same way they've slept for a week now, but it's the first time she's been so aware of the space between them. A lot of space, she reasons, but she would be grateful for a little more. Even when she closes her eyes, she can see the backlit outline of his body behind the screen. Just as he could see her, she realizes, recalling his uncomfortable silence a few moments ago. She pushes the thought from her mind, determined not to linger on it.

"Dawn," she echoes, propping herself up to blow out the candle on her bedside table before burrowing back under the duvet. She hears Leopold do the same with his candle, and darkness engulfs them, sleep following soon after.

# Daphne

Daphne sleeps fitfully that night. She tosses and turns in the large bed she and Bairre share, earning annoyed, sleep-drenched groans from him every time she does, but she can't help it. The knowledge that she's sleeping beneath the same roof as her mother keeps her thoughts turning. In just a few hours, Violie and Leopold will be off away from Friv and the empress, but until then . . . what if the empress isn't wasting time? What if right this moment, she has one of her people sneaking into their bedroom, armed and ready to kill them both while they sleep?

It wouldn't be the right move, Daphne knows. Her mother is too smart to be so hasty. But that knowledge doesn't ease her mind.

After a while, Daphne's thoughts turn from defensive to offensive. What if, rather than waiting for her mother to attack Violie and Leopold, Daphne simply killed her mother? She has the advantage here; she knows the lay of the Frivian castle better than her mother or her guards. And while her mother may suspect that her loyalties have shifted, she surely wouldn't be expecting Daphne to kill her, would she?

What if tonight is the best chance she has to kill her

mother? What if doing so is the only way to save Beatriz from whatever she's facing in Cellaria? What if it's the only way to protect Violie and Leopold and Bairre? What if it's the only way to protect herself?

Could she do it?

Daphne isn't sure, and she hates that. She wasn't trained to hesitate; she was trained to identify threats and eliminate them.

"Ow," Bairre grumbles as she shifts again, accidentally kicking him as she rolls onto her side. "Daphne, at this rate I'll be one giant bruise by morning."

"Sorry," she says for what she would guess is the twelfth time. "Did I wake you?"

"No," he says with a tired sigh, propping himself up on his elbows. "In order for you to wake me, I'd have had to be able to fall asleep at all, and that's been an impossible feat with you tonight. Even without all the squirming and kicking, I can practically *hear* you thinking."

Daphne rolls toward him. In the faint moonlight shining through the window, she can just make out the lines of his face, his star-touched silver eyes glinting as he runs a hand through sleep-mussed hair.

"I don't think I can kill her," Daphne blurts out.

Bairre frowns, looking down at her. "Who?" he asks before shaking his head. "Silly question, I suppose. Killing your mother while she's a guest in Friv would be shortsighted."

"I know that," Daphne says. "But if she tries to kill any of us—"

"That would also be shortsighted," he reasons. "And you've come to the conclusion that she wouldn't risk it."

Daphne purses her lips. He's right, she knows he's right, logically. But emotionally?

"But if she does?" Daphne asks.

Bairre looks at her for a long moment and sighs. "If we truly believe she poses an imminent threat, I'll do it."

Daphne blinks. "You'd . . . kill my mother?" she says slowly. She's seen Bairre kill before, but only when they were attacked by assassins in the woods, never in a planned, organized way. She wonders if he knows what he's offering.

"If it meant you didn't have to?" he says. "In a heartbeat, Daph."

Daphne laughs, the sound coming out choked. "Your hands are much cleaner than mine, Bairre," she tells him. "There's no need to protect my sensitive soul."

"Maybe not," Bairre says softly. "But she's your mother, and despite everything, I know you love her. I don't want you to carry that weight around with you—even if it is necessary, it would still haunt you."

Daphne wants to argue, but she suspects he's right. "I'll sleep better tomorrow," she tells him after a moment. "After Leopold and Violie are gone and there are two fewer people to worry about."

It occurs to Daphne that even with Violie and Leopold gone, there will be plenty of others she cares about who her mother could hurt. Bairre, of course, and Cliona. Haimish and Rufus. King Bartholomew, who might not be a very good king but is, Daphne believes, a good man nonetheless. Even Lord Panlington and Aurelia, neither of whom Daphne particularly likes, but who Cliona and Bairre love. If her mother hurt them, Daphne would still feel it.

When she arrived in Friv, things were so much simpler. She cared about herself, her sisters, her mother, and no one else. Certainly no one in Friv, of all places. The armor she wore was solid and strong, impenetrable. But slowly, bit by bit, these people have turned her armor into little more than silk chiffon. They've made it so *easy* for her mother to hurt her, and Daphne hates them a little bit for that—she hates *Bairre* a little bit for that.

But as she looks at Bairre, her silver eyes finding his in the dark, she knows she doesn't actually hate him at all. Not even close. And that's the problem.

The silence that has wedged itself between them is broken by the quiet sound of a door opening and closing in the sitting room outside their bedroom.

"Bairre," Daphne says, dropping her voice to a whisper.

"Someone's outside," he whispers back, throwing the covers off and climbing out of bed, silent as a falling star. "Stay here."

But Daphne is already jumping out of bed herself, grabbing for the dagger she keeps under her pillow, brushing past him to the door.

"You're unarmed. Unless you're planning on glowering at them until they keel over, allow me," she replies. Bairre looks like he wants to argue that, but the sound of two sets of footsteps coming toward their door stops him short. He gives Daphne one brief nod and reaches for the doorknob. When Daphne nods back, he opens the door and steps aside so Daphne can launch herself through it, dagger in hand, tackling the closest figure to the floor. In seconds, her dagger is at his throat.

"Pas!" the other intruder shouts, but Bairre already has a firm hold of him, pinning his arms behind his back.

It isn't that Daphne doubts Bairre's combat abilities—or her own—but she can't imagine her mother would send assassins who weren't highly capable in their own right. These two haven't put up any sort of fight at all.

Daphne manages to maneuver to her feet, pulling her intruder with her and keeping a knife to his throat. It's difficult to get a good look at his face in the dark, but he's young—near her own age—with suntanned skin and wide, dark brown eyes that remind her of a deer in a hunter's crosshairs.

She's seen him before.

"Pas," she says, repeating the name the other intruder called him. Something in her mind clicks into pace. "Prince Pasquale."

He gives as much of a nod as he can with her dagger still pressed to his throat, and after a second longer of searching his face, she lets the dagger drop.

"And you," he says, hand reaching up to massage his throat, "can only be Daphne."

"How did you get past the guards?" Daphne asks. It isn't the biggest question on her mind, but it's the one that reaches her lips first.

Pasquale manages a shrug. "I admit I don't have a fraction of your sister's training, but she did teach me a thing or two about sneaking around castles."

Daphne ignores the pang in her chest at the mention of Beatriz and glances over her shoulder at Bairre, giving him a nod. He releases the intruder he was holding—another boy, with hair a couple of shades lighter than Pasquale's and a deep crease between his brows as he glances between Daphne and Pasquale.

"This is Ambrose," Pasquale says, nodding toward the other boy. "He's with me, and he was—*is*—a friend of Triz's."

*Triz's.* It strikes Daphne as strange to hear her nickname for her sister in the mouth of a stranger. She doesn't think she's ever heard anyone call Beatriz that apart from her and Sophronia.

She looks between Pasquale, Ambrose, and Bairre before her eyes dart to the tall clock in the corner. It's nearly five in the morning. She lets out a small sigh. "There's a lot we need to catch each other up on," she says, making her way back to her room to grab her cloak from the wardrobe, getting Bairre's, too, and passing it to him as she returns. "But it'll be best if we wake Violie and Leopold first, to save you from having to repeat yourself."

# Violie

Violie is already awake when the soft knock sounds on the main entrance to the suite of rooms she and Leopold are sharing at just after five in the morning. During the year that Violie worked as a servant, she grew accustomed to rising early to get as much cleaning and cooking done before the royalty and nobility she worked for woke up. It is, she finds, a difficult habit to break now that she is acting at being royalty herself.

Most mornings since she's become Sophronia, she busies herself by reading some of the Frivian books left in the bookcase in the sitting room. Her Frivian was perfectly serviceable when she was acting as a common-born servant, but she has found it helpful to broaden her vocabulary, and reading has helped her to do that. Occasionally, she files away words to ask Daphne, Cliona, or Bairre to define, but mostly she can figure them out from the context.

Today, though, she is bustling about the rooms while Leopold sleeps—dead to the world around him—ensuring that everything they'll need for their journey is packed and ready to go. She is about to wake him up when the knock at the door comes.

Violie grabs her dagger from her bedside table as she makes her way toward the door. She knows it's most likely Daphne, and that anyone sent by the empress certainly wouldn't bother knocking, but one can never be too careful.

Sure enough, when Violie opens the door she finds Daphne standing there, and her grip on her dagger loosens. But Daphne isn't alone. Bairre is at her side, with two familiar faces just behind them.

"Ambrose, Pasquale," Violie says, careful to keep her voice quiet as she ushers the four of them into the room and closes the door behind them. As soon as that's done, she gives both boys a quick, fierce hug. "I can't say I thought our paths would cross again," she admits.

"I hoped they might," Ambrose says with a smile. "Though I can't say I would ever have guessed I'd find you a princess the next time they did."

"Playing at one," she corrects. "And not for much longer."

Just then, Leopold appears in the doorway to their bedroom, bronze hair wild, hand raised to his mouth to cover a yawn. He blinks, taking in the sight of Ambrose and Pasquale in their receiving room. For a moment, he looks as if he suspects he's still asleep.

"Ambrose?" he asks, making his way toward them. "Pas?"

The three boys greet one another with firm hugs of their own.

"They arrived at our door just moments ago," Daphne says when Leopold and Pasquale break apart. Seeing the two of them side by side, it's still difficult for Violie to detect the family resemblance. They're only cousins, she supposes, but they couldn't look more different—Leopold broad-shouldered and strong-jawed, with the sort of golden good looks one would expect in a young king, Pasquale with his hair so dark a brown it's nearly black, and though he's a few inches taller than Leopold, he holds himself in a way that makes it look like he's trying to make himself smaller.

At least, that's how he used to stand. Looking at him now, Violie notices that Pasquale holds himself a little taller, stands a little surer.

"Beatriz—is she safe?" Violie asks him.

Pasquale glances at Daphne, whose face remains inscrutable, before looking back at Violie. "We don't know," he admits. "We escaped from the Bessemian palace and were on our way here—Beatriz spoke to you, then, didn't she?" he asks, looking at Daphne, who gives a jerky nod. "We reached an inn for the night; Ambrose and I stayed in one room, Beatriz and Gisella in one down the hall."

"Gisella?" Daphne interrupts, frowning.

"Oh," Ambrose says with a strained laugh. "There is more to catch you up on than we realized."

"Gisella is my cousin," Pasquale supplies. "Once, I considered her and her twin, Nicolo, to be friends. He and Beatriz . . . well . . ." He trails off, cheeks reddening.

Daphne rolls her eyes and mutters something under her breath that to Violie's ear sounds like *shameless*.

"Long story short, Nicolo and Gisella betrayed us and Nicolo took the Cellarian throne after my father died. They're the reason Beatriz and I were banished to the Sororia and Fraternia in the mountains in the first place."

Events are clicking together in Violie's mind, but Pasquale isn't done.

"Gisella came to Bessemia just after we arrived, hoping to smooth things over with your mother, but she was imprisoned there instead. She helped Beatriz brew a poison to use on the empress, and in exchange, Beatriz promised to release her from the dungeon."

"I take it the poison didn't work, then?" Daphne says.

"It did, just not on your mother," Pasquale says. "Nigellus attacked Beatriz and she used it on him instead."

"Nigellus is dead?" Violie asks, and Pasquale gives a quick nod.

Margaraux said Nigellus *paid the ultimate price for his foolishness,* so she isn't surprised at the news, but Nigellus has been the most powerful empyrea in Bessemia since before Violie drew her first breath, and it is difficult to imagine that a man like that could simply die. But to hear Pasquale tell it, he isn't just dead, but killed, and by Beatriz no less.

"Gisella double-crossed us," Pasquale says, getting back to the story. "At the inn, we woke up early that morning to find them gone and a note."

Ambrose reaches into the knapsack he carries, bringing out a folded piece of paper and passing it to Daphne. Violie peers over her shoulder to read it as well.

*Pas,*

*I won't ask forgiveness for this, but it's the only way. Run, now, before the empress realizes I didn't kill you. Never set foot in Cellaria again.*

*—S*

"Your mother was telling the truth, then," Violie says to Daphne, who nods.

"Apparently," she says, folding the letter again.

"Your mother . . . ," Pasquale says to them before trailing off, his face turning a shade paler. "Wait . . . how did you know the poison didn't work on her?"

"Because at this very moment, she's in a guest suite down the hall," Daphne says. "Which is why you can't stay here."

"They can't come with us, either," Violie points out. "Considering that we're heading to Cellaria, where half the country wants him dead."

"Ah, but the other half wants to see him on the throne," Daphne counters. "That's certainly better odds."

"You're going to Cellaria?" Pasquale interrupts, looking between them. "For Beatriz?"

Daphne nods. "According to my mother, she returned there of her own volition to marry King Nicolo after you were tragically killed," she says. "Even before you arrived, I knew that wasn't true."

Pasquale, still pale, shakes his head. "In Beatriz's own words, she wouldn't marry him if he were the last person in Cellaria. And she told him so after threatening to throw him out a window."

Daphne gives a snort. "Always dramatic," she says, but

there is more than a little fondness in her voice. "I've been trying to get in touch with her again using stardust, but I haven't had any luck. Do you have any idea why that might be?"

Pasquale and Ambrose exchange a look. "No, but there is one more thing you should know—she's an empyrea."

Daphne's dark eyebrows arch. "Gisella?" she says. "A Cellarian empyrea—I never thought I'd see the day—"

"No," Ambrose says. "Beatriz."

For a moment, Daphne stares blankly at Ambrose, then at Pasquale as if expecting him to correct Ambrose. When he doesn't, she laughs, the sound coming out half hysterical. "You're joking."

"We're not," Ambrose says. "Before he . . . died, Nigellus was training her. He said she had the gift to take stars down from the sky without killing them . . . or perhaps the gift to rebirth stars, it was too soon to say."

"That's impossible," Bairre says—the first words he's uttered since entering the room.

"Apparently not," Pasquale says. "But Nigellus also believed it was killing her to use her gift. Each time she did, she became more ill."

Daphne doesn't respond, her expression drawn tight.

"Still," Pasquale says slowly, "I thought, given that she'd been kidnapped, she might view using her gift as worth the risk to her health. Beatriz isn't the cautious sort."

"That's an understatement," Daphne says. "So why didn't she? If she's an empyrea, why not wish to be out of Cellaria? Why not wish herself here?"

"Unless she can't," Ambrose suggests. "What if there's

something keeping her from using her magic? Maybe it's also keeping her from being able to communicate with you."

"Your mother," Leopold suggests quietly.

"She didn't know," Pasquale says. "That Beatriz was an empyrea, I mean."

Daphne reaches up to rub her temples, giving a humorless little laugh. "One thing I am absolutely sure of, Pasquale, is that my mother always, *always* knows everything."

"If that's true, Beatriz is in more danger than I thought," Pasquale says, his face turning a shade paler. "When are we leaving?"

"We?" Ambrose echoes, gaping at Pasquale. "Pas, Gisella said it herself—if you set foot in Cellaria again—"

"If I had my way, I'd never set foot in Cellaria again," Pasquale interrupts, his voice coming out harsh. "A week ago, I'd have said Nicolo was welcome to it, but he can't have Beatriz, Ambrose."

"From what I understand," Daphne interjects calmly, "my sister isn't your problem, Prince Pasquale."

Pasquale whirls to face Daphne. "Then you understand very little, Princess Daphne," he says. "For one thing, contrary to how you view her, your sister isn't anyone's *problem*."

Daphne blanches, looking, for the first time in Violie's memory, truly shocked. "That isn't . . . I didn't mean it like that."

Pasquale looks at her for a moment before softening slightly. "I know," he says. "It's true that Beatriz and I are married only in the most technical of senses, but we are friends, and we promised we would take care of each other. She's upheld her end of that promise time and time again, and it'll take more than a threat from my power-mad cousins to keep me from doing the same now. So, I will ask again: When are we leaving?"

Violie clears her throat. "Now," she says. "I'm sorry you won't have the chance for more rest—"

"I don't need it," Pasquale interrupts, glancing at Ambrose. "You don't have to come with me, Ambrose. The empress never saw you in person—you'll be safer staying here."

Ambrose shakes his head. "No, I go where you go, Pas," he says. "Though I'd have preferred a bath and a night's rest in a real bed," he adds in a murmur, earning a grin from Pasquale.

"You'll need to take stardust with you, and a lot of it," Daphne says. "Do you have an issue with using it?" she asks Pasquale.

Again, Pasquale and Ambrose exchange a look. Both of them were born and raised in Cellaria, where using magic and stardust is a sin of the highest order. Under Pasquale's father's reign, people were burned at the stake for breaking that law.

"No," Pasquale says, his voice coming out sure. "We'll take as much as you can spare."

"Take this, too," Daphne says, holding out her left wrist and unhooking the bracelet there—the same one Sophronia wore, Violie remembers. The one holding a single wish, more powerful than mere stardust.

"No," Violie says. "You should keep that. If your mother—"

"My mother knows exactly what it is," Daphne interrupts. "And I doubt she'll let me keep it if she views it as a threat to her—I'd be shocked if she wasn't conspiring to steal it even as we speak. Stars, if we didn't know Sophronia's and Beatriz's bracelets worked just as she said they would, I'd suspect they were tricks, meant to make us feel safer than we were."

"Why *did* she give them to you, then?" Leopold asks. "If she hadn't, Sophronia wouldn't have been able to save my life, and Beatriz wouldn't have saved Lord Savelle, complicating her plans in Cellaria."

Daphne turns to Violie with a furrowed brow, but before she can ask the question on her mind, Violie shakes her head. "She didn't tell me all of her plans," she says. "She only told me what I needed to know, and that certainly wasn't part of it."

For a moment, Daphne just stares at the bracelet in her hand; then she shakes her head and tries again to pass it to Violie. "Take it, for Beatriz," she says.

Violie shakes her head. "If I try to give that to Beatriz, she'll likely break my nose all over again for putting another one of her sisters at risk, and I doubt she'd offer me stardust to heal it this time. Keep it."

Daphne hesitates a moment, the bracelet outstretched toward Violie, but when Violie makes no move to take it, Daphne lets out an annoyed huff and reclasps the bracelet around her own wrist.

---

Daphne and Bairre go to gather the necessary stardust, leaving Violie, Leopold, Ambrose, and Pasquale to finish packing and make their way down to the stables, where the stablemaster has saddled two horses for them under Daphne's instruction and is quick to saddle two more. Just as the four of them are ready to mount their horses, Daphne and Bairre return, each carrying a bulging leather satchel.

"Courtesy of the rebellion," Daphne says, passing her satchel to Violie while Leopold takes his satchel from Bairre.

"Thank Cliona for me, then," Violie says.

Daphne snorts. "Oh, trust me, when she discovers it's missing, I'll be giving you the lion's share of the blame," she says before her smile slips and she grabs hold of Violie's hand, squeezing it. "Be careful, Vi."

"The same goes for you," Violie says. In truth, if she had to choose between trekking across the continent into a hostile country to rescue an imprisoned princess and sleeping beneath the same roof as Empress Margaraux for one more night, it would be an easy choice. But even if she doesn't envy Daphne her role, she knows that if anyone can survive the empress, it's Daphne. She has more practice than almost anyone else, after all. "Anything you want me to tell Beatriz for you?" she asks.

Daphne opens her mouth to answer, then closes it again, releasing Violie's hand and taking a step back. "Plenty," she says. "But bring her back here so I can tell it to her myself."

Violie nods. "I will," she says. "Try not to get yourself killed before then."

# Beatriz

In the day following her conversation with Nicolo, Beatriz hasn't seen him—not even at mealtimes in the banquet hall, surrounded by courtiers; his seat always remains empty. But the court itself seems like a different one entirely than the court Beatriz left mere weeks ago, and nowhere is that clearer than in the banquet hall.

Before, King Cesare lorded it over the hall from his seat on the dais, drunk, belligerent, and sometimes dangerous, surrounded by a court that was desperate to find favor with him and terrified of what would happen when that favor inevitably turned sour. It had made for a fraught atmosphere, but Beatriz never realized just how fraught it was until she saw the court without King Cesare's influence. Without any royal influence at all.

She thought they might be lighter, freer—or else, more desperate to scramble to fill the vacuum of power Nicolo's absence opened up—but as Beatriz enters the banquet hall for breakfast two days after speaking to Nicolo, every eye in the room turns toward her, expectant and relieved, and she realizes that in the wake of losing a tyrannical king, replaced with an ambivalent upstart who's more absent than not, the

Cellarian court isn't lighter or freer at all. They're aimless, unused to being without a strong source of power to guide them, however violent that guidance often was.

The only person in the banquet hall *not* looking at Beatriz is Gisella, who sits to the left of Nicolo's chair on the dais, the plate in front of her loaded with toast smeared with a mix of soft cheese, honey, and herbs, layered with paper-thin slices of blood oranges, which Beatriz has been craving since the last time she was in Cellaria. Gisella takes a bite of her toast and glances up at Beatriz, her expression a practiced sort of empty that tells Beatriz she's still fuming about Beatriz's telling Nicolo's council that story about how she'd crawled through a sewer—not the ladylike, pristine image Gisella tries so hard to maintain.

"Gisella," Beatriz says, sitting down in the seat on the other side of Nicolo's empty chair.

"Your Highness," Gisella replies.

"Just think—soon you'll be calling me Your Majesty! Won't that be a fun change," Beatriz says, unable to resist needling her even though she knows it's as smart as tugging at a viper's tail.

Puzzlement clouds Gisella's expression, but she tries to hide it by taking a sip of her steaming-hot coffee. She glances out at the court breakfasting before them, pretending not to watch their every move. No one is close enough to overhear them, though, and Gisella must realize this, because when she lowers her cup, a smile is pasted onto her face.

"You've had quite a change of heart," she comments.

"What can I say? I'm an eternal optimist," Beatriz says, smiling as a servant places a plate with her own orange toast before her. He bows and backs away, and when he is out of earshot, Gisella snorts.

"Is that what you're going with?" she asks. "You're going to pretend you're happy to be here, like I didn't drug, kidnap, and blackmail you into that seat."

Beatriz shrugs. "Obviously, I'd rather you'd *not* done any of those things, but I'm going to become Queen of Cellaria, Gisella. I consider that a silver lining. You, however, miscalculated." She pauses, taking a bite of her toast and resisting the urge to let out a sigh of pleasure. The only thing she's missed about Cellaria, she thinks, is the food, but while she's here she plans to enjoy it as much as she can. Another silver lining.

"Did I?" Gisella asks, her voice tight even as her smile remains fixed in place, for the benefit of their audience. "What, exactly, did I miscalculate?"

Beatriz smiles, inclining her head toward the banquet hall full of courtiers. "You made me a saint, Gisella," she says. "And now a queen. And you believe I won't use the power you've given me to destroy you?"

Gisella's smile slips—a gratifying achievement for Beatriz until she sees the expression that hides beneath. Not fear or doubt but pity. More than that, it's the fact that Gisella tries to *hide* her pity with a worried frown that makes Beatriz suddenly lose her appetite and push her mostly uneaten toast away.

Nigellus told her that for her mother's wish to rule Cellaria to come true, Beatriz would need to die on Cellarian soil, by Cellarian hands. The truth clicks into place, and Beatriz wants to kick herself for not putting it together sooner. She asked about the details of Nicolo's deal with her mother, but she didn't think Gisella would have made a deal of her own.

"There was more to your deal with my mother," Beatriz infers.

Gisella doesn't speak for a moment, and that silence is all the answer Beatriz needs. "Eat up, Beatriz," she says finally, her voice hollow. "We can't have you passing out at the altar, can we?" Without waiting for a response, Gisella finishes her coffee in one final sip and pushes away from the table, sweeping out of the room without a backward glance.

Beatriz doesn't return to her rooms, though she knows she can't go far without the guards Nicolo assigned her coming up with some excuse to drag her back. It's part of the illusion Nicolo and Gisella have orchestrated to ensure that everyone in Cellaria believes she is here of her own free will, not as a prisoner. Even the guards have been told they're to prevent her from going too far for her own safety, rather than out of worry that she'll run.

Right now, running is the first thing Beatriz wants to do, but since that isn't an option, she makes her way down to the sea garden, one thought repeating in her mind. Her mother enlisted Gisella to kill her and Gisella agreed. Knowing Gisella, Beatriz suspects she won't fail, especially since her strength lies in poisoning, which has always been a weakness of Beatriz's. If Daphne were here, maybe she could avoid whatever Gisella has planned, but Beatriz is alone.

When she reaches the sea garden, it is all but deserted, with only a few courtiers strolling through the shallow water, along paths that cut through the jewel-bright corals and anemones and other sea creatures cultivated for the garden. Beatriz shucks off her slippers, leaving them on the sand as she wades in, her guards—as ever—just behind her.

Even though it's winter in Cellaria, there is only the barest chill in the air and the water lapping at Beatriz's ankles is more refreshing than bracing. As she makes her way down a sandy path, her mind turns.

She could tell Nicolo her suspicion that Gisella is planning to kill her. With everything she knows, it's more than a suspicion, and she can make him see the truth as well. His trust in Gisella already seems fractured—she can use that. But Nicolo isn't some sentimental fool, even if he *does* care for Beatriz. He betrayed her once and he'll betray her again, especially if her mother has offered Gisella something tempting to lure her into murdering Beatriz. Something like naming Nicolo her heir after she dies childless—a promise the empress would never actually follow through on, but one that would be tempting to both Gisella and Nicolo nonetheless.

She could tell both Nicolo *and* Gisella the truth about everything—her mother's plans to take all of Vesteria for her own, Sophronia's death, her true mission in originally coming to Cellaria. It could serve to break the illusion of whatever promises the empress has made and show how little the empress can be trusted, but again it requires more faith in Nicolo and Gisella than Beatriz is comfortable placing in them. And, knowing her mother, she's devised contingencies for that.

No, Beatriz needs to do something her mother won't expect of her, and that means doing *exactly* what she's been raised to.

Beatriz looks around at the courtiers in the sea garden, taking in the new faces. One of those new faces is familiar, as if summoned from Beatriz's musings.

"Your Grace," she says, calling up a bright smile as she approaches the Duke of Ribel, who bows deeply in return.

Beatriz thought him handsome at breakfast the other day, but here in the garden, as he stands in the golden sunlight, his tan skin glows and the waves of his dark brown hair are tousled by the sea air. His trousers are cuffed just below his knees to avoid the tide and his white linen shirt is rolled up at the elbows, baring strong forearms that Beatriz has to force herself not to stare at. She doesn't think she's ever found forearms a particularly attractive body part before, but there is a first time for everything.

"Your Highness," he says, rising from his bow with a smile, his blue eyes glinting. "It's nice to see you up and about." At her confused look, he continues, "My cousins said you were exhausted after your ordeal in Bessemia, which was why you were not much seen."

"Ah, yes," Beatriz says, and it takes every ounce of self-control not to roll her eyes. "I'm feeling much better, and I've always loved the sea garden."

"As have I," he says. "I missed it in my time away from court."

Beatriz mentally sifts through the decade of gossip that made its way from her mother's spies in Cellaria to her schoolroom in Bessemia, her memory catching on the information she seeks. The Duke of Ribel left court several years back, after he became a target of the late king's temper one too many times. Beatriz suspects that the reason for that is King Cesare's jealousy of the much younger, handsomer, more charming man who was a rival to his throne. She suspects it's the same reason King Cesare was so cruel to Pasquale, why he gave Nicolo the position of cupbearer and hurled goblets at him when he felt like it.

"How long were you gone from court?" Beatriz asks him as they begin to walk together, side by side down the path, her guards a few steps behind them. They'll tell Nicolo about this, she's sure, and she welcomes it. Let Nicolo know that he can kidnap her and force her into marriage, but he can't control her. And, after their last conversation, let him worry what she might do if he refuses her demand for an equal partnership—let him wonder if she might find a new king of Cellaria to give her what she wants. After all, Nicolo's hold on the throne is tenuous, and the Duke of Ribel has every bit as much of a claim to it as Nicolo does, both of them nephews of the last king.

"Five years. I left just after my father died and I inherited the dukedom. I was twelve. My guardian—an uncle on my mother's side—thought it would be unsafe for me here."

"He was likely right," she tells him. "I wasn't a member of King Cesare's court for long, but I was here long enough to see the effect it had on Pasquale, Nicolo, even Gisella. I don't think it was any place for a young person with any proximity to power."

"From what I've heard, it wasn't safe for you, either," he says, his voice softening.

Beatriz laughs, shrugging. "I wasn't here long enough to have had too many issues. Until the end, I suppose."

"Until you helped a condemned traitor escape from the dungeon and found yourself banished to a Sororia?" he asks.

Beatriz nearly misses a step but catches herself, offering the duke a bashful smile. "I didn't understand what we were doing," she says, the lie rolling off her tongue.

"Ah, of course, it was Pasquale's idea, wasn't it?" he asks, echoing the lie that Gisella and Nicolo planted to keep Beatriz's name clean and allow her to marry Nicolo. "I must say, it doesn't sound like the cousin I remember."

It wasn't at all like Pasquale, in truth. He'd only gone along with her mad plan because she'd asked it of him, convinced him that everything would be fine. But now here they are, her a prisoner in Cellaria, him somewhere in the world, trying to survive without his name, title, or any money. It is, she supposes, better than the time they spent in the Sororia and Fraternia, but not by much.

"People change, Your Grace," Beatriz says.

"Call me Enzo, please," he says. "*Your Grace* sounds so stuffy, and I hope that you'll consider me a friend, Your Highness."

"Then you must call me Beatriz," she says, taking the opportunity to survey him. He's using her, she knows that, but to what end? She assumes, based on the information she heard at the council meeting she attended with her mother in Cellaria, that he's going to make a play for the throne, and she knows he's already amassed some support. Perhaps, like Nicolo, he thinks marrying her, a saint in the eyes of the Cellarian people and the way to maintaining a prosperous alliance with Bessemia, will make him a more appealing option for king. If that's the move he's intending to make, he'll be disappointed, but Beatriz sees no reason she can't use him in return. "And I hope we can be friends, Enzo. I suppose we both know how lonely court can be."

They reach the start of the path where the sea meets the shore, and Enzo turns toward Beatriz, lifting her hand to his lips and kissing it, lingering a half second longer than seems appropriate.

"Good day, Beatriz, I hope we meet again soon," he says.

# Violie

Violie, Leopold, Pasquale, and Ambrose ride hard until midday, aiming to put as much distance between themselves and the empress as possible so that any trackers she sends after them will have difficulty following. In eight hours of riding, they've crossed into Bessemia, and they stop for a short break near Lake Asteria, eating the packed lunch Violie swiped from the kitchens—a mix of apples, hard cheeses, and fresh bread—and letting the horses graze and rest.

While the others chat about the journey, Violie takes an apple from her saddlebag and palms one of the thirteen vials of stardust Daphne gave them, walking far enough away that she'll be out of earshot. She finds a boulder by a small stream and perches on it, sitting cross-legged and taking a bite of the apple, looking at the vial of stardust in her hand as she chews, thinking over whether now is the right time to use it.

She's being impatient. She knows she's being impatient. But it's been days since Daphne tried to reach Beatriz, and now that they have more information, Violie suspects Beatriz was drugged for the journey to Cellaria, which might have made it impossible for Daphne to speak with her. And she would have made it back to Cellaria by now. If she *had* been drugged for the journey, she wouldn't be anymore.

It's a lot of ifs, but the more Violie turns over the sequence of events in her mind, the more sure she is. Even from a distance she can hear Pasquale's voice, Ambrose's laugh. She considered telling the others her plan while she formed it during their ride, but all it would accomplish is getting their hopes up, and Violie doesn't want to do that just to have to dash them again if it doesn't work.

She takes another bite of her apple, then another, but she knows she's procrastinating.

"What are you . . ." Leopold's voice jerks Violie from her thoughts, and she looks up to find him approaching her through the woods, his eyes on the stardust in her hand. "Is that one of the ones Daphne gave us?" he asks slowly. "To use in Cellaria to help get Beatriz out?"

Violie closes her hand over the vial, feeling her face heat. "We have twelve more vials," she points out. "I think Daphne gave us more than enough." Even as she says the words, though, she knows she has no way of knowing that. It isn't as if she has any experience staging a rescue mission in a hostile country. Leopold simply raises an eyebrow, and she sighs, telling him her theory about Beatriz being unconscious and therefore unreachable when Daphne tried.

"For all we know, Daphne is trying again now," Leopold points out.

That, Violie hadn't considered, but of course Daphne will try again. If she has to use all the stardust in Friv, Daphne won't stop until she reaches her sister. And if Beatriz said anything to Daphne that Violie and the others would need to know, Daphne would pass it along. She, unlike Violie, can access more stardust with relative ease.

Violie lets out a long exhale. "I don't like it," she says finally.

Leopold moves closer, sitting beside her on the boulder. "You don't like trusting Daphne?" he asks. "I know her loyalty has been wobbly in the past, but—"

"No, I trust Daphne," Violie interrupts, shaking her head. "But I don't like relying on her—not *just* her. I don't like relying on anyone." She pauses, considering what she's just said, and Leopold, for his part, lets her think. "I've always worked alone," she says. "And it's always turned out perfectly well that way. But this"—she gestures to the woods in the general direction of where Pasquale and Ambrose are—"this is new to me."

Leopold nods slowly. "For what it's worth, I thought we made a good team before," he says, though there's an uncertainty to his voice that's new.

"We did," she says quickly. "But I suppose before, for the most part, I asked—or maybe assumed—a lot more trust of you than you asked of me."

Leopold gives a half smile. "You trusted me about Daphne, when I told you I trusted her," he points out. "And I know that couldn't have been easy."

She snorts. "No, definitely not, but you were right in the end."

"And trusting you has never led me astray," he replies.

The words steal Violie's breath. She shakes her head. "Sophronia trusted me," she says after a moment.

"She did," he says. "She trusted both of us, and I don't think she regretted that in the end."

For a moment, Violie doesn't quite know what to say. No matter what Daphne claimed Sophronia's spirit told her during the northern lights, she doesn't think she'll ever feel like she's truly earned Sophronia's forgiveness. If Violie hadn't stolen the royal seal from her bedchamber, if she hadn't used it to forge a declaration of war on Cellaria, it wouldn't have sparked the mob that arrested and beheaded Sophronia. Forgiveness will always feel just out of reach. "You must miss her terribly," she says, hoping to change the subject.

It's Leopold's turn to fall silent. When he speaks, his voice is soft, but sure. "I do. I think I probably always will. But I've gotten to know her better in death than I think I ever knew her in life."

"That isn't true—"

"I don't mean it as an insult," he says quickly. "But in all the letters we shared over all those years, I think we were both lying in a way. Each of us was showing the other the parts we wanted them to see—she was using her training even then, and I . . . well, I wanted her to see the Leopold I wanted to be, someone smart and brave, someone worthy of being king."

"You are all those things, Leo," Violie tells him, resisting the urge to reach for his hand. They're friends, she tells herself, and it wouldn't be the first time they've shown each other comfort, but here and now, with Sophronia's shadow heavy on them, it would feel wrong.

"I like to think I've *become* that person," he says. "Sophie was becoming the person she wanted to be too. In the end,

I hope she felt she got there. I loved her, but I'm starting to think it was a half-formed type of love, built more on hope than anything solid because *we* were still half formed. Do you know what I mean?"

Violie swallows, thinking of the Leopold she knew in Temarin, the one who traveled with her to Friv, not just heartbroken but soul-broken, seeing everything he'd known to be true ripped away from him. He isn't the same person he was then. And Sophie, had she survived, likely wouldn't be the same person now either.

"I do," she says slowly. "But I don't think that makes what the two of you shared any less real."

"No," he agrees. "I believe the man I'm becoming would have loved the woman she would have been, and there is a part of me that will always be angry that that future was taken away from us."

Words escape Violie again. She feels the urge to defend Sophronia, but defend her against what? Leopold has a point, and if Sophronia were here, Violie knows she would agree with him. "We'll make the empress pay for that," she says finally, the only thing she can think to say. She is drowning in a sea of complicated emotions, reaching for anger—trusted and familiar—to keep her afloat.

Leopold laughs, but the sound comes out harsh. "I wish I could think of it like that," he says, shaking his head. "Like there was a price I could extract from Margaraux that would heal that wound, that would balance the scales, that would make the world feel just and right again, but there isn't. I'm not here, standing against her, to get some sort of revenge, Violie. I'm here to stop her from hurting anyone else."

Violie looks at him for a long moment. She assumed anger was driving him, like it's driving her. Not because she thinks it will balance any scales, but because anger has *always* driven her. It's only now, in this moment, that she realizes it isn't the same for everyone. She envies him that, but at the same time, she doesn't know who she is without her anger—at the empress, at the world, at herself. She doesn't know how she could survive without it to fuel her.

Silence stretches between them for a long moment, and when Pasquale shouts their names and says they should get going, Violie is relieved.

In the evening, they reach a fork in the road with a crudely crafted signpost pointing out where each tine leads. The path to the right takes them west, toward Temarin, the path to the left takes them east toward Hapantoile. The path straight ahead takes them through the Nemaria Woods and into Cellaria. To Beatriz.

Violie doesn't hesitate before starting down the path straight ahead, but Leopold pulls his horse to the left. Pasquale and Ambrose come to a halt, looking between them.

"We're going to Cellaria," Violie says over her shoulder, trying to keep patience in her voice when she doesn't feel particularly patient. She would wager everything she owns that all three of them received a far better education than she did—surely they can read a simple signpost.

"Going through Hapantoile will be less suspicious," Leopold argues.

Violie pulls her horse's reins, bringing the mare to a stop. She turns, looking at Leopold over her shoulder, then toward Pasquale and Ambrose. She snorts. "I'd argue that would be extremely suspicious," she points out.

"Which is exactly why Margaraux will think you're too smart to go that way," Leopold counters.

"There's no reason to waste time in Hapantoile; Beatriz—" Violie starts.

"Will survive the day's delay stopping in Bessemia will cost us," Leopold says, his voice decisive.

"We don't know that—"

"Violie," Ambrose says, surprising her. She turns back to him and sees an unexpected softness in his face. "How long has it been since you've seen your mother?"

*A year and a half,* Violie thinks immediately, but she doesn't say it aloud. Instead, she tamps down the way her heart lifts at the thought of seeing her mother and raises her chin, keeping her expression carefully cool. "You said Beatriz healed her. I'll see her when this mess with the empress is through."

As she says the words, she knows they're all thinking the same thing—that this mess with the empress very well may never be through, that just because her mother has been healed doesn't mean she's in any less danger, especially now that the empress knows Violie betrayed her. But she trusts that her mother can fend for herself, and she knows she has the help of the other women at the Crimson Petal.

What Violie doesn't say aloud, what she barely allows herself to even think, is that as desperate as she is to see her mother, she doesn't want her mother to see *her*. Does she know what Violie has done over the last year and a half, the people she has hurt, the damage she has caused? She is largely responsible for bringing an entire country to ruin, for the siege that killed not just Sophronia but countless others. She did it to save her mother, but Violie knows her mother will not be moved by that knowledge, and she doesn't want her mother to look at her and see the person she's become. She'd rather her mother remember her as she was, even if it means never seeing her again.

The other three exchange a look that Violie can't read before Pasquale finally clears his throat.

"When we were in Hapantoile before, when Beatriz healed your mother," he says slowly, "everyone at the Crimson Petal was grateful, and the madam there made it clear their loyalty was to Beatriz—that she believed a debt was owed."

Violie scoffs, hoping to hide how the words clench at her heart. The madam at the Crimson Petal, Elodia, had been a grandmother of sorts to Violie when she was growing up, a woman as shrewd at business as she was loyal to the woman who worked for her. She wasn't one to swear that loyalty to an outsider, but if she'd offered it to Beatriz, it was too valuable a gift to pass up. Still . . .

"We aren't dragging my mother into this, or Elodia, or any of the others there," Violie says, her voice firm. "They have plenty of troubles of their own, and who sits on what throne has nothing to do with them."

"Normally, I'd agree with you," Pasquale says, his voice low. "But Beatriz's life is on the line, and I will take every bit of help I can get, from every corner offering it, if it means saving her."

"We aren't asking anyone at the Crimson Petal to charge into Cellaria with us," Leopold adds, looking between Violie and his cousin. "But if there's a chance to gather more resources, more intelligence about what is waiting for us, more time to formulate a plan—"

He breaks off, a frown creasing his forehead as he looks at Violie, noticing the spark in her eyes as a plan comes to her, half formed and tentative, but a plan nonetheless. A plan they will need the help of the Crimson Petal to execute, because she knows that courtesans can find an open door just about anywhere in the world, even in palaces, and they are always, *always* underestimated.

"Vi . . . ," Leopold starts, but Violie is already digging her heels into her mare's sides, urging her forward and steering her down the left tine of the fork, toward Hapantoile, to her mother and her home, joy and dread going to war inside her as she gathers her words.

"I know how we can get into the Cellarian court," she says, her words curt.

# Daphne

The empress spends most of her first full day in Friv resting, but Daphne knows that her mother has eyes and ears everywhere, so she isn't surprised when she receives a pointed summons, demanding that Daphne join her mother in her rooms before dinner. She knows it will be about Violie and Leopold's sudden departure from the castle.

"This isn't Bessemia. She has no power to issue orders as if Friv is hers," Bairre mutters from his place sitting cross-legged at the foot of their bed, watching as Daphne bustles around their bedroom, fussing with her hair in the vanity mirror, checking that her gown is pristinely pressed and fitted. If she has a hair out of place, her mother will notice. Daphne can see her, amber eyes fixed on any imperfection she perceives, nostrils flaring, mouth pursed. That look has haunted Daphne's nightmares for years, and she wishes she could say that that fear has gone away these past weeks, but it hasn't.

She knows there are bigger issues at play than how she looks, but it feels like one small thing she has control over.

"I think you'll find that my mother believes she has power

*everywhere* she goes," Daphne tells him, pinching her cheeks to bring color to them. "But we have power too—enough that we know she hasn't sent scouts out of the castle to find Violie and Leopold. Not yet, at least."

"And that worries you more than if she *had* sent scouts," Bairre says.

Daphne's eyes find his in the mirror and she turns to face him, smoothing her hands down the front of her velvet skirt. "My mother is always a step ahead," she says softly. "So yes, I would prefer to know the direction in which those steps are heading."

Bairre pushes himself up to stand, crossing the room toward her, his expression so somber that Daphne has to fight the urge to smooth the furrow in his brow away with her fingers. "I'm not worried about Violie and Leopold," he says, reaching a hand up to cup her face, his calloused palm against her cheek. "I'm worried about you."

Daphne forces a smile, trying not to give away her own fears, not only for herself, but for him, too. "We could always run," she says. "Leave Friv, leave Vesteria altogether. Head somewhere warm—a tropical island where no one has even heard the name Empress Margaraux before."

Bairre smiles too, but it doesn't reach his eyes and she knows he is only humoring her. "We could spend our days lying out on a beach, sunburn the biggest threat we face."

"Paradise." Daphne says the word on a sigh, wanting that life so badly it hurts. But then she thinks about Beatriz, about Violie and Leopold, Pasquale and Ambrose, about Cliona, Rufus, Haimish—even King Bartholomew and Lord Cadringal and everyone else in Friv who doesn't yet realize the threat her mother poses. About Friv itself, a country she was prepared to hate but has come to love. About the rest of Vesteria and what it will become if her mother gets her way.

Daphne knows she can't find paradise while the world around her burns, and looking up at Bairre, she knows he feels the same.

"Stars above, I wish we could be happy in paradise," he says, taking the words from her.

"So do I," she tells him. Then she kisses him all too briefly on the lips and pulls away, steeling herself to do battle with her mother. When she reaches the door, she pauses, turning back toward him.

"Do you have any more stardust?" she asks.

Bairre frowns. "We gave all of it to Violie and the others," he says.

"But can you get more?" she asks. "I want to try to talk to Beatriz again tonight."

Bairre opens his mouth—to argue, Daphne expects, to tell her that it's foolish of her to try again when her attempts haven't worked the last dozen or so times she's tried. But instead, he catches himself. "Do you think this time will be different?" he asks.

Daphne hesitates. Her mother said Beatriz had gone to Cellaria, but Daphne knows her sister wouldn't have gone without a fight. Her mother would have had an easier time of it drugging her, and if she'd been drugged, Daphne wouldn't have been able to reach her. It's possible that if she tries again, it will work. But does she truly believe that, or does she just want to try again out of habit and a growing sense of desperation? She casts her thoughts to Beatriz, several worlds away.

"I think . . . I think it'll work this time," she says quietly. "I just . . . feel it."

She half expects Bairre to laugh at her, but he doesn't. He just nods. "I can call in a favor," he says.

"Thank you."

---

"They're *gone*?" Empress Margaraux asks, eyeing Daphne over the top of her steaming teacup, brows raised.

Though she appears shocked, Daphne knows her mother well enough to know she isn't truly surprised.

"I'm afraid so," Daphne says, sipping her own tea. The sounds of laughter and music from the banquet hall below float up through the open window to the empress's sitting room, only serving to highlight the cold quiet.

Daphne would much rather be there, with Bairre and Cliona and the other Frivians, toasting and dancing before dinner is served, but instead she is here, struggling to perform a dangerous balancing act with her mother. She clears her throat and continues, spinning the story she and Violie devised.

"Leopold gave his excuses to Bartholomew—apparently he was alerted that one of his brothers had suffered a grave injury and he wanted to see for himself that he was safe," she said. "Violie elected to join him."

At that, the empress gives a short laugh. "Of course she did," she says, shaking her head. "I don't suppose you've managed to learn *where* his brothers are hiding?"

"I haven't," Daphne says, forcing a smile. It is the truth, too. When Leopold sent his brothers away from Friv for their safety, he wasn't certain he could trust Daphne, so Daphne arranged for Haimish to take them to a location only he, Leopold, and Violie would know. Haimish is Bairre's friend, and more hers than Leopold's, but his loyalty is, above all else, to Prince Gideon and Prince Reid. Now that she has more firmly earned Leopold's trust, she supposes she could have asked for the true location of his brothers, but she didn't see the point in that; she knew that sooner or later, her mother would ask her this very question, and the less Daphne has to lie about, the better. She continues. "Surely Violie will tell you when she returns—unless you don't trust her?"

She asks the words idly, tilting her head to one side to regard her mother with what she hopes is an innocent expression.

The empress smiles. "Come now, Daphne, I raised you better than that—we trust no one."

"Of course not, Mother," Daphne says. "But I could hardly follow along, could I? And I'm sure you wouldn't have hired Violie if you didn't understand who she is and how she operates."

Her mother makes a noncommittal noise in the back of her throat. "At any rate, I'm not concerned with Leopold or that girl, whatever name she's calling herself now. Temarin is mine, after all, and if he has an ounce of sense in that brain of his, he won't try to take it back. What I still do not have is Friv."

Daphne tries to hide her expression by taking another

sip of tea. "As I shared in my letters and I'm sure your spies have told you, Friv is on the verge of a civil war and it is only a matter of time before it's vulnerable." A shade of truth, if not all of it. "I've been urging things along, stoking tensions between Bartholomew's court and the rebels—though they are one and the same in quite a few cases. Now that I'm officially princess of Friv and queen-to-be, I'll be able to redouble my efforts. Patience, Mama. Friv *will* fall."

The empress's nostrils flare, but that is the only visible reaction she has to Daphne's words. "If I truly believed you had the matter well in hand, I wouldn't have dragged myself up here in the dead of winter, Daphne," she says.

The words pierce through Daphne's armor, wounding her. Despite everything Daphne knows to be true of her mother, despite how much she tells herself she doesn't need or want her approval, the words still sting.

"The situation in Friv is complicated," she says tightly. "But I don't believe anyone could do a better job of driving it to war—not even you."

The empress's eyes spark, and a cruel smile curls over her lips. "I'd like to see that for myself," she says. "You mentioned in your letters that Lord Panlington was heading the rebellion?"

Daphne nods even as she curses her past self, so anxious to impress her mother that she'd told her far more than she should have. She was such a fool.

"I've issued an invitation for him to join me for lunch tomorrow and he's accepted," the empress says. "You'll join us."

Daphne's stomach sours, but she manages to maintain her smile. "Of course, Mama."

"You'll bring your husband, too," the empress adds.

Daphne laughs. "That's hardly necessary—Bairre doesn't know anything about anything."

When her mother's red-painted lips purse, Daphne knows she's misstepped. For a moment, her heart stops, panic turning her blood to ice.

"My spies tell me differently," the empress says slowly. "But then, I think you know that, Daphne."

Mind awhirl, Daphne takes a moment to gather herself.

"I'm sure your spies have told you that Bairre fancies himself part of the rebellion," she says carefully. "But he's nothing more than a pawn."

Daphne knows her mother won't believe her, but she doesn't need her to. She needs the empress to misunderstand the reason for Daphne's lie, so she lets a blush rise to her cheeks as she glances away, biting her lip. She summons the way Sophronia always used to look when she spoke of Leopold in their mother's presence, like she is trying—and failing—to hide just how much Bairre means to her.

Her mother clicks her tongue. "Oh, Daphne," she says. "I raised you better than that."

Daphne pretends confusion. "I don't know what you mean, Mama," she says, forcing a bright smile that doesn't actually feel forced at all. Better that her mother believes her a lovesick fool whose loyalties have shifted because of tender feelings for her husband than the truth.

"I'm sure you don't," the empress says, not even bothering to make the words sound true. "But all the same, I expect you and your husband at lunch tomorrow, and I'm sure you don't wish to disappoint me."

At that, Daphne's smile does feel strained, the souring in her stomach all too real. "Of course not, Mama," she says before standing. "We should get to dinner—the Frivians are beasts; if we tarry too long there won't be a crumb left."

Saying the words makes Daphne's skin crawl, but she knows she needs to maintain the illusion, now more than ever, that she detests Friv, that she views the people who live here as less than human.

Dinner passes in a blur, Daphne barely able to maintain small talk with the nobles seated near her as she keeps an eye on her mother across the table, noting who she's speaking to and doing her best to read her lips without anyone—her mother especially—taking note. As far as Daphne is able to tell, though, her mother is also only engaging in small talk, speaking about the weather with Lord Fulcher and about the design of her gown with Lady Uster. The empress is wearing what Daphne and her sisters used to call her *court smile,* the one that can brighten a room and entrance anyone she directs it at. The one that can fall away in an instant as soon as a door closes behind her, like a mask dropping at the end of a masquerade.

Daphne knows her mother well, though. She can see the subtle flare of her nostrils when she takes her first sip of Frivian ale, the nearly imperceptible flinch at Lord Fulcher's thick highland accent, the way her eyes linger disparagingly on Lady Uster's gown, pretty but unforgivably plain by her mother's standards. The empress's revulsion for Friv and its people is clear, to Daphne if no one else, and while that angers her, she's also deeply embarrassed by it—in no small part because she knows she acted the same way when she first arrived in Friv.

Daphne thought the stars would all tumble from the sky before the day came when her mother would mortify her like this, but the woman across the table isn't the untouchable goddess Daphne always viewed her mother as, a flawless, looming figure who could do no wrong and whose word was law. Instead, each time Daphne looks at her mother, she's struck by how *sad* she is.

Still dangerous, of course, but painfully human.

By the time dinner is over, Daphne feels a bit light-headed from one too many mugs of ale. She knows she should have kept her wits about her better, especially with her mother so close, but it feels nice, for just a moment, to enjoy the alcohol buzzing through her veins, the heavy feel of Bairre's arm around her shoulders, the way her body fits so perfectly against his as they stumble back to their rooms, Bairre every bit as tipsy as she is. They say good night to the guards outside their rooms and Daphne tries to ignore the knowing look the guards share, as if they know exactly what Daphne and Bairre will be getting up to tonight.

They're wrong, of course. As much as Daphne would like to spend the rest of the night wrapped up in Bairre, she won't. Now, more than ever, it's important that their marriage remain unconsummated, to prevent her mother from taking control of Friv should anything happen to Daphne. Should anything happen to both of them, she corrects herself, the thought sobering her. She glances sideways at Bairre as he opens the door to their rooms and ushers her inside, his hand at the small of her back.

Her conversation with her mother wasn't a shocking one, all things considered, but it felt like a bucket of ice water over her head all the same. If Daphne had been any less selfish, she would have tried to send Bairre off to Cellaria with the others, but she knows Bairre would rather have cut off his own hand than leave Friv. She loves him for that.

She loves him.

The thought is fuzzy and ale-soaked, but it sticks in her mind like tar. She loves him.

Also not shocking, but also like being soaked with ice water.

She should tell him as much. The words rise to her lips—*I love you*—but before she can give voice to them, Bairre reaches into the pocket of his coat and pulls out a vial of stardust.

"Do you want privacy?" he asks her.

Daphne blinks before remembering their earlier conversation—she's going to try to talk to Beatriz again.

"No," she says, taking the vial from him. "Will you stay with me?"

"Of course," he tells her.

He shrugs out of his coat and helps her out of her own, hanging them side by side in their wardrobe. She walks from their sitting room to their bedroom, Bairre at her heels, and sits down cross-legged on their bed, her velvet gown surrounding her like a flower's fallen petals. After a brief hesitation, Bairre sits next to her.

Daphne looks down at the vial of stardust, turning the cool glass over in her hands. She's tried so many times to reach Beatriz that she's lost count. What if she's too late, what if her mother was lying and Beatriz is already dead? What if this attempt doesn't work either, if she is never able to speak to her sister again? The thought turns her stomach and she clutches the vial tighter in her hand.

*No*, she thinks. The stars themselves aren't going to keep her from her sister, not again.

She unstoppers the vial and smears the dust over the back of her hand, letting her eyes flutter closed.

"I wish I could speak to Princess Beatriz Soluné."

Everything is still and silent, Bairre's presence beside her the only thing Daphne is aware of. *It didn't work.* Disappointment seeps through her. She is just about to open her eyes when she feels a shift, her sister's presence as recognizable as the sound of her own name.

"Beatriz," she says, though she knows her lips don't move.

"Daphne?" Beatriz's voice is as clear as if she were standing next to Daphne.

At the sound of her sister saying her name, Daphne feels the tension go out of her, a breath filling her lungs completely for the first time in more than a week. Distantly, she's aware of Bairre's hand on her back, anchoring her.

"You're alive," she says, relief overwhelming her until she's dizzy with it.

"I'm alive," Beatriz confirms. "Fine, more or less, just in Cellaria—"

"I know," Daphne interrupts. She doesn't know how long this connection will last and she doesn't want to waste time. "Mama made it sound like you went of your own volition, but I knew that wasn't true, even before Pasquale confirmed it."

Beatriz pauses as she processes this. "You've seen Pas?" she asks finally.

"Yes, he and Ambrose are fine. They're on their way to you now, along with Violie and Leopold."

At that, Beatriz lets out a low curse. "Why would you send him here? They'll kill him in Cellaria," she snaps.

Irritation flares. It strikes Daphne as almost funny that she can go from being relieved that her sister is alive to so annoyed with her in just a few seconds, but it's hardly the first time her feelings toward Beatriz have swung so wildly.

"Considering that Mama is in Friv, there seem to be few places he can go where someone *doesn't* want him dead," Daphne replies, her words sharp. "I thought he had a better chance in Cellaria, and I ought to add that I doubt I could have stopped him even if I'd wanted to." Beatriz sighs, and Daphne feels herself soften. "He's fine, Beatriz. I didn't have the chance to get to know him well, but he seemed to know what he was doing. And at any rate, Violie is with him."

"That does make me feel better," Beatriz admits after a moment. "I'm sorry I snapped—I didn't realize Mama was there in Friv. How are you?"

A sharp laugh forces its way out of Daphne. "Alive," she says. "Trying to stay that way."

"Does she know your allegiances have shifted?" Beatriz asks.

It's a question Daphne has pondered herself, but she can't

come to a conclusion. It feels as if she and her mother are acting out an elaborate play each time they talk, speaking lines and pretending to be other people. But is that because her mother knows of Daphne's betrayal? Or is it because her mother has *always* been playing a part with her and Daphne is merely recognizing it for the first time?

"I don't know," Daphne admits. "She arrived when she received word Sophie was alive. She wanted to see it for herself."

At that, Beatriz laughs truly, and the sound wraps around Daphne like a warm hug. "I would give anything to have seen her face in that moment," Beatriz says.

"One day, I'll describe it to you in great detail," Daphne promises. "What about you? I'm imagining you being kept locked away in a tower somewhere in Cellaria."

"It isn't quite so bad," Beatriz says. "I'm managing things as best I can. Nicolo wants to marry me, and I think I can use him. It's Gisella who concerns me. I believe Mama's given her instructions to kill me. It's part of the wish she made with Nigellus before we were born—we have to die on the soil of the land Mama is conquering, by the hand of someone from there. *By Cellarian hands, on Cellarian soil,* is what he said about me."

So Daphne will need to be killed by Frivian hands, on Frivian soil. Which might explain why her mother hasn't made her move yet.

"And you can't simply . . . wish your way out?" Daphne asks.

There's a pause. "Pasquale told you?" Beatriz asks.

"He said you were an empyrea. I confess, Beatriz, I can scarcely believe it," Daphne says.

"Neither can I," Beatriz admits. "Especially since I can no longer do it."

"Oh," Daphne says, feeling herself deflate. "Nigellus must have told Mama—perhaps she's given you something that's muting your powers?"

"No," Beatriz says. "I have no illusions about who Nigellus was, but I know he didn't tell Mama anything about me. It wouldn't have been in his best interests to."

"Then why—"

"I killed him," Beatriz interrupts. "Nigellus, I mean. He was trying to wish on the stars, to take away my gift, and I . . . I couldn't let him do that."

Daphne goes still, words leaving her. She knows Beatriz had the same training she did. They learned how to kill side by side, with poisons, with daggers, with their bare hands if necessary. Daphne herself has killed her fair share of people since coming to Friv—the assassins in the woods; Ansel, who held a dagger to Prince Gideon's throat; Eugenia in her sickbed. But try as she might, she can't imagine Beatriz doing the same. But she did.

"I have to wonder if it's a punishment from the stars," Beatriz says when Daphne doesn't respond. "They gave me this gift, and now they've taken it away because I killed him."

"From what you've told me, Triz, if the stars hold his death against you, then I curse the lot of them."

Beatriz doesn't respond, but Daphne can feel her smile. "What, then?" she asks finally.

"I don't know," Daphne says. "But I'd wager I'll have a better chance of discovering what happened here. And when Pasquale and the others reach you, they'll have enough stardust with them to get you out no matter what power you may or may not have."

"It's dangerous," Beatriz says.

"It's worth it," Daphne replies, just before the magic cuts out and Daphne is alone in her head once more.

# Beatriz

Beatriz opens her eyes to meet the stares of a dozen ladies of the Cellarian court, including Gisella. Daphne certainly could have picked a more opportune moment to reach her than during the dinner party Gisella insisted Beatriz attend with her and her friends—though *friends* is certainly a loose term from what Beatriz can see. Still, perhaps, Beatriz reasons as she notes that most of the stares are intrigued rather than fearful, she can use this to her advantage.

She heaves a dramatic sigh, touching the back of her hand to her forehead and casting her gaze upward—where the night stars would be shining down if they weren't ensconced indoors, in Lady Pignalle's dining room.

"The stars," she says, letting her eyes drift closed. "I'm sorry, they're just so loud tonight, I can hardly concentrate." She opens her eyes again and drops her hand, turning her attention back to Lady Pignalle, who'd been speaking before Daphne interrupted Beatriz's thoughts. "I'm sorry, Adriella—you were telling us about your husband's new racehorse?"

"I . . . ," Lady Pignalle says, her eyes darting to Gisella, then back to Beatriz. "Yes, Your Highness. Descended from King Cesare's prize stallion."

"Ah," Beatriz says. Even now, the sound of King Cesare's name alone is enough to make her feel ill. "Well, the late king did have excellent taste in horses."

It's such an inane comment that Beatriz wants to roll her eyes, never mind that she's the one saying the words. Why Gisella insisted she come tonight, she has no idea; she has to assume it's an attempt to bore her to death. But when she glances at the other girl across the round dining table, Gisella is watching her with curious eyes.

"Your Highness," another one of the ladies says—Lady Traversini, a woman about five years older than Beatriz. "If I may ask . . . what are the stars saying?"

The question prompts a flurry of whispers from the rest of the table, and Beatriz is shocked that the woman is bold enough to ask it. There is nothing outright heretical about it, even by Cellaria's standards, but were King Cesare still alive, it might very well be enough to earn her a thorough and likely violent interrogation, if not outright execution. Now, under Nicolo, things are more lax. Not lax enough that Beatriz can easily access stardust, unfortunately, but more lax all the same.

Beatriz knows how to play a role, so she offers Lady Traversini a bright smile. "They say there is change coming," she says.

"Of course there is," Gisella says, sipping from her goblet of red wine. "Cellaria will be blessed with a new queen soon, after all. What a change that will be."

The words pool like tar in Beatriz's stomach. She doesn't

need the reminder that her wedding to Nicolo is looming ever closer, and that as soon as it's done, Gisella will kill her. Looking at her now, Beatriz struggles to imagine it. She and Gisella have been at odds, but they were friends once. She should know better than to be so sentimental, but when she tries to imagine their situations reversed, she doesn't think she would be able to kill Gisella, even after everything. But she's underestimated Gisella before, and that isn't a mistake she intends to make a third time.

Daphne said Pasquale and Ambrose were heading to Cellaria, with Violie and Leopold in tow. Though she knows Cellaria isn't safe for Pasquale, her heart lifts at the thought of seeing him again—a possibility she hadn't allowed herself to hope for before. And as afraid for him as she is, she knows he's safe with Violie. The real question is whether or not they'll arrive before her wedding, before Gisella sees her promise to the empress through.

Beatriz still hasn't seen Nicolo since their conversation in the servants' corridor—and it's getting more and more difficult for her to believe it's an accident. He's avoiding her, and she understands why. She can still feel the ghost of his breath against her cheek, his dark gaze on her, his stubbled cheek beneath her palm. She was using him, pulling out every last trick she'd learned from her training with the courtesans, but she would be lying if she said it didn't affect her.

Her feelings for Nicolo had been a fire, bright and hot but young enough to smother without much trouble. Or so she'd thought. In that moment in the servants' corridor, she could feel them banking to life again, threatening to burn her from inside.

She knows who Nicolo is, she knows he's a coward and a snake, that he betrayed her once and will doubtless do it again if she lets him. Sometimes, though, her body has a tendency to forget that.

*Beatriz, you shameless harlot,* Daphne's voice whispers through her mind as she paces her sitting room that night. For a moment, she thinks Daphne has used more stardust to speak with her, but it's only a memory of the countless times her sister has chided her for letting her feelings get the better of her.

She thinks of Daphne, cold and calculating. From across the continent, Beatriz decides to borrow those qualities, wrapping them up in layers of softness and charm. Nicolo has ignored her for too long, and while neither of them may like it, he *is* her best chance at getting out of Cellaria before Pasquale reaches her and likely loses his head in the process.

Crossing to her desk, she scribbles a brief note.

*You've been working too hard and you must relax sometime. Join me for dessert in my rooms?*

Beatriz takes the note to the door that leads from her sitting room to the main hallway, opening it to find two guards stationed just outside. She passes the note to one of them with a bright smile.

"Have this delivered to the king, please," she says. "And ask the kitchen to send up red wine and some of those delightful citrus tarts."

Just twenty minutes later, Beatriz's guards announce that the king has arrived, opening the door to her sitting room and ushering Nicolo inside. He's flanked by his own guards, but they remain outside, leaving Nicolo and Beatriz alone.

In the twenty minutes since she sent the note, Beatriz has transformed herself, changing out of the modest pale rose brocade dress she wore to dinner and into an emerald-colored evening gown with off-the-shoulder sleeves and a daringly low neckline. While the jewelry box and cosmetics case she used when she was in Cellaria before weren't placed in her rooms along with her extensive wardrobe, there were plenty of other, more ordinary items to use. A long gold chain with a ruby pendant further highlights her décolletage, and she has touched up her face with a hint of kohl around her eyes and a swipe of red lip paint.

The way Nicolo's eyes widen slightly when he sees her, the brief hitch in his step, tells Beatriz her efforts were not in vain.

"Nico," she says, offering what she hopes appears to be a guileless smile. "I'm so glad you came. I was beginning to think you were avoiding me."

"Not at all," Nicolo says, stepping forward to close the distance between them. She offers him her hand and he bows over it, brushing a kiss across her skin. Belatedly, she realizes she's supposed to curtsy to him, as king, but she can't bring herself to. Not when it's just the two of them. She doesn't think her body will let her. "But it is busy being king," he says, rising again, though he keeps hold of her hand, tucking it into the crook of his elbow.

"Well, as we discussed, I would like to help you with that," she says, keeping her voice light.

Nicolo laughs. "Let me get some wine first, will you?" he says, escorting her into the adjoining dining room.

While Beatriz was getting ready, her maids brought the citrus tarts she requested up from the kitchens. Two places are set on either side of the table, each with a goblet already full of red wine, with the half-full bottle at the center. Beatriz instructed the maids that tonight, she and Nicolo would be serving themselves, which she's sure will set the court gossip mill aflame for at least the next few days.

Nicolo holds one of the chairs out for her, and once she's seated, he takes the other. Beatriz lifts her wine goblet toward him.

"To us," she says.

Nicolo's brow furrows in something like suspicion, but he echoes her toast and they both take a sip.

"You're in a very good mood today," he comments as he picks up one of the tarts, each one barely bigger than a single bite. Beatriz does the same. He takes a bite, chews, swallows before speaking again. "It's unnerving."

Beatriz snorts. "Why? Because I'm being held here against my will, forced into marriage with a man who's betrayed me several times? While I suppose that's enough to make anyone a bit peevish, I've decided to look on the bright side of things."

"And what is the bright side?" Nicolo asks warily.

"The food," Beatriz replies without a second's hesitation. He glances up, a second tart halfway to his mouth, surprised. "The food in Cellaria is far superior to anything found in Bessemia."

Nicolo smiles at that, popping the tart into his mouth. He follows it up with a sip of wine before leaning back in his chair to look at her. "Why does it feel like you're trying to seduce me?" he asks finally.

Beatriz is prepared for this. She knows if she tries to flatter him with lies, he'll see straight through them. She embraces the truth, mostly.

"Because I am," she tells him, shrugging. "What other power do I have here, Nico? Apart from the fact that you want me? Of course I'm going to use that, and you're a fool if you expected anything less."

For a moment, Nico doesn't say anything. Instead, he takes another sip of wine, mulling her words over.

"It doesn't suit you," he says finally.

A sudden worry nags at Beatriz, but she struggles not to show it, masking her insecurity in faux confusion. "The lip paint?" she asks, touching her fingers to her bottom lip, tracking the way his eyes follow the movement, lingering there.

"Powerlessness," he says. "I've seen you with the world at your feet, Beatriz, and I've seen you after you took a fall that few people would manage to rise from. Even then, you weren't powerless. Pretending to be so now, *that* is what doesn't suit. You could sooner convince me you were an empyrea."

It is an ironic choice of words, but Beatriz is the only one who knows that.

She laughs, letting the sound come out hard. "You and your sister have kidnapped me, you're responsible for killing Pasquale, you have my every step trailed by guards because you *know* if I had half a chance, I would run. You've taken every bit of control over my life, and yet you *still*—"

Nico interrupts her. "What were you doing with my cousin in the sea garden yesterday?"

Beatriz pauses, noting the flicker of envy in his eyes at the mention of Enzo. That, too, she expected, and she allows her mouth to curve into a true, spiteful smile.

"Hedging my bets," she tells him. "I've given you my terms, Nico. Should you not find them amenable, I'm sure he will. My marriage to Pasquale has already been annulled; I'm sure I can get ours annulled as well—assuming, of course, it takes that long for him to rally his supporters and dethrone you. I heard gossip even in Bessemia that he's a far more popular choice for king than you are. Perhaps the coup will happen before the wedding."

Nicolo looks at her for a long moment before reaching for his wineglass. He lifts it toward her like he's toasting her, a small smile curling at his lips. "There you are," he says with a knowing smile. "Not powerless at all."

Beatriz doesn't know whether Nicolo is giving her a compliment or simply reminding her that he sees through her. She should know better by now, should have learned how to hold her tongue. But she thinks she could sooner pull the sun down from the sky than keep her thoughts to herself, no matter how many times it's gotten her in trouble.

Nicolo drains his wine goblet and sets it on the table with a thud that echoes throughout the quiet room. He surveys her for a moment, dark brown eyes glowing in the candlelight.

"Very well," he says, sitting back in his chair. "We have an agreement—when we marry, you'll become queen, not queen consort."

Beatriz blinks. Whatever she'd expected him to say next, that wasn't it. "And we'll go to war with Bessemia," she says.

Nicolo nods. "Stars help me if I try to stand in your way, but it won't be an easy fight."

"Of course not," Beatriz says, mind whirling with what this means, how she can use it to her advantage. Chiefly, it means she doesn't need Pasquale to risk his life to rescue her any longer. He and Ambrose can run as far as they can, settle somewhere far away and safe. It's all she wants for them—peace. She refocuses on Nicolo. "Easy fights don't beget kings and queens of legend, do they? If we can conquer Bessemia, the whole of Cellaria will praise you as its king. Any doubters will be silenced."

Nicolo nods slowly. "*If* we can conquer Bessemia," he echoes.

Beatriz hesitates. She shouldn't push her luck tonight, not when he's agreed to her terms, but once again, she can't help herself.

"There is one more thing I need before I agree," she says, leaning across the table, gratified when his eyes drop to the display of her cleavage. She'll take every advantage she can get in this moment. "Gisella, banished from court. Permanently."

Nicolo's eyes snap back up to hers, surprise clear on his face. "Gisella?" he asks. "What for?"

Beatriz raises her eyebrows. The list of Gisella's sins against her is long enough on its own without telling Nicolo about her conspiring with the empress to murder her, but it isn't enough. She knows it isn't enough. Even if they are at odds right now, Gisella is still Nicolo's twin, and that is a bond Beatriz understands better than most would. So she reaches for the bottle of wine at the center of the table and refills his glass, then her own, before taking a sip.

"The arrangement between you and my mother—there's more to it than you know," she says. "And I suppose it's time you knew the truth."

Beatriz doesn't tell him everything. She makes no mention of being an empyrea, and she doesn't tell him that Pasquale is still alive, but she tells him the outline of her mother's plan, the truth of her attempt to rescue Lord Savelle, what she is certain are the details of her mother's true agreement with Gisella.

"You believe your mother tasked my sister with killing you?" he says slowly when she finishes, disbelief clear in his voice.

The rest of it, she notes, he accepts easily enough. It isn't entirely surprising—she's sure he had suspicions. He saw her expertise with disguises firsthand, and not many princesses make a habit of staging jailbreaks or escaping Sororias. He seems to understand exactly who Beatriz is and what she's capable of—it's his twin he underestimates.

"According to my mother's empyrea, her wish to conquer

Cellaria can only be fulfilled if I'm killed on Cellarian soil, by Cellarian hands," Beatriz says. "And Gisella stopped just short of outright confirming that hers are the hands my mother enlisted to do it. You aren't so naïve, Nico, that you don't believe her capable of it?"

Nicolo pauses. "I'm not," he says finally. "But let's assume your suspicions are correct—banishing her won't help. Gisella doesn't need proximity to kill you."

Beatriz knows he's right. Gisella had a part in poisoning King Cesare and Nigellus, even if she didn't directly administer either poison herself.

"What do you suggest, then?" she asks.

"Keep her close," Nicolo says. "Watch her, be ready for whatever strike she may make. I know my sister—she isn't one to attack face to face."

"No," Beatriz agrees. "She prefers to stab people in the back—metaphorically, to the best of my knowledge, though I can't say I'd be surprised if she did so literally."

A smile flickers over his face. "All the same," he says. "The best solution, it would seem, is to never show her your back. At least not until after we've conquered Bessemia and she has a chance to . . . reevaluate her choices."

Beatriz is tempted to push him further, but this time she does succeed in holding her tongue. He's right, more or less, though she knows the safest option would be to kill Gisella before Gisella can kill her. She isn't foolish enough to say that to Nicolo, however. That, she knows, would be too far to push him.

For now, she'll simply have to mind her back *and* her front and keep Gisella as close as she dares.

"Very well, then," Beatriz says, lifting her glass toward Nicolo. "We have a deal."

Nicolo raises his glass as well. "To us, then, and the future of the Cellarian empire."

The clink of her goblet against his echoes throughout the room, sounding to Beatriz's ears like the chains she once wore around her wrists.

# Violie

Violie, Leopold, Pasquale, and Ambrose arrive in Hapantoile just after noon the following day, crossing through the gleaming gold gates that guard the city to the west. It has been two years since Violie was here, and it occurs to her as they pass through that the girl who left is not the same one who is returning. She knows she's harder around the edges—she's seen too much not to be—but she also knows that despite the horrors she's experienced in Temarin and Friv, and despite the lives she's taken and the desperate decisions she's made, she's a kinder person as well.

As they make their way in silence through the bustling city streets, Violie's thoughts turn again to what her mother will think of her. Since they made the decision yesterday to come to Hapantoile, she's thought of little else. In the deepest corners of her heart, Violie had reconciled herself to the fact that she would never see her mother again. She hadn't quite made peace with it, but she'd accepted it. Now, though, faced with the imminent surety of seeing her mother again, Violie is overcome by nerves.

She must have some idea of what Violie has done these

past years. Will she be disappointed in her? Horrified? Will she know that everything Violie did, at least in the beginning, she did for her? Will that make it better, in her mother's eyes, or worse?

Violie is terrified to know.

She is desperate to know.

The streets of Hapantoile are still as familiar to Violie as the sound of her own name, and she leads her new friends through them until they reach the Crimson Petal—a whitewashed town house with red curtains in the windows and a gleaming black door complete with a rose-shaped knocker. The wooden sign hanging from the second floor is discreet, but in Violie's memory it was never discreet enough for everyone in the neighborhood not to know exactly what happened within the town house's walls.

Violie pulls her horse to a stop in front of the brothel, and after a moment, Pasquale pulls alongside her.

"I could go in first, if you'd rather," he offers.

Violie hears the trace of compassion in his voice, which sounds too near to pity for her tastes, so she shakes her head and swings down out of the saddle, her boots hitting Bessemian stone for the first time in years. Pasquale does the same, and she passes him her reins without a word and makes her way up the front steps to the lacquered black door she's passed through countless times. Tempted as she is to simply enter her home as she always has, she doesn't. Instead, she lifts her hand to the brass rose knocker and knocks three times.

A moment passes, Violie's heart thundering in her chest, before the door opens, revealing a frail-looking woman in her seventies with hair more gray than red now. Her pale skin is creased in places, but clear and luminous, her rosy mouth curved into a ready smile. She isn't beautiful in spite of her age but *because* of it. When her blue eyes meet Violie's, they widen in recognition.

"Elodia," Violie says, trying to smile, but she feels the smile falter on her face, killed by the nerves wracking her. Though they share no blood, Violie has known Elodia for the entirety of her life. She's the closest thing Violie has to a grandmother.

"Oh, Violie," Elodia says, folding Violie into her arms and peppering her face with kisses. "Welcome home."

*Home.*

The word echoes through Violie, and she hugs Elodia back for a moment before pulling away. "Is my mother here?"

For the space of a heartbeat, Violie fears the worst—Pasquale told her Beatriz had cured her mother of Vexis, but countless things could have befallen her between then and now. What if she is too late?

But Elodia turns her head to the entry hall behind her. "Thalia, fetch Avalise at once."

A sound halfway between a sob and a laugh pushes past Violie's lips, and before she knows what she's doing, she's walking past Elodia, into the Crimson Petal's expansive entry hall, past the startled young woman she doesn't recognize, who must be Thalia. A grand stairway dominates the space, its polished gold railing and red-carpeted steps curving up to the second-floor landing.

"Mother?" she calls out, her voice reverberating through the hall. Suddenly, her nerves are gone, her fear is gone; all that's left is the bone-aching need to see her mother's face, to feel her arms around her.

Her mother appears at the top of the stairs, still in her nightgown with a velvet dressing gown pulled over it, her blond hair sleep-mussed. When she sees Violie, she lets out a cry that sounds, vaguely, like Violie's name, and then she is running down the stairs and Violie is running up them. They meet somewhere in the middle, in a collision of arms and tears and babbled words that are only half audible. Violie would like nothing more than to linger here for eternity, but after a moment, she forces herself to pull away, to study her mother's face.

Vexis certainly took its toll, making her skin more sallow, her hair thinner, her eyes underlined with dark circles, but she is here and alive and that is all Violie could ask. She feels her mother taking inventory of her as well, her thumb coming up to brush over her cheek, a soft smile curving at her lips.

"Oh, my darling girl, look at you. All grown-up," she breathes. "I always knew the stars would bring you home to me."

Violie has never put much stock in the stars. It's difficult to grow up in Vesteria and not be aware of them, but she's never tailored her life to a horoscope or stayed up all night to track their travel across the sky and beg their help. Now, though, she feels her mother's faith wash over her, and whether or not the stars played any part in reuniting them, she is grateful all the same.

Violie would like nothing more than to spend days on end with her mother, catching up and celebrating the fact that they have both survived this long, against all odds, but there is no time. Elodia shows them to a stable at the end of the block where they can keep their horses for the night at the cost of a few asters; then she shows them to rooms on the top floor, usually reserved for guests paying to stay longer than a few hours, and leaves them to bathe and change into fresh clothes, with the agreement to regroup for lunch in an hour.

When Violie arrives in the sitting room in a borrowed spring-green day dress that's too big in the chest and hips, with her wet hair in a haphazard braid drawn over her shoulder, Leopold is the only one there. He stands near the burning fireplace in a clean white shirt and loose dark brown trousers, arms crossed over his chest. His own hair is still damp, lying flat against his head. He hears her enter the room and spins to face her, the lines of tension in his face smoothing out when his eyes meet hers.

"This is . . . not what I expected," he admits, glancing around the sitting room.

Violie follows his gaze and laughs. It's true that nothing about the room outright proclaims it's in a brothel and it could just as easily fit into any of the grand manors that line Bonairre Street, but there is a sultriness to the deep red velvet sofa crowded with an assortment of plush pillows, the black lace cloth draped over the low table, the smoked glass that surrounds each wall sconce, casting the room in a dim, hazy light even though it's the middle of the afternoon.

"I'm not sure I even want to know what you expected," she says, smiling.

He laughs, shaking his head. "I wasn't expecting a place that felt . . . like a home. But I can see you growing up here," he says.

"Well, I wasn't allowed in half the rooms," she says, shrugging. "And after dark, I had to stay in my room—at least one of the women was always off duty and stayed with me, sometimes my mother, sometimes one of my . . . aunts, as I called them."

Leopold gives no indication of judging her or her upbringing, but in his silence, she feels the need to defend it all the same. An old habit, she supposes. It wouldn't be the first time she's had to. "I always had a full belly, a roof over my head, and I was surrounded by people who loved and protected me. I wouldn't trade my childhood for anything," she tells him, her voice perhaps a touch too firm.

"I believe you," he says, eyes darting around the room again.

She wishes she could see it through his eyes, know what he thinks of it, but all she can see is the sofa where her mother used to braid her hair and tell her stories; the hard corner of the low table that she slammed her knee into when she was seven, leaving a faint, jagged scar; the place near the door where her mother reached out to steady herself the first time the Vexis made itself known, stealing her balance and strength in an instant.

She wishes she could stay here forever, and she wants to flee at the next available opportunity. She doesn't know which urge frustrates her more.

"Your mother looks like you," Leopold says, breaking the silence.

It isn't the first time Violie has heard that, but his words feel like a warm blanket draped over her shoulders. "Elodia always joked that my mother created me out of whole cloth. No one is sure who, exactly, fathered me, but he left little trace of himself. The only thing I didn't inherit from my mother is my eyes."

In the silence that follows, Violie hears him wondering. Her eyes are star-touched silver, which means she was wished for, like Sophronia, Daphne, and Beatriz. Like Bairre, too. Leopold doesn't give voice to his question, but Violie answers it all the same.

"My mother was... entertaining a gentleman. Some duke or earl or other, she says, though she's never said who. After he fell asleep she lay awake, struck by a sudden *need* for a child. She always wanted to be a mother, she said, but in that moment, she said she needed it more than her next breath. She needed *me*. The room was dark, with only moonlight shining in through the window, just bright enough to catch on something jutting out from the pocket of the gentleman's discarded coat. She got out of bed, crouched down beside it, and realized it was stardust. She didn't think twice about it—she took it, she crossed to the window, she looked up at the stars, and she used it to wish for me."

"Was he your father, then?" he asks.

Violie laughs. It isn't a question she hasn't asked herself, but the truth is, there is no way to know for sure, and even if there were, her mother claimed not to remember the man's name. But Violie doesn't explain that to Leopold. Instead, she settles on a simpler truth. "It doesn't matter," she says. "I'm my mother's daughter, and that is enough for me."

It's at that moment that the door opens and her mother enters the room, followed seconds later by Elodia, then by Pasquale and Ambrose. They take seats around the room, Violie sitting between her mother and Elodia on the sofa.

"I don't have to ask why you're here," Elodia says, reaching into her pocket and producing a stiff cream-colored card the size of her hand, emblazoned with gold leaf. She hands it to Violie. "I take it you're on your way to Cellaria?"

"What makes you say that?" Leopold asks, but Violie's attention is on the card, reading over Elodia's shoulder. She can speak Cellarian passably well, though reading it is a different skill. But she doesn't need to read Cellarian to recognize the shape of Beatriz's name. She frowns, passing the letter to Pasquale, who reads it, his expression going from surprise to fury.

"It's an invitation," he says, looking up at Violie. "To the wedding of Princess Beatriz of Bessemia and King Nicolo of Cellaria. Where did you get this?"

"One of our patrons is the Cellarian ambassador," Elodia says with a shrug. "Suffice to say it . . . fell out of his pocket while he was visiting just last night."

"When is it?" Leopold asks.

"Three days," Pasquale says. "Can we reach Vallon in time?"

"Just," Leopold says. "But we can hardly stroll into a royal wedding without a plan."

Violie shrugs. "A royal wedding will mean an influx of visitors and overworked staff. We couldn't ask for a better distraction when we sneak into the palace to find Beatriz," she says, looking to her mother. "Is Graciella still here?"

Graciella had come to the Crimson Petal just a few months before Violie left, a young woman in her mid-twenties who'd already become notorious among Cellarian courtesans as a favorite of King Cesare. Several of the other women at the Crimson Petal wondered why she would possibly leave a position like that behind to come here, but from what Violie has heard of King Cesare since then, she can guess what made Graciella anxious to leave. It would only have been a matter of time before his favor soured, and she'd be lucky to walk away with her freedom and her life.

Violie glances across the room at Pasquale, the polar opposite of everything she's heard about his father, and wonders if the name sounds familiar to him, but he shows no sign of recognition.

"She is," Violie's mother says.

"Good," Violie says. "I'd wager she knows a discreet way into the king's bedchamber. Nicolo isn't a fool, from everything I've heard about him—he'll keep Beatriz close so he can watch her and prevent her from escaping. The queen's chambers will connect to his, won't they?" she asks Pasquale, who looks confused but nods.

"Yes, they connect," he says. "Will it be that simple?"

"Likely not," Violie says with a wry smile and a shake of her head. "But the simpler the plan is, the more room we'll have to . . . improvise when something goes awry."

Violie feels her mother and Elodia exchange a look over her head. "What is it?" she asks, glancing between them. "Is Graciella all right?"

"She is," Elodia says quickly. "But we have a new girl as well—you met her briefly when you arrived."

Violie frowns. "Thalia," she recalls, though she was in such a hurry to find her mother that she remembers little of the woman—just a blur of auburn hair and tan skin and startled eyes.

"Unfortunately, she's the only one we could take in," Elodia says, which confuses Violie until she realizes that Elodia isn't speaking to her. She's speaking to Leopold.

"Elodia," Violie's mother warns, her voice sharp. "Surely they have enough on their plate without—"

"Beatriz isn't his responsibility," Elodia interjects, her eyes never leaving Leopold. "They are."

"Who?" Leopold asks, looking as confused as Violie feels.

"The refugees," Elodia says coolly. "We could take in Thalia—her husband was a palace guard, killed by the same mob that killed your wife, and she has two young children in her care—but there are more Temarinians coming into Hapantoile every day, looking for safety and stability they can no longer find at home."

"But why would they come here?" Violie asks. "Bessemia is the one responsible for the upheaval in Temarin."

"Where else would you have them go?" Elodia asks. "To Cellaria, which has made no secret of its hatred of Temarin? To Friv, a country they can only reach by purchasing passage on a ship, which few can afford? Bessemia may be the belly of the beast, but even the belly of the beast offers warmth and shelter."

Leopold goes progressively paler as she speaks, horror

flooding his face, but Elodia isn't done. "Perhaps, Your Majesty, your time would be better spent helping the people who still call you king than interfering in another country's troubles."

Leopold swallows, an angry red flush stealing over his cheeks. He's quiet for a moment, but Violie can tell he's considering his words carefully. "I was not a good king, madam," he says quietly. "And ignorant as it seems to have been, I believed the Temarinian people were better off without me leading them. I'd believed the empress's reign was unchallenged. Word of any unrest didn't make it to Friv."

"Few things make it to Friv," Elodia says with a snort. "But just because the empress's control is unchallenged by you doesn't mean it has been peaceful. Do you not know your people, Your Majesty? Did you believe they would accept the empress's rule without fighting back?"

"I'm glad they are," Violie puts in, but Elodia levels her with a hard look and Violie immediately regrets speaking.

"Him I expect naïveté from," she tells Violie, inclining her head toward Leopold. "But you should know better. Fighting back may sound noble, but the battles that have cropped up between the Bessemian troops and the Temarinian rebels have rendered the country dangerous. Villages have been razed to the ground by the empress's troops for fear they were housing rebel forces. And the rebels have caused damage of their own—I heard tell of a fire set to burn a Bessemian encampment that spread to destroy a nearby farm and acres of crops. Crops Temarin couldn't afford to lose as winter settles in. It's the common people who find themselves caught in the middle of a fight they never asked for."

Leopold absorbs this. "If Thalia wishes to speak with me herself, I would be honored to hear her."

"And say what?" Violie asks him, sure she knows the answer already but hoping desperately that she's wrong.

Leopold looks at her with heavy eyes and a stubborn set to his jaw that she's come to recognize as the look he gets before he does something foolish and brave.

"To apologize profusely for both my reign and my abandonment," he says. "And to swear on each star in the sky that I won't rest until I reclaim every last grain of Temarinian soil and make it safe to call it home once more."

It's precisely what Violie was afraid he would say, but she knows she could sooner prevent the stars from shining than keep him from returning to Temarin. Still, she can't resist trying.

"You'll be killed as soon as you cross the border," she says.

Leopold shrugs. "Then I'll die a king rather than live a coward."

"You aren't a coward," she protests.

"Then it's time to stop running like one," he says.

Frustration rises up in her throat, and she only barely manages to tamp it down. "I promised Sophronia I would keep you safe—"

"Sophronia released you from that promise," Leopold interrupts, his voice gentle. "And she knew better than anyone that there are more important things in this world than being safe. If she were in my position, she would do the same."

He's right. Violie knows he's right, and she hates him for it. She hasn't kept him alive these past weeks, hasn't come to know him and care for him and let him get close enough to care for her in turn, just to let him die on some noble, impossible mission. She gets to her feet, ignoring the startled looks from her mother, Elodia, Pasquale, and Ambrose.

"Then die, just like she did," she tells him, regretting the words as soon as they leave her lips. "But while the world will remember her as a martyr, they'll remember you as a fool."

Leopold holds her gaze, unflinching. "Better that than a selfish coward who let his people suffer in his stead."

The desire to throttle sense into him is so overwhelming that the only way to resist it is to walk away, ignoring the others calling her name as she does, leaving the room and closing the door firmly behind her. Before anyone can come after her, she walks downstairs to the foyer, taking her coat from the hook and tying it around her shoulders, then slipping her feet into the worn boots she left by the door. Then she leaves the Crimson Petal and steps out onto the bustling streets of Hapantoile.

# Daphne

Lunch with the empress and Lord Panlington is set up in Lord Panlington's private rooms, on the other side of the castle from the royal wing, where Daphne and Bairre's rooms as well as the empress's temporary lodgings are. Daphne's stomach is tied in knots during the entire walk over. Bairre is at her side, and despite her earlier protests to her mother, she's glad to have him with her. He knows what to expect, and after her conversation with her mother the night before, she hopes the empress will underestimate him.

"You told Lord Panlington what your mother was planning," Bairre murmurs to her as they pass through the busy castle hallways. "He isn't unprepared to meet her, and Lord Panlington is a smart man, more than capable of holding his own, even against the empress."

He must feel the anxiety coursing through her, but despite his words, she isn't reassured.

"Lord Panlington has no affection for me," she points out, shaking her head. "He tolerates me out of necessity, and because I've proven myself too much of a nuisance to ignore or outright kill. But that doesn't mean he's our ally. If my mother means to sway him to help her claim Vesteria—all it would take would be a few false promises that he couldn't see through. Do you think, if she promises him troops to help dethrone Bartholomew tomorrow, he won't be tempted to take them despite everything I've told him about her?"

Bairre considers this. "You always say people underestimate your mother, but I believe in this case you may be underestimating Lord Panlington. He sees through just about everything, in my experience with the man."

Daphne is tempted to agree with that assessment. Her dealings with Lord Panlington himself are recent, but she's seen his work through the actions of the rebellion, and through Cliona. He isn't a fool to be easily led.

At least, Daphne believes that until they reach Lord Panlington's rooms and a maid leads them through the regal but sparse sitting room and into a similarly decorated dining room, where her mother is seated at a round table, dressed in a Bessemian blue-and-gold gown, with Lord Panlington seated to her left, appearing utterly besotted.

"Oh, there you are, darling," the empress says, tearing her attention away from Lord Panlington and fixing Daphne with a full, glowing smile.

There was a time not long ago when Daphne dreamt of her mother's beaming smile being directed at her. Growing up, it always felt like a rare gift, not often bestowed but worth working for. Even now, it still warms her, and she has to remind herself that like most parts of her mother, it's a lie.

"I hope we didn't keep you waiting," Daphne says, matching her mother's smile as best she can. Her eyes slide to the clock standing in the corner—two minutes shy of one o'clock, their arranged meeting time. Daphne kicks herself for not realizing her mother would be early, that she would want to take advantage of any extra time she could get with Lord Panlington.

"Not at all, Your Highnesses," Lord Panlington says, getting to his feet and offering Bairre and Daphne a shallow bow. "Your mother was simply telling me a charming story about a time when her father encountered a wild boar while selling his hats on the road."

Daphne's smile begins to feel even more forced. She knows her mother's stories, what each one aims to accomplish, and more than that, she knows that her mother never *ever* mentions her father, Daphne's grandfather. In Daphne's experience, her mother has done everything in her power to distance herself from her common origins and has certainly never purposefully *reminded* anyone of them. But with Lord Panlington, it is perhaps a perfect ploy, a way for him to see her as a simple tailor's daughter rather than a powerful empress scheming to take Friv for her own.

"Oh?" Daphne says, gaze moving to her mother. "The way you were giggling, I thought for sure you were telling Lord Panlington of the time you arranged for your bathtub to be filled with champagne after your minister of the treasury cautioned you against reckless spending, simply to prove a point."

For just an instant, the mask drops and Daphne glimpses the ire in her mother's eyes before she pulls the mask back into place, offering a bland smile. "Not to prove a point," her mother corrects, managing to soften the sharpness of her tone, if only barely. "To prove that I was correct—our treasury could tolerate a bit of reckless spending, it *couldn't* tolerate his thieving."

It's the truth, and at the time, Daphne applauded her mother's handling of the situation, reveled in how red the minister's face grew when her mother insisted that, should the champagne required for her baths be too much, she would need a full breakdown of the palace accounts to see what else could be cut and immediately found the sums that weren't adding up. But it doesn't matter that it's the truth. Daphne can see in Lord Panlington's expression that the image of a bathtub filled with champagne has suitably counteracted the folksy tale the empress has spun for him of her humble upbringing.

"Of course, Mama," Daphne says, injecting her voice with a spoonful of honey as Bairre pulls out the chair directly across from the empress and Daphne lowers herself into it with all the grace she learned from watching her mother. Bairre takes the seat beside her.

Lord Panlington must notice the tension, because he clears his throat, motioning for a servant girl, who appears between Daphne and Bairre and fills their cups with steaming tea. Daphne adds a cube of sugar and a splash of milk to hers, taking a sip, knowing better than to broach the elephant in the room first.

Lord Panlington gives the servant girl a nod, dismissing her. As soon as the door is closed behind her, leaving the four of them alone, he speaks. "Your mother, Princess, seems to be under the impression that I'm the head of some rebel faction in Friv. Where in the name of the stars would she have gotten that idea?" he asks, eyes heavy on her.

Daphne silently curses herself. She might have told Lord Panlington of her mother's plans to conquer Friv with her help, but she didn't exactly explain that she'd already told her mother all about him and his part in the rebellion. If she could go back, she wouldn't have, but she learned of Lord Panlington's true allegiances when she was still loyal to her mother, back when Sophronia was alive and the thought of going against the empress had been as ridiculous as the stars going dark.

"I might have mentioned it," Daphne says, careful to keep her voice neutral. "Back when I thought you might be responsible for the attempts on my life."

It isn't the truth, but it's a lie Lord Panlington has no trouble believing.

At that moment, the door opens again and Cliona strides through, red hair coming loose from its plait, freckled cheeks flushed, and midway through pulling off a pair of leather riding gloves. She hasn't bothered to change out of her riding habit, and Daphne doesn't miss the way the empress's brown eyes narrow, sweeping over Cliona and immediately finding her wanting.

"Sorry I'm late," Cliona says, not sounding sorry at all as she finishes removing her gloves and takes the seat on Daphne's other side, flashing her father a quick, bright smile that he returns easily. "My ride was so invigorating I lost track of time."

"How you manage in this dreadful weather is beyond me," the empress says, any trace of the flash of disdain she showed replaced by the friendly mask that Daphne finds so discombobulating.

"It's a talent," Cliona replies. Daphne is impressed with how perfectly Cliona matches the empress's tone, the same measure of sweet gentility but with an undercurrent of condescension.

"Empress, I don't believe you've met my daughter yet," Lord Panlington says. "Cliona, this is Empress Margaraux."

"Of course, Daphne's mother," Cliona says, and Daphne has to smother a smile at her friend's boldness, at the way the empress ever so slightly flinches at being referred to as *Daphne's mother* rather than by her long list of titles. "We're all so glad you could pay us a visit—Daphne has accumulated so many supporters here in Friv. The people just adore her. You must be so proud."

Now, *that's* a bridge too far, and Daphne subtly kicks Cliona under the table to communicate as much.

"Actually, before you joined us, we were discussing her suspicions that you tried to have Daphne killed," the empress says, artfully dodging any confirmation that she is, in fact, proud of Daphne.

Cliona laughs, pouring herself a cup of tea and taking a sip of it black. "I can't imagine where she got that idea."

"The time you and Mrs. Nattermore held me hostage at knifepoint and freely discussed how best to kill me?" Daphne suggests airily. "Or the number of times you've threatened to kill me since?"

"I forget how sensitive you can be," Cliona replies, waving a hand. "I made some jokes here and there, but we weren't responsible for the assassins—any of them."

"My daughter might believe that, but I don't see why I should," the empress says, her voice still conversational even when her eyes dart between Cliona, Bairre, and Lord Panlington with an air of severity.

"Because, Your Majesty," Cliona says, lowering her voice to a conspiratorial whisper, though she's heard by everyone at the table, "if the Frivian rebellion wanted your daughter dead, we would do it ourselves, and we wouldn't fail."

A silence falls over the table as Cliona and the empress hold each other's gazes, neither moving, blinking, or—as far as Daphne can tell—even breathing.

Then the empress laughs. It isn't the sort of laugh Daphne has seen from her mother before, not a stoic chuckle or demure giggle that doesn't quite reach her eyes. Instead, she throws her head back with the force of it, her shoulders heaving. She laughs with her entire body and, after a moment, the rest of the table joins in, some of the tension dissipating.

"I see why my daughter has grown fond of you," the empress says, but though the words sound complimentary, Daphne can hear the condemnation in them as well, the reminder that in becoming *fond* of Cliona or anyone else outside of her mother and sisters, Daphne has failed.

Lord Panlington looks between his daughter and the empress with a faintly bewildered expression, no doubt understanding each word that has passed between them but failing to grasp the full meaning of what is being said. "Should we cut through the nonsense and speak plainly, Your Majesty?" he says to the empress, who gifts him with a benevolent smile.

"I would prefer that, Lord Panlington. I would like to help you and your rebellion, but in order to properly overthrow

King Bartholomew, you require more resources than you currently have at your disposal—in terms both of weapons and of people to wield them. Am I correct?"

Lord Panlington's jaw tenses, but after a moment he gives a nod.

"I have resources," the empress says. "Unfortunately, I also have a vested interest in keeping Friv's monarchy firmly in place. My grandchild will one day sit on that throne—I can't have it broken to pieces by the time they arrive, can I?"

At the mention of grandchildren, Daphne feels herself flush, and she is sure that if she were to let herself look at Bairre, his cheeks would be red as well. She knows her mother has no intention of letting either of them live long enough to have children, but it serves her purpose just now to pretend. And, Daphne realizes when her mother glances at her, then Bairre, it serves another purpose as well. She feels, suddenly, like virginity is written all over her face, and surely over Bairre's as well. If her mother had suspicions that they had not consummated their marriage, they've all but confirmed them.

"The goals of the rebellion have become more . . . flexible, as of late," Lord Panlington says carefully. "While we'd insist each clan have full authority over their lands, we would be amenable to a ruling family that serves as a figurehead, of sorts. But Bartholomew's reign is poisoned. After the force—and, if rumors are to be believed, magic—he used to take the throne, he'll never be accepted by all of Friv, and he is . . . unwilling to negotiate with the rebellion about restructuring power, at any rate."

Empress Margaraux sips her tea, dark brown gaze on

Lord Panlington over the rim of her cup, before she sets it down on its saucer with a decisive clink. "My daughters have been reared as future queens, Lord Panlington. Taught to rule countries fairly and honorably, to navigate them through hardships and see them prosper. I'm aware that Prince Bairre was not born to be a king. Perhaps he would be all too happy to shirk his responsibility and play figurehead, but I raised Daphne to be better than that."

Daphne allows herself to glance sideways at Bairre to see if her mother's words, as true as some of them might be, have wounded him, but if so, he gives no outward sign of it. Instead, he watches her mother with calculating eyes.

"My *responsibility*," he says, his voice colder than Daphne has ever heard it, "is just as it always has been and always will be regardless of the title attached to my name—to Friv."

"Hmm, that is *admirable*," the empress says with the sort of smile that reminds Daphne of the way one might smile at a child showing off a horrendously done drawing. She turns her attention away from him and back to Lord Panlington. "What you're offering is insufficient," she says.

"And yet it is all I can offer," Lord Panlington replies with a shrug. "You can keep your funds—Friv has always survived and thrived without help from outsiders. This time will be no different."

Daphne doesn't know whether or not he's bluffing, but she's grateful for his refusal all the same. She doesn't doubt that any promises her mother offered would no doubt be retracted just as easily, but she also knows better than most that her mother can be persuasive.

The empress laughs softly, shaking her head. "I confess

I'm disappointed, Lord Panlington," she says, leaning across the table to pick up the half-full pot of tea. She pours some for herself, then inclines her head to Lord Panlington's empty cup, which he nods and pushes toward her. Suspicion suddenly slithers through Daphne—her mother doesn't pour her own tea, let alone offer to pour for someone she views as beneath her. "Daphne had such high hopes for a partnership between us. Didn't you, Daphne?"

Lord Panlington looks to her, confusion furrowing his brow, but Daphne's gaze lingers on her mother's hands as they pour tea into Lord Panlington's cup, at the faint sprinkle of white powder that falls from the ruby ring on her right middle finger.

No one else notices. They are all staring at Daphne, waiting for an answer to a question she can't quite remember. But Daphne notices. Her mother *let* her notice. She swallows. "Yes, of course," she says, feeling as if someone else has taken over her body. "But I suppose your goals are wholly unaligned after all."

Her mother passes Lord Panlington's cup of tea back to him, and words rise up in Daphne's throat. She should say something, should stop him from drinking what she's sure is poison. But if she does, if she finds a way to warn him or stop him from drinking it, her mother will know for certain that her loyalties have changed, and that would put not just Lord Panlington in danger, but everyone Daphne cares about. Perhaps attempting to poison Lord Panlington would be enough to force King Bartholomew to have her imprisoned, but she wouldn't stay there long. She is an empress, after all. He would be unable to hold her.

Daphne feels as if she has no choice but to watch as her mother lifts her teacup toward Lord Panlington.

"To the tragedy of failed partnerships," she says with a wry smile.

Lord Panlington appears slightly unnerved, but he returns her smile and clinks his teacup with hers before they both take a sip.

Daphne watches, frozen in her seat, as Lord Panlington swallows and sets his cup down, a third of the tea gone. Daphne doesn't know for sure what poison her mother used on him—a white powder could be anything from arsenic to sleeping dust—if it's anything at all. Daphne isn't sure this isn't a test of her own loyalties. Perhaps the white powder was nothing more than confectioners' sugar.

She tells herself that's exactly what it is, and as their lunch progresses and Lord Panlington shows no sign of being poisoned, she almost manages to convince herself it's the truth. But not quite. As the rest of the table falls into a somewhat stilted conversation, with Lord Panlington, Cliona, and Bairre making halfhearted suggestions as to how the empress should spend her next couple of days in Friv and the empress giving noncommittal answers, Daphne stays silent. Watching. Waiting. Desperate to shout for help but unable to open her mouth.

It happens just as the servants come to clear away their plates—all empty, apart from Daphne's, which she barely touched. Lord Panlington moves to stand, but before he straightens fully, he collapses back into his chair, his hands flying to his chest, just to the left, where his heart, Daphne knows now, is beating far, far too fast. His eyes bulge, the whites of his eyes flushing red, mouth agape—half shocked, half pained.

In a blur of movement, Cliona is at his side, yelling to a servant to call for a doctor, but it's too late for that. Daphne watches, stunned and horrified, as Lord Panlington grasps his daughter's hand in a white-knuckled grip, struggling to speak, before that grip goes slack and his lifeless body slumps back in the chair.

Cliona lets out a scream when she realizes; Bairre moves to her side to guide her away from the body, and Daphne averts her eyes, unable to look at her friend in this moment, knowing she could have stopped it. Her gaze, instead, lands on her mother, who meets it across the table. No one else in the room is paying either of them any mind, and the empress lifts her chin a fraction of an inch and gives Daphne a brief, chilling smile.

# Beatriz

Keeping her enemies close was not a novel idea to Beatriz when Nicolo suggested it—it's a lesson her mother instilled in her as well—but putting it into practice with Gisella proves to be more of a struggle than Beatriz anticipates. The day gets off to an auspicious start, with Beatriz extending an invitation to Gisella to join her in her rooms, where Beatriz has a wedding gown fitting. Gisella accepts, as Beatriz knew she would, and just after lunch, the guards outside her door knock twice before announcing Gisella's arrival.

She's early, stepping into Beatriz's sitting room before the dressmaker and her seamstresses arrive, but Beatriz welcomes her all the same. It made little sense to have her maids lace her into all the layers of a day dress only to have to change into the wedding gowns the dressmaker is bringing, so Beatriz is wearing only her chemise with a plush brocade dressing gown over it. Gisella, on the other hand, looks as put together as she ever does, in a fashionable sapphire gown that hugs her frame, with her pale blond hair up in a coiling braided style reminiscent of a crown.

There is no audience once the guards close the door behind Gisella, so Beatriz doesn't waste energy on politeness. She looks Gisella over for a moment, channeling Daphne's cool gaze. She chooses not to speak, instead watching Gisella struggle for a moment in the uncomfortable silence. That, much as she loathes admitting it, is a trick she learned from her mother.

"The dressmaker isn't here yet?" Gisella says finally, looking around the room as if she might find the dressmaker and her seamstresses hiding behind a sofa.

"You're early," Beatriz says coolly, lowering herself into the armchair and crossing her legs at the ankles. She ignores Gisella, reaching for the volume of poetry she left open on the end table. She waves a hand dismissively. "Help yourself to water or wine. I'm sure you know where things are by now."

Gisella doesn't move, though. Instead she stares at Beatriz for a moment before giving a derisive scoff. "Is this how things will be, then?" she asks. "You intend to ignore me like a petulant child who was refused a piece of cake?"

Beatriz looks up at Gisella with a blank expression. "I'm sorry, perhaps you're more up to date on your etiquette than I am," she says, voice dripping with condescension. "What *is* the proper way to treat someone who is planning on killing you in the near future? Should I greet you with hugs and kisses? Ask how your day is going as if I care?"

Gisella says nothing at first. Instead, she crosses the room to the sideboard, rifling through the cabinets until she finds a bottle she likes. She picks out a goblet and gives a heavy pour, taking a long sip before turning to face Beatriz once more.

"You can pretend to be a victim if you like," Gisella says, her voice level and bone-cold. "But you understand how the world works, Beatriz. You know the rules of the game of power better than anyone. You can treat me like the villain, but if our positions were reversed, if killing me were the only way to protect yourself and your sister, would you do anything differently?"

Beatriz glares at her, hating that she's right. Or rather, that she *thinks* she's right.

"I wouldn't," Beatriz agrees. "But I can guarantee you that I wouldn't be stupid enough to believe my mother's promises to be worth more than the air she spoke them with."

At that, Gisella smiles, taking another sip of wine. "Oh, you don't have to worry about me there," she says. "It isn't as if my promises are worth all that much either, as you well know. The empress and I have the same goals, up to a point, but my loyalty certainly won't outlast her usefulness."

That surprises Beatriz. Gisella has betrayed her before, and she isn't fully surprised that she plans to eventually cross the empress as well, but . . .

"And how does killing me fit into your goals?" she asks, unsure whether she wants to hear the answer. She may be masking it with ice and snark, but discussing her imminent death with Gisella is unnerving.

Gisella doesn't respond right away. Silence stretches between them for so long that Beatriz begins to suspect Gisella won't give her an answer at all. Just when she's given up on expecting one, Gisella surprises her.

"Every movement requires a martyr," she says finally, her voice soft. "And you'll make such a lovely one."

Frost ghosts over Beatriz's skin, leaving goose bumps in its wake. She suppresses a shudder.

"And what movement is that?" she asks.

Gisella only smiles, and Beatriz knows she wouldn't have given an answer, even if they hadn't been interrupted at that moment by the arrival of the dressmaker and her seamstresses.

***

The dress fitting itself passes in a blur of silk and tulle as Beatriz tries on the dozen gowns the dressmaker brought—some form-fitting, some voluminous, some trimmed in feathers, others in jewels, and one in fresh red rose petals, sprayed with gold to hide where they've started to brown. Now that they have an audience, she and Gisella are careful to maintain their smiles, and Gisella offers compliments and critiques for each gown she tries on.

"It has to be the skirt on the sixth gown, with that rippling train, but with the rose bodice from the tenth gown," Beatriz says after she's stripped of the final gown and one of the seamstresses helps her back into her dressing gown. "But I'll want the roses as fresh as possible—could they be sewed onto the bodice the afternoon of the wedding?"

"We'll get the last one on as you're entering the chapel, Princess," the dressmaker vows, scribbling notes in her notepad.

"Oh yes," Gisella says, her voice gushing, though Beatriz hears the sarcasm lurking underneath. "The dress must be as flawless as my future sister-in-law. Nothing less will do, Madame Favioli."

Beatriz glances at the dozen gowns being packed away by the army of seamstresses, each one some shade of Cellarian red—blood red. If she isn't careful, this won't only be her wedding dress, it very well may be the dress she dies in.

# Violie

Violie walks through Hapantoile for more than an hour, doing her best to get lost in the city that raised her. It's a losing battle. She knows the streets too well for them to swallow her up, though as she tries to disappear into the crowds, she notices how much has changed in her absence. Some shops have closed, other new ones opening in their place. Houses have been repainted, their gardens and window boxes abloom in new colors. One road has been repaved entirely—a relief, she's sure, remembering the pothole that claimed more than its fair share of carriage wheels.

The biggest change, though, is the people. She hadn't noticed when they arrived, too caught up in the prospect of seeing her mother again to pay attention to much else, but now she's acutely aware of the energy vibrating through the city. Hapantoile has always been lively and busy, but now there is a franticness in the air that is new and disconcerting.

Before long, she can pick out the Temarinians as well. Hapantoile has always had high turnover, with people moving to and from the city in droves, meaning even Violie's neighbors when she was growing up rarely stayed for longer than a few years. But she finds she can tell the Temarinians apart with ease. There is something skittish in their eyes as they push through the crowd, a protective hunch to their shoulders, an invisible wolf still nipping at their heels.

Violie soon realizes just how lucky Thalia is to have found a job at the Crimson Petal. The closer she gets to the palace, the more beggars she sees on the street, holding tin cups out to those passing by, who largely ignore them. Violie didn't bring her satchel, but she finds three asters in the pocket of her cloak and drops them into three tin cups at random. The sound of the coin hitting the tin is hollow and leaves Violie swarmed with nagging guilt.

Leopold shouldered the blame readily for what befell Temarin, allowing Elodia to lay the fault at his feet, but Violie knows that isn't fair. If there's blame to be assigned, much of it lies with her. Yes, Leopold was too oblivious to notice the rot at the heart of Temarin until it came for him, but Violie is the one who fed it.

Under Empress Margaraux's orders, Violie worked to weaken Temarin even before Sophronia arrived, intercepting letters when she worked for the duchess and sending the empress reports of Queen Eugenia's every move, along with everything she could discern about Leopold. And when Sophronia arrived, Violie was the one to finish what she couldn't.

What would have happened if Violie hadn't forged that letter from Leopold, declaring war on Cellaria? Would it have changed anything, or was the empress's plan too far along to be stopped? She'd allied with Eugenia by that point, hadn't she? Temarin would have torn itself in two with or without Violie's assistance.

Perhaps, she thinks, if the empress's plan had been executed as it should have been, with Leopold dead beside Sophronia, the empress wouldn't have met with so much resistance from its people. She would have been viewed as the savior she intended to be, her armies welcomed with gratitude rather than violence. But Leopold lived, and in doing so, he created enough uncertainty that a rebellion had blossomed.

With a sinking stomach, she understands why Leopold wants to return—not just out of guilt but out of hope—and an apology is the least of the debts she owes, not just to Leopold but to Temarin as well.

Violie returns to find Leopold still in the upstairs drawing room, but now the others have gone and only Thalia is there, sitting in the armchair with her back to the door so she doesn't notice when Violie slips inside. Leopold does, though his eyes don't waver from Thalia as she speaks, her voice soft, but with a quiet power behind it. She's speaking Temarinian, and Violie realizes that she's in the middle of the story of what brought her and her children to Hapantoile.

It's a hard story, with no lack of suffering, and one Violie doesn't particularly want to hear, but Leopold leans toward Thalia, bracing his elbows on his knees and listening intently. In the firelight, Violie can make out that his right cheek is distinctly pink—like he's recently been slapped, and hard. Thalia's doing, Violie guesses.

"I will carry your story and the memory of your husband with me always, Mrs. Eaves," Leopold says when she's finished, his voice solemn. "Had I known the suffering you and other Temarinians would feel in the chaos that followed the coup . . ." He trails off, only then looking at Violie before turning his attention back to Thalia. "When Kavelle fell and my wife, Sophie, was executed, I couldn't see past my own loss. I had my reasons for going into hiding, but whether it was the right choice or the wrong one, the journey changed me into someone who is no longer content to put my safety over the safety of others."

Violie watches as Leopold rises from his chair and drops to one knee in front of where Thalia sits, bowing his head.

"You have my apology, but I know it's little comfort. Perhaps a vow will be worth more to you—I swear in the name of all the stars above that I will take back control of Temarin, and if it is the last thing I do in this world, I will see you bring your children safely home."

Violie can't see Thalia's face and she's too far away to hear the words Thalia murmurs, but Leopold hears them, his mouth tightening as he gives a nod.

"I swear it," he tells her.

Thalia begins to rise, and Violie slips out of the door as silently as she came in, embarrassed to have witnessed the private moment. She returns to her room and sits crosslegged on her bed, and when a knock sounds at her door a few moments later, she calls to come in, knowing before he enters that it's Leopold.

When he closes the door behind him, he leans back against it and for a long moment, they just look at each other.

"We'll leave at dawn," she says finally.

Leopold pushes away from the door, shaking his head. "I told you, I can't go with you to Cellaria—"

"You and I," Violie interrupts, stopping him short, "are going to Temarin. Pasquale and Ambrose will have to rescue Beatriz on their own."

"They'll need your help," Leopold protests.

"You need my help," Violie retorts.

Leopold gives a halfhearted smile. "I did, once," he says. "And I know I wouldn't be standing here now without you, but you've taught me well. I can do this on my own."

Violie isn't sure he's wrong about that. The naïve boy he was when they fled Temarin is gone, and the man standing before her now is strong, savvy, and more than capable of taking care of himself. She can't pretend she's going with him for his sake.

"You wish to atone for the ways you betrayed Temarin," she says softly. "So do I. But I'm not sure how much help I'll be—I was trained to destroy countries, Leopold, not put them back together again. Do you have a plan?"

"Right now my plan is to return to Temarin and see for myself what is happening there," he says.

"If what Elodia said is true, the empress's men and a Temarinian rebellion are fighting one another," Violie points out. "It's possible the Temarinians will rally around you when they learn you're alive, but if this Temarinian rebellion is anything like the last one, they may want you dead even more than the empress."

Leopold absorbs this with surprising ease. "Then I'm Levi again," he says, noting the common name he went by after fleeing Temarin.

It's still dangerous, Violie knows, but Leopold knows that too. She nods. "We'll have to tell Pasquale and Ambrose our plans have changed," she says.

Pasquale and Ambrose aren't surprised when Violie and Leopold tell them they'll be parting ways instead of continuing on to Cellaria and Beatriz with them.

"It's the right thing to do," Pasquale says as they eat supper together in the kitchen. The Crimson Petal couldn't close for the evening without raising suspicions, so Elodia and most of the other women who work there are upstairs in the sitting room, greeting and flirting with the clients who are visiting. In an hour or two, the clients will speak to Elodia and coin will exchange hands, at which point couples will move to more private rooms, but now the sounds of music and conversation and laughter waft through the walls.

Violie's mother did take the evening off—not unusual, given her recent illness—and she's sitting at the supper table with them, quiet but with a deep crease in her brow as she looks down at the bowl of parsnip soup in front of her, which she has yet to touch.

"You can get to Beatriz on your own," Violie tells Pasquale and Ambrose. She's careful not to phrase the words as a question, but Ambrose must hear the uncertainty in her voice anyway, because he laughs.

"The difficulty will be in not being recognized once we're in Vallon," he says. "Graciella was kind enough to draw up a thorough map of how she was brought to the king's chambers covertly, and since even Pasquale had no inkling the woman existed—a true feat considering the swiftness of gossip in the Cellarian palace—it seems like the surest way to get into the palace without being noticed."

"Getting out will be trickier," Pasquale acknowledges.

"Take all of the stardust Daphne gave us," Violie says, but Pasquale is already shaking his head.

"We couldn't do that," he says. "You'll need it as well."

"She gave it so that we could rescue Beatriz," Violie says.

"Of course you should take it."

Pasquale and Ambrose exchange a look.

"Do you"—Leopold begins tentatively—"feel comfortable using it?"

Pasquale lifts a shoulder in a shrug, but his cheeks darken. "I have before," he says. "To get Ambrose and Gisella out of the dungeon before we fled Hapantoile the first time."

"It may bring trouble, if we're caught with it in Cellaria," Ambrose says.

*Trouble* is an understatement. Violie isn't sure if King Nicolo has the same inclination toward burning people to death as King Cesare did, but possessing stardust has been a capital crime since long before King Cesare's great-grandfather was born. Still . . .

"If someone is suspicious enough of you to be searching your belongings, you'll already be in enough trouble that the possession of stardust will hardly signify," Leopold points out. "Take it from a king who's been in hiding before. Carrying stardust is going to be the least of your concerns."

"Besides," Violie adds, "I don't see a way you can succeed in escaping the palace with Beatriz if you *don't* use stardust.

If anything, the fact that it's outlawed is a boon—no one will be prepared to stop you or use stardust of their own."

Pasquale nods slowly. "You're right," he says. "And Beatriz will know how to use it—as I said, I've only used it once, and Beatriz told me exactly how to word my wish."

"You should take a vial, though," Ambrose offers.

Violie shakes her head. "It isn't *for* me," she says.

"But you're the only one of us star-touched," Ambrose points out. "If you need to reach Daphne or try to reach Beatriz for any reason, you'll have it. Even if you can get stardust in Temarin, it won't be the Frivian kind and it won't have the same effect."

Violie opens her mouth to protest but quickly closes it again.

"He's right," Leopold says softly from beside her. "We all have the same goal—to sever the empress's hold on the continent and her daughters. It will help if we can coordinate."

Violie hesitates a moment longer before nodding. "Fine," she says. "If Beatriz can't get you all out of Cellaria with twelve vials of stardust, she wouldn't be able to do it with thirteen."

Violie's mother clears her throat, stirring her parsnip soup idly though she still doesn't eat any. "Alternatively," she says softly, "all four of you could sail away somewhere the empress couldn't find you rather than storming into danger."

Violie looks at her mother, surprised, though that surprise is quickly chased away by shame. The last time she left, she told her mother she had secured a job working for a duchess in Temarin—not a lie, but not the full truth, either.

Her mother had no idea about the training Violie had received or the danger she was facing as a spy. And that danger was nothing compared to what she and Leopold face now, marching back into a country where almost everyone wants him dead for one reason or another.

She reaches out to take her mother's hand, squeezing it tight. "We can't do that," she says.

"I know," her mother tells her with a sad smile. "But I had to suggest it anyway." She slides her gaze from Violie to Leopold. "Elodia was harsh with you earlier and she's too proud to apologize, but I will on her behalf."

"No apologies are necessary," Leopold says, shaking his head. "I was a terrible king, even before the siege."

"You weren't," Pasquale says, his face clouding over. "A foolish king, perhaps, and a naïve one from what I've heard, but my father was a terrible king and there's a difference between neglecting your role and abusing it."

Violie is confused for a moment until her mother sighs. "Graciella shared more than a map with you, I take it."

Now Violie understands. When Graciella first arrived at the Crimson Petal, she was skittish and quiet, but in time she shared details about King Cesare, what he did to her behind closed doors and what he did to others while his court egged him on.

"Killing him is one thing I'm grateful to my cousins for, I'll admit," Pasquale says softly. "I believe Graciella took some comfort in the manner of his death when I relayed it to her. He didn't go quickly or quietly in the end."

"Nicolo and Gisella killed him for their own reasons,"

Ambrose says, shaking his head. "It wasn't some noble choice, Pas."

Pasquale doesn't agree. "I'm not keen on defending them for most of the choices they've made, and I'm not naïve enough to believe they poisoned my father for purely selfless reasons, but I also don't believe it was purely a pragmatic, self-serving decision either. Both things can be true. And Gisella spared our lives, in case you're forgetting."

"I'm not," Ambrose says. "But one small mercy doesn't change anything in the grand scheme of things."

Violie agrees with Ambrose. She might not have met Gisella personally, but from everything she's heard, the few redeeming qualities she might have aren't nearly enough to make her someone worth sympathizing with. A small voice in the back of Violie's mind scoffs at that thought—after all, could the same not have been said of her mere months ago? She pushes that voice away before she can examine it too closely.

"It might," Pasquale says, his voice quieting as his eyes drop away from Ambrose, focusing instead on the table between them. He studies the grain of the wood, tracing its whorl with his thumb as he considers his next words. "It might change everything if it means there's a line she won't cross, not even for all the power in Cellaria. I think Gisella and Beatriz are far more alike than either of them cares to admit."

Ambrose smiles slightly. "Please, promise me you'll say that to Beatriz's face when we see her again. I'd give just about anything to see her reaction."

They leave early the following morning, and when they say their goodbyes to the women of the Crimson Petal, Violie struggles to keep her emotions from spilling over. It's already too difficult to release her mother from their embrace, to smile when Elodia tells her how proud she is. It's more tempting than Violie wants to admit, even to herself, to leave again. Once, she *wanted* to leave, to see the whole wide world and everything it had to offer. Now, that might still be true, but she finds she has a better appreciation for what she's leaving behind here—it isn't a life she wants for herself, but it is family and acceptance and love, and she knows now how lucky she is to have those three things together. Luckier than those born in palaces.

She is still thinking about her home and her mother as they ride out of the bustling city of Hapantoile and back into the Nemaria Woods, where they pause for more goodbyes and well-wishes before going their separate ways, Pasquale and Ambrose south to Cellaria and Violie and Leopold west to Temarin.

# Beatriz

That night, Beatriz decides to finally sneak out of the lavish rooms that are her prison. She's made no attempt up until now, but that doesn't mean she hasn't been considering it. She and Nicolo have negotiated terms, and if all goes to plan, she'll be queen of Cellaria in two days' time and going to war with her mother soon after that, but Gisella is still a threat and a variable, and Beatriz hasn't given up her search for stardust that might fix whatever is wrong with her magic.

Beatriz wants options, so she's been monitoring how often the guards change shifts, which guards are more lax in their duties, the layout of the private corridor that contains only her suite and Nicolo's. Tonight, she decides upon returning to her rooms after dinner, the stars have aligned and she won't waste the chance.

She bids good night to her guards—Tomoso and Ferdinand, who will be changing shifts in roughly half an hour—and tells them not to allow anyone to enter, including her maids. She's so tired, she explains to them, that she'll make do undressing herself for the night.

At the mention of her undressing, both of their faces turn

Cellarian red and they stutter out their own good nights, and Beatriz has to smother a giggle.

Once she's alone in her room, she strips off her evening gown and the layers of petticoats and corsetry underneath, leaving it all in a heap on the bench in front of her bed. Then she finds the maid's uniform she's collected in pieces—the kerchief and apron taken when a maid had removed hers after Beatriz insisted the fire be left burning far too long, turning the room into a virtual furnace; the dress she stole after *accidentally* spilling wine on a maid and insisting the girl change into one of her ever-so-slightly-out-of-date day dresses as an apology; the slippers she got by insisting the maids remove theirs before entering her room and subtly kicking one pair under the sofa when they were distracted. Each piece of the uniform came from a different maid, and while each might have thought it strange that their clothing had gone missing, they couldn't fathom that a princess would be stealing their work uniforms.

The dress is slightly too tight across the shoulders, the shoes a size too big, but Beatriz can manage, and when she glances at her reflection in the mirror, tucking the last of her distinctive red hair underneath her kerchief, she's satisfied she looks nothing like herself. She wishes she had access to all the paints and creams in her full cosmetics case to perfect the illusion, but given the circumstances, she'll do.

Besides, after a week of flawless prisoner behavior, she doubts her guards or anyone else will be expecting any different of her tonight.

The last thing she takes is truly hers—a ring from her jewelry box, a heavy gold thing with an emerald roughly the size of a peach pit. She slips it into the pocket of her apron and does her best to smooth away the lump.

She watches the clock and paces her sitting room, listening for the sound of approaching boots, the low exchange of words between the two sets of guards as they switch places. Patricchio and Alec are on duty now, and both guards, she knows, have a habit of indulging in a couple of glasses of wine with their supper.

Once she's sure Tomoso and Ferdinand have gone, she slips out the door, smile at the ready for Patricchio and Alec.

"The princess has gone to bed," she tells them, softening the edges of her Cellarian accent so that she sounds more like a commoner than a noble. "She asked not to be disturbed until morning."

"I was hardly expecting she'd be up for a game of chess, was I?" Alec grumbles, but neither he nor Patricchio spares her more than a passing glance, and she makes her way down the hallway, relief flooding through her.

Beatriz follows a group finishing their shift out the servants' exit, careful to keep her distance lest they look too closely at her, and when she steps out of the palace, she takes a deep breath, enjoying the kiss of the night air on her skin and in her lungs. She hasn't exactly been imprisoned indoors since she agreed to play nice with Gisella and Nicolo, but there is a world of difference between promenades around the sea garden with guards shadowing every move and this.

*Freedom.*

*Temporary freedom*, she reminds herself as she strolls

away from the palace and through the streets of Vallon. She will have to return to her gilded cage—fleeing now, with no weapons or money or horse, would only see her swiftly caught and returned to Nicolo, destroying any trust she's spent the last few days earning with her good behavior. This freedom is only hers for a matter of hours, but she intends to make the very most of it.

She never spent time in Vallon during her first stay at the palace—everything she wanted came to her, after all—but she's seen maps and overheard servants talk about the places they go, the shops they frequent. She knows that there is an apothecary near the castle, one that is open late enough to cater to servants during their off hours, and she sets about looking for it, meandering down busy streets lined with various shop fronts and public houses.

Beatriz could ask for directions, she supposes—the chances of anyone recognizing her out of the context of her life in the palace are slim—but for the time being she's enjoying the act of wandering, of aimless steps and the sense of exploration.

How many nights did she spend like this in Bessemia, her sisters at her side, wandering down the streets outside the palace in Hapantoile, blending in with a crowd and pretending, for just a moment, they were like any of the other people around them? No duties weighing heavy on their shoulders, no empress mother guiding their every step, no future already decided for them. The longing to go back to that simpler time wraps around her heart and holds fast. It's been more than a month now since Sophronia's death, but Beatriz still can't quite conceptualize the fact that she will never see her again. And Daphne . . .

Beatriz's breath catches. She can't let herself imagine a future where their paths cross again either—it will hurt too much when that hope is dashed once more. All she allows herself is the wish that Daphne survives, that she lives out a long life, happy and free, even if Beatriz can't be a part of it.

Her eyes light on a squat whitewashed building with soft glowing windows and a bright yellow awning rippling in the evening breeze. On the black lacquered door is a cowery flower, painted in gold—the Cellarian symbol of the apothecary. Triumphant, Beatriz makes her way to the door and rings the bell beside it.

"Come in, but hurry up—we're closing soon," a woman's voice calls out, and Beatriz pushes the door open, triggering the tinkling of a second bell above her head. She won't need more than a moment of the woman's time.

The apothecary is just shy of middle age, with sun-kissed skin and wild black hair pulled into a haphazard bun at the nape of her neck, frizzy pieces escaping to frame her sharp face. She stands behind a glass counter lined with glass jars of various sizes, filled with liquids, powders, and even some whole items like frog legs and tiger teeth, a rag in hand. She glances up at Beatriz, taking her in with startling shrewdness.

"I don't know you," the apothecary says, straight to the point.

Beatriz smiles. "I recently took up work in the palace," she explains, maintaining the common Cellarian accent she used with her guards.

The woman doesn't return Beatriz's smile. "And?" she

asks when Beatriz doesn't continue. "I told you, I'm closing. If you want something, you'd best get to the point."

Beatriz drops her smile and steps toward the counter, making a show of biting her lip and glancing around the room. It may inflame the woman's impatience, but it's a necessary ruse.

"I... heard that you can get things most wouldn't carry," she says carefully.

The woman's expression still doesn't shift. "I have the broadest selection of medicines and herbs in the city, that's true. What. Do. You. Want," she says, enunciating each word as if Beatriz is a wayward child.

But Beatriz can't say it outright. She's bluffing, after all—she doesn't *know* that this apothecary has stardust, but from what she's overheard around the palace, if anyone will have it, it will be her. And someone in Cellaria *must* have it. After all, if there is a demand for stardust, there will be a supply, laws be damned. And she can't imagine that there aren't plenty of people demanding stardust here. If she's right, she might be able to use the stardust to unlock her stifled magic, but if she's wrong... well, King Cesare might be dead, but possessing stardust in Cellaria is still a crime punishable by death, and she isn't keen to test Nicolo's feelings on that.

She proceeds carefully with the story she's rehearsed in her head—one inspired by the story Violie told her.

"My mother," she says, clasping her hands in front of her and wringing them. "She has Vexis—the doctor says she doesn't have long left, that there is no hope for her. But I heard..." She trails off again. "I heard that *you* might have a cure."

The apothecary's expression doesn't waver. "There is no cure for Vexis," she says, her tone softening somewhat. "You were given bad information."

Beatriz blinks rapidly, summoning ersatz tears, and closes the distance between them, until she is just on the other side of the glass counter. "Please, I will try anything. *Anything*," she says. "I have five younger siblings—the youngest still an infant, and our father is gone. If my mother dies . . ." She trails off once more, choking back a fake sob.

"I have nothing for you," the woman says again, but this time, Beatriz hears the thread of uncertainty in her voice, the temptation.

She digs her hand into the pocket of her apron, pulling out the emerald ring and placing it on the table between them. She doesn't speak, instead letting the apothecary look the ring over. She picks it up, eyes widening, and turns it over in her hand.

"Where did you get this?" she asks, awe in her voice.

Beatriz meets her eyes. "From a very important person," she says. "Someone it would be considered a grave crime to steal from, a crime that would cost me my life." The apothecary lets out a long exhale, setting the ring back between them, her fingers lingering for a moment on the stone. "I told you I was desperate," Beatriz says, her voice quiet. "There is no risk I will not take, no price I will not pay, to save my mother's life. Tell me again that I am beyond your help and I will walk out that door and trust the stars to guide me to someone who will."

The woman holds her gaze but doesn't speak. *Won't*

speak, Beatriz realizes after a moment, not even to lie to her again. Suddenly, Beatriz is sure that she *does* have stardust, that she is on the cusp of giving it to her, but not quite there yet. She can't even blame the woman for her hesitance—she knows how many Cellarians King Cesare saw burned on the slightest suspicion of using stardust. But Beatriz has one last card to play.

"Fine, then," she says, the words coming out bitter. She drops her gaze, pockets the ring again, and turns away from the apothecary, walking toward the door. She counts her steps as she goes. One, two, three . . .

"Wait," the apothecary says when Beatriz's hand is on the doorknob. "Lock the door and draw the curtains. I have what you're seeking."

Not ten minutes later, Beatriz is making her way back to the castle, without the emerald ring but with the smallest vial of stardust she's ever seen, the glass bottle the same size as her smallest finger, tapered at the bottom to a point. She didn't dare keep it in her pocket, in case a guard stops her. Instead, the apothecary helped her tuck the vial into her braided hair, hidden beneath her kerchief, secure and out of sight. The apothecary also gave her explicit instructions on how to use the stardust, how to phrase her wish just so, and warned her that even if she does everything right it still might not have the effect she wishes.

*Stardust is tricky,* she whispered as she unlocked the door and ushered Beatriz out onto the street again.

But Beatriz knows that well by now. Still, there is a chance it will work and that is enough for her.

She reenters the castle through the servants' quarters, just as she left, then climbs the stairs and winds through the hallways, unstopped by the guards on duty until she reaches the door to her rooms, where Patricchio and Alec are still on duty. When they see her, Alec scowls.

"What are you doing back?" he asks.

Beatriz smiles and approaches, pushing her kerchief up just enough to reveal a bit of her hair while keeping her vial of stardust safely concealed. She watches with some satisfaction as the guards take her in with fresh eyes, that glimpse of hair enough to see her for who she truly is.

"P-Princess," Patricchio says, stumbling over her title. "What are you . . . you shouldn't be—"

"King Nicolo gave strict orders," Alec interrupts, his face turning a violent shade of red.

Beatriz's smile widens. "Of course he did," she says sweetly. "And he will be so terribly disappointed in you should he learn that you let me by, won't he? He assigned you such a simple job, after all." She clicks her tongue. "But *I* won't tell him. Will you?" she asks, looking between them. "He might be a bit cross with me, but I daresay he'd be much angrier with you two. You'd likely find yourself without jobs at the very least."

The men look at each other, flustered. Finally, Patricchio turns back to her and clears his throat. "There's no reason the king needs to know, Your Highness."

"Provided it doesn't happen again," Alec adds.

"It won't," she says.

Alec pushes the door open for her and she reenters her room, pausing just before the door closes behind her. "Oh, and Alec?"

"Yes, Your Highness?"

She channels Daphne into the sharpness of her smile, making it strong enough to draw blood. "Contrary to what you said earlier, I'm *always* up for a good game of chess, but I should warn you I never lose."

She notes the way he swallows, blanching. "Yes, Your Highness," he says, and closes the door.

# Daphne

The morning after Lord Panlington's sudden death—a heart attack, the court physician called it—Daphne makes her way to the chapel, looking for Cliona. In all the chaos, she wasn't able to see her friend. Guards pulled Daphne away, rushing both her and Bairre from the room and returning them to their quarters until they could ascertain that there was no threat to them. During Bairre's pacing and worrying about Lord Panlington in the hours that followed, Daphne couldn't bring herself to tell him about her mother's hand lingering over Lord Panlington's teacup, the fine powder dropping into the dark liquid from her ring. She knew if she did tell him, he would ask a question she couldn't answer.

*Why didn't you stop her?*

It was a question that kept her up all night, tossing and turning. A question that lingers in her mind even now as she steps into the frigid chapel, empty apart from a single figure sitting in the front pew, red hair peeking out from beneath a black mourning veil.

Daphne's heart aches as she makes her way down the aisle and slides into the pew beside Cliona, who keeps her head bowed, hands clasped in her lap. Daphne knew little of Lord Panlington and liked even less, but he was Cliona's father all the same, and she can feel the grief rolling off her in waves, along with something else Daphne realizes too late is anger.

"You knew," Cliona says, still not looking at her. Her voice is a thread-thin thing, but Daphne still feels it like a dagger pressed to the back of her neck.

She swallows. "Cliona..." She trails off. Years of training in manipulation and charm tell her to lie, to make excuses, to persuade Cliona to see her side of things, to understand why she had to let her father die. But how can Daphne do that when she doesn't understand it herself?

Cliona waits a moment for a response, but when Daphne doesn't give one, she turns her head to look at her for the first time. She looks at Daphne like she's never seen her before, like they're strangers, and Daphne feels that like a punch to her stomach.

"I knew your mother was responsible," Cliona says. "I knew it as soon as the life left his eyes. You told me what she was capable of, and I *knew* she'd killed him. But when I returned to my rooms to find her waiting for me... I wasn't expecting her to confess to it. To tell me that you helped her."

"I didn't—" Daphne begins to protest before biting her tongue. Her mother designed this, she realizes. Yes, she was annoyed that Lord Panlington didn't agree to ally with her, but that wasn't why she killed him. After all, whoever fills his shoes in the rebellion won't be any more inclined to give the empress power in Friv. No, Daphne sees now the real reason the empress did it, why she let Daphne see her use the poison. It wasn't a test at all, it was a trap. The empress has always sought to isolate Daphne and her sisters, preventing them from having any friends outside of one another, and she only let them have that because it was inevitable. Daphne never minded it growing up—her mother and sisters were all she wanted—but now she feels Cliona slipping away. No, wrenching herself away.

She tries again, suddenly desperate. "I'm sorry, Cliona, I should have said something, should have stopped her. I thought it was a test, to see if my loyalties were still to her. I thought if she knew they weren't . . ." She trails off again, and this time Cliona doesn't wait for her to finish. She laughs, the sound broken.

"You made the decision to let my father *die* in order to prevent your mother from being disappointed in you?" she asks.

"No," Daphne says, but deep down she knows Cliona isn't wrong, not completely. "But if she knows I've turned against her, it puts everyone in danger—"

"Oh, wake up, Daphne," Cliona snaps, her voice echoing in the empty chapel. "Everyone is in danger now. Is my father not proof enough of that? The only one you're protecting is yourself."

Daphne shakes her head. "I'm protecting you," she says. "And Bairre, and my sister, and—"

"I don't want or need your protection," Cliona says, voice cracking. She gets to her feet and hastily wipes a black-gloved hand under her eyes to catch what Daphne realizes are tears. She wants nothing more in that moment than to reach out, to comfort her hurting friend, but she knows she's the last person Cliona wants comfort from, so instead she balls her hands into fists in her lap. When Cliona speaks again, her voice is cold. "What I need is people I can trust, Daphne. And that no longer includes you." She slips out of the pew and starts back up the aisle, and Daphne moves to follow her.

"Cliona, there are bigger things at play here—"

"Stay away from me," Cliona says without turning around. "The last thing you need is another enemy."

Daphne stops short at the words and watches Cliona's back as she exits the chapel, closing the door firmly behind her and leaving Daphne wholly alone.

Daphne tells herself that Cliona just needs time. She's grieving and hurt, but Cliona has always been a shrewd and pragmatic person. In time, she'll be able to see why Daphne couldn't save her father. But as she leaves the chapel and begins to wind her way through the palace hallways, her guards at her heels, she begins to worry that something between them has been irreparably broken—that *she* broke it. She tries to envision another outcome to that fatal lunch but can't see her way to any she could accept.

But still, Cliona's words haunt her. *You made the decision to let my father die in order to prevent your mother from being disappointed in you?*

Once, not too long ago, the thought of disappointing the empress was enough to make Daphne nauseous. She thought, with Sophronia's visit during the northern lights, that the empress no longer had that hold on her, that Daphne no longer needed her approval. Now, though, she suspects that she will never be free of that desire. Perhaps it will always linger, no matter how irrational and impractical it might be.

But that doesn't mean she has to feed it.

She stops short at the thought, her two guards nearly walking into her before catching themselves.

"Princess?" one of them asks, his voice uncertain. His name is Tal, and Daphne suspects he's in league with the rebels, as many guards are. The other guard, Dominic, stays silent, but then, Daphne doesn't think she's ever heard Dominic speak.

She turns to face them both, a sudden determination warring with wariness within her.

"I've changed my mind," she says. "We aren't returning to my rooms after all—I need to speak with my mother."

Her mother, Daphne learns, is visiting the castle's glasshouse—a vast structure set up in the east garden that contains an array of flowers, trees, and crops from across Vesteria, sheltered from Friv's harsh winter climate. Daphne isn't surprised that her mother has chosen to spend her morning there—even in Bessemia, her free time was often spent in her rose garden, nurturing and pruning her collection of delicate flowers.

There aren't many roses in Friv's glasshouse, but Daphne knows exactly where they are. She instructs her guards to wait outside the glasshouse doors, where the empress's guards are lingering, and steps inside, the blast of warmth a welcome respite from the frigid outdoor air. Daphne meanders by citrus trees and potted orchids, through a metal archway trellised with fragrant jasmine, past beds of wrinkled cabbages and feathery carrot tops, until the scent of roses hits her and she catches sight of her mother's bright blue skirt among all the greenery.

The empress is crouched before a rosebush, its pale pink flowers closed in tight buds, the branches tangled and overgrown. In her hands, she holds a pair of pruning shears.

"Surely the gardener will handle that," Daphne says.

Her mother doesn't startle at the sound of her voice. Instead, she peers over her shoulder at Daphne with raised eyebrows.

"The gardener doesn't know the first thing about pruning roses. Clearly," she says, turning back to the rosebush and giving a decisive snip. A withered branch laden with thorns falls to the ground. "I sent Bartholomew this plant as a cutting from one of my own rosebushes, you know. It was a gift, to celebrate your betrothal to his son. This rosebush is almost exactly your age."

Daphne has never shared her mother's passion for roses, but she eyes the bush thoughtfully. "Is that not old for a rosebush?" she asks.

"It is," her mother confirms. "Most don't live past a decade, though I'd wager the stardust used to keep this glasshouse temperate has a hand in extending the plants' life-spans." She shakes her head, and Daphne doesn't need to see her face to know her mouth is curled in disgust. In her mother's mind, using magic to keep plants alive is cheating.

Apparently, using magic to conquer a continent is not.

"Still," her mother continues, rising to her feet, shears in hand, "I'm afraid it is at the end of its life cycle. It's lived sixteen years, but it won't see seventeen, no matter what help it's given."

Daphne knows her mother isn't only talking about the rosebush. She's talking about *her*. And about Beatriz as well. Her eyes go again to the shears in her mother's hand. Perhaps those should be considered a threat, but Daphne doesn't feel threatened. Not here, not like this. Her mother may want her dead, but she can't be the one to kill her. *By Frivian hands, on Frivian soil.*

At any rate, she has her own weapons close at hand. A dagger in her boot, another holstered to her forearm beneath her gown and cloak, should she need them.

But she won't. Not yet.

"Why did you kill Lord Panlington?" she asks, drawing her eyes back up to meet her mother's.

Her mother smiles. "Lord Panlington was an obstacle," she says, shrugging. "I do hope whoever takes over leading the rebellion will be more amenable to my desires. If someone else takes over at all—it's just as likely that without a strong leader they'll fall to chaos and your path to claiming Friv will be even easier. You ought to be thanking me, Daphne."

Daphne chooses her next words carefully, but all the same, they threaten to choke her as she gives them breath. "You're lying."

The empress's brows arch higher. "Am I?"

"If that were your aim, you wouldn't have confessed to Cliona. You wouldn't have told her I knew what you were doing. Cliona was loyal to me, and therefore so was the rebellion. That loyalty has been integral to our plans since I arrived in Friv; you had nothing to gain by severing it."

"*Our* plans?" her mother repeats, and while her tone is light, Daphne hears the danger just underneath. The impulse to appease her rises up, the desire to tell her mother exactly what she wants to hear, to prove to her that she's a good, dutiful daughter, that she's worthy.

This time, though, Daphne doesn't feed it.

Ever since her mother arrived in Friv, they've been engaged in a careful dance, she realizes. Daphne has been pretending that nothing has changed, that *she* hasn't changed, and her mother has been pretending to believe her. In some ways, Daphne suspects she's been pretending to believe her mother's belief, another layer to their precarious tower of illusions.

Now, though, Daphne decides to raze that tower to the ground.

"*Your* plans," she corrects, forcing herself to meet her mother's gaze. She lifts her chin an inch and forces herself not to cower. "I suppose they stopped being my plans the moment I learned you killed Sophronia."

The empress isn't shocked by the accusation. She clicks her tongue. "Oh, Daphne," she says, the name heavy with disappointment. "You've been listening to poisoned whispers. A Temarinian mob killed Sophronia."

This, too, is part of the dance of illusions, Daphne realizes. Her mother doesn't even bother to make her denial sound convincing.

"A Temarinian mob," she echoes. "Including a young man

named Ansel? I caught him kidnapping Gideon and Reid, you know—the Temarinian princes. He had plenty to say about his associations with you."

"All lies," her mother says, sounding bored.

"And Eugenia was lying too, I expect? And Violie?" Daphne asks.

The empress shakes her head, looking at Daphne with pity that makes her skin crawl. "This world is full of people who want to hurt me, Daphne," she says. "But I never imagined my own daughter would be among them. I didn't know there was such hatred in you toward me, that you would believe these people's lies."

The empress turns to go, to walk away from Daphne, but Daphne isn't done.

"And Sophronia?" she asks. "Was she lying too?"

Her mother freezes, but she doesn't turn around. Daphne doesn't care—she couldn't stop the words flowing from her now even if she wanted to, though these next words are a lie, close enough to the truth that in Daphne's mind they barely count as one. "Frivian stardust is stronger than other kinds," she says, taking a step toward her mother, then another. "It's strong enough to allow communication between those of us who are star-touched. I used it to speak with Beatriz and Sophronia on the day she died, as they were leading her up to the guillotine."

She studies her mother's back, searching for any twitch or tension, but if her mother is troubled by her words, she doesn't show it. Daphne continues. "She told Beatriz and me then that you were responsible for her death, that you were determined to kill all three of us to claim Vesteria." This is the part that isn't wholly true—Sophronia didn't blame their mother then, and even if she had, Daphne wouldn't have been ready to hear it.

"Your sister was a fool," the empress says. "I didn't believe *you* were one as well."

Daphne ignores the sting those words cause. "And Nigellus?" she asks. "Was he a fool when he confirmed your plans to Beatriz, when he explained to her the details of the wish he made for you seventeen years ago?"

The empress lets out a long exhale, her shoulders sagging. When she turns to face Daphne again, the cold apathy in her expression is gone, replaced with a look so full of desolation that Daphne's heart clenches and she has to force herself not to take a step toward her. This is just another mask, she reminds herself, but a small part of her wonders if it isn't. If this, finally, truly is her mother at last.

"You want the truth, Daphne?" she asks, her voice a thin thread pulled taut, to its breaking point. It isn't a voice Daphne has ever heard from her mother, and that frightens her more than anything else the empress has said or done so far. The empress doesn't wait for an answer. She crosses back toward Daphne, each step slow and measured.

"When I was eighteen, I was assisting my father during a visit to some clients who lived at the palace in Hapantoile and wished to comission new gowns. To you, that palace is simply home, I suppose, positively mundane, but for me that day . . . I'd never seen anything like it. Every inch of it seemed to glitter in my eyes, and oh, the people! The courtiers dripping in jewels and silks, moving through the world without a care. They knew nothing of what it felt like to go hungry when their father's business had a bad week, or to worry that they might not be able to afford enough firewood to keep them warm in winter. I hated them for the unfairness of it all, but I envied them even more. I don't suppose you know anything about that sort of envy," she adds, giving Daphne a level look. And while Daphne is no stranger to envy, she can't claim to relate to how her mother felt then.

The empress doesn't wait for an answer. "As we went from one apartment to the next within the palace, by pure chance, we passed by the emperor and his attendants. My father bowed and I curtsied, along with all the other courtiers and servants present, and by pure chance, the emperor's attention caught on me. *Me*," she emphasizes with a short, sharp laugh. "A scrawny young thing barely out of girlhood, in a plain cotton dress and scuffed-up shoes. An errant weed with the audacity to crop up among orchids."

Daphne has never heard this story from the empress herself, but she's heard it in snippets of gossip, passed through the halls of that same palace in Hapantoile. She knows what happens next, but she certainly doesn't want to hear the details. Not from her mother, about her father, even if he was a man Daphne has no memory of.

"He made you his mistress," she says.

The empress nods. "It was my first real taste of power," she says. "And I wanted nothing more than to drown in it, to let it sink beneath my skin and into my lungs, changing me from the girl I was into the woman I was so desperate to be. A woman who wanted for nothing, who made people listen. But no one listened to me then. Not really. What power I had as the emperor's mistress was secondhand, contingent on the whims of a man whose whims were ever-changing. Yes, it was more power than I'd ever had before, power I was lucky to have by virtue of a pretty face and being in the right place at the right time, but it wasn't enough. I wanted—*needed*—more."

"So you went to Nigellus," Daphne says.

"He wasn't the court empyrea then," her mother says. "He was nothing before I found him, just a hermit living alone on the edge of the Nemaria Woods, but even then I'd heard stories of his power. People he'd helped swore that he was the most powerful empyrea in Vesteria. I thought it merely an exaggeration—all I cared about was that he was an empyrea with no connection to court, no loyalty to the emperor."

It occurs to Daphne that it isn't quite true that Nigellus was nothing before her mother—he had his power, he had work that he did well. Her mother didn't create him by shining a beacon on him, but she suspects that in the empress's mind, that's exactly what happened.

"The emperor gave me an allowance, as well as plenty of gifts—gold and jewels each worth a small fortune—but when I offered everything I had in exchange for Nigellus's help, he refused me. I thought what I asked for was too much, but instead of closing the door in my face, he ushered me in and laid out his terms. As I would come to learn, Nigellus had little interest in wealth or even power—he craved knowledge, to understand what the limits of his magic were and to push them, simply for the sake of it. In my court, he would be able to do that without worrying that the crown would punish him for sacrilege or heresy. Some of his ideas were . . . unpopular, to say the least. Including the plan we came up with together—not only wishing for me to conceive heirs with an infertile king, which forced him to annul his marriage to the then-empress and marry me, but tying each of your fates to the fate of another country. When you were killed, the country would fall, and it would be mine for the taking. I was aware of the sacrifice it would require, but I was only nineteen. The cost of losing children I had no desire for in the first place didn't haunt me. It was a price I was happy to pay. Then."

Daphne watches her mother as she speaks, searching for the cracks in her facade—and it has to be a facade, surely. But the empress herself taught Daphne that the best lies are built on truths.

"Is this the part where you tell me you regret it?" she asks, crossing her arms over her chest, her voice so thick with sarcasm she knows she sounds more like Beatriz than herself. "That once you became a mother, you loved us and you tried to change the magic Nigellus cast?"

The empress laughs, shaking her head. "Stars, no, I never regretted it," she says. "I don't expect you to understand, of course. You were born to power, born to privilege, and you've never known anything else. And as little as you know about powerlessness, you know even less about motherhood."

The empress doesn't say the words unkindly, yet they act as a lit match thrown onto the tinderbox of Daphne's anger. It flares inside her, threatening to consume her whole. Yes, her life has been a privileged one in many ways, but her mother has perfected the art of making her and her sisters feel powerless. She said it was to force them to become stronger, to help them grow, but Daphne wonders now if it was cruelty for cruelty's sake, aimed to do nothing more than make them feel small, to make herself feel large.

And while it's true that Daphne is not a mother and has no desire to change that fact anytime soon, that doesn't make her ignorant.

But Daphne is not Beatriz. She doesn't have Beatriz's temper or her impulsiveness, so she keeps the inferno of her anger deep inside, careful to betray no outward sign of it. The anger is what her mother wants, she knows, and the second she gives it to her, Daphne loses.

"Perhaps," she says, matching her mother's cold tone. "But I know that mothers are supposed to protect their children, not sacrifice them at the altar of their own ambitions."

The empress inclines her head, acknowledging the point even if she doesn't appear troubled by it. "I lost no sleep over Sophronia, and I won't pretend I did," she says. "And when I had Beatriz brought back to Cellaria, to the fate awaiting her there, I did so without a second thought." She pauses, taking a step closer to Daphne and closing the distance between them. Daphne struggles not to flinch as her mother's cold, ungloved hand rests against her cheek, the touch unnervingly tender. "But you . . ." She gives a heavy sigh. "Daphne, I've had countless opportunities to have you killed, and I haven't been able to take any of them. Because you're different—you're special to me."

Those last words are ones Daphne has always wanted to hear from her mother. Even now, knowing everything she does, the sound of them still worms its way into her heart, tangling there. She forces herself to take a step back, pushing her mother's hand away from her face.

"You hired assassins," she says, grasping for reason, and she sees the truth of it in her mother's face as soon as the words leave her lips. She *did* hire those assassins. Her mother *did* try to kill her. It isn't a surprise, after everything, but it still manages to shock her.

"I did," the empress says slowly. "It was foolish of me to do it so soon—with Prince Cillian dead and you still unmarried, I knew it was too soon to guarantee my plan would work. But I also knew, my dove, that the longer I waited, the harder it would be for me. And every time I received word that you had eluded them, that you had triumphed over them in the end, I was so *relieved*. I tried so hard to keep my distance from you and your sisters, but with you . . . with you, Daphne, I never stood a chance. Despite all of my best efforts, I love you too much to let you meet the same fate as your sisters."

Daphne feels herself waver. These are the words she's always wanted to hear, the approval she's always worked so hard for. Of course her mother knows that, of course she's using that desire against her now, baiting a trap. She wishes that knowing her mother's motivations rendered that bait useless, but it doesn't. Not entirely, at least.

She knows there are two ways this conversation can go—if she rejects her mother's overture outright, she declares herself a threat, and she knows how her mother deals with threats. Logically, her mother has no reason not to have her killed now that she and Bairre are married. Most of Friv loves her, that's true, but there are surely plenty who don't, plenty who would be eager to take her mother's coin and deliver a dagger to her heart, a poison to her morning tea. No, while Daphne doesn't believe that her mother has changed her mind out of love, something *is* causing her to stay her hand, at least for now. And if Daphne can dance to the empress's tune a little longer, a little *better* than she has thus far, she might still be able to beat her at her own game.

"Then let me come home," Daphne says, making her voice hesitant. Her mother will suspect if she changes her mind too quickly, if she sets aside all her anger and suspicions in the blink of an eye.

The empress frowns, looking truly confused for the first time today. "Home?" she asks.

"To Bessemia," Daphne clarifies. "If you're serious about sparing me, let me come home. Away from Frivian soil and Frivian hands. Make me your heir officially, give me a future outside the cursed one you and Nigellus planned for me."

"You have a husband here," the empress says.

Daphne shrugs. "We can invite him, too, or not," she says. "But if you're truly giving up on using me to conquer Friv, there is no reason for me to stay. Instead, name me your heir, and eventually, Bairre and I will rule Friv and Bessemia together, as will our heir, your grandchild. If you're giving up on ruling it alone, surely that's an excellent consolation prize."

The empress's expression remains placid, but Daphne knows her mind is whirling, looking for holes in Daphne's logic and finding none big enough to walk through.

"Very well," the empress says finally. "I'll speak with Bartholomew about it over dinner, but I expect you'll need to convince your husband to join us. He's quite attached to Friv."

Daphne smiles tightly. She knows her mother isn't inviting Bairre out of kindness or with any thought to Daphne's desires—he's to be a hostage, someone the empress *can* harm or even kill if Daphne steps out of line.

# Beatriz

All day, as Beatriz attends to the myriad appointments to go over details of her wedding tomorrow, she struggles to think of anything other than the vial of stardust hidden in her room. She elected not to use it the night before—it was late, she was tired, and she wanted to take the time to consider how exactly to phrase her wish and also ensure that she is ready for the aftermath.

If it works.

It *has* to work.

She was careful in hiding the stardust, knowing the risk if anyone were to find it while cleaning. Beatriz doubts Nicolo would have her killed if she was found with the stardust, but she remembers the maid who was executed after finding the stardust she created the last time she was in Cellaria, and she doesn't want to put anyone else in danger.

Nowhere seemed safe enough, considering how thorough her maids were in their cleaning, but Beatriz eventually lit one of the thick candles on the mantel above the fireplace in her sitting room. She waited for the surface of the candle to soften, then pressed the pointed end of the vial into the wax until the entire thing sank inside. Then, when the softened wax was barely cool enough to touch, she used her fingers to smooth the wax over the top of the vial until it looked just as it had before.

Getting it out will prove a challenge, she knows, but if all goes according to plan, she won't have to answer for the mess she makes when she removes it. She'll be gone.

"Princess?"

Beatriz's thoughts are jerked away from the stardust and the candle and she pastes a smile on her face as she focuses on the present—in the palace's vast kitchen with the royal pastry chef in front of her, watching and waiting for a reaction to the slice of cake Beatriz took a bite of some time ago. Vanilla cake layered with lemon raspberry jam and topped with a light lemon frosting.

"It's perfect," she says with a smile. "And I'm sure the king will agree. He does *adore* raspberries."

Gisella cuts her a bemused look but says nothing. All day, as Gisella has accompanied her on these last-minute wedding errands, she's been quiet, not offering more to any conversation than agreeing with any opinions Beatriz offers. At first, her silence was a relief—the last thing Beatriz wants to do is make casual conversation with a girl planning to kill her—but as the day has gone on, Beatriz has found it more and more unnerving.

The pastry chef beams and curtsies before excusing herself—no doubt eager to get started on what Beatriz is sure is a mammoth project to complete in just over twenty-four hours. As soon as she's gone, the palace's head chef, Ovellio, approaches with a thick square of parchment, passing it to Beatriz with a smug smile.

"The menu for the wedding feast," he says, bowing. "I trust it will meet with your approval?"

Beatriz skims each of the ten courses, and though she only just ate lunch, the menu makes her hungry all over again. It isn't enough to make her consider staying, but it's close. Perhaps when this is all done, she can persuade Ovellio away from Cellaria, to work for her.

Wherever it is she ends up.

"You've outdone yourself, Ovellio," she says, handing the menu back to him. "It will surely be a feast no one will soon forget."

"Thank you, Your Majesty," he says, smile deepening. He bows again, then backs away to return to work.

"Where are we off to next?" Beatriz asks, turning toward Gisella, who still seems worlds away.

"The chapel," Gisella says simply before starting toward the door that leads out of the kitchens. Beatriz follows, eyeing Gisella's back as they walk, her pale blond hair done in an elaborate plait that swings with each step. Beatriz's two guards, who waited outside on Gisella's orders while they spoke to the chefs, fall into step behind her, their boots tapping against the stone floor in perfect rhythm.

Gisella's silence shouldn't bother her, Beatriz thinks, hurrying to catch up. Whatever it is she's plotting, whatever secrets she's hiding doesn't matter to Beatriz. She'll be gone before any of them can take shape. Tonight, after she uses the stardust to wish her magic unblocked, the first thing she'll do is wish herself far away from Cellaria, and once she's gone, she'll never spare Gisella another thought.

*Every movement requires a martyr,* Gisella told her. *And you'll make such a lovely one.*

The words have been gnawing at Beatriz, giving her the peculiar sense that she's staring at a tapestry too closely, seeing the fine needlework but missing the entire effect of the piece. One thing she knows, though, is that she'd be a fool to underestimate Gisella. Not many people can say that they outmaneuvered the empress and lived to tell the tale, but Gisella has.

It's more than Beatriz herself has ever managed, she realizes with a mixture of irritation and grudging respect.

An idea occurs to her. Perhaps a reckless one, but if everything goes according to plan tonight, she'll never see Gisella again, and if it doesn't . . . well, she'll be dead soon enough no matter what. It's early in the afternoon, and Beatriz needs to wait until the stars are out before she makes her wish. Five hours, give or take.

"I don't think I can make another decision without more coffee," Beatriz tells Gisella, faking a yawn.

Gisella's brow creases in suspicion, but after a moment she gives a brief nod. "Fine," she says.

"My rooms are closer—allow me to play hostess," Beatriz says, making a sudden right down the palace corridor that leads to the royal wing.

She feels Gisella's suspicion rolling off her in waves, but that's to be expected. She simply needs to present a decoy.

"I received a letter from my mother," she lies, thinking quickly. "Perhaps when you read her words yourself, you'll understand just how dangerous the game you're playing is."

Gisella scoffs, but Beatriz knows her curiosity is piqued. "If you insist," Gisella says.

When they reach Beatriz's receiving room, her guards wait outside and Beatriz sends the maid who is dusting the bookshelf for coffee and pastries. Both Beatriz and Gisella are all smiles, maintaining the illusion of friendship between them, but when the door closes and their audience is gone, Gisella's smile slips off her face and she turns toward Beatriz.

"Well?" she asks. "Where's the letter?"

Beatriz's own smile widens. "And here I thought you weren't interested in what she had to say," she says, collapsing into an armchair with another fake yawn.

"I'm mostly interested in how it got to you," Gisella says, shrugging. "You must know all your letters are inspected."

Beatriz did suspect that, not that anyone she cares about has been foolish enough to send her letters. She shakes her head. "You truly have no idea who you're dealing with, do you?" she asks with a laugh. "My mother has spies everywhere."

It's only half a bluff—Beatriz knows her mother's network of spies is extensive, but by the same token, if she had so many Cellarians at court to do her bidding, why depend on Gisella to assassinate Beatriz? Perhaps she simply knows how capable Gisella is at killing, but perhaps it's more than that. Perhaps the stretch of her mother's reach is an illusion the empress imprinted upon her and her sisters, one she's never had leave to question. Her mother does have spies, this she knows, but Beatriz suddenly suspects they're fewer and less powerful than her mother has made them seem.

"Let's enjoy our coffee before we wade into such unpleasantness," Beatriz says to Gisella.

Gisella eyes Beatriz for a moment, lips pursed. Finally she sighs and crosses toward the armchair beside Daphne's, lowering herself into it. "You're making everything so much more difficult than it needs to be," she says after a moment.

"Because I want coffee?" Beatriz asks dryly.

"Because you insist on fighting even after you've lost," Gisella says. "It must be exhausting."

Beatriz considers this for a moment. Even if she didn't have the stardust, even if she didn't have a plan, she knows she would still be fighting. She can't help it.

Her thoughts are interrupted by the maid returning with a small, gilded cart on wheels, which holds a brass pot of coffee and three small plates piled high with an array of pastries. Beatriz thanks her and dismisses her for the afternoon and the maid leaves with a curtsy, shutting the door behind her.

"You and my mother have that in common," Beatriz tells Gisella as she pours herself a cup of coffee and helps herself to a dainty tea cake topped with pink icing and dried flower petals. "Finding me difficult, that is. And yes, I suppose it is exhausting, but if the day comes when I am well and truly beaten, Gigi, I'll rest easy knowing I made things as difficult for you as possible. And then I'll take great pleasure in haunting both you and my mother for the rest of your sad, joyless lives."

Gisella absorbs her speech with a placid smile, taking an idle sip of her coffee. "I can't speak for your mother, but I don't think my life will lack joy by any means," she says. "All the more so knowing that I'll need to give your ghost a show and keep you properly entertained."

Beatriz grits her teeth and pops the entire tea cake into her mouth before she can say something she'll come to regret.

"I will miss you, though," Gisella says, as casually as if Beatriz were planning a weekend away in the country.

Beatriz tries not to choke on her tea cake. She swallows and offers Gisella a pointed smile. "I missed you before," she replies, matching Gisella's tone. "But I can assure you, my aim will be better next time."

Gisella's expression catches somewhere between a scowl and a laugh and she tries to hide it behind her cup of coffee, taking another long sip that drains the cup. She sets it back on its saucer.

"Well?" she asks. "Where's this letter?"

Beatriz holds up her coffee cup, still half full. "I'm not done yet," she says. "But if you're so impatient, get it yourself—in my desk, top left drawer."

Gisella gets to her feet and crosses the room, turning her back to Beatriz—a mistake she should have known better than to make. Beatriz sets her own cup down, making not a single sound as the cup hits the saucer; then she is slipping her feet from her slippers and crossing the room quick and silent, grabbing the now-empty brass coffeepot from the cart as she passes by. Gisella is just opening the drawer when Beatriz swings the coffeepot. Gisella is turning toward her, and the coffeepot strikes Gisella's temple with a dull clang. Gisella drops, but Beatriz is ready for that, catching her unconscious body before she hits the floor with a sound that would alarm the guards outside.

Her combat instructor taught her and her sisters that maneuver while the empress looked on, eyes shrewd and judgmental, and Beatriz feels a little thrill, thinking that if her mother could see her now, she would surely regret that.

She wastes no time dragging Gisella into the dining room, closing the door behind her and pushing her into a high-backed chair with carved wooden arms. She goes to her bedroom and pulls out a nightgown, tearing the linen into strips. She uses them to bind Gisella to the chair, using the last strip as a gag. Then she sits down across the table from Gisella and waits.

# Violie

The first time Violie rode from Hapantoile into Temarin, she did so alone, with just enough coin to afford her a moderate room in a shabby inn and a single change of clothes packed into a satchel with some bread, cheese, and cake her mother had packed for her. It hadn't mattered that the empress was employing her—a servant traveling any more comfortably could have been seen as suspicious, and any companions she might be traveling with had the potential to see through her lies.

Ansel had met her in a small village near the border—a surprise to Violie, though he'd apparently been acting on orders to wait for her for days. He'd been the one to provide her with forged letters of reference from a reclusive Temarinian count, and they'd hitchhiked the rest of the way to Kavelle in a farmer's wagon. They'd arrived in the city smelling like hay, having spent those hours wrapped up in each other's arms simply because it had been a way to pass the time.

When Violie and Leopold cross into Temarin, she can't help but think about Ansel. She didn't mourn his death when Daphne told her about it. After everything that had happened, she'd have killed him herself if she'd been given a chance. But now the thought of him sends a pang into her heart. Her feelings for him were a shallow puddle, born more of convenience and the need for security in a strange new world than anything else.

They were so similar when they first met, she realizes. Both angry at the world and desperate for more from life, both ready to burn the world down if they could turn a profit from the ashes. Violie agreed to work for the empress to heal her mother, yes, but she knows deep down that if her mother hadn't been sick, she'd have done the same for a bag of gold and a way out of the life she'd been born into. And in Ansel, she'd seen her ambition and ruthlessness mirrored.

They took different paths from there, but now she spares a thought for the person he might have been, and the person she might have been too. When the moment passes, though, she banishes Ansel from her thoughts for good and turns to Leopold.

"I don't suppose you've developed a plan now that we're in Temarin?" she asks him. "You know you can't simply march into Kavelle and declare yourself king again."

"Of course I know that," Leopold says, scoffing before he falls silent for a moment. "But I wouldn't say I have a plan, no," he adds. "I've been thinking about my family's allies who weren't at court when the siege happened, those who might still be alive."

Violie opens her mouth to dispel any ideas he might have about that, but he starts speaking again.

"After the siege, those courtiers would have either sworn allegiance to Empress Margaraux or been executed by her army. And I'd wager good money that none of them took the latter option."

Violie closes her mouth, surprised he saw the logical truth before she pointed it out. "Some might decide to ally with you, but at best, their loyalty would be a fickle thing you couldn't depend on. At worst, they'd turn you over to the Bessemian soldiers before you had a chance to take off your cloak."

Leopold nods. "That's a dead end, then," he says. "But I have no other allies in Temarin. I don't think I *ever* had true allies here. I had sycophants. I didn't know the difference then, but I do now."

Violie considers this, her mind catching on the memory of Leopold with Thalia, the striking sight of a king bowing before a commoner, asking for forgiveness and promising to atone.

"You have a gift with people," she says after a moment. "When you lived in the palace, surrounded by sycophants as you called them, you didn't have much opportunity to use it, but the way you spoke with Thalia—it didn't matter her station or yours or the fact that I'm fairly certain she slapped you across the face before I arrived. You truly listened to her, and treated her with respect and honor. If we had the time, I'd suggest you speak to every Temarinian individually in the same way."

"But that could take years," Leopold says. "And it isn't something I can summon. I just spoke to her the same way I'd speak to you. The same way I spoke with Daphne and Beatriz when we spoke of Sophie."

"That's exactly my point," Violie says. "You spoke to Thalia the same way you spoke to princesses."

Leopold still appears confused.

"It's something you've done even before we officially met, you know," she says, annoyance twinging through her when she realizes she has to mention the ghost she so recently banished from her mind. "With Ansel," she says.

The name hangs heavy between them. "Treating him as anything more than a clod of dirt was a mistake," Leopold says, his voice hard. Violie can't blame him for the anger in his tone—Ansel was the head of the rebel faction that executed Sophronia, and he'd been behind the kidnapping of Leopold's brothers as well. Leopold has every reason to hate him. Still . . .

"The mistakes weren't yours," she says. "They were his. You invited him to dine at your table when you thought he was just an unemployed fisherman. You listened to his concerns and tried to help him. He met your kindness with cruelty, but that wasn't your doing. I'm only saying that if the people of Temarin could see you the way I have, the way Thalia and plenty of others have at this point, I believe they would rally behind you."

As soon as the words are out of Violie's mouth, she pulls her horse to a stop. Leopold follows suit a beat later and looks at her in confusion. "What is it?" he asks.

"We need people to know you, to know that you aren't the spoiled king who fled when Temarin needed him. We need them to know that you're here, ready to fight for them, to make up for your mistakes. We can't show that to every person individually, but whispers will travel farther and faster than we ever could."

Leopold still looks confused.

"We'll make our way to Kavelle," Violie says. "Careful to avoid the detection of the Bessemian army, and with a few stops along the way. In villages and towns where you can meet with a handful of people—people I can ensure are open-minded. They'll tell stories about you to their friends and neighbors, who will spread the stories further. Anyone who wishes to join our party is welcome to. By the time we reach Temarin, we could have an army at our back. Or, should my plan fail miserably, it will just be us."

Leopold takes this in, nodding slowly. "If that's the case," he says, his gaze on her softening, "there's no one I would rather fight beside."

Violie smiles, the words warming her, but she shakes her head. "Much as I appreciate the sentiment, Leo, I'd like for us to not die, so let's try to recruit an army, shall we?"

The first town Violie and Leopold arrive at sits just south of the Amivel River. They ride around its perimeter, giving it a wide berth and looking for signs of a Bessemian presence. They don't have to look hard. A Bessemian flag waves from the guard tower, the gold sigil of the sun against a pale blue background. It's unsurprising that the Bessemians have a stronghold here, given how close the town sits to the Bessemian border, and there's no telling how many soldiers will have made themselves at home within the town's walls.

They find a small copse of trees to the east, and when they're inside, they dismount.

"You stay here," Violie tells Leopold, passing him her reins, which he takes without complaint. She's surprised by how quickly he acquiesces. She expected him to insist on blazing into the town himself, determined to be the hero, but instead, he nods.

"I'll see that the horses graze and drink," he says. It's only then that he pauses. "You're no novice when it comes to going unnoticed, I know that, but I'm still asking you to be careful."

"I will be," she assures him, though they both know it's a hollow promise. If she were truly to be careful, she wouldn't walk into a town occupied by their army. But then, if he were being careful, they wouldn't be in Temarin at all.

Violie finds she can slip into her Temarinian accent as easily as an old cloak, getting past two armed guards standing at one of the town's entry gates with an empty smile and a story about visiting her cousins from a village in the south. The guards don't give her a second look before letting her in. They certainly don't think to check for the dagger in her boot.

Once inside, Violie takes a moment to get her bearings. She's seen enough towns and cities in Vesteria that she understands the general layout. While Hapantoile was crammed full of public houses and shops for everything from ribbons to horseshoes, the smaller towns she's visited usually only have a single public house, which acts as a hub for the community.

When Violie finds it, the sun has just started to set and the public house is already filling up, with a dozen townspeople scattered around the main room—a group of three women gathered near the fireplace with their knitting and mugs of mulled wine; two men hunched over a table too small for them, laughing over their ale; a family of four supping on bowls of soup at a booth in the corner; and a trio of teenagers only a couple of years younger than Violie, sitting at the bar and making jokes with the barmaid, oblivious to her irritation.

Violie feels curious eyes on her as she makes her way to the bar, greeting the barmaid and ordering a mug of ale. In a town this small, strangers are uncommon, she'd wager, and cause for wariness even before so much of Temarin became a battlefield. Violie casts her gaze around the room, smiling when she catches someone's eye, and sipping at her ale. She chooses an empty seat in the far corner, largely obscured by a pillar and far enough from the rest of the patrons that no one will think she's eavesdropping.

Slowly, the townspeople realize she means them no harm, and their attention fades, meandering back to their own conversations. And while Violie isn't close enough to anyone to hear what they're saying, their body language gives her some idea.

The knitting circle, for instance, is tense, though that tension doesn't seem stretched between its members. Their words are hissed more than spoken, and the conversation is stilted and wary. The laughing men are loose enough, though judging by their flushed skin and glassy eyes, the ale they're drinking isn't their first or even second round. The daughter eating dinner with her parents is young, four or five, and seemingly oblivious to the simmering argument between her parents, who speak only to her and not each other. The teenagers, she suspects, are frightened, their raucous laughter both a mask and a balm for that fear.

She is considering whether to approach the drunken men or the knitting circle when the door bangs open, the sound of wood slamming against wood thunderously loud. As soon as Violie hears the click of their boot heels against the public house's wooden floors, she knows they're soldiers. Five of them, she counts, without looking up. She imagines herself melting into her chair, blending in with the shadow cast by the pillar half hiding her from view. She thinks herself small and easy to overlook.

"A round of ale, girl!" one soldier shouts to the barkeep in Bessemian. The barkeep understands nevertheless and hastens to pour five mugs of ale. Even from where Violie sits across the pub, she can see the barkeep's hands shaking.

Everyone else in the public house has fallen silent, the tensions Violie noticed moments ago heightened. Even the child has gone still, staring at the table in front of her with intent eyes.

"We're celebrating, aren't we, boys?" the same soldier continues, a grin stretched over his face that Violie instinctively wants to slap off. The other soldiers grin as well, cheering in assent. The man Violie picks out as their leader claps one of them on the shoulder and laughs. "We caught the thieves who were stealing from our armory."

The soldiers cheer again, but Violie's attention is drawn to the group of teenagers at the bar, standing a mere five feet from the soldiers. One of them inhales sharply at the soldier's news, though he keeps his gaze focused on the wooden bar top. He's careful to keep his face angled away from the soldiers so they don't see the fear flash there, but Violie can see it perfectly. It's a fear she felt before, when she learned about the coup planned to capture and kill Sophronia and the other nobles, and then again when she discovered that Daphne had orders to kill Leopold shortly after they'd left Eldevale together for Prince Cillian's starjourn. Dread, fear, and helplessness.

But Violie was never truly helpless in those situations. Both times she'd set out to save the people she cared for, and she knows with shocking certainty that this boy will do the same.

"And we caught them just in time for the baron's visit tomorrow—I'm sure His Lordship will take great pleasure in seeing them punished."

*The baron.* Violie hadn't expected that the empress would send a nobleman to fight in Temarin, though baron is a relatively low rank. Perhaps this baron had some military talent that made him volunteer for the role. But while Violie studied the names and details of Temarinian courtiers before the empress sent her here to spy, there was no need for her to learn anything about Bessemian nobility. Daphne and Beatriz might know who the baron is, but Violie hasn't a clue.

The boy Violie is watching knows, though. He tenses

further at the title, his knuckles turning white around the mug he holds. The soldiers watch him and his friends as well, expecting something, but Violie can't tell whether or not they receive it. The leader watches too, and Violie realizes with growing dread that he understands exactly what he's doing. He's taunting the boy on purpose, to what end Violie can only begin to guess.

As the soldiers laugh and drink, oblivious to or enjoying the discomfort of the rest of the room, Violie takes a closer look at the boy and his friends.

She'd dismissed them immediately because of their youth, though she knows they aren't much younger than her. Older, certainly, than she was when she started working for the empress. It wasn't that she thought them incapable, though, just that word of Leopold's return and promise to reclaim Temarin would hold less sway coming from their mouths. But looking now, she realizes it isn't only one boy upset at the news from the soldiers—they all are. The other boy and girl with him are simply better at hiding their simmering anger.

Violie sweeps her gaze across the room again. All the townspeople are angry, she knows, but most of their anger is drowned out by fear. But while she's sure the youths at the bar are afraid, the anger rolling off them is too strong to leave room for much else.

She lifts her ale to her lips and takes a small sip as the soldiers put on their show to assert their power and intimidate. They don't so much as glance in her direction, and they speak to no one else, not even the barmaid to settle their tab. But against the din of their laughter and shouts, Violie's mind is working quickly, her plan shifting and growing.

Leopold will be furious with her, since what her new plan entails is the very antithesis of caution, but she knows that if he were in her place, he wouldn't hesitate.

# Beatriz

When Gisella begins to stir, Beatriz straightens up, smothering a yawn. "Oh, good," Beatriz says when Gisella opens her eyes, groggy and confused. "It's been some time since I knocked someone unconscious and I was beginning to think I'd done some serious damage, which wasn't my intent. This time."

Beatriz watches with no small amount of satisfaction as Gisella remembers what happened before she passed out. Of course she tries to struggle at the scraps of fabric binding her to the dining chair. Of course she tries to scream before realizing how effective the gag Beatriz fashioned out of another bit of fabric is. When she's finally satisfied that she's properly trapped, she opens her eyes fully and looks at Beatriz with pure loathing.

Beatriz matches the loathing with a cold smile. "Perhaps now you're more amenable to a proper chat."

Gisella rolls her eyes and tries to speak again—likely something along the lines of *How can I chat when you've gagged me?* Though it's impossible to say for certain.

"Unfortunately, you and Nicolo ensured that I never

had access to anything sharper than a butter knife," Beatriz continues, fiddling with an item in her lap and drawing Gisella's gaze there. Her face goes slightly paler when she realizes what it is. "But you were asleep for a few hours, and that was plenty of time to fashion something suitable for my purposes."

Beatriz holds up the wooden leg she's broken off one of the dining chairs. She used the hard edge of one of her silver hair combs to sharpen the already tapered shape into a fine point. It took time and a good bit of work, but Beatriz is confident that she can do some damage with it if she exerts enough pressure.

Beatriz stands, moving toward Gisella, who flinches. Her fear makes Beatriz's smile widen, and she holds up the makeshift stake, pressing the point of it to the delicate hollow of Gisella's throat.

"I want to know the full extent of your arrangement with my mother," Beatriz tells her. "And if I suspect you're lying or holding anything back, I won't hesitate to use this."

Gisella glares at Beatriz as she roughly yanks the gag from her mouth, letting it hang around Gisella's neck, just above the stake.

"Well?" Beatriz prompts.

"You know already," Gisella says, her voice calmer than it has any right to be given the circumstances. "Your mother gave me my freedom and I agreed to kill you—on Cellarian soil, with my own hands. I'd intended to do it quickly, but now I'm rethinking that."

Beatriz presses the pointed tip of the wood against Gisella's throat hard enough that she feels the skin break.

Gisella lets out a quiet cry, more shocked than pained, but that's exactly what Beatriz wants. For now.

"You've lost your mind," Gisella says, struggling harder against her bonds, but when Beatriz tightens her hold on the stake, a reminder of the damage it can do, Gisella goes still.

"And you seem to believe lying to me is in your best interests," Beatriz counters. "Try again. You told me yourself there was more at play."

"I was goading you," Gisella scoffs.

"Your freedom has been promised to you already, and if you didn't believe me, you had to know Pas would keep his word," Beatriz says. "You're many things, Gigi, but I don't believe you're a poor negotiator. What else did my mother promise you?"

Gisella meets her gaze for a moment before relaxing, her shoulders slumping. She even leans into the stake's point, as if daring Beatriz to use it.

"I'd rather hear about *your* plan, Beatriz. What do you imagine will happen when someone discovers you've kidnapped me, that you've tied me to a chair and drawn blood? As you yourself have pointed out several times, I'm not a princess, but I don't think it will go well for you, attacking the king's sister."

"Perhaps not," Beatriz counters with a smile. "But we both know that Nicolo won't be too upset by it, will he?"

Gisella's eyes flash.

"Besides, I don't plan on staying long," Beatriz adds, gesturing to the dining table, where the remains of the candle are, the vial of stardust laid out and glittering among the chunks of wax. But where surprise and horror showed clearly on Gisella's face when she discovered her bindings and Beatriz's stake, now there is only amusement.

"Oh, that must have been difficult to get your hands on. I'm impressed, though I'd caution against celebrating too soon," Gisella says.

*She's bluffing,* Beatriz thinks. She has to be. But the more Beatriz stares at her, the casual way she sits, the small smile on her lips, the confidence in her eyes...

"What are you talking about?" Beatriz asks, unease worming into her gut.

Gisella's smile stretches wider, and suddenly, Beatriz feels like the other girl is the one with a weapon. "If magic could rescue you, Triz, surely you wouldn't need stardust to escape. You could have disappeared the first night you were conscious here, the moment you saw a star shine through the window. Don't tell me you didn't attempt it."

Beatriz feels ice slither through her veins.

"I don't know what you're talking about," she says, her voice coming out surprisingly level, but Gisella is having none of it.

"You think using stardust will go differently? Go on, then. Try it."

Beatriz shakes her head. "You really don't want me to know about your agreement with my mother," she says.

"Beatriz, I don't even have to tell you what I had for breakfast," Gisella says. "You made a grave miscalculation. You've showed your hand and emptied your arsenal, believing you had an escape hatch. But whether it takes a moment or an hour, soon you'll realize you're trapped here, with me, with no way to escape the consequences coming for you. I'd recommend untying me now, before you do anything even more foolish."

Dread pools in Beatriz's stomach, but she tries not to show her uncertainty. She pulls the gag back up into Gisella's mouth, stifling her protest, and then she tucks the stake between her upper arm and rib cage as she snatches the vial from the table, using both hands to open the stardust. Perhaps it is a bluff, she thinks, but something in her gut says it isn't.

With shaking hands, she empties the stardust onto the back of one hand. Since it's only stardust, she needs to keep her wish small and simple. She won't take chances asking for something too big, especially not now. Wishing to be outside the palace won't work, and she no longer feels confident about using the stardust to restore her own magic. Her best bet is on wishing for the tools to escape.

Beatriz clears her throat, a new plan coming to her. "I wish my hair were the same color as Gisella's," she says. It's a simple plan, disguising herself as Gisella to walk past the guards outside her door, but it's the best plan she has now.

She waits for the change in the air that she feels when using magic, the quiet buzz that fills her, the tingle at her scalp she's felt in the past when using stardust to alter her hair color. It doesn't come.

"It didn't work," Beatriz says, more to herself than Gisella, but even with the gag in place, she can feel Gisella's smugness.

Beatriz grabs her stake again, pressing it to Gisella's throat before removing the gag.

"What did you do?" Beatriz demands, panic finally sinking in.

"Nothing," Gisella says quickly, but when Beatriz presses the stake harder, in the exact same place she drew blood before, Gisella's eyes widen. She realizes that Beatriz is backed into a corner now, not helpless so much as desperate. "It was your mother. Before we left the palace, she gave me a potion to give you, to knock you unconscious."

"Yes, I remember that," Beatriz says through clenched teeth.

"But it had something else in it. She said it was from an empyrea—something that would keep you from using magic—whether that's your own or stardust."

Beatriz's jaw tightens and she presses the stake tighter to Gisella's throat. "She knew?" Before Gisella can answer, Beatriz laughs, shaking her head. "Of course she knew. She knows everything."

Did Nigellus make the poison? Beatriz wonders. She doubts it. If he had, he wouldn't have been so desperate to take her magic from her. What would have been the point, if the poison he made would do the job in a few hours' time? Who, then?

An answer doesn't come, but it doesn't matter. Gisella is right—Beatriz has made a massive miscalculation. The escape route she was counting on to take her out of Cellaria has disappeared, and now she's trapped in a room, holding the king's sister hostage, the day before Beatriz is supposed to marry him.

"Fuck," Beatriz bites out.

# Daphne

Daphne avoids Bairre for the rest of the day following her conversation with her mother, trying to decide how best to approach the question of their venturing to Bessemia. She can't tell him the truth, she knows. It isn't that she doesn't trust him, but unlike her, he hasn't spent the bulk of his life learning to hide every emotion. Daphne can read on his face each thought that crosses his mind, and her mother will be able to as well. The empress needs to believe that Daphne trusts her, that she believes the lie that she is too special, too loved to meet the same fate as her sisters. And the only way Daphne can convince her of that is if she lets herself believe it too.

The prospect terrifies her. It's a role that fits her like a second skin, one that will swallow her up if she lets it. She'll just need to keep it up until her mother lets her guard slip, until Daphne can get close enough to her to kill her.

She'll get one chance at it, and even if she *does* manage it, she knows she likely won't live much longer. One doesn't simply kill an empress and walk away. But she knows her mother won't stop. She won't stop until she gets everything she wants, until Daphne and Beatriz are dead, and likely plenty of other people besides, including Bairre.

Daphne skips supper, returning to her room in the evening and busying herself with preparing to leave Friv. Servants will handle the packing, but Daphne wants to sort through her things herself, picking out what she will take with her and what she will leave behind.

As she riffles through her wardrobe, fingering the plush velvets and soft ermines, a pang of sadness goes through her. When she first came to Friv, she hated everything about this place, particularly the fashions necessitated by the cold weather. She longed for the pastel silks and flowing chiffons she wore in Bessemia, dresses that floated around her like clouds and bared her shoulders to the warmth of the sun. She would have given anything for her mother to summon her home.

But now *home* is exactly where she stands, and she doesn't want to leave. She wants nothing more than to stay here, to spend the rest of her days in Friv, exploring its stark wilderness and all the magic within it, walking every inch of this land until she knows all of its secrets and stories. In another life, Bairre would tell them to her as they lived out their lives together.

"Daphne?"

Daphne drops her fingers from the gowns in her wardrobe, turning to face Bairre, who stands in the doorway of their bedroom as if her thoughts summoned him.

"You weren't at supper," he says, looking at her with worry in his eyes. "Should I have something sent up?"

Daphne shakes her head. Even the thought of food turns

her stomach. She doesn't know how to begin this conversation, how to spin this story that she knows will hurt him. Daphne has always lied as easily as she breathes, but now her lies stick in her throat, threatening to choke her.

"We're going to Bessemia," she blurts out.

Surprise and confusion battle on Bairre's face, always so easy to read. "Why in the name of the stars would we do that?" he asks.

Daphne looks down at the floor in front of her, studying the pattern of leaves woven into the rug. "My mother and I have come to . . . an understanding," she says. "She's agreed to spare me and to spare Friv."

Bairre laughs, but when Daphne doesn't join him, he stops short. "You're joking," he says. "What about Beatriz? And Leopold and Violie? Does this truce extend to them, too?"

Daphne is ready for this question, even if the answer she needs to give tastes like ash in her mouth. "They can handle themselves," she tells Bairre. "My mother is a pragmatic person, Bairre. I've thrived more in Friv than she expected, I have more allies than she imagined possible. We laid our cards out on the table and she realized that Friv isn't worth the effort it would cost her to take it now. She even seems to respect me for it." She knows if she tells him about her mother's claim to have been swayed by love, he won't believe it. Not after Daphne learned that the empress killed Sophronia. This, though, is a more believable temptation. "She's content to know that her descendants will rule Friv, even if she never does. And she's going to officially name me her heir. One day, together, we'll rule Friv and Bessemia."

"I don't want that," Bairre says, shaking his head.

"I do," Daphne tells him softly. The best lies are close to the truth, after all, and there is a part of Daphne that *does* want to rule, that was raised to do it, that believes she would be good at it. There is a part of her that craves power, a seed planted by her mother. She decides to water it. "This is what I want, what I've always wanted, Bairre. You knew that from the moment we met."

Bairre stares at her like he's never seen her before, and she struggles to hold on to her mask, to seal away the pain that lances through her at that look.

"She's lying to you, Daphne," he says, his voice coming out raw. "You have to see that."

Daphne bites her lip, considering her next words carefully, hewing as close to the truth as she dares to. "I don't trust her," she admits finally. "Which is why we have to go with her to Bessemia. She can't have me killed there, not in a way that would get her Friv. As long as I'm not on Frivian soil, I'm safe. I don't trust her, but I trust that."

Bairre continues to look at her, a dozen thoughts flickering over his face before his jaw tightens. He gives a single nod. "All right."

Daphne blinks. She expected him to fight her, to tell her how selfish she's being, how aligning with the empress is the worst possible idea and he will absolutely *not* be coming to Bessemia with her. She was even ready to threaten to tell Bartholomew about his involvement with the rebellion if he didn't.

"All right what?" she asks.

"All right, we're going to Bessemia," he says, as if it's the simplest thing in the world.

A laugh forces itself past her lips. "You don't want to go to Bessemia," she says.

"No, I don't," he agrees. "But you're up to something, and you're asking me to join you, and there's only one answer I can give to that."

Daphne opens her mouth to respond, then closes it. "I told you what I'm up to," she says, trying even harder to keep her face impassive, her words bland, to give him no hint of anything beneath the surface. But Bairre's gaze only sharpens; he is no longer looking at her like a stranger.

"And I know you," Bairre says, his voice softening. "I know you aren't telling me everything and I know you have a reason for that. But I trust you, and I trust that you know what you're doing."

Her shoulders sag and she drops her head into her hands. "You were supposed to hate me," she tells him. "I wanted you to see me as my mother's daughter."

The bed Daphne is sitting on shifts as Bairre sits down beside her. "I'm sorry," he says, not sounding sorry at all. His hand comes to rest on her back, an anchor Daphne tells herself she doesn't want. "I know you too well for that."

He's right, but also wrong. She shrugs his hand off and stands up, desperate to put some distance between them. She needs him angry at her, angry enough that the empress will detect it, thinking her influence has put them at odds, that Daphne is well and truly isolated, just like the empress wants her to be.

"My mother killed Lord Panlington," she blurts out, striding toward the fireplace and crossing her arms over her chest. She keeps her back to him, not wanting to see his face or to let him see hers, since apparently he can read her just as well as she can him.

For a moment, Bairre is silent. "Did she tell you that?" he asks.

Daphne shakes her head. "I saw her do it," she says. "She put powder in his tea and he drank it. I didn't try to stop him."

Silence again, this time longer, louder.

She finally turns to look at him. "I could have," she said. "All it would have taken was a word. I didn't even have to speak, really—I might have stood up from my seat under some pretense and tripped, knocking his cup over. I could have saved him, but not without tipping my hand to my mother before I was ready. I let a man die to protect myself. *That's* who I am, Bairre."

He shakes his head. "I don't believe you."

Daphne shrugs. "Ask Cliona, then. She knows. I'm sure she'll be thrilled to tell you just how like my mother I really am."

Bairre considers this for a moment before pushing himself to his feet. He starts toward the door and leaves without looking back.

After Bairre leaves, Daphne doesn't let herself fall apart even for a moment. She can't, or she won't know how to pull herself together again. Instead, she paces the room as the light outside her window fades, pale moonlight spilling across the floor. More than anything, she wants to be with her sisters, to hear their voices again and remind herself that she isn't alone, that she hasn't been since the three of them came into the world together. But that isn't true. Sophronia is dead and Beatriz is lost to her.

Daphne thinks about Beatriz—is she still held captive in Cellaria? Have Violie and the others reached her yet? Daphne is sure she would know if Beatriz had been killed, but it could still be too late. She very well may never see her sister again.

Her steps falter, and she comes to stand in the center of the room, struck by that thought, by the prospect of a world without her in it. Daphne has always been one to think through everything, to consider each move carefully before acting, but tonight she doesn't. She moves on instinct.

She searches the room top to bottom until she finds a small vial of stardust tucked at the back of Bairre's desk. She uncorks it as she walks toward the window, stopping in front of it and staring out at the endless sky stretching to the south, littered with stars. Normally, Daphne enjoys finding constellations, the puzzle they present. Tonight, though, she lets her eyes take in the sky in its grand, messy entirety. No order, only chaos.

"Please," she says, her voice barely louder than a whisper as she empties the vial of stardust onto the back of her hand, a smear of glittering black against her pale skin. "I wish to speak to Beatriz."

Daphne feels the sharp needle of her sister's irritation and she's grateful for it.

# Beatriz

When Beatriz feels Daphne's presence in her head, she doesn't know whether to thank the stars or curse them.

"Daphne," she says, realizing from Gisella's look—surprised and wary, as if Beatriz truly has lost her mind—that she said the words out loud. "We really need to work on timing."

"What's wrong?" Daphne asks. Her sister's voice in her mind is brusque and pragmatic, wasting no time on pleasantries or silly questions, and while Beatriz has often rolled her eyes at Daphne's cold composure, right now her levelheadedness is a steady ship in stormy waters and Beatriz is grateful for it.

Gisella tries to speak through the gag, her alarm clear even if her words aren't, but Beatriz presses the pointed stake harder to her throat.

"Shut up," Beatriz snaps.

"Who are you talking to?" Daphne asks. "Because I *know* you aren't telling *me* to shut up."

"It wouldn't be the first time," Beatriz points out before catching Daphne up, as quickly as she can, on how she found herself with the King of Cellaria's sister as a hostage the night before her wedding, with no plan and, more importantly, no magic to help her.

"Mama knew about my magic somehow," Beatriz finishes. "Gisella says she drugged me with something that blocks my magic and any used around me. Which ruins my plan for escape, but I'm . . . recalibrating."

"Mama is always two steps ahead of us," Daphne says. Beatriz can imagine her face, disappointed and resigned. "She's bringing me back to Bessemia—she thinks I've allied with her, that I truly believe she'll spare me out of love. As long as she keeps thinking that, she'll let her guard down. And the second she does, I'll kill her, Triz. Can you hang on a little longer?"

Beatriz looks at Gisella, furious and gagged, her wrists and ankles still bound to the dining chair. Beatriz can't imagine how she'll come out of this—even Nicolo won't be able to help her when his court discovers that she kidnapped his sister, that she attempted to use stardust. And when Nicolo realizes that she was trying to run, to go back on their agreement, she doubts he'll even try. He might even cheer for her execution too.

But she can't tell Daphne about that. Her sister would only worry. She thinks about their last conversation with Sophronia, how she had the chance to say goodbye. Perhaps Beatriz should do the same now, but she doesn't know whether that would be a kindness or a curse. Would it have been better if Sophronia had given them false hope for her? Made promises she knew she couldn't keep? Beatriz isn't sure.

"Don't worry about me," she tells Daphne, making the selfish choice in her mind. *She* can't stand to say goodbye, much as Daphne might deserve to hear it.

For a beat, Daphne is quiet, but when she speaks again, her voice is sharp. "That wasn't an answer," she says. "I'm not losing another sister, Triz."

Beatriz closes her eyes. She should have known Daphne wouldn't allow her to bluff her way out of this. She takes a breath. If this is the last moment she has with her sister, Daphne will never forgive her for tainting it with lies.

"I'm backed into a corner," Beatriz tells her, choosing the truth. "There is no way out of it without magic—magic I can't access."

Daphne says nothing, but Beatriz can practically hear her thinking, even from the other side of Vesteria.

"Maybe I can," she says finally.

# Daphne

Daphne can feel Beatriz's skepticism, but she doesn't have time to explain the wild, desperate idea that came to her. She hurries to her side of the bed, to the potted fern there. Grabbing the plant firmly by the base of its stem, she pulls it out of its pot. Then she digs her fingers into the dirt at the bottom of the plant and sifts through the roots, caring little for the mess she makes of it, until she finds the wish bracelet her mother gave her when she left Bessemia. After Violie refused to take it, Daphne hid it carefully in case her mother sent one of her spies to retrieve it.

It very well might not work. The magic in their bracelets was strong enough for Beatriz and Sophronia to rescue other people, transporting them from one place to another in the snap of a finger, but both of her sisters were in the same room as the people they were trying to save. Daphne isn't.

"Daphne?" Beatriz asks.

Daphne turns the bracelet over in her hands, knowing she has to hurry before the connection between them breaks, but she isn't sure what to wish for. Will the stardust be enough to transport Beatriz all the way to Bessemia? And will Beatriz be any better off there, defenseless and alone, surrounded by her mother's allies? There are too many pitfalls if she goes that route.

But there's another wish she can make, she realizes.

It may not work—but then all of this is a desperate last attempt, and Daphne knows that even if it fails, she'll never regret using her wish like this, doing everything she can to save her sister.

"Beatriz," she says, placing the wish bracelet on her desk and taking a heavy book from the shelf beside it. She lays the book on top of the stone and places both hands on the cover. "I love you. Meet me in Bessemia. We'll take Mama down together."

"Daphne, what are you—"

Daphne presses all of her weight on the book, feeling the stone crumble under the pressure. "I wish Beatriz had full, unimpeded access to her magic again."

# Beatriz

*I* wish Beatriz had full, unimpeded access to her magic again.

Beatriz hears her sister's words and feels the echo of them deep in her bones, thrumming through her and drowning out everything else.

Almost.

Gisella squirms beneath the point of the stake, apparently worried that Beatriz has gone too mad to care about the sharp bit of wood at her throat.

Beatriz *doesn't* care—she's only vaguely aware of her own body hurtling toward the window, the clatter of the wooden stake against the wooden floor, the much louder sound of Gisella's chair crashing to the floor as she hurls herself backward, the wooden chair splintering. Beatriz doesn't care about any of it—she throws open the curtains she drew earlier and braces her hands on the windowsill, heaving deep breaths of evening air, feeling like she's been drowning until this moment and now she can't breathe deeply enough.

Gisella must have gotten her hands free, because she removes the gag and screams, but still Beatriz doesn't turn around, not even when the door to the dining room swings open and the heavy boots of her guards approach, not even when they take stock of Gisella still half bound to the broken chair, the empty vial of stardust and the smear of it on the back of Beatriz's hand—evidence of the fact that she used it.

Beatriz is barely aware of any of it. She's held in rapture by the light of the stars just coming into view in the darkening sky. She feels their light against her skin wrapping around her like an embrace. She feels their magic in her heart, burning hot and spreading to the rest of her, unbearable and euphoric all at once.

When one guard reaches her, wrenching her arms around her back and dragging her out of the room, Beatriz doesn't fight. Instead, she stares at the stars until she can no longer see them, and she smiles.

Daphne's wish worked—she can feel her magic at her fingertips once more, begging to be used. And as soon as she stands in the light of the stars again, she'll indulge it, no matter what it costs her.

The guards bind Beatriz's hands and leave her on the sofa in the sitting room, muttering to themselves in bewilderment as they go to free Gisella. They've been guarding Beatriz since she returned to Cellaria; surely they realized they were keeping her imprisoned as much as they were keeping her safe, but she's still a princess of Bessemia, soon to be the Queen of Cellaria, and so they don't know what to do with her—take her to the dungeon? Surely not.

While they're untying Gisella, Beatriz marvels at the magic she still feels rushing through her from her brief moment at the window. Daphne's wish worked—that much she knows. Even experiencing what she did, even feeling the magic still tugging at her in this windowless room, she can't quite believe it.

Beatriz can't wait to throw her arms around Daphne and thank her—and she will. As soon as she gets out of this palace, she's going to Bessemia to find Daphne.

"Is she securely detained?" Gisella demands of the guards, walking into the sitting room as she rubs her wrists where they were bound and are now chafed and an angry red. Gisella doesn't wait for the guards to answer her, looking at Beatriz with narrow eyes. "Good. Then fetch my brother at once—both of you."

"Surely one of us should stay with you, Lady Gisella," one guard says.

"That isn't necessary," Gisella says coolly. "Go. Now."

They hasten to obey her, hurrying out of the room and closing the door behind them firmly. When they're alone, Gisella turns to fully face Beatriz, and in the soft glow of the fireplace, the place on her throat where Beatriz drew blood stands out even more starkly, a smear of crimson against her fair skin. Beatriz hopes it will leave a scar—something for Gisella to remember her by.

"What," Gisella says through clenched teeth, "in the name of the stars was *that*?"

Beatriz knows she needs to play this carefully. If Gisella suspects she has her power back, she'll have Beatriz sealed away in a dark room for the rest of her days. But Gisella saw her reaction; she knows *something* happened to her to cause that.

"My sister is dead," Beatriz bites out, summoning tears to her eyes that come readily enough. She's always been good at crying on command.

"That isn't news," Gisella says, frowning.

"*Daphne* is dead," she clarifies. "She used Frivian stardust to slip inside my head in her last minutes. I *felt* someone plunge a knife into her heart; I felt it like it was happening to me." She chokes out the words.

Something akin to sympathy flashes over Gisella's face, gone quickly but not quickly enough.

"Don't tell me you're going to offer condolences," Beatriz snaps at Gisella, knowing that pure sobbing grief won't be believable. She needs to pretend shock, to lean into anger. "The only thing you're sorry about is that her assassin managed to kill her before you could kill me."

Gisella swallows, glancing away from Beatriz. "Well, I wasn't going to stab you in the heart," she says after a moment. "That's an ugly, painful way to die. I intended to let you die in your sleep."

"How kind," Beatriz says, each word dripping in acid.

Gisella shrugs. "I never claimed to be kind," she says.

Beatriz stares at Gisella for a moment. Blasé as she tries to sound, something in her expression cracks. But Beatriz isn't inclined to allow her even an ounce of self-pity.

"Tell me," she says. "Will your deal with my mother hold if I'm killed before I marry Nicolo? I'm supposed to die a queen, after all. Not a traitor and heretic. It won't be easy for her to use my death as an excuse to invade Cellaria if my death is warranted."

Gisella laughs. "You think Nicolo will order you executed?" she asks.

Not before she has a chance to see the stars long enough to make a wish, Beatriz hopes. "I think that's far more likely than him marrying me now," she says.

"Oh, Beatriz," Gisella says, shaking her head. "You don't understand anything at all, do you?"

Before Beatriz can ask what she means, the door opens and Nicolo enters, flanked by Beatriz's guards. He takes in the scene—Gisella's bloodied throat, Beatriz's bound wrists. His dark brown eyes are pensive, though he doesn't look at all surprised.

"Leave us," Nicolo tells the guards, his voice surprisingly mild. "And if you speak a word of what happened tonight to anyone, you'll regret it until your final breath—which won't be very long in coming."

The guards mumble their assent and offer deep bows before leaving the room. When they're gone, Nicolo is quiet for a minute more. Deciding which of them he wants to hear the story from first, Beatriz realizes. She resolves not to give him a choice.

"Did you not tell me to keep Gisella close? I was simply following your advice," Beatriz tells him, keeping her voice light. She's managed to wrap Nicolo around her finger before, though doing so with Gisella present is infinitely more challenging.

"She brought stardust into the palace," Gisella interjects. "And used it."

Beatriz frowns, schooling her expression into one of bewilderment. "I absolutely did not," she says.

"If you don't believe me, look at her hand," Gisella tells her brother.

Nicolo approaches Beatriz, expression unreadable. The guards bound her hands in front of her, so when he takes hold of her wrists, there's no hiding the glittering dust smeared on the back of one of them.

"Fake stardust," Beatriz tells him, a story taking shape as she tells it. "It looks convincing, doesn't it? I told you that your sister wanted me dead, and since you refused to help me, I took matters into my own hands. It was quite a ruse, convincing Gisella I'd procured stardust when actually it was just a bit of crushed pearl and ash from my fireplace." She sighs. "Yes, fine, I knocked her unconscious and tied her to a chair for a few hours. I don't think you can truly fault me for that, all things considered. But I wanted us to come to an . . . understanding before the wedding and I thought if I tricked her into believing I had stardust at my disposal, she'd be more amenable to my demands."

"Demands like her not killing you," Nicolo says.

"Precisely." Beatriz beams at him, gratified to see his own lips curve like he's fighting a smile.

Gisella sees it too. "Nico, you can't be such a fool to believe that," she says. "When the most obvious explanation is that she used stardust to try to escape."

"If I did," Beatriz says slowly, pursing her lips as if a thought has just occurred to her, "why would I still be here? As you said, I used it." She holds up her bound wrists as proof. "If I used it, what did I wish for?"

Gisella opens her mouth to reply but then quickly closes it again. There's no answer she can give, not without explaining to Nicolo that Beatriz is an empyrea with a smothered gift. She could go down that road, but if she didn't tell Nicolo the truth from the start, it will certainly sound like an opportunistic lie now. Gisella must realize this too, because she changes direction.

"She still kidnapped me," Gisella tells him. "She knocked me unconscious, held me hostage for hours, put a makeshift weapon to my throat, and *cut* me." She gestures to the gash in her throat. "Besides which, she was trying to escape the day before your wedding. Can you imagine what a fool you'd have looked like if she'd succeeded?"

"Oh, I wasn't going to escape," Beatriz says, laughing. "Why would I, Nico, after everything we discussed?" She lets the words hang heavy in the room, certain that Nicolo doesn't want Gisella to know about the agreement they came to. She sees the warning in his eyes even at the mention of it. Beatriz smiles.

"No, that wouldn't have been prudent at all," Nicolo agrees before turning to his sister. "Well, you're the injured party this time, Gisella. What would you have me do?" he asks her.

Gisella's eyes have been darting between Beatriz and Nicolo. Beatriz is sure she has plenty of questions on her tongue, but none that she'll voice until she and Nicolo are alone. She considers his own question for a moment.

"It's less than twenty-four hours until the wedding," Gisella says. "Are you still intent on going through with it?"

"I am," Nicolo says.

"Then I believe we should ensure that nothing else goes . . . amiss," Gisella says. "I can brew a draught that will make her sleep until just before the ceremony. To keep her from causing any further trouble."

"I'm not taking anything she brews," Beatriz protests. "She wants me dead."

"I do not," Gisella says, scoffing like the idea is ludicrous. Beatriz herself is aware that she sounds paranoid, but she isn't willing to take chances and she needs to get out of Cellaria *tonight*. She can't do that if she's drugged.

"What would you suggest?" Nicolo asks Beatriz. "You did attack her, after all, and if you try to escape again the night before the wedding, Gisella is right—it would make me look like a fool."

"Of course," Beatriz says, swallowing back a sharper retort. She thinks through what she can give up right now and what she can't. She summons the way she used to smile at him, when she was so foolishly infatuated. "I do want to marry you, Nicolo, and I want the future we discussed. But if it would help ease your mind, I'll agree to take a sleeping draught on one condition."

"And what might that be?" he asks.

"Gisella takes the same potion I do," she says. "I want her to tell the guards exactly what ingredients she needs within my hearing, then I want them to fetch those items for her. I want her to brew it here, where I can see everything she does."

Nicolo considers that, but Gisella's face has soured. It will mean Beatriz has to wait another day and hope that she's able to see the stars before she marries Nicolo, but at least she can be sure she'll wake up tomorrow.

Nicolo nods once, decisive. "A fair compromise," he says, looking to his sister. "Do you find it agreeable?"

Gisella looks like she wants nothing more than to say no, but she must realize she can't do that without all but confirming she's planning to assassinate Beatriz, because she gives a loud exhale. "Fine," she says. "I agree."

# Violie

When the group of youths leaves the public house, Violie leaves too, following them down the dirt path that leads away from the establishment and past a row of single-story stone houses with thatched roofs and smoking chimneys. At the end of the lane, they keep walking, passing through a gate and into a field. Violie can't follow without being seen, so she hangs back and watches as the trio enters a small, dark barn on the far side of the field. Moments later, the soft glow of a candle appears in the window on the second story.

She can't say for certain that only the three of them are in the barn, but she would wager good money on it, so she quickly hurries across the field herself. She finds the door and hesitates—should she knock? Or would that only put them on edge? Is barging in better or worse?

Before she can decide, she hears soft footsteps behind her and doesn't have time to turn before a rough burlap sack covers her head, a rope pulling tight around her neck to secure it. Violie knows better than to scream, but she does fight, throwing her weight back and trying to dislodge her attacker, hands fumbling for the dagger in her boot, but whoever put the bag on her head is quick to bind her arms as well.

"Who are you? Why are you following us?" a voice snaps in her ear—male, she guesses, and young. One of the group she followed, she realizes, relaxing slightly. He asks the question in Bessemian, assuming Violie is one of them. Which she is, she supposes, but that doesn't make her his enemy.

"I mean you no harm," she replies in Temarinian, keeping her voice calm.

"That," another voice says—this one coming from in front of her with a higher cadence; the girl, she thinks—"isn't an answer to either question."

Violie takes a breath. "The answer to the first question is long and I'd rather give it in more comfortable circumstances," she says. "But to answer your second—I've come to keep you from foolishly running headlong into the trap those soldiers clearly laid out for you at the public house."

Silence follows her words.

"Get her inside," the girl says finally, her voice hard. "Quick, before she's seen."

Hands grab Violie's arms, hauling her forward. Though the bag over her head keeps her from seeing, she feels the moment she steps into the barn, the soft grass beneath her boots giving way to packed dirt. A door closes behind her just as the hood is roughly pulled from her head. Violie blinks, her eyes slowly adjusting to the warm glow of a lantern, held by the boy she first noticed in the tavern, with the white-knuckled hands and the bare fear in his face. His hair is dark where the other boy's is fair, but there's a striking similarity to the shape of their faces and the blue of their eyes.

Now his fear is gone, replaced with cool anger.

"Did they send you?" he asked.

The Bessemian soldiers, he means. Violie shakes her head.

"I'm not with them," she says in Temarinian.

A hard smile slashes across his face. "You can drop the act," he tells her. "You speak Temarinian well, but there's no hiding the accent."

Violie blinks in surprise. She's always taken great pride in her language skills, and no one has ever critiqued her accent before. But then, the Temarinian accent she learned was polished and noble, designed to blend in with others at the palace and in Kavelle, should she have need to use it. Perhaps it's harder to hide her natural undercurrent of Bessemian here, where the way of speaking highlights her flaws.

She lets out a low breath. "I told you that who I was is a long story," she says, giving her wrists an experimental tug, but they're securely bound with a length of coarse rope. "Yes, it's true, I was born in Bessemia, but I am not aligned with the soldiers who have your friends." She glances between them, meeting each of their gazes in turn before continuing. "I'm with King Leopold."

She lets the words sink in, stunning them at first, though the shock quickly gives way to disbelief.

"King Leopold's dead," the girl says, scoffing. "Only fools believe otherwise."

"He isn't," Violie corrects. "Though not for lack of trying on many people's part—none more so than Empress Margaraux. Which is why I'm here and he's not. If they find him, he'll be sitting right beside your friends in whatever prison they've set up, though I doubt they'd wait for whoever *the baron* is to kill him."

The three of them exchange a look, and for a long moment, no one speaks.

"If King Leopold isn't dead, he's a traitor," the blond boy says. "If the soldiers want to kill him, they can go ahead. We won't mourn him."

Violie expected this, but there is still a small part of her that wants to defend Leopold. They have only heard stories of who he was, and she can't fault them for any low opinion based on that. And there is no way to change that opinion with her words, she knows.

"No," she agrees. "I don't suppose you would. You owe him no more loyalty than you owe the empress, do you?"

The girl looks like she wants to protest that but quickly closes her mouth.

Violie continues. "But he owes you—he owes all of Temarin a debt he is eager to repay. And he's going to begin by freeing your friends from the Bessemian soldiers."

Another stretch of wary silence follows that, but this time the look the three of them exchange is charged with something different—hope.

"Not friends," the dark-haired boy says quietly. "My sister—our sister," he adds, nodding toward the fair-haired boy. Brothers, Violie realizes, which explains the resemblance.

"And mine as well," the girl adds. "Daisy and Hester. Our parents told them to be careful, that tweaking the soldiers' noses wasn't worth what would happen if they were caught, but of course they didn't listen. They never do."

Violie remembers what the soldiers said, how it sounded like the thieves they caught had been giving them trouble for some time.

"I'm guessing it wasn't their first time robbing the armory," she says slowly.

"No," the dark-haired boy says. "The fifth time this month."

Violie is impressed—especially since after the first time, the soldiers would have been on high alert. Still, continuing to rob them was foolish, and it was only a matter of time before the thieves' skills were hindered by rotten luck. Foolish, she thinks, but incredibly brave. Not unlike Leopold himself.

"And do you know where they were hiding the spoils of their theft?" she asks.

Again, the three of them look to one another, having a conversation without words.

"How do we know you're telling the truth?" the girl asks. "You could be a spy, sent by them to get us to lead you to the weapons our sisters stole—that makes an awful lot more sense than a dead king returning."

Violie knows she's right, but she has no real proof on her. Even if she were to bring them to Leopold, how would they know he's who he claims to be? She doubts they ever saw him in person, certainly never got close enough to know his face.

"I told you the story of who I am is a long one," she says. "And if you don't mind, I'd appreciate having the use of my hands and a comfortable place to sit while I tell it."

Another beat of hesitation before the dark-haired boy takes hold of one of Violie's arms and she feels the cold metal of a knife at her wrists an instant before the ropes binding her are cut.

Violie holds nothing back in the story of her last few years, beginning with the moment she broke into Nigellus's palace laboratory to steal stardust when she was fourteen, desperate after her mother had fallen ill with Vexis, which was sure to kill her. Sitting cross-legged on a bale of hay while the three youths—who introduce themselves as Helena, the girl; Louis, the fair-haired boy; and Sam, his dark-haired brother—watch her with wary eyes. Those eyes grow warier when she tells them the truth of her initial involvement with the empress, and Violie wonders if perhaps being that honest was a mistake, but no—Leopold is owning his mistakes; the least she can do is own hers as well.

She tells them about coming to Temarin and ingratiating herself in the palace ahead of Sophronia's arrival, and then she tells them about Sophronia herself: the fearful princess anxious to do as her mother raised her to, until she saw the effect that would have on the Temarinian people. She tells them about Sophronia's soft heart and sharp mind and how, terrified of the empress as she was, she defied her in order to protect Temarin. She tells them how, in one of Sophronia's final acts, she saved King Leopold, and in doing so forced him to become a better man and a better king.

"I don't see why we should care," Helena says in the silence that follows Violie's recounting of Sophronia's execution and the way Leopold's screaming her name was drowned out by the cheers and jeers of the crowd. "The royalty and nobility never cared for us."

"No," Violie agrees, thinking about how she saw the Temarinian palace when she'd first arrived, the courtiers dripping in jewels and silks and sipping never-ending glasses of champagne while those who lived in the city just outside the palace walls starved to death. Perhaps Sophronia would disagree with her if she were here—Violie is sure she would—but Violie has no tears to spare for most of the nobility killed when the rebels laid siege to the palace. If the rebellion had been orchestrated by Temarinians demanding change from those who kept them pinned beneath the heels of their boots, Violie might even have applauded them for fighting back, but instead the rebels were directed by Empress Margaraux, their motive chaos, disguised as comeuppance. "I won't tell you that Temarin was a paradise before the siege—I saw enough of it to know that wasn't the case. But this? Now?" she asks. "Is this any better?"

She knows the answer to that and doesn't wait for them to provide it.

"Of course not. Of course it's worse, or your sisters wouldn't be imprisoned, awaiting judgment by whoever *the baron* might be." The three of them exchange a heavy look at the mention of his name, and Violie files that away in her mind with growing dread. "But I'm not asking you to choose between two untenable situations. I'm asking you to help King Leopold create a better Temarin, one that serves everyone, not only those elite few born into the right families. He isn't only here to tear out the weeds of the Bessemian invasion—he's here to plant seeds too. And he needs your help to do it."

Silence follows her words until Louis breaks it, clearing his throat. "What happened next to King Leopold?" he asks. "After Queen Sophronia was executed?"

Violie manages a small smile. "Will you let him tell you himself?"

The village entrances are guarded by Bessemian soldiers, and while Violie, as a visitor, might be able to get past them without suspicion, Helena, Louis, and Sam won't. If Violie is right about the guards laying a trap by taunting them about their sisters' imprisonment, leaving the village at this time of night in the company of a stranger will only paint a larger target on their backs, and should someone decide to follow their trail, it would lead them directly to Leopold.

Unlike the Bessemian soldiers, though, Helena, Louis, and Sam have lived in the village their whole lives and know every last cracked window and loose stone. In particular, they know that one such loose stone can be found in the north side of the wall that surrounds the village, at the bottom, obscured by an overgrown blueberry bush in Mrs. Hastel's garden. When the stone is removed, it reveals a tunnel that stretches beneath the wall, offering an escape for anyone small and fearless enough to fit through it.

Violie herself barely manages, dragging her body through the soft earth on her elbows, clods of dirt flaking down into her face, making it unwise to open her mouth to pant at the exertion. By the time she glimpses the opening ahead, all of her muscles burn, and despite the winter chill in the air, a thin layer of sweat covers her skin. When her head breaks through to the surface, she finally lets herself breathe deeply, wiping the back of her dirty hand over her dirtier face and blinking around at her new surroundings.

A small copse of woods, she notices, and a familiar one at that.

"Took you long enough," Helena whispers, not bothering to hide her grin.

Violie allows the girl her smugness—in a few years' time, Helena will either grow into her lanky limbs and find her own difficulty fitting through that tunnel, or she'll be dead. Either way, she can take her joy where she can find it.

Louis and Sam climbed into the tunnel before Violie as well, and now they stand nearby, speaking in low voices that Violie can't quite make out. She glances around the copse of trees, searching for a sign of Leopold or their horses. Surely, she would hear the horses if nothing else, she thinks with growing dread.

"Are we alone here?" she asks, her voice coming out sharp as she looks at the trio.

Sam shrugs. "There was an old beggar, but when Louis and I told him we had no coin or food to spare, he left."

"A bit odd to see a beggar with two horses, though," Louis adds. "I wonder why he didn't just sell one of them—that would get him money quicker than waiting in the woods for people to pass by."

Violie closes her eyes and forces herself to take a deep breath. "How long ago was this?" she asks slowly.

"Ten minutes?" Louis guesses. "Right before Helena showed up. You took a really long time."

Violie ignores that. "Which way did he go?"

Sam and Louis both point east, and without saying another word, Violie starts off in that direction. After a few seconds, the other three fall into step around her.

"What's wrong?" Helena asks. "Why are we chasing a beggar instead of meeting King Leopold?"

Violie doesn't answer, allowing the words to hang in the air until, seemingly at once, they realize.

"The beggar *was* King Leopold," Louis says, reaching out his hand to give his brother a light smack to the back of his head.

"Ow!" Sam replies. "How was I supposed to know? He didn't *look* like a king. He was hunched over and old."

"You saw his face?" Violie asks, knowing the answer before he gives it.

"Well, no," Sam says. "He kept his hood up. But I heard his voice and he *sounded* old."

"He was *pretending*, you fools," Helena says, shaking her head. "Just like in a folk song—the king pretending to be a poor peasant, rewarding the people who help him and punishing those who don't. You failed *that* test."

As the three of them dissolve into bickering, Violie wonders if she made a mistake. The two drunken men at the tavern might have come with their own challenges, but surely nothing so bad as this.

"Shh," she hisses, and the three of them fall quiet immediately. That, she thinks with some satisfaction, is likely not an effect she would have had over the drunks. "Unless you intend to run him off to another village for help, stay quiet."

It's a bluff—Violie knows Leopold would never leave without her—but it's a bluff that works. Silence falls over them as they hurry through the trees and into a wide-open meadow. As Violie's eyes scan the space, her heart sinks. There's no sign of Leopold or the horses.

"Maybe the soldiers caught him," Sam says quietly.

Before Violie can snap at him to be quiet, Helena jabs him sharply in the ribs, punctuating the move with a warning glare. Sam gives a brief yelp before falling silent, shooting Violie a sheepish look.

Violie tries to ignore Sam's words even though a large part of her knows how likely it is that he's right. No, she tells herself. Leopold is an excellent tracker and hunter and as such, he also knows how to hide his own tracks. She looks around, taking note of the walled village, the open meadow, the copse of trees behind them. If she were in his shoes, what would she do?

She turns sharply, the others stumbling to keep up with her as she quickens her pace. Instead of walking back into the copse of trees, though, she goes around it to the east, scanning the horizon until she catches sight of a blur of white in the darkness—her horse, there, behind a boulder beside a stream. She breaks into a run, heart beating quickly, but it isn't until she sees Leopold crane his head over the top of the boulder at the sound of her footsteps that she realizes how tightly fear had wound through her at the thought of losing him. But when she sees his face, the fear snaps and the next thing Violie knows, he's caught her in his arms and her own are wrapped around his neck.

"I told you not to move," she says, even though she understands why he did, would have done exactly the same in his position.

"And I told you to be careful," he replies. "So why do you look like you clawed yourself out of your own grave?"

Violie pulls back, looking down at her dirt-caked dress and skin. She can't see her face and hair, but she's sure they are in a similar state.

"Never mind that," she says, shaking her head. "I've brought our first recruits."

He glances over her shoulder, eyes narrowing when he catches sight of Helena, Sam, and Louis. "You've brought children. They can't be older than Gideon."

Gideon, the elder of Leopold's two younger brothers, is safely ensconced somewhere in the Silvan Isles after Leopold went to great lengths to find him and protect him from this war with the empress. But while Gideon is fourteen, close in age, she would guess, to the three youths, it occurs to Violie that he would find little in common with them.

"They need help," Violie says, rather than trying to explain that to him now. "And we can give it."

The other three finally catch up with Violie, looking at Leopold with wide, uncertain eyes.

"Sorry we thought you were an old beggar," Louis says, the words coming out in a nervous rush.

Leopold smiles, the expression tense. He's nervous, Violie realizes with a touch of amusement. "I wanted you to think I was an old beggar. You have nothing to apologize for."

Helena clears her throat. "I don't know how to curtsy or bow," she admits.

"That's perfectly fine," Leopold tells her. "I don't particularly like strangers curtsying and bowing to me anyway."

Violie's eyes cut to him—is that true? she wonders. But

as soon as she questions it, she knows it is. She looks at them and clears her throat. "I know I said Leopold would tell you the rest of his story, but why don't we save that for after we free your sisters?" she suggests, feeling Leopold stiffen beside her.

"What happened to your sisters?" he asks.

"The Bessemians caught them," Helena says. "They've been stealing from the armory they set up in town after the siege."

"They turned the grain storehouse on Mr. Oville's farm into a makeshift prison, but our sisters won't be there for long," Sam adds. "The baron is coming tomorrow and he'll punish them, maybe even kill them."

*There it is again,* Violie thinks. The mention of the mysterious baron, with an undercurrent of dread that raises the hairs on the back of her neck even if she doesn't yet understand why.

"And who exactly," Leopold says slowly, his dark brown eyes moving between Helena, Sam, and Louis, "is the baron?"

# Daphne

Harsh, cold light slashing across her darkened vision wakes Daphne, her eyelids blinking rapidly as she tries to adjust to her surroundings. The last thing she remembers is standing before her bedroom window, gleaming stars before her and her sister's voice in her head. She remembers pressing the wish bracelet her mother gave her between the windowsill and a book, the words passing her lips as she crushed the stone and released its magic—*I wish Beatriz had full, unimpeded access to her magic again*—and then she remembers nothing at all.

"Daphne?" a voice asks. The last few times she's come to like this, Bairre has been close at hand, but now it isn't his voice that greets her, it's her mother's.

Just turning her head causes a bolt of pain in her neck, but Daphne manages. Her mother is sitting in a chair beside her bed, still in her gown from the last time Daphne saw her, with her jet-black hair pulled back in a simple knot at the nape of her neck. As far as Daphne can tell, her face is free of cosmetics, making her mother look older than she usually does, but even so, at thirty-five her mother is not an old woman by anyone's standards, except maybe her own.

Even through the fog rolling through her head, Daphne understands this illusion her mother has crafted for her— the image of a worried mother, holding vigil at her beloved child's bedside with little care for her own needs or vanity. It's a charming illusion, but an illusion all the same. She opens her mouth to ask where Bairre is before closing it quickly again—that won't be what her mother wants to hear, and Daphne still needs to tread carefully. Especially since she doesn't know if her wish worked, if Beatriz has gotten her powers back. *Meet me in Bessemia,* she told Beatriz. If her wish worked, she'll see her sister soon enough.

She settles on a different question, one no less pressing than her husband's whereabouts.

"What happened?"

"No one is quite sure, my darling," the empress says, leaning forward and taking one of Daphne's hands in both of hers. "A maid came into your apartments late last night to ensure that the fire in your sitting room was properly banked, and she happened to see you through your open bedroom door, collapsed on the floor in front of the window. Your head was bleeding—it appeared you hit it on the windowsill somehow."

Daphne can imagine it, how after making the wish, she collapsed, knocking her head on the way down. She reaches for her head, and though she doesn't find a wound, the place above her eyebrow is tender.

"The physician had to use common stardust," the empress says, noticing the move and wrinkling her nose in distaste. "Apparently Bartholomew has allowed his empyrea to roam about wherever and whenever she wishes, so she was unavailable to heal the wound properly. Imagine if you'd been more badly hurt! You might have ended up permanently scarred."

It isn't lost on Daphne that her mother views having a scar on her face as a worse fate than any other injury that could have befallen her. Even so, the information about the Frivian empyrea is more concerning. "Aurelia still hasn't returned to court?" she asks. "Where is she?"

The empress scoffs. "Bartholomew hadn't the slightest idea, if you can believe that. There's a reason warlords make such poor kings, Daphne. The man has no idea what's going on in his own court."

Part of Daphne is inclined to agree with her mother on that—while Bartholomew has always been kind to her and tried to rule Friv fairly, she knows he's very far out of his depth. Even since before Daphne or her mother set foot in the castle, he was surrounded by enemies and none the wiser about it.

Still, Aurelia's extended absence from court nags at Daphne. There's been no sign of her since she tried to convince Cliona to bring her Gideon and Reid. Daphne expected her to lie low at first, since whatever she planned for those boys hadn't been ordered by Lord Panlington in service of the rebels like she told Cliona, but Daphne thought she'd have returned by now, especially with Lord Panlington dead.

"I'll ring for the doctor," her mother says, giving Daphne's hand a final squeeze before releasing it and reaching for the bellpull beside Daphne's bed, giving the velvet rope a sharp tug. "What on earth happened?"

Daphne swallows. "I don't quite remember," she says, staying as close to the truth as she can. "I was sleeping, but I remember waking up and wanting to fetch an extra blanket. I must have tripped getting out of bed." She frowns as if searching her memory. "I do remember stumbling," she says. "And bracing my hands on the windowsill, but I suppose I didn't catch myself in time."

"I suppose not," the empress says. "What an unfortunate accident, but you're awake now. Are you well? I intend for us to leave for Bessemia by the afternoon."

Any move, even breathing, makes Daphne's body ache inside and out, and the thought of being jostled around in a carriage is unbearable, but Daphne suspects she could be at death's door and her mother wouldn't change her plans. "I'll be better when we reach Bessemia," she says with a smile. "I'm looking forward to being more fully healed by an empyrea there—you have replaced Nigellus, haven't you?"

"Empyreas don't exactly grow on trees, Daphne," the empress says airily. "But a search is certainly underway. Can you survive without one, or would you be more comfortable if we delayed our trip?"

Daphne understands that her mother isn't so much asking a question as demanding a particular answer.

"I'm fine," she tells her, ignoring her pain and forcing herself to sit up, smothering any outward sign of discomfort as she does.

"Good girl," her mother says.

Just then, a knock sounds at Daphne's bedroom door

and the court physician enters. It's only when Daphne feels herself deflate that she realizes she expected Bairre to enter with him—does he know she's awake? Does he know what happened last night? She remembers what her mother said—a maid found her, not Bairre. He never came back to their rooms at all. Unease weaves through her. He might be angry with her, but avoiding her this way isn't like Bairre. What if something is wrong?

She stays quiet, letting the doctor check her pulse and her head until her mother excuses herself and leaves the room. Only then does Daphne turn to the doctor. "Has my husband been updated about my recovery?" she asks.

The doctor looks down at her, perplexed. "I believe every effort has been made to find him, Your Highness, but I've been told he isn't currently in the castle."

"Oh?" Daphne says, trying to hide her growing worry. "Were you told where he is?"

The doctor clears his throat, looking uncomfortable. "I believe he went into town last night, Princess. He hasn't yet returned."

Daphne schools her expression into one of practiced disinterest. "Oh, of course. I remember now—he told me as much yesterday, I simply forgot." She understands that the doctor's discomfort is about more than Bairre's going out last night—it's who he was with. Daphne would wager every jewel in her collection that he was with Cliona, that it's the implications of her husband's spending the night out with a woman who is not her. "He and Lady Cliona had plans—they are old friends, you know."

The doctor shows some relief at the words. "As soon as

they arrive, I'm sure they'll both be distressed at your injury, Princess," he says.

Daphne knows Cliona won't be, but she smiles, relieved that Bairre is safe but also annoyed. She knows it shouldn't bother her, that she *told* Bairre to speak with Cliona, to hear from her own lips what Daphne did to Cliona's father. These are merely the consequences of Daphne's own actions—consequences she was aware of, that she even wanted. Getting what she wanted shouldn't hurt, but it does.

When the doctor leaves and Daphne is alone, she ignores the doctor's advice that she rest and forces herself out of bed. Every muscle in her body protests. If all that happened to her was hitting her head on the windowsill, surely the rest of her wouldn't hurt this badly, would it? She thinks about the one time in her life when Nigellus pulled a star from the sky to make a wish, to end the drought that had overcome the whole of Vesteria. He didn't get out of bed for days afterward. Is that why she feels this way?

The bracelet her mother gave her wasn't the same as an empyrea making a wish, but perhaps in wishing for Beatriz to get her own empyrea power back, with Beatriz herself in her head, some of the consequences of that magic rebounded onto her.

*The bracelet.* Dread coils in Daphne's belly. In all the confusion of the morning, the bracelet itself slipped her mind. She remembers using the book to crush it, but she passed out before she could clean up the mess left behind. The maid must have found her with the book and the broken bracelet still on the windowsill. Which raises a further question—was her mother telling the truth about what she knew of Daphne's accident, meaning the maid hid the full context of it from her? Or did her mother know more about what Daphne had done than she let on? If she knows Daphne used her wish, can she guess what she'd used it for?

Daphne turns that question over in her mind as she hobbles across the room, willing the tightness in her muscles to loosen with every step she takes. She feels as if she and her mother are still circling each other in that elaborate dance, only now Daphne has been blindfolded and the steps of the dance have changed without her realizing.

The doctor left three vials of stardust on her bedside table to help with any pain, but when Daphne limps toward them, taking one and uncorking it, she doesn't use it to wish away her aches or the pounding in her head. She smears the stardust over the back of her hand and wishes to speak with Beatriz again.

Nothing happens, just as it did before. She clutches the empty vial tight in her hand, resisting the temptation to throw it against the wall.

The door behind her opens and Daphne whirls around, half dreading to see her mother again, but instead Bairre stands in the doorway, his face drawn and eyes wild. When he sees her, his eyes sweep over her and the tension leaves his shoulders, but the wild look in his eyes doesn't quite fade.

"What happened?" he asks. "Am I allowed to know that much?"

The sharpness in his words feels like a well-placed punch, but Daphne knows it's more self-defense than anything else.

"Do you want to know?" she asks, perching on the edge of the bed to lessen the pain in her aching legs. "I'm sure Cliona told you everything last night. I'm surprised to see you here at all after that."

She doesn't mean for her own words to come out bitter, but they do. It was so much easier, she thinks, when she kept everyone at arm's length. Now that she's let him in, it's hard to go back to the distance she so carefully maintained before.

Bairre doesn't say anything for a moment. "Cliona did tell me everything," he says slowly. "And I don't know how to look at you right now, much less talk to you about Lord Panlington. I can't believe you would sit silently and let him die. If you expect me to assuage your guilt and tell you that you did nothing wrong, I can't do that."

It's no more or less than what Daphne expects, but she still feels the words like a dagger. This is what she's always known would happen, since the first moment she met Bairre—that one day he would see her for who she truly is and walk away.

"I fully intend to discuss it further, but not when you're recovering from what sounds like a bad head injury," he finishes.

Daphne looks up at him, surprised. "Discuss it further?" she asks.

Now Bairre looks confused. "You allowed your mother to kill a man right in front of you—a man you might not have liked but certainly didn't hate. And, if nothing else, you know Clíona loved him, and that I did too, in a way. I don't believe you would have done that without a reason, even if it's a reason I don't agree with."

Daphne continues to stare at him, too shocked to speak.

"Right now, though," Bairre says, misreading her silence, "I want to ensure that you're all right. I'm sorry I wasn't here last night. If I had been—"

"Don't," she interrupts. A large part of her wants to tell him the truth about her injury, how she spoke with Beatriz and used her wish to give her sister her magic back, though she doesn't know if the wish succeeded. But she can't—the more Bairre knows, the more danger he's in from her mother. "I'm fine. A little sore, perhaps, but I'll live. We're leaving for Bessemia today."

It's Bairre's turn to go speechless. "You're in no state to travel—the doctor said he doesn't know how serious your injury is."

Daphne shrugs. "We'll monitor it, then," she said. "And make use of stardust should it prove a problem."

When Bairre doesn't look convinced by that, Daphne lets out a long sigh. "Getting to Bessemia is more important than anything else," she tells him.

"But why—"

"I know my body," she says, snapping more than she means to. "And I know my fate. I'm not asking for your opinion or permission to do what needs to be done. We leave for Bessemia today."

Bairre stares at her a second longer, like she's a cipher he doesn't have the key to. "Is that how things are to be?" he asks her finally, his voice low.

*It's how things have to be,* Daphne thinks, but the words lodge in her throat, threatening to choke her. Instead, she gives a curt nod.

"All right," he says. "Cliona will be joining the trip as well, then."

Daphne blinks. "What?" she asks.

Bairre lifts a shoulder in what she imagines he means to be a blasé manner, but she sees the tension in it. Try as he might, he can't hide how much he cares, which is precisely the problem. Because if she can read him this easily, her mother will be able to as well. "She asked last night and I wanted to discuss it with you, but since we aren't seeking opinions or permission, I've changed my mind."

Daphne knows she can fight him on this, and she knows that even if he remains stubborn, it's up to her mother who is invited to Bessemia, and Daphne can convince her that Cliona's presence is more trouble than it's worth. But she also knows that she's asking for—or more accurately, demanding—blind trust from him. She's willing to grant him the same. And despite the current state of their friendship, Daphne does trust Cliona as well, and she'll need all the allies she can get to take down her mother.

"Fine," she says. "But if she intends to kill me, ask her to wait until after we cross into Bessemia, otherwise she'll play right into my mother's plans."

When Bairre's brow furrows in confusion, she elaborates. "I have to die by Frivian hands on Frivian soil for her to gain control of Friv," she reminds him.

"Cliona doesn't want to kill you," Bairre says, though he doesn't manage to make the words sound convincing.

Daphne shrugs, remembering the way Cliona looked at her in the chapel, the harsh bite of her voice. *The last thing you need is another enemy.* "All the same," she says, "make sure she knows what's at stake."

"We all know what's at stake, Daphne," he says, shaking his head. "This isn't only your fight. You aren't the only one with something to lose."

Daphne opens her mouth to retort but quickly closes it again. He's right—she knows he's right. If her mother's plan succeeds, Friv will fall to ruin. Her mother has no love for this country, no understanding of it. She sees it as just another gem in her crown, and if she manages to conquer it, every person and creature who calls Friv home will suffer.

"I'm tired," she says instead, the words true enough. "I doubt I'll sleep in the carriage, so I'd like to take a nap before we go." She doubts she'll be able to sleep, but she knows she can't keep arguing with him.

Bairre hesitates a moment before nodding. "I'll stay with you," he says.

"That isn't necessary," she says, standing up to pull the duvet back so she can crawl into bed once more.

"After last night, I beg to differ," he says, crossing to sit in the armchair her mother vacated earlier.

"Right now, I think I'd prefer another head injury to you pestering me," she says, aware even as she says it that she doesn't mean it. Bairre seems to know that as well, because the ghost of a smile flickers over his mouth.

"I'm not asking for your opinion or permission," he replies, parroting her own words back to her.

Already, she regrets saying that. Not only because he continues to use it against her, but because it's a half-lie.

She rolls onto her side to look at him. "I always want your opinion," she says softly. "Even when I do hate hearing it."

Bairre looks surprised at the admission, but after a moment he nods. "As I want yours, Daphne," he says. "And I'm not going anywhere, no matter how hard you try to push me away."

The words surprise her. Beatriz has always called her a ruthless bitch, and even with Sophronia, there were times when she would look so wounded after Daphne had said something unkind, when she wouldn't speak to her for days. The only reason either of them ever forgave her was because they were sisters, but Daphne has never expected that loyalty from anyone else. No one else is supposed to be able to love her, she thinks. Her mother didn't raise her to be loved.

"We made vows to each other beneath the stars," Bairre continues.

"But you didn't choose me," she reminds him. She can't help herself. As perfect as his words are, she can't bring herself to believe them.

"Not at first," he agrees. "But for as long as I've truly known you, I've chosen you. And I'll keep choosing you, even if the stars go dark."

Daphne doesn't know how to respond. She has never

been good at expressing her emotions, and now especially she's terrified of saying the wrong thing. But perhaps she can give him a sliver of honesty.

"If my mother realizes how deeply I care about you, she'll destroy you. Do you understand that?" she asks softly.

Understanding flickers behind Bairre's eyes. "Then hate me," he says. "Give me as much vitriol as you need to. I can take it, Daphne."

Daphne shakes her head. "I need you to hate me back."

One corner of Bairre's mouth lifts. "I hate you," he says, but Daphne hears *I love you* instead.

"I hate you, too," she tells him softly. "So much it scares me."

Bairre shucks off his shoes and coat and climbs into bed beside her, pulling her back to his chest.

"I know who you are, Daphne," he tells her, his voice quiet in her ear. "And I'll remember it even if you forget."

They stay like that, neither one speaking, for an unknowable stretch of time, until Daphne falls asleep with the rhythm of his heartbeat matching her own.

When afternoon comes, Daphne lets herself be dressed in a traveling dress and cloak, her maids maneuvering her limbs like a doll's, each movement aching. They don't pack much for her—after all, as far as they know the trip will only be a visit, and the weather is so different in Bessemia as to render her Frivian wardrobe unwearable—but Daphne instructs them to bring her jewelry box and cosmetics case. The weapons hidden within are ones her mother knows about, but they might still prove useful.

Finally, she, Bairre, and Cliona are loaded into what Daphne suspects is the same Frivian carriage she and Cliona traveled in from Hapantoile what feels like a lifetime ago, when the two of them were strangers. They feel like strangers again now as the carriage sets off, following the powder-blue-and-gold carriage her mother has to herself and the retinue of smaller carriages containing her entourage. Silence swamps the three of them as they make their way toward the castle gates.

"I'm surprised you chose to join us instead of your mother," Cliona says, her voice pointed though she doesn't look at Daphne, instead keeping her green gaze focused out the window.

"My mother prefers to travel in solitude," Daphne says. It used to bother her as a child, when her mother would force Daphne and her sisters into a different carriage for long trips, claiming they irritated her nerves, but now Daphne is grateful for it. She doesn't know how she would survive the long trip to Hapantoile in such close proximity to her mother, both of them masked in layers of secrets.

"I envy her that," Cliona says under her breath, but the carriage is too small to keep the words to herself.

"Cliona," Bairre says, his voice a warning. "It will be a long trip if you start already."

"Oh, give her more credit, Bairre," Daphne replies. "I don't think she'll struggle to fill two days with insults, will you, Cliona?"

Still, Cliona doesn't look at her. She also doesn't answer

her question, instead keeping her gaze steadily out the window.

In the silence that stretches out as the Frivian castle disappears behind them, Daphne suspects she would prefer two days of insults from Cliona to two days of this.

# Violie

Violie stifles a yawn as she peeks through the linen curtains drawn shut over the single window in the inn room she is sharing with Leopold, watching the late-morning light cut through the village's quiet streets.

"You should try to sleep more," Leopold says as her yawn triggers one from him as well. She glances over her shoulder to see him sitting up on the threadbare sofa he insisted on sleeping on in order to give her the narrow bed. Though, really, given the time that stretched from when the innkeeper led them to this room and when bright morning light woke them, *napping* is a more accurate word.

"Do you think I'd have an easier time of it than you?" she asks, stepping away from the window and into the center of the room, exhaustion weighing her limbs down.

"I suppose not," he admits, rolling his shoulders and tilting his head this way and that—trying to rid himself of the crick that surely took up residence in his neck after hours of contorting his body to fit on the sofa. "But I expect you'll hear the baron's arrival long before you see it through the window."

Violie crosses her arms over her chest and looks at him.

"You're saying it the same way everyone else seems to now," she points out. "*The baron*. Like he's a villain in a folk song."

"Are you so sure he isn't?" Leopold replies.

No, Violie isn't sure about that at all. After what Helena, Sam, and Louis told them about the baron yesterday, she's sure the baron has inspired plenty of monsters in the imagination of those whose paths he's crossed. She remembers a tale Helena told, about the last time the baron had visited the village and how the smell of burning flesh had lingered in the air for weeks after he'd left.

"You're sure you don't know who he is?" Violie asks. "They did say he was a Temarinian who'd allied with the Bessemian army."

"I knew plenty of barons," Leopold said, shrugging. "And I can't say I have difficulty imagining any one of them turning against Temarin to save themselves. But that level of depravity? I'm not sure how any of them could be capable of it."

Violie bites her tongue, not pointing out the obvious fact screaming through her mind, but Leopold realizes it anyway, a flash of red stealing over his cheeks—embarrassment and anger.

"But then, I'm not very good at seeing threats for what they are, am I? My own mother was capable of far worse than I could ever have imagined," he says quietly. "And Sophie—she had a change of heart, but I didn't see her for who she truly was either."

"And me," Violie adds quietly.

Leopold's eyes find hers and he considers that for a moment, leaning back against the arm of the sofa. "I didn't see you at all when you were pretending to be a servant, I'll admit," he says. "But from the moment we met in the cave after the siege, I've known who you are, Vi. And I've known exactly what you're capable of."

Violie holds his gaze for a beat longer, a protest rising up in her throat—he doesn't know half of the terrible things she's done now, and he certainly had no idea of them in the cave, before he saw some of them firsthand—but then, he isn't claiming he knows what she's done. He's saying he knows who she is and what she could be, and she wonders if he might be right about that. How can he be, though, when Violie feels like she doesn't even know herself that well?

*Then who am I?* she wants to ask him, but she forces the question down, afraid the answer will either hurt her or disappoint her. She drops her eyes from his and clears her throat.

"Let's go over the plan again," she says instead, perching on the edge of the bed, facing him.

He turns toward her, placing his bare feet on the wooden floor and leaning forward, resting his elbows on his knees. "We know the plan, Violie. It isn't a terribly complicated one," he tells her. "The simplicity is the point."

That doesn't make her any less nervous. She's no stranger to plots and plans, but all of her plans used to involve her alone, and there was comfort in knowing that she had total control over every piece. Then she had to bring Sophronia into a plan, and from there she couldn't go back. Her plots involved Leopold and Beatriz and Daphne and all the people *they* were plotting with. Even then, though, she understood who she was putting trust in and knew they were capable of doing what they needed to.

This time she doesn't have that luxury. All it will take is for one person in the village to break, one person to fail, one person to betray them, and everything will be ruined.

The sound of a trumpet breaks the silence—coming from a distance, but still loud enough to make Violie and Leopold both startle.

"I told you we'd hear him before we saw him. I may not know who he is, but I've never met a nobleman who didn't insist on drawing attention to himself," Leopold says when the trumpet finishes, pushing himself to his feet with a heavy sigh. "The baron is almost here."

Heart still racing from the shock, Violie stands and goes back to the window, once again peering through the space between the curtains carefully so that no one realizes the room is occupied. If she squints and stands on tiptoe, she can only just make out a cloud of dust rising in the distance, beyond the village's wall.

"Then we'd better get ready," she tells Leopold.

Twenty minutes later, Violie is downstairs, behind the bar of the tavern and dressed in a borrowed shift and apron, both a size too big for her. Janellia, the barmaid they belong to, stands beside her, walking Violie through a hasty tour of the bar. It isn't the first time in Violie's life that she's had to pretend to be a barmaid, and she knows she can find her way around with little trouble, but she can tell by Janellia's rambling words and shaking hands that she's nervous, and

Violie decides it's best to let her continue on and distract herself from the baron's imminent arrival.

"And the pistol?" Violie asks when Janellia has shown her the contents of every cabinet and drawer.

Janellia's face goes a shade paler, and she swallows before bending down to open a wooden crate beside a keg of ale, revealing a pistol nestled among loose hay.

It turned out that before Daisy and Hester were caught vandalizing the Bessemian army's armory, they managed to steal ten pistols, six shotguns, five broadswords, ten daggers, and two crates of bullets, storing them deep in a cave outside the village. When Helena, Louis, and Sam led Violie and Leopold there the night before, they were both stunned. Violie understood precisely why the soldiers in the tavern had been so proud of themselves for apprehending the two girls—they'd caused more than enough trouble.

If the plan works, she is very much looking forward to meeting Daisy and Hester.

Violie reaches for the pistol, turning it over in her hands. Her own is already holstered at her thigh, but this one she hands to Janellia. She hopes the barmaid won't need to use it, though given how much interaction they'll be having with the baron, it seemed prudent to be sure she could defend herself.

Janellia is eyeing the pistol like it's a hissing snake. She reaches out a hand, but it shakes even more now than it did before, and Violie pulls the gun back.

"I can do it," Janellia says, making a valiant effort to force confidence into her voice, but Violie shakes her head.

"No," Violie says softly. "All you have to do is wait for

them to arrive and introduce me as your visiting cousin when they ask who I am. After that you can excuse yourself."

Janellia frowns. "Won't they be suspicious?"

Violie laughs despite the tension heavy in the air around them. "Not if you blame *female issues*," she says. "Men are usually too uncomfortable to be suspicious when those are brought up."

Janellia's cheeks redden, but she gives a small, fierce nod.

"Then you retreat to the kitchens and let me deal with them. Stay close to Ferris," Violie says, naming the cook she met briefly at dawn, bleary-eyed and bone-tired. "I think he may be more dangerous with his paring knife than you'd be with a pistol."

Janellia gives a brief, wan smile as Violie puts the pistol back into the crate, hoping she won't have cause to require a second pistol, but grateful to know it's there if she does. She watches Janellia busy herself with polishing glasses, feeling vaguely unmoored—the Violie of six months ago wouldn't have wasted time and energy coddling a frail-nerved barmaid. She would have rolled her eyes and snarled at Janellia to sort herself out and stop being cowardly. It strikes her suddenly that Leopold has had just as much of an impact on her as she's had on him these past weeks.

*I've known who you are, Vi. And I've known exactly what you're capable of.*

Leopold's words come back to her, but before she can decide how she feels about them, the sound of more than a dozen heavy boots approaches the door of the tavern and Janellia's eyes find hers across the bar.

Violie sucks in a breath and gives the girl a final

encouraging smile just as the tavern door swings open and a man who can only be the baron walks in.

He's flanked by soldiers, all of them dressed in gold armor, emblazoned with the Bessemian sigil of the entwined sun, moon, and stars over their breastplates, but even though he's of utterly unremarkable height and build, Violie knows the baron by the way he walks, with an air of nobility and grace that the soldiers around him couldn't match if they practiced every day for a decade. Her eyes find the heavy gold chain that hangs from his thick neck, dangling down over his breastplate, then the small charm that hangs from the chain. That, Violie recognizes instantly, her vision floods with red and it's all she can do to remain still, behind the bar, with a pleasant smile pasted to her face, when she wants nothing more than to launch herself across the tavern and claw the chain from the man's neck, even if she has to decapitate him to do it.

A gold ring, set with a sapphire the size of a quail's egg. She watched from the crowded servants' balcony as Leopold slipped that ring onto Sophronia's finger in the palace chapel beneath the light of the Lovers' Hands. She saw it every day after, winking at her from Sophronia's left hand as she signed letters and sipped tea and folded together ingredients to bake cakes. The baron is wearing Sophronia's wedding ring like a trophy, and Violie knows he would only display it so proudly if he was the one who removed it from her cold, dead finger.

An elbow digs into Violie's ribs and she jumps, realizing Janellia has nudged her.

"Are you all right?" Janellia whispers, but Violie doesn't

know how to answer that. She gives a nod anyway, not taking her eyes off the baron as his group seats themselves at the largest table in the tavern, placing himself at its head. It's only then that he reaches up to remove his helm, followed a beat later by the other soldiers, though Violie's eyes are stuck to the baron, the dread in her stomach congealing as he lowers the helm and looks her way with beady dark brown eyes and a sneering mouth and recognition hits her like an anvil to the head. The baron is Duchess Bruna's husband—Leopold's uncle, by marriage, not blood, and Violie's former employer.

She finds herself holding her breath as his eyes slide over her and to Janellia beside her, no sign of recognition in them. It isn't surprising, she reminds herself as she tries to calm her mind: the baron was rarely at court and when he was, he was drunk more often than not. He and Duchess Bruna hated each other and took no pains to hide it—he resented that she'd kept her title when she married him, and she resented that he'd lost the bulk of her dowry and allowance at the gambling table.

The baron isn't drunk now, though—his eyes are clear and sharp as he looks around the tavern, saying something to the soldier at his right.

"You don't look all right," Janellia whispers.

Violie forces herself to breathe, her mind working quickly. She doesn't think the baron recognized her, but she can't be certain of that, or that his memory won't be jogged when she takes their order and serves them ale laced with poison.

"I'm fine," she tells Janellia in a rush of air. The soldier the baron spoke to is making his way over now, and she doesn't have much time. "Get a message to the king—tell him the baron is his uncle, that he may know me. Mind your face," she adds, snapping more than she means to because the look of horror that has come over Janellia could very well give their game away. Obediently, Janellia smooths a smile over her face, and Violie hopes she's the only one who notices the tension in it.

"Jennie, who's this?" the soldier asks as he comes to stand on the other side of the bar, leaning his elbows on the waxed wood. His eyes travel over Violie, but not with suspicion, merely curiosity.

Janellia doesn't correct him about her name, instead reaching beneath the bar to start counting out flagons for the twelve soldiers and the baron. Thirteen in all.

"My cousin," she tells him as she sets the flagons on the bar top. "Violet is newly widowed and staying with me while she gets back on her feet."

In times of war, young widows aren't a rarity, and sure enough, the soldier accepts this without question. "We'll take the usual, but make it quick—the baron is in one of his moods."

One of the flagons slips from Janellia's fingers, clattering to the stone floor with a sound that echoes through the tavern, loud enough that everyone seated at the baron's table looks over. Janellia swallows, hurrying to pick it up, but when she rises again, flagon in hand, Violie puts a hand on her shoulder.

"Oh, cousin, you really ought to be resting in your condition," Violie says.

"What's wrong with her?" the soldier asks, eyes narrowing.

Violie summons a blush to her cheeks, lowering her voice to an embarrassed murmur. "It's her monthly courses, sir," she tells him. "She took a tincture for the pain, but it hasn't done much good, apart from making her nauseous."

The soldier's suspicion gives way to confusion, then discomfort. He clears his throat. "You—what was your name?"

"Violet," Violie tells him.

"You'll bring us our ale—and keep our flagons full for the evening. Can you manage that?"

Violie nods. "I may be new here, but I've worked at taverns before," she says. "I'll be over in a moment."

The guard glances at Janellia, then back at Violie. "Hurry," he says, the word curt and dismissive before he turns and goes back to the baron, leaning down to speak in the man's ear, likely recounting the conversation with Violie.

Unease slithers through her—what if he does recognize her? But even if he does, it changes nothing. The plan is too far along now, and she has to do her part so that Leopold and the others can do theirs. She thinks again about how fragile their plan is, how one person can ruin it all. She refuses to let that person be her.

"Go," she tells Janellia, keeping her voice a whisper. "Get word to Leopold if you can but keep yourself safe."

Janellia doesn't need to be told twice. She presses the empty flagon into Violie's arms and hurries through the door that leads to the kitchen, leaving Violie alone with the baron and his soldiers, who are now watching her with impatient eyes, but not wary ones. Not yet.

Violie busies herself with filling each flagon from the keg of ale, watching the sheer, iridescent film that covers the bottom of each flagon disappear into the amber liquid, the remaining rainbow sheen covered by a layer of fizzing white foam.

The apothecary was bleary-eyed and bewildered to find that Violie, Leopold, Helena, Louis, and Sam had let themselves into her kitchen just past midnight, but when Violie explained to her what she needed, she was eager to help, fetching vials of galling root, dried frostberries, and crypt snake venom. Violie watched the woman with interest as she mixed the ingredients together in a mortar and pestle and boiled them in a pot of water over an open flame before straining the clear liquid into a jar and passing it to Violie with instructions on how to use it.

As Violie sets each of the thirteen poisoned flagons on the tray and carries them to the table, though, she worries she didn't use enough in each flagon. If it had been up to her, she'd have taken no chances and doubled the dose, but when it had come to a vote, she'd been the lone voice in favor of killing the lot of them. Leopold had a good point in that the baron would make a better hostage than a corpse, but that was never Violie's concern. In her experience with poisons, it's much better to overdo the dose and be left with a body than underdo it and be left with thirteen armed men who are ill enough to know they've been poisoned and conscious enough to retaliate.

She concentrates on the feel of her pistol holstered to her thigh as each man takes a flagon of ale from her tray while she makes her way around the table—small comfort as it is, given the odds at play. The final flagon goes to the baron, but as he reaches for it, pale fingers curling around the brass handle, his eyes meet hers and his gaze lingers.

"Have we met before, girl?" he asks. His voice is barely recognizable now, not slurred or shouted but somehow even more dangerous.

"No, my lord," Violie says, dropping her eyes. "I only arrived yesterday to stay with my cousin."

"Hmm," he says, but he doesn't lift the flagon from her tray, and she can still feel his eyes searching her face. "And where were you before?" he asks.

Violie prepared for this question, memorizing the name of a village in the Alder Mountains where few traveled and even inventing a name and occupation for her dead husband, should anyone ask, but rather than give the name she planned, she decides to improvise. If the baron believes he's seen her before, perhaps she can sate his curiosity without raising his suspicions.

"I grew up in Kavelle, my lord," she tells him.

"In the palace?" he asks, his grip on the flagon tightening slightly.

Violie laughs. "Oh no, my lord, but my mother was a seamstress and sometimes the nobility hired her for odd jobs and she would bring me along for an extra pair of hands."

"Hmm," the baron says again, but his grip relaxes and he lifts the flagon from the tray. "Perhaps that was where I saw you," he says, shaking his head. "My late wife required a new ensemble for each hour of the day, it seemed. We'll require stew as well—your cook knows what I like."

Violie bobs a quick curtsy, relief surging through her, and she turns away and retreats.

She steps into the kitchen and relays the message about the stew to the empty space, the cook disappeared along with Janellia, pitching her voice loud enough to be heard by the baron and his soldiers. She takes a deep, steadying breath, trying to calm her racing nerves. Then she returns to the tavern's main room and finds the baron's pistol pressed to her chest.

"You," he says slowly, his voice low. "Oh, I remember you."

# Beatriz

Beatriz feels as if she is floating in a dark sky, her body buoyant and tingly, her mind too soft for thoughts to find purchase. She imagines herself a star, the entire world spread out beneath her but too far away to see more than the barest shapes. If she is a star, she isn't alone—there are other stars all around her, twinkling and so bright they're nearly blinding. One of them, she knows in the deepest part of her soul, is Sophronia, and that thought alone manages to stick, filling Beatriz with warmth.

Is she dead? The idea flickers through her, but she can't summon any kind of shock or horror or even relief about it, and a second later the thought has disappeared, blown away like dandelion fluff in the wind.

Something pulls at her arm—do stars have arms?—but after a second she forgets about that, too, until it happens again. And again.

She comes to suddenly, bright white light flooding her vision, sea-tinged Cellarian air filling her lungs, the feeling of her cotton nightgown and linen bedsheets against her cool skin. Her life comes back to her in fragments, sixteen years filtering into her memory in a single second, dizzying her.

Gisella's hand is locked on her arm, the grip a vise. Beatriz stares at it a moment.

"If you don't remove your hand," she says, her voice coming out in a rasp, "I'll remove your head."

Gisella scoffs but does release Beatriz, taking a step back from the bed.

Beatriz's bed, she remembers. She took the potion Gisella gave her and barely managed to change into her nightgown before the drug pulled her under.

"We took the same dose," Gisella says, seemingly more to herself than Beatriz. "But perhaps you have a weaker constitution, since it affected you more."

The sound of her voice grates on Beatriz and she rolls away from Gisella, covering her ears with a pillow, which Gisella swiftly rips away from her. *Perhaps,* she wants to say but can't form the words, *my constitution was already weakened from the sleeping draughts you gave me to get me from Bessemia to Cellaria.*

"The wedding is beginning in an hour," Gisella says, tugging the quilt off Beatriz as well.

Beatriz would happily murder her—if she could summon enough strength into her body to do more than lift her arms.

More memories come to Beatriz—speaking to Daphne the night before, her sister wishing for Beatriz to have her magic back, the feel of that magic flooding through her. She can't feel it now, but then she can't feel much of anything now through the drugged haze that envelops her. She remembers insisting that Gisella swallow the same potion she gave Beatriz, watching Gisella closely as she mixed the ingredients the guards brought for her to ensure that Gisella didn't take the opportunity to kill Beatriz like the empress had instructed her to. After that, she remembers nothing at all.

"You're going to have to drag me down the aisle," Beatriz says when she manages to find words. She's in earnest—she doesn't think she can stand on her own, much less walk—but Gisella glares at her, apparently assuming she's intentionally being difficult. After a second, she seems to realize Beatriz is being serious and a brief flash of guilt crosses her face before it's gone, replaced by cool indifference.

"It should wear off in an hour's time," she says. "I'll send for extra maids to help you get out of bed."

She turns away from Beatriz, walking to the door that leads to the sitting room. As soon as she's gone, Beatriz turns her face to the window, where a scant few stars have already appeared in the purpling sky. She searches for the magic, summons it to the surface, but it feels like trying to summon wind in a crypt.

It isn't like before, she tells herself. She can *feel* the magic. But it's just out of reach. Her fingertips can graze it, but she can't quite grab hold.

The door opens again and Gisella returns, followed by no fewer than a dozen maids with matching cheerful expressions.

"I told them you indulged a bit too much last night," Gisella says with an affectionate shake of her head. "You certainly aren't the first bride to do so, but you'll need a bit of extra assistance getting ready tonight. Help her stand," she adds to the maids, and two of them step forward, gently taking hold of each of Beatriz's arms and pulling her to her feet. Even with their support, she sways and her knees threaten to buckle.

Gisella looks her over, lips pursed, before she addresses the maids again. "I'm afraid we only have an hour, but I trust you'll do your best to make her look like the future Queen of Cellaria she is," she says.

As the maids move her limbs like a doll to dress her in the layers of chemises and stays and petticoats and, finally, the frothy lace wedding dress that surely weighs more than Beatriz herself does, the fog of her mind begins to clear and she feels more and more like herself. There are no windows in the sitting room, so she can't feel the tug of her magic, but she suspects if she could, it would come to her willingly now.

The maids move on to styling her hair and painting her face—all while Gisella observes from the nearby sofa, glancing up from a book every so often to offer a suggestion or critique. Beatriz is barely aware of any of them. She's thinking about the geography of the palace, the long winding halls that will lead from her rooms to the chapel. Halls lined with windows that should offer a passing glimpse of the stars.

She could make a wish then, she thinks. It would have to be quick—picking out a star, concentrating on it, giving voice to her wish—but she could do it. Gisella would realize what she was up to, but she wouldn't be able to stop her.

Or.

Beatriz imagines herself entering the chapel, dressed in this ridiculous monstrosity of a wedding gown, the eyes of all the most influential people in Cellaria on her, watching her call upon the stars and break their most serious law, disappearing before their eyes.

If Daphne were here, she would tell her to be practical, but Daphne isn't here and Beatriz has always loved a spectacle.

# Beatriz

Gisella stays close to Beatriz's side as guards escort them down the halls and stairways that lead from her rooms to the palace chapel on the first floor. Beatriz is sure Gisella expects her to make another escape attempt, but Beatriz keeps a serene smile plastered on her face as they walk, six maids trailing behind her to hold up the heavy, jewel-encrusted train of her gown.

She doesn't remember much about her wedding to Pasquale. She'd barely had a chance to get her bearings in her new country and drank far too much wine before the ceremony itself, so the entire evening is a blur in her memory. One thing she remembers with startling clarity, though, is being introduced to Nicolo and Gisella. If she could go back to that night now, there are a lot of things she might do differently, but she would begin by throwing her wine in their faces.

"Nervous?" Gisella asks now, and while she tries to inject the words with casualness, Beatriz can hear the tension lurking beneath.

Beatriz smiles at her the same way she did that night, like Gisella is merely an amusing stranger. "It isn't my first wedding," she tells Gisella. "Perhaps we should see about getting you married next, Gigi—it hardly seems fair that I get to have all the fun. I'll discuss it with Nicolo and offer a few suggestions. I hear Baron Farini has found himself widowed again."

Beatriz intends to be gone before she has another private conversation with Nicolo about anything, but the bluff is worth it to see the disgust and horror that flicker over Gisella's expression. Her brown eyes cut to the guards walking in front of them, then the guards behind them, before she stops short.

"I need a moment with Princess Beatriz," she says, with a sweet smile that sours slightly when the guards look to Beatriz for confirmation. She gives a quick nod. The maids and guards step away, and Beatriz is struck by the fact that should Gisella forgo her plan and try to kill her *before* the wedding, her wedding gown has rendered her a sitting duck. It's so heavy she doesn't think she can take so much as a step on her own.

"You're planning something," Gisella says quietly.

"What could I possibly be planning?" Beatriz asks, rolling her eyes skyward, hoping the dramatics mask the secret she's keeping, the power flowing through her. "Without magic, without a weapon, without anything at all?"

Gisella's eyes narrow and she stares at Beatriz for a second. "I need you to trust me," she says, still keeping her voice soft.

Beatriz snorts out a laugh. "You can't be serious," she says. "You've made it very clear that you're going to kill me as soon as your brother's ring is on my finger."

"Have I?" Gisella asks. "When? When did I tell you that?"

Beatriz opens her mouth and closes it again. She's sure Gisella said as much. She confirmed that the empress gave her orders, she even discussed the manner she considered doing it in . . . but has she actually said she was going to?

"Are you denying that my mother's ordered you to kill me?" she asks as her thoughts spin.

"I'm not denying that," Gisella says. "But I have no loyalty to your mother, no more than I had to you or to Pasquale. Certainly no more than I have to my brother."

That catches Beatriz by surprise. "Considering the lengths you've gone to in order to see him on the Cellarian throne, that's hardly reassuring."

Gisella's smile is brittle. "And what, exactly, has that gotten me, Beatriz? Abandoned in a Bessemian prison? A role as nanny for his wayward fiancée? We were supposed to rise together, but he left me behind the first chance he had—just as you said he would."

Beatriz recalls their conversation after Nicolo had been named Cesare's heir mere hours before Cesare died, how Beatriz warned her that Nicolo would turn on her, that the further Gisella tried to climb the further she would fall.

"You insinuated yesterday that he was making plots with you," Gisella says. "I won't ask you what they are because I know you won't tell me, and in the end, they won't matter."

Beatriz knows they won't matter, but not for whatever reason Gisella seems to think. "Because you have plots of your own?" she guesses, fitting together pieces of what she knows and trying to see the full picture. "Much of the court isn't happy with Nico, but they'd be far less happy to see you on the throne in his stead."

Gisella makes a scornful sound. "If I were alone," she says.

And just like that, the final piece of the puzzle slides into place. "The Duke of Ribel," she says. "If the two of you marry, it would consolidate power." She's speaking more to herself than Gisella now. "The only thing in the way would be Nicolo."

"And you," Gisella adds mildly. "Should you decide to make yourself a nuisance. But you don't intend to do that, do you?"

Despite Gisella's casual tone, Beatriz knows it's a loaded question. It strikes her as almost funny that the fates of countries aren't always decided on battlefields or in throne rooms, but in quiet hallways like this, between desperate women with everything to lose. Still, she's walked this path with Gisella before and it has never worked out in her favor.

"I have no reason to trust you," she says. "And a good many reasons not to."

"You don't have to trust me," Gisella tells her. "I assume whatever you're planning will take you out of Cellaria?"

Beatriz only stares at Gisella, careful not to let her expression betray anything. After a second, Gisella sighs.

"I expect you never to return," she says.

Beatriz says nothing, struggling to make sense of what, exactly, Gisella is up to, but when Gisella turns to call the guards and maids back, Beatriz finds her voice.

"The throne you're fighting for isn't yours," she says. "It's Pasquale's."

Gisella turns back to her, eyes sharp. "If he wanted it, he should have fought for it," she says. "But we both know he doesn't want it at all, so why shouldn't it be mine? Why is he or anyone else more deserving of it? Because of blood? I have as much royal blood as Nicolo. Because he's a man?" She tsks. "Come, Beatriz, you and I are the same at the heart."

"What in the name of the stars would make you believe that?" Beatriz asks.

"Because we want so much more than we were born for."

"That's hardly a fair comparison, considering *I* was born to die," Beatriz points out.

"You were born to further your family's position, no matter how it affected you," Gisella corrects. "All girls are raised like lambs to the slaughter in some way or other. You and your sisters aren't unique in that."

"Perhaps not, but I've never stepped on others to escape my fate," Beatriz retorts.

Gisella laughs. "Haven't you?" she asks. "Your hands aren't clean, Beatriz. The servant girl who was executed for possessing the stardust you created? The empyrea you killed in Bessemia?—yes, I know about that. And Pasquale—had you not dragged him into your schemes, he would be sitting quite securely on the throne now."

Beatriz stares at her, unable to say a word. Fury burns through her, all the hotter because she knows that Gisella is speaking the truth. Her hands aren't clean, and they'll get bloodier still before she's through. She holds Gisella's gaze for a moment longer before looking away.

"Guards," she calls out. "We're ready to proceed."

The chapel is dark when Beatriz enters, lit only by the moon and stars shining down through the glass ceiling. It isn't enough to see much more than two steps in front of her, but she doesn't need to. She can feel the stars dancing on her skin, calling to her with the sweetest soundless music. She felt them briefly the night before, but now it overwhelms her in the best way, like an embrace from a long-lost friend. She takes as deep a breath as she can in her tightly laced wedding gown.

The first constellation Beatriz picks out is the Thorned Rose—one of the constellations that hung overhead when she took her first breath more than sixteen years ago. In a way, it might be fitting to use it now for that reason alone, but tonight Beatriz doesn't need beauty or the thorns that accompany it. A different power courses through her as she puts one foot in front of the other, down the long, plushly carpeted aisle.

At the front, she can just barely make out the shadowy shape of Nicolo, waiting for her. A brief stab of pity goes through her. He has no idea what he has walked into tonight, soon to be betrayed not just by her but by his twin as well. Beatriz doesn't think Gisella would go so far as to have him killed, but the second the thought crosses her mind she takes it back. There are no lengths Gisella wouldn't go to for power, and she's too smart to let a threat go uneliminated.

Except, she thinks, for Beatriz herself. Gisella is letting her go. Whether that is because, despite everything, Gisella does care for—or at the very least respect—her, or because

Beatriz has simply made herself too much of a nuisance, she doesn't know. She likely never will know.

The Twisted Trees move through the sky to the east, symbolizing friendship, but that isn't the right constellation for Beatriz to pull from either. The branches of the Twisted Trees entangle like the lives of friends, and the last thing Beatriz wants to do is inadvertently tie her life to anyone in this stars-forsaken chapel.

Beatriz steps up onto the dais at the front of the chapel, coming to stand beside Nicolo, just as a new constellation catches her eye, edging into the sky from the South—the Glittering Diamond.

It's another one of Beatriz's birth constellations, symbolizing strength. She could certainly use a bit of that tonight, she thinks.

She's dimly aware of Nicolo taking hold of both of her hands, of the archbishop's droning voice reciting a passage from the scriptures, of the eyes of hundreds of people on her, but the bulk of her attention is on the Glittering Diamond, arcing across the sky. It's moving quickly; there is no time to waste.

She draws a full breath into her lungs and casts her gaze upward, picking out the largest star at the center of the constellation.

"I wish—"

Her words are interrupted by a high-pitched scream. It's too dark to make out more than vague shapes, but Beatriz sees what looks like a woman bolting upright in one of the middle pews, the figure next to her slumping forward, unmoving. Almost perfectly in sync, the sound of dozens of swords being drawn from their scabbards cuts through the silent chapel, starlight glinting off silver blades. And then chaos rears its head.

Someone—Nicolo, she realizes—yanks at her arm, pulling her back behind the altar. It offers only the illusion of safety, without any kind of defense at all. Nicolo's eyes are wild, his face panic-stricken and shocked.

He truly did not expect this.

Nicolo shrugs his jacket off, reaching for the dagger holstered at his hip. Beatriz's eyes follow the movement, mind spinning.

"Stay here," Nicolo grits out.

But Beatriz is tired of being told what to do by him, his sister, or anyone else. There is little left for her to lose now, so she balls her right hand into a fist and slams it into Nicolo's nose, sending him stumbling back, his grip on the blade loosening as it clatters to the stone floor. He curses, hand on his nose as he struggles to regain his balance, looking even more perplexed now.

"What in the name of the stars—" he begins, but Beatriz doesn't let him finish. She scrabbles for the dropped dagger, her fingers closing around the hilt just as a new scream joins the cacophony filling the chapel.

"Beatriz!"

She knows that voice, she realizes with dawning horror. Somewhere amid the bloodshed of what Beatriz is quickly realizing is a coup orchestrated by Gisella and Enzo, is Pasquale.

Nicolo realizes it too, recognition cutting through the shock in his eyes. "Pasquale is dead," he says, though it sounds more like a question than a statement.

He isn't wrong, though. If Pasquale is truly in the middle of the melee that's broken out in the chapel, he is as good as dead.

"Is this his doing?" Nicolo continues, his voice barely audible over the sound of swords clashing and the shouts of triumph and pain.

Despite the danger surrounding them and the thought of Pasquale in the carnage, Beatriz laughs. "You think Pasquale is behind this?" she asks incredulously. "You have no idea, do you? What's been unfolding right underneath your nose? In your own court? In your own family?"

She sees the realization hit him, not so outlandish an idea that he struggles to grasp it. "Gisella." He says his twin's name like a curse.

"Gisella," Beatriz confirms. "You aren't walking out of this chapel alive, Nico."

He opens his mouth—to argue, she's sure—but he closes it again, apparently realizing the truth of her words. He looks at Beatriz for a moment, and she can see the thoughts racing through his mind, searching for a way out of this and finding none. Moving fast as lightning, his hand grabs hers, still holding the dagger. She tries to wrench away from him but he holds fast, his eyes somber as he pulls her hand up to bring the dagger to his throat.

Confusion floods her. "What are you—"

"I'm not getting out of this chapel, Beatriz, you said it yourself. But you are if you use me as a hostage."

That only unnerves her more. "I don't need a hostage," she tells him, pulling her hand away and the dagger with it. Reluctantly, he lets her go. "You would do that?" she asks him.

Nicolo shrugs, looking away from her with discomfort clear in his eyes. "If it weren't for me, you wouldn't be anywhere near this mess," he tells her. "It seemed to be the least I could do."

He isn't wrong about that, but the gesture still moves her. She tries to peer around the altar, but from her position she can't see the stars—she can't reach her magic. She needs to stand, but doing so will make her a target, and she's sure she'll be dead before she can utter even half of her wish.

*Her wish.* She had one prepared for the Glittering Diamond—*I wish I were in Hapantoile*—but she can't use that now and leave Pasquale here. She could wish both of them away, but she doesn't know who else might be with him—Ambrose, Violie, Leopold, someone else altogether. And even if she succeeds in getting herself, Pasquale, and whoever he's with out of this place, she couldn't do it. It was one thing to escape a wedding, but running away from what very well might be best described as a massacre when she has more power to stop it than anyone else present is something entirely different. Just moments ago, Gisella reminded Beatriz of all the blood on her hands. She might not be able to wash them clean, but the stars can damn her before she adds another drop—even if that blood belongs to Nicolo. Her eyes find his and she tightens her grip on the dagger.

"You're going to follow my lead," she tells him.

He barely has time to nod before she grabs hold of his

arm with her free hand and jerks them both to the side of the altar until she's standing behind him while he kneels, both of them facing the battle, with the dagger's sharp edge pressed to his throat.

"Drop your swords or I'll slit his throat!" she shouts out as loudly as she can to be heard over the sounds of fighting. Her words echo through the room, drawing hundreds of eyes to her, their swords stalling in midair before falling limp at their sides.

"Change of heart?" Nicolo hisses.

She ignores him. In truth, Beatriz doesn't fully know what she's doing, but she has the stars now and the full attention of the room. Even the courtiers fighting to overthrow Nicolo don't want him dead—not like this at least, beheaded by a hysterical woman in a story they won't be able to spin to add to their own mythos. Beatriz holds the narrative now, so she holds the power.

She searches the crowd, but it's too dark to see much. She knows, though, that Pasquale is out there somewhere. Overhead, the Glittering Diamond has left the sky. Now there are only the Twisting Trees, the Dancing Bear, the Clouded Sun. Beatriz doesn't have time to be picky about the constellation she pulls from now—any one of those will have to do the job—but some unknowable force whispers through her.

*Patience,* it says.

Patience has never been Beatriz's strength, and now seems like a terrible time to practice the skill, but she lowers her eyes from the stars, looking out at the chapel, which has become a battlefield. The Cellarians think her a saint, she muses. *Saint* wasn't among the identities her mother trained her to take on, but she knows the rules of it all the same. She draws herself up to her full height and squares her shoulders.

"You dare spill blood in the light of the stars?" she asks, her voice stern.

"The stars cursed Cellaria the moment that imposter took the throne," a man in the front counters, earning a scattered cheer from the rest of the chapel. "Surely they'll be glad to witness us righting that mistake."

"Yes, fine, he's been a shit king," Beatriz replies, and despite the tension in the chapel, there's a bout of choked laughter from an unseen place at the sound of the word *shit* leaving the sainted princess's mouth. *Good*, Beatriz thinks, feeling more confident. "Do you think Duke Ribel will be a better one? I don't see him among your numbers—is he too cowardly to fight for his throne?"

"Beatriz," Nicolo warns, but again Beatriz ignores him. She knows that taunting Enzo would be a foolish thing to do if she planned on staying in Cellaria long enough to face the consequences for it.

"Your Highness, if you wished to speak with me, you needed only ask," a familiar voice says, and Beatriz follows it up to a small balcony on her right, high above the chapel floor. Beatriz can just barely make out Enzo leaning over the railing, Gisella beside him. Even from a distance, Beatriz can see the irritation on Gisella's face, but Beatriz knows that despite what she might pretend, Gisella isn't immune to the sight of her twin with a blade to his throat.

Beatriz schools her own expression into a bland smile. "How kind of you to attend my wedding, Your Grace!" she shouts up to him. "Though I do wish you hadn't tried so hard to upstage me."

"Oh, I could never upstage you, Princess," he replies. "In that dress, particularly. Under different circumstances, I'd call our king a very lucky man."

Beatriz knows that if she didn't have a dagger to Nicolo's throat, he wouldn't be able to resist a retort.

She widens her smile, instilling it with every ounce of charm she can manage. "Whatever family squabble this may be, Enzo, it has nothing to do with me. For these past weeks I've been held in Cellaria against my will, bullied and blackmailed into a marriage I did not want, and pushed toward a throne I have no interest in laying claim to. I thank you for liberating me from my situation, but I hope you'll agree that we should settle this in a more civilized manner before all this fighting ruins what you yourself have pointed out is quite a lovely gown." She hopes that by returning his playful banter, despite the dozen or so bodies already bleeding out on the chapel floor, she'll incline him more to agree to her terms, but he purses his lips. "Surely Nicolo here is willing to discuss a truce?" She looks down at Nicolo, kneeling in front of her, who hesitates just long enough for a man toward the front of the chapel to shout out.

"The stars will fall before we'll accept the duke as king," he says, the words followed by a roar of approval from what Beatriz imagines is roughly half of the chapel.

"Better him than the usurper king we have now!" someone else shouts. "Go ahead, slit his throat, Princess. Save us the trouble." More cheers follow that, and Beatriz tightens her grip on the dagger, wondering if perhaps she's in over her head. But she is a saint, she reminds herself, if only in their eyes.

"The stars have already cursed Cellaria, dooming you to centuries without starshowers, with mad kings and cruel kings and now an incompetent one," she says, shaking her head. "To spill a drop more blood in their chapel would invite more misery for every person who calls this land home."

"Who says?" someone asks, skepticism clear in their voice.

"The stars have chosen me as their messenger," she replies coolly. "Do you dare to question that? In their chapel? Under their watch?" She casts her gaze skyward, partly for an added touch of theatrics but mostly to see the stars. The Slithering Snake has made its way into view—appropriate, Beatriz supposes, given all the betrayal at play. Perhaps . . .

*Not yet*, the voice whispers through her again, and this time it almost sounds like Sophronia.

"As you say, Princess," Enzo calls from the balcony, his smile cold. "Cellaria is no stranger to curses from the stars. We've managed to survive and thrive for centuries without their blessed favor raining down on us, haven't we? You think we still fear offending them? Kill him and see for yourself. The stars may not bless us, but they don't curse us either. They've abandoned us, just as they always have, and only children believe differently."

A tense silence follows his words, and Beatriz can see some of the men in the chapel shifting uncertainly. What Enzo is saying is sacrilege, but he knows that. The sacrilege is the point. Because while some men are uncomfortable with the way Enzo is speaking, others are nodding along, rapt at someone putting their own long-borne feelings into words.

"The stars haven't abandoned Cellaria," another voice says, one that Beatriz has missed so sorely that hearing it again is a lance through her heart.

The crowd parts for Pasquale as he makes his way down the aisle toward her, dressed as a servant and holding a clean sword at his side.

# Violie

As the baron's soldiers bound Violie's wrists, panic and fury swarmed her, but only for a moment. They were replaced by satisfaction when the soldiers searched the kitchens and found no cook, no Janellia. The satisfaction turned to smugness when the baron ordered his men to search the inn in its entirety and found it empty.

The baron didn't hesitate in slapping the smugness off her face—she can still feel the ache in her chin where one of his heavy rings collided with her jaw. She can't see her reflection, but she can feel the swelling and the trickle of blood drying on her skin.

"Where is everyone?" the baron snarls at her, shoving her backward into a wooden chair. Without the use of her hands she nearly tumbles out of it, but another soldier is there, yanking her arms roughly back so that they're secured behind the chair, nearly dislocating her shoulder in the process.

Violie doesn't answer the baron. Instead, she smiles. "I don't know what you mean, my lord," she says, her voice coming out sweet and simpering.

A soldier approaches the baron, saying something Violie can't hear.

"Search the village," the baron snaps at him. "I want every house scoured from top to bottom and every man, woman, and child gathered in the square."

The soldier bows his head and hurries to follow the order, but when he reaches the tavern door, the baron calls after him.

"Wait," he says, and though the word is intended for the soldier, the baron's eyes stay on Violie as he steps toward her. He shoves the skirt of her gown high enough to bare the pistol holstered to her thigh, unsheathing it and showing it to the soldier. "And thoroughly check anyone you do find for weapons."

The baron passes the pistol to another soldier nearby as the first slips out the door.

"Well, General?" the baron asks the man. "Is that one of yours?"

The general's face goes a shade paler and he gives a quick nod. "It's one of the pistols that was stolen from our armory, Your Grace."

"By the thieves you were so proud of finally capturing?" the baron asks. "I don't believe it's a coincidence she has it."

The general clears his throat, eyes moving between Violie and the baron. "And . . . who is she, my lord?"

Violie finds that she's interested in the baron's answer too—who, exactly, does he believe she is? Queen Sophronia's former lady's maid seems the most likely answer, but she can't imagine that alone would have earned her this treatment. Though, given the baron's notorious hatred of Duchess Bruna, perhaps it's merely Violie's association with her that raised his suspicions.

"Do you not recognize her?" the baron asks, a mocking lilt to his voice. "I do hope one of you is wise enough to have the latest dispatch from Hapantoile?"

A few soldiers fumble, hands searching pockets and satchels, but the baron is the one who finally pulls a folded square of papers from his sleeve, unfolding them and smoothing them out on the table. He shuffles though them, and from Violie's vantage point, she can make out letters written in Bessemian, picking out words like *border, captured,* and *attack* as he searches for what he's looking for. When he finds it, Violie's stomach drops.

There, taking up an entire page, is an illustration of a woman who can only be Violie herself, from the shoulders up. The likeness isn't perfect, and Violie takes particular exception to the size the artist drew her ears, but Violie sees herself in the image all the same, and she sees the soldiers look from the illustration to her with dawning recognition.

"I hadn't thought about that," the general says, shaking his head. "Of course I saw the dispatch, but the message claimed she and King Leopold were en route to Cellaria."

Violie didn't think her dread could deepen, but at the mention of Leopold, it does. Is there another page with his image sketched on it? She tells herself it doesn't matter if there is—Leopold was always going to be recognizable in Temarin, he knows to keep himself hidden. It's Violie who was supposed to be safe, whose talent has always rested on her ability to disappear into a crowd, to become anyone she needs to in order to get what she wants. An ability that has now been snatched away from her, leaving her vulnerable, visible, and trapped.

"A clever lie, though, about working at the palace," the baron comments, shaking his head. "I very nearly believed it."

Violie laughs; she can't help it—if this is the only card she has to play, she'll play it, even if she doesn't know to what end it will serve her. "That wasn't a lie, my lord," she tells him. "Though I'm not surprised you don't remember me—I don't believe I ever saw you sober in the year I worked in your household, as your wife's lady's maid. If you weren't stumbling around the apartment her brother gifted her, where she permitted you to stay, raving after losing a fortune at the gambling table, you were passed out for days on end, unable even to get out of bed without vomiting all over yourself. How much has changed in a few short months."

The baron's face hardens and his fist clenches at his side, but before he can strike her again, he catches himself. "We all gamble, girl," he says, his voice cold. "And I made the right call when it counted."

"By allying yourself with the empress?" Violie asks, laughing. "I wouldn't go claiming the pot just yet, my lord. The game is only halfway through."

The baron glares at her, eyes narrowing. "I suppose my fool-brained nephew is somewhere nearby?"

The lies spill easily from Violie's lips. "King Leopold?" she asks, blinking. "Last I saw him, he was boarding a ship somewhere east—he didn't care where, so long as it got him out of Vesteria. I did try to convince him to come with me, but, well, you know Leopold—he's never met a fight he hasn't fled from. I think the stars will go dark before he sets foot in Temarin again."

The baron looks at her for a long moment, a sneer

curling his upper lip. "You know, I just might believe you," he says slowly. "But if that's the case, what could possibly have brought you back here? Surely not any sort of loyalty to Temarin—the dispatch said you were Bessemian, born and raised, though you speak the language well, I admit."

Violie opens her mouth to answer but quickly closes it again when words don't come. She's always been one to have an excuse or explanation at the ready, but now? The baron is right. There is no other reason for her to be here, fighting against her own people for a country she has no loyalty to. Not one the baron will believe, at any rate.

"Because it's right," she says finally, the words tasting as silly as they do true.

The baron laughs. "Now you even sound like Leopold," he says. "And I'd wager I know exactly where he is—how many soldiers are guarding the prison, General?"

"Four seemed sufficient," the general says after a moment's hesitation.

"Four would certainly be sufficient to keep watch over two sixteen-year-old girls," the baron agrees, cutting a sharp look at the general. "But I fear it was woefully insufficient against King Leopold, the villagers he gathered, and the weapons they stole from your armory."

The general lets out a low curse.

"Never fear, though, General," the baron says, his eyes tracing over Violie in a way that makes her skin crawl. "As the girl pointed out, I'm a gambling man, and I believe we've just upped the ante enough that Leopold will be forced to come to the table."

Violie barely has time to process that before the general

nods to the soldier behind her and she's unceremoniously yanked to her feet again. Her mind swims as she's roughly shoved toward the tavern door, the baron at her back and his shotgun pressed between her shoulder blades.

"If Leopold wishes to play at being the hero, let him," the baron says, low enough that only Violie can hear him. "He let his feelings for a girl destroy him once, after all. He'll do it again."

Violie fears he's right, but she manages to keep her expression disinterested. "You might be right, if King Leopold had any feelings for me. But I'm not Queen Sophronia—as you yourself pointed out, I'm a servant and a spy. No one a king would surrender for."

The baron smiles like he knows something Violie doesn't. "I suppose there's only one way to find out, isn't there?"

The pain in Violie's jaw is still sharp, as is the jab of the baron's rifle between her shoulder blades as he forces her to walk ahead of him down the silent streets, but she feels as if she is floating outside her body, watching another girl being marched through a deserted village, knowing that the stranger who wears her face won't see sunrise. *Hoping* she never sees sunrise, because the alternative is infinitely harder to bear.

*Was this how Sophronia felt?* Violie wonders. Did she walk across the scaffold to the guillotine feeling like she was watching herself from above, feeling strangely, impossibly at peace with the promise of death looming before her? At least Sophronia didn't die alone—she died with her sisters' voices in her head. Violie thinks that would be comforting, but she isn't sure she wants comfort. And, at any rate, she would much rather die alone, just as she has lived for most of her life. If she dies alone, she thinks, it will be easier for Leopold. It will mean there is less of a chance he'll do something foolish and brave, just as his uncle expects him to.

A part of her isn't sure Leopold won't fall into his uncle's trap without a second thought. He always acts first and thinks later, driven by his feelings rather than logic. She knows he's changed over the past weeks, but thinking about the boy she's been traveling with, the boy who's been at her side through challenges, successes, and failures, Violie knows he's still the same Leopold at heart, the one who screamed at the top of his lungs as he watched the blade of the guillotine fall on Sophronia's neck, knowing the scream put him in danger of discovery.

He feels too much, loves too deeply, and that is a trait Violie couldn't strip from Leopold if she wanted to—and she never wanted to. She just didn't want those emotions to cloud his judgment. As a king, Leopold needs to keep his emotions in check. He can't let how he feels about any one person outweigh his duty to his country. Even if that one person is her.

Violie stops short in the middle of the street, throwing herself backward against the baron and taking him by surprise as her head collides with his nose. She braces herself for the sound of his shotgun going off, the impact of a bullet ripping through her flesh—given where the gun was pressed, she knows it would give her a quick death, but the shot never comes. Instead, she only hears the sound of the baron's nose breaking from the impact of her head, followed by his snarled curse as two sets of hands grab her by the shoulders, forcing her to keep walking.

"Keep hold of her—she's no good to us dead," the baron says, his voice coming out sharp and nasal. Even though her plan to force him to kill her here and now has failed, Violie still takes some pleasure in knowing she injured him, if only superficially.

"That was a valid attempt," he adds as they start walking again. "But you've given away the game now, girl. If you thought to save him from the choice, you've confirmed my suspicion that it will be a difficult one for him."

Violie doesn't answer. Instead she keeps her gaze ahead, toward the low gate and the grain storehouse just behind it. It's a low, squat building barely wider than it is tall, with a sloping, thatched roof. At first glance, it's abandoned, with no sign of armed villagers, a rebel king, or Bessemian guards, but as they draw closer, Violie sees a slumped figure in the shade of the grain house, the Bessemian sigil of his armor glinting in the moonlight.

"Search the granary," the baron barks. "They can't have gone far."

Half the soldiers dash forward to follow the order, one of them pausing to check the fallen soldier, but when he drops the soldier's hand while checking the pulse, Violie surmises he's dead. Unsurprising—if the guard had lived, Leopold would have known better than to leave him there. Unless there are more bodies inside the granary, Violie would wager the other four guards are being kept as hostages.

"No one's inside," a soldier announces, appearing at the

granary's entrance, the others at his back. "And the girls are gone."

"That's fine," the baron says, shoving Violie roughly to two of his soldiers, who catch her before she stumbles to the ground. "Tie her up in their stead—King Leopold will be back any moment now, I'd wager."

"I never thought I'd see the day you won a wager, Uncle." Leopold's voice comes from behind them, booming strong and clear even from a distance. He stands on the other side of the gates the baron and his soldiers pushed Violie through, three dozen villagers around him, armed with pistols, shotguns, swords, and even some makeshift household weapons—one woman, Violie notes, holds a fire poker. "Though I suppose there's a first time for everything."

The baron snarls at him. "You've always been a fool, Leopold, but surely you know you're outnumbered—my men are waiting outside the village, and once I—"

"Your men *were* waiting outside the village," Leopold says, his voice quiet but no less powerful. "Many of them surrendered willingly when they realized who I was and assisted in detaining those who didn't. Which is to say that *my* men are now waiting outside the walls of the village."

Violie can't see the baron's face, but she's sure he's gone a shade paler. "Be that as it may, I have her." The baron gestures to Violie.

Leopold follows the gesture, his eyes finding Violie's, and in that look, she sees an apology she has no use for.

"You do," Leopold agrees. "If you'd like to discuss exchanging hostages, I have a good many of your men that I could offer to trade—"

"What good are a smattering of soldiers to me now?" the baron interrupts. "When you say yourself you have me surrounded. No, my terms are simple, Leopold: you surrender, or she dies."

Leopold absorbs this for a moment, not surprised—or at least not showing it if he is. He looks at his uncle; then his gaze moves to Violie and lingers.

"It's all right, Leo," Violie says, her words cut off by a soldier shoving her forward, her knees hitting the dirt. She would fall on her face if it weren't for a soldier grabbing her shoulders and holding her in place as a second brings his sword to the side of her neck.

"Violie," Leopold says, the anguish in that single word cutting her deeper than any sword could.

Anguish because he knows as well as Violie does that the bargain the baron is presenting is no bargain at all. Violie told him she was no one to Leopold, and while that isn't true, in the grand scheme of things, weighed against the lives and freedom of Temarin and her people, she is no one.

"I've surrendered too many times already, Uncle, and put my wants and feelings ahead of the country I swore to protect when I took the throne," Leopold says, and though he's speaking to the baron, his gaze lingers on Violie, the words for her more than anyone else. "I won't do it again. Not for anyone, as much as I wish I could."

"It's all right," Violie tries to tell him, but the blade against her throat presses harder and the words die a whisper.

Leopold must hear them, though—or at least understand on some other level—because he gives one final nod before looking to the baron and raising his sword.

"Attack!" he shouts at his army, which pushes forward, flooding through the gate with a shout. With so many voices, it's difficult to understand, but Violie thinks they're shouting *For King Leopold*. It's the last thing she hears before the soldier's blade cuts through her skin and she falls to the ground, her vision filling with stars as blood pools around her.

# Beatriz

Beatriz watches Pasquale as he walks toward her, joy, relief, and fear doing battle inside her. She knows this is the worst possible place for him to be at this moment, but she's so glad to see him safe and alive.

"The stars don't bless us because we refuse their blessings," Pasquale says as he comes down the aisle, his voice loud and more sure than Beatriz has ever heard it. "We outlaw them and we punish those who seek to accept the blessings they find."

"Cousin," Enzo says, craning his head to see Pasquale from his place on the balcony. "I'm relieved to see that the rumors of your death were unfounded."

He does manage to sound relieved, but Beatriz doesn't believe it for a moment. She swallows down the myriad of feelings rushing through her, masking them with a cool smile she borrows from her mother.

"Did Lady Gisella not mention that?" she asks, her voice innocent though she can't hide the jagged edge beneath the surface as she realizes that the only way through this is to do exactly what her mother taught her—sow chaos and let mistrust bloom thick enough to divide the factions of the Cellarian court further.

"She didn't," Enzo says after a moment, and though his tone is still mild, Beatriz smiles, knowing she's hit her mark.

"I don't think she's told you much of anything, Enzo," she says, playfully, before looking down at Nicolo. "And she's told *you* even less."

"Beatriz," Gisella says, a warning that Beatriz has no intention of heeding.

Beatriz ignores her, focusing instead on Pasquale, now just in front of the dais she stands on. If she weren't occupied with holding Nicolo in place and her knife at his throat, she could reach out and touch Pasquale. "I'm glad to see you, husband," Beatriz says to him, letting real warmth infuse her words. "Though it makes me wonder how many other old friends I might have here that I don't know about."

"You have a tendency to make friends everywhere, Beatriz," Pasquale replies, though surely he must know what Beatriz is truly asking—how many others are in the castle? Pasquale can't answer, though. Not verbally, at least, but his left hand lifts to scratch his nose—one finger. One other friend in the chapel—Ambrose, she'd bet, though he's even less suited to battle than Pasquale is, far more comfortable with books than blood.

"Perhaps I do," Beatriz says, filing the information away in case she needs it to make a quick escape. "Though I admit the quality of many of those friends does leave something to be desired."

Pasquale climbs onto the dais to stand beside Beatriz,

and she releases Nicolo's shoulder—still keeping her blade hard against his neck—and grasps Pasquale's hand tightly, borrowing some of his strength and lending him some of hers in turn before she looks out at the crowd again, addressing them.

"Whether you are friends or foes, the truth of it remains the same—this little coup you're staging, the childish squabbles over who gets to sit on a shiny metal chair and wear a pretty crown? They're meaningless. Because in a few days or weeks or perhaps months, should luck be on your side, my mother is going to send an army across the border and crush your defenses like ants beneath the heel of a boot. And you'll be too busy fighting one another to notice until it's too late. I know that because I was meant to help her do it. And Gisella knows it for the same reason. She conspired with my mother to drug me and return me here. To assassinate me when the time came so that my mother had cause to lay siege to Cellaria."

A murmur goes up throughout the chapel.

"She's lying," Gisella says, but no matter how clear and sure her voice is, it isn't enough to erase the doubt Beatriz has raised.

"Which part?" Beatriz asks her with a laugh. "Which part, exactly, is the lie?"

For a beat, Gisella doesn't say anything, but finally she finds her voice. "Yes, fine, I did conspire with Empress Margaraux," she admits, the words sounding like they're being dragged from her mouth by force. "And yes, everything Beatriz is saying is technically true, but I was never going to hold up my end of our bargain. I lied to her to secure my own freedom after *she* had me imprisoned in a Bessemian dungeon."

She finishes by jabbing an accusatory finger in Beatriz's direction.

"And you expect anyone to believe that?" Beatriz asks with a harsh laugh. "When you yourself admit that you have no sense of honor? No loyalty?"

More murmurs arise at that.

"I am loyal to Cellaria!" Gisella shouts, but in the silence that follows, Beatriz knows that she lost the fight the moment she lost her temper. How many will tell the story of tonight and describe her voice as *shrill,* her manner as *hysterical*? Gisella knows it too—how can she not? She grew up in this court, watched plenty of women before her make the same mistakes she just did, likely swearing to herself that she would never be so foolish. There's a reason that Cellaria has never had a woman on its throne and that even Gisella, for all her scheming and ambition, has always tried to pull strings from behind a curtain rather than make a play for the throne herself.

Watching Gisella realize her mistake, Beatriz expected to feel triumph or pride—how many nights has she fallen asleep imagining the moment of Gisella's downfall?—but instead all she feels is *sad*. Years of Gisella's plotting, of carefully creating alliances, of cultivating power so slowly and meticulously that no one noticed what she was doing until it was too late, and it all ends like this—with a single display of unregulated emotion. A shrill voice doing more damage than the bloodshed that reigned just moments before.

Never mind that nearly everyone in this chapel was all

too happy to bend the knee to King Cesare through his many temper tantrums. Never mind that *his* temper tantrums had a habit of ending in executions. But the second Gisella let her temper show, the respect of the men who were ready to slaughter one another under her clever manipulation disappears like mist in sunlight.

Despite everything, Beatriz pities Gisella in this moment. More than that, she's angry on her behalf. If she removes her own personal feelings from the equation, she can see that Gisella would make a better ruler of Cellaria than Nicolo, who floundered the second she left his side. Better than Enzo, who was too cowardly to stay in the same city as King Cesare during his reign, let alone try to remove him from the throne like Gisella did. Beatriz has to admit that Gisella would even make a better ruler than Pasquale, for the simple reason that he has never *wanted* power.

Gisella, she thinks, might just have been the best ruler Cellaria could ask for, if King Cesare and all the kings that came before him hadn't nourished a populace too ignorant to see it.

Gisella's eyes meet hers, and even though Gisella must know she's lost her following, must have noticed even Enzo inching away from her, trying to put as much distance between them as he can on the small balcony, her brown eyes are steely, her chin lifted. A queen, even without a crown.

An equal, Beatriz realizes.

Thinking quickly, Beatriz looks to Pasquale beside her and gives his hand a squeeze. She still can't believe he's here, and while she would rather he were somewhere far, far away and safe, she's grateful for his presence.

"Pasquale, you have the strongest claim to the Cellarian throne," she says, loudly enough to be heard in the back pew of the chapel. "King Cesare disinherited you, yes, but I don't think anyone present would argue the fact that he was not in his right mind at the time." She pauses for dissenters, but after some uncertain glances, no one speaks, so she continues. "Do you want to be king?"

She knows his answer before she even finishes the question, but in this she can't speak for him. And he doesn't need her to.

"As dearly as I love my country and as much as I have missed being home," he says, his voice as loud and sure as her own, "I believe I can better serve Cellaria away from the throne and the court."

He's being more polite than the courtiers listening to him deserve—Pasquale was miserable at court, and while she's sure he does love Cellaria, she doubts he's missed it. Still, it's a good speech and his voice doesn't waver once—a feat she isn't sure he would have been capable of the last time he stood before his court, drowning in the shadow his father cast.

Beatriz tears her eyes away from him and drops the dagger from Nicolo's neck, urging him to stand on her other side. He no longer looks confused, but his eyes are still wary as he looks from Beatriz, to Gisella and Enzo, to the crowd.

"And you, Nico?" she asks, using his nickname intentionally. "You once told me you wanted to see more of the world. Surrendering your crown by choice and going willingly into exile will allow plenty of time for that."

Nicolo reaches up to touch the aforementioned crown, his brow furrowed but his eyes as calculating as ever. Searching for ways forward, weighing each one carefully in the space of a few seconds. He inclines his head toward her slightly, a small smile tugging at his lips, like they've been playing chess and she's finally put him in checkmate. He lifts the crown off his head and looks at it for a moment before passing it to Beatriz. She has to release Pasquale's hand to hold both the crown and the dagger, and the crown is by far the heavier of the two.

She turns her attention to the balcony, where Enzo is leaning on his elbows over the balcony, a stone-faced Gisella beside him.

"Your Grace," Beatriz begins.

"I'll save you the trouble, Princess," Enzo says, his voice bored. "I very much *do* want to be king, and have no interest in relinquishing my claim. Which is lucky, I suspect, as we're quickly running through anyone with a drop of royal blood in their veins."

It isn't lost on Beatriz that he's ignoring Gisella altogether, whose claim to the throne is stronger than his and every bit as strong as Nicolo's.

"Seize the three of them," Enzo orders.

With no one else to heed, the crowd moves toward the dais, uncertain but dangerous all the same.

"Beatriz," Pasquale says. "Do you have a plan here?"

"She has the same plan I do," Nicolo says through gritted teeth. "Not to die."

That is, more or less, the gist of Beatriz's plan. She casts another desperate look toward the stars, and what she sees steals her breath. There, moving overhead, is the Empyrea's Staff, the constellation that represents magic, the one that

Nigellus pulled a star from the moment she was born. The one that is, quite literally, a part of her.

*Now*, the voice inside her whispers, not a moment too soon.

And looking around at the frenzied chapel, the mob of Cellarians broken by decades—maybe even centuries—of inept kings, by wars stemming from bitter jealousy that ruined them, by the knowledge that no matter what their lore tried to tell them, the stars had forsaken them, Beatriz knows *exactly* what to wish for. Not an escape hatch at all, but a miracle.

She turns her face toward the sky and breathes deeply, her eyes finding a star in the constellation. Not a small one this time but the largest one she sees at the very top of the staff's shape. She lets emotion flood through her—fury at Enzo, at the guards and courtiers following his orders, at her mother. At the stars themselves, even. She lets the fury course through her and then she opens her mouth.

"I wish . . . ," she begins. Pasquale shouts at her, calling her name, telling her to stop as he realizes what she's doing, but she ignores him. ". . . For the stars to bless Cellaria once again and forevermore, just as they do the rest of Vesteria."

If she'd had the time, she would have found a way to word her wish better, but the stars hear her all the same. They brighten until the entire night sky is a pure, blinding white, a mirroring pain lancing through Beatriz's head—a pain she knows will only get worse. Everyone around her is screaming, cursing, crying, but Beatriz keeps her gaze on the white sky, watching the impossible brightness of the stars fade, until the dark sky is visible once again.

"What did you do?" Nicolo asks her, his voice more awed than accusatory. Everyone else in the chapel is staring at the sky as well, slack-jawed and wide-eyed—in some mix of terror and wonder. Faces Beatriz can see clearly now, she realizes, because the stars are still brighter than they were before she made her wish.

Beatriz doesn't have time to answer Nicolo's question before the stars answer it for her. A lone star streaks across the sky, a trail of light following behind it.

"Was that—" Pasquale begins, but before he can finish, another star falls. Then another. Then they are falling in groups of two or three at a time, flickering across the sky as they make their way to the ground. To *Cellaria*.

It is the first starshower in five centuries, and Beatriz summoned it.

The shocked silence in the chapel gives way to murmurs, to shouts as people point up at falling stars, to cheers. Some sink to their knees in prayer. Others openly sob. Among them, one voice rises above the rest.

"All hail Saint Beatriz!" a man shouts.

Other voices echo him until the entire chapel is praising her name. Or rather, almost the entire chapel.

Her eyes find the balcony again, catching sight of Enzo, his face white as the sky was moments ago. He alone looks terrified of her, and she can't blame him for that.

"Seize the usurper," Beatriz says, and the mob turns, starting toward the door that must lead to the staircase to the balcony, but Gisella is closer and quicker. In the blink of an eye, she has a penknife to Enzo's throat.

Gisella is nothing if not an opportunist, Beatriz knows,

but then, so is Beatriz herself. She offers Gisella a sharp smile.

"Bring him to me," she orders.

As Gisella and Enzo make their way downstairs to the chapel, Beatriz wavers on her feet. Pasquale is quick to steady her with an arm around her shoulders.

"You shouldn't have done that," he tells her.

"Of course I should have," she says, though already she's feeling the consequences of the wish, the toll the magic takes on her body. The last time she wished on a star, she coughed blood and Nigellus told her that continuing to use magic would kill her. Will this be it? she wonders. Will this be the wish that ends her life? If so, she'd better make sure it counts for something.

She forces herself to shrug off Pasquale's arm, to stand up straight and tall, to ignore the darkness swarming around her, trying to draw her under. Beatriz knows that to show weakness now would change the story being written with every breath she takes, that it would transform it from a tale of power and triumph to a tale of tragedy. They may call her a saint, but she will not let herself become a martyr.

She focuses on her breathing, on standing on her own two feet, and ignores the pain refracting through her like shards of a broken mirror.

"Is she all right?" Nicolo asks Pasquale, his voice low, though not low enough for Beatriz to miss.

"No," Pasquale tells him through gritted teeth at the same time Beatriz says, "Yes."

Before Nicolo can ask any further questions, Gisella enters the chapel through the side door, forcing Enzo in ahead of her with the sharp edge of her penknife against his throat. Her expression is guarded, and there is no sign of the girl who lost her temper, no sign of the girl who before that threatened and betrayed Beatriz and made no apologies for either.

Above all else, Beatriz knows, Gisella is smart. Smart enough to know when she's been beaten and conniving enough to get into the good graces of whoever bested her, to live to scheme another day.

"Bow," Gisella tells Enzo, and when he hesitates, she digs the blade into his neck until a bead of blood blooms against his skin and he finally acquiesces, bowing deeply to Beatriz. Gisella herself manages as deep a curtsy as she can while keeping Enzo at knifepoint.

Beatriz doesn't care about Enzo—no more than Gisella did, she supposes. He was only ever a vessel for Gisella's ambitions, just as Nicolo had been once. Instead, Beatriz surveys Gisella, wary and calculating.

She may regret this, she thinks, but that has never stopped Beatriz from acting before.

Beatriz summons every scrap of her theatricality and fakes a great shudder that races through her entire body, throwing her head back and looking at the stars with dramatically wide eyes. She sucks in a large breath and holds it for a few seconds before letting herself collapse forward onto her hands and knees.

"Beatriz!" Pasquale shouts, and drops down beside her.

"I'm fine," she says, though she makes no effort to sound fine. Instead, she lets her exhaustion and pain color her words, leaving her sounding as drained as she feels.

Pasquale helps her to her feet, and she lets him before looking out at the crowd of courtiers staring at her in rapt attention.

"The stars have a message for Cellaria," she says, pitching her voice a tad lower and giving it an ominous quality. "They have declared that one person and one person alone is fit to rule this land and have promised that as long as this person and their heirs—chosen or born—sit upon the Cellarian throne, they will shine down on Cellaria, and Cellaria will prosper."

She feels the attention of everyone in the room like a tangible thing against her skin, and despite the pain in her head and the sharp ache in her body, the power that comes with that attention is delicious. She shifts her gaze to Gisella, who must know Beatriz is acting but appears as rapt as anyone else.

"The ruler the stars have chosen is Queen Gisella, the first of her name," she says.

Genuine surprise and confusion play over Gisella's expression, but they're gone as quickly as they appear, replaced with a more practiced look of humble shock.

"Surely, I am undeserving," Gisella murmurs, bowing her head, and the performer in Beatriz respects Gisella for how easily she embraces the role of the chosen one. "I conspired with the enemy, you said it yourself, Princess Beatriz."

"The stars know this," Beatriz says with a benevolent smile. "They have seen everything you've done, but they've also seen inside your heart, and they know that every act you have taken has been in the interest of Cellaria." While Beatriz hasn't communed with the stars, she believes it's true—Gisella has killed a king, she's betrayed Beatriz and Pasquale several times over, she's made deals with enemies, and Beatriz is sure there are far more sins than she knows about. But Gisella has never acted against Cellaria's best interests. Still, Beatriz isn't foolish enough to hand Gisella unfettered power that can later be wielded against her.

"But," she adds, and notices a flicker of unease in Gisella's eyes. *Good,* she thinks. "Should you ever betray the stars or your country, the stars vow to cast Cellaria's sky into darkness forevermore. Is that understood?"

She holds Gisella's gaze, communicating the greater threat wordlessly. *I have made you queen and I can make you nothing just as easily.* Gisella hears the threat as clearly as if Beatriz spoke it aloud, and she purses her lips.

"It's understood," she says, bowing her head again. "I vow before the stars and every soul present that I will dedicate my life to seeing Cellaria through every triumph and every difficulty, to steering her into a bright future and ruling justly and fairly, for the rest of my days."

Beatriz has thought before that Gisella lies as easily as she breathes, but these, she knows, are the truest words she's ever spoken. And that is enough.

With the last vestiges of her strength, she drops into a deep curtsy. "All hail Queen Gisella. Long live the queen."

The crowd echoes the words, men dropping to their knees, their swords clattering to the floor beside them, women curtsying and clasping their hands to their hearts. Even Enzo drops to his knee, though if he hopes for mercy from Gisella, Beatriz suspects he'll be disappointed.

Rising from her curtsy is the most difficult thing Beatriz

has ever done, her muscles screaming as she comes to stand. She loses her balance, but both Pasquale and Nicolo steady her. Gisella launches into a speech that she has likely practiced in the mirror since childhood, but Beatriz has heard and seen enough. She makes her way down from the dais on unsteady feet, Nicolo and Pasquale at her heels, and only just manages to make it out the door and into the empty hallway before finally giving in and letting the darkness swallow her up.

# Violie

As the battle rages around Violie, all she sees are the stars, the constellations moving across the sky in their slow but steady parade. She never learned them as well as Leopold and the princesses of Bessemia, but she knows enough to pick out the Hero's Heart, the Glittering Diamond, and there, toward the southern edge of the sky, she sees the Empyrea's Staff. She feels her eyes growing heavier, the ground around her damp with her blood, but she keeps her eyes on the stars and tries to stop her mind from wondering what will happen next.

Her mother used to tell her that when she died, she would take her place among the stars, but as Violie got older, she scoffed at the idea—only children would believe such a fantasy. Now, though, she hopes it's true. That when she loses enough blood and her heart slows to a stop and the world goes dark for her, she will awaken again in the sky, surrounded by stars. Sophronia will be there, she thinks, and one day her mother and Elodia will join her too. One day she'll see Leopold again, and Beatriz, and Daphne, and the others she's come to care for.

She believes it because now, veering toward the end of her

life far sooner than she ever expected, she has no choice but to believe. The belief comes easily, and as she takes a deep breath that floods her lungs with pain, she tells herself she's ready to die, ready to leave this world behind with the confidence that it isn't truly the end.

As she lets the air out of her lungs, something catches her eye to the south—a star plunging down over the Alder Mountains. The trajectory of its fall, it almost looks like... her thoughts trail off as another star falls, then another, all of them appearing to streak past the Alder Mountains, landing in Cellaria.

*Impossible,* she thinks, but her eyes say differently.

*Beatriz,* she thinks a moment later, and she would laugh at the realization if everything didn't hurt so badly. Beatriz has caused a starshower in Cellaria—Violie would stake her life on it, precious little as it may be worth now. Warmth spreads through her—Beatriz did it, she got her power back, and what a miracle she's created with it.

Violie is so taken by the sight of the stars falling that she doesn't realize the battle around her has ceased until Leopold crouches beside her, taking her hand in both of his.

"Violie, someone went for the physician," he says, but Violie barely hears him. Some distant part of her knows it's too late, that she's too far gone and if there is something she needs to say to Leopold, now is the time to do it, but she can't tear her eyes away from the sky.

"It's a starshower," she manages. "In Cellaria."

"She's delusional," another voice says, one Violie doesn't recognize. "She isn't going to make it, Your Majesty."

"No," a third voice says, this one filled with awe. "No, she's right—look."

Violie feels the attention shift off her, everyone looking to the sky—everyone except Leopold, who keeps his focus on her, his grip on her hand tight enough that she feels it, even as the feeling of everything else fades.

A thought breaks through her clouded mind, sharp as a freshly forged dagger—when Sophronia died, she died at peace because she'd done all she could, said all she needed to. But Violie is not at peace. Words claw at her chest, demanding breath to voice them that she can't muster. Her body aches somewhere deeper than physical pain, demanding she get up, demanding she keep fighting. She can't die like this, not without seeing the empress fall, not without doing everything she can to help Daphne and Beatriz triumph, not without seeing Leopold sit on the throne he's earned—without seeing the king he's become reign. Not without discovering the feel of his lips against hers and discovering for sure whether the love she feels for him is platonic or romantic, not without finding out whether it's reciprocated.

Violie is not ready to die, and if these truly are to be the last moments of her life, she won't spend them stoic and serene. If this is how she dies, she intends to do it wholly as herself. She'll fight, with every scrappy, stubborn, sharp-edged part of her.

She sucks in a deep breath that pains her lungs so badly she can hardly stand it; then she searches the falling stars.

If one of them came her way . . . She can barely finish the thought, but she latches onto it as best she can. Violie knows she isn't Beatriz, with the power to call down stars, but she *is* star-touched. There is stardust in her veins, just as there is in every empyrea. And while Violie has never asked anything of the stars, never put any stock in their miracles, she does so now. After all, if Beatriz could cause the stars to fall over Cellaria, surely Violie can draw one to her now.

*Please,* she thinks, but when Leopold sucks in a breath, she realizes she spoke the word out loud. *If I have a miracle in me, let it come now. You gave me my life, and I have so much left to do before I'm done with it.*

Violie's eyes close and darkness surrounds her, but as everything else fades, Leopold's hand in hers is constant, an anchor she can't bear to release.

*The stars aren't done with you yet,* a voice whispers through Violie's mind, a voice that sounds like Sophronia's. *Though soon you might wish they were. Dying is less painful than living.*

"Look out!" The shout cuts through the darkness surrounding Violie, and her eyes fly open just in time to see the bright light barreling toward her from above—the star that hits Violie square in the chest, engulfing her body in a blinding white heat that feels like it's burning her alive.

It hurts like no pain Violie has ever felt before, but the pain tells her she's alive, so she endures.

# Daphne

Daphne sleeps most of the way to Bessemia, not yet fully recovered from unleashing Beatriz's magic. She has vague memories of a brief stop at an inn—just long enough for a meal and a few hours' rest—before the second leg of their journey, when she promptly fell asleep again. Though she wishes she didn't feel like death, she can't deny that sleeping for more or less a day and a half straight has been preferable to suffering in awkward silence with Cliona.

When she finally does stir, it's to the bright sunlight of late morning, and she realizes her head is resting on Bairre's shoulder. He must feel her move, because he glances down at her with a half smile.

"Cliona says we're getting close," he says.

Daphne straightens up, blinking the exhaustion from her eyes to find Cliona studiously avoiding her gaze and instead staring out the window. Daphne glances out the opposite window, taking in the familiar terrain of the Nemaria Woods. She and Cliona met somewhere near here, she recalls, in a clearing to the south of Hapantoile on the day she said goodbye to her sisters.

She remembers her initial impression of Cliona, back

when she believed the other girl to be an unassuming noblewoman with a clever wit and a curse for lying badly. Daphne underestimated her. She wonders what Cliona thought of her that day, and just how much Cliona underestimated her in turn.

*If I could go back,* Daphne thinks, *I would do so much differently.*

She would give help to Sophronia when she asked for it. She would tell Bairre the truth earlier. She would believe Beatriz about their mother and leave no words unspoken between them. But Cliona . . . all of their missteps and misunderstandings and mistrust—she wouldn't change any of that. For girls as sharp-edged as they are, there was never a smooth path to friendship.

But she also wouldn't change the fact that she allowed her mother to murder Cliona's father. She has replayed that lunch over and over in her mind, has even seen it acted out again and again in her dreams over the last couple of days, and she knows that no matter what she'd done, she would have lost someone or something that day. And to her, Lord Panlington was the most acceptable sacrifice.

Cliona doesn't see it that way, though, and perhaps she never will. Nothing Daphne can say will change that, but she tries nonetheless.

"When I met Cliona," she tells Bairre, aware that Cliona can hear every word even if she pretends not to, "I already knew everything about her—or so I thought. My mother's spies were no match for hers and her father's, I suppose."

At the mention of her father, Cliona's shoulders stiffen, but Daphne pushes on.

"There was nothing in any of the intelligence I read about Lord Panlington or his daughter being involved in the rebellion, much less his leading it. I sat across from her in the carriage to Friv and thought she was just another empty-headed socialite whose father spoiled her rotten. That made it into the dossier," she adds. "How dearly Lord Panlington loved his only daughter. He hid many things, but he couldn't hide that."

Cliona's face is still stubbornly turned toward the window, but Daphne catches her lifting her hand to her cheek to wipe away a stray tear. Daphne addresses her directly now.

"As soon as I learned you and he were part of the rebellion, I told my mother," she says. "I knew it presented the perfect opportunity to sow discord in Friv, that if King Bartholomew knew his closest friend and advisor had betrayed him, it could be the key needed for a civil war that would leave Friv vulnerable to my mother's attack. That's what I regret—that I told her anything at all about you or him. That is what I would change if I could. That is the real choice I made that led to his death, Cliona. And I will always regret that."

Cliona says nothing, but Daphne doesn't expect her to. She looks out her window again and sees the white stone towers of the Bessemian palace appear over the treetops, pale blue flags fluttering in the wind, emblazoned with a golden sun.

Daphne lets out a soft breath. She's home.

The fanfare around the empress's return—and to some extent, Daphne's—passes in a blur, but Daphne watches Cliona's and Bairre's reactions more than she watches the crowds that line the streets in Hapantoile, shouting and waving as they pass. She can almost see the city through their eyes—how it's so big that Eldevale could fit within it at least three times, how the buildings are taller, the roads paved and smooth, the tidy shops and houses in neat rows. Daphne knows it's nothing like any place they've seen because until a couple of months ago, Friv was nothing like any place *she'd* ever seen. She wonders if they're already missing their country the way she missed Bessemia in those days.

She can't blame them if they are—she herself finds that she's missing the unrefined edges of Friv, how even in the country's capital, the wild woods encroached on all sides, how the snowcapped mountains loomed to the north like sleeping giants watching over the city, how crisp the very air tasted.

All too soon they arrive at the palace, and that, too, is something new to Bairre and Cliona—bigger, newer, more elegant than the castle in Friv, which for most of its existence was first and foremost a fortress. Daphne knows that in past centuries the Bessemian palace has acted as a fortress itself, that it did its duty of protecting the people within while war raged outside its walls, but looking at its delicate spires and polished white stone walls, she can't imagine it. Surely it would crumble under the slightest breeze.

The empress disembarks from her carriage first, handed down by a footman in a resplendent blue silk gown that somehow doesn't have a single wrinkle despite the hours of travel.

Another crowd has formed along the palace steps, cheering for the empress as she ascends the marble stairs and falling silent when she reaches the top and turns to face them, lifting a hand. When she speaks, her voice carries enough that even Daphne can hear her from inside the carriage.

"I am happy to be home and happier still to find such a warm welcome," she says, beaming at the crowd, which hangs on her every word, just as Daphne does even still. When her mother speaks in front of a crowd like this, she never fails to hold them in the palm of her hand, a skill Daphne has tried so hard to mimic but has never managed quite so well. This is her mother's gift, Daphne knows. Diplomacy, strategy, politics, and statesmanship were all skills the empress had to learn as she went, but this is the charisma that first drew the emperor's attention and held it, that lured allies to her when she should have had none. Daphne has always been awed by this facet of her mother, but now it terrifies her just as much. "My journey to Friv was a fruitful one, and I discovered that our beloved Princess Sophronia—now Queen Sophronia of Temarin—is indeed alive."

She pauses as the cheers rise up again, this time deafening. Daphne feels many eyes turn to her carriage, no doubt expecting that Sophronia is inside. She knows with an aching certainty that they'll be disappointed to realize it's only her. Not that she can blame them for that. But she waits, listening to her mother's next words, curious how she'll choose to spin the myth of Sophronia being alive without ever producing her in the flesh.

"Unfortunately," the empress continues when the crowd falls silent again, "the Temarinian usurpers who attempted to kill her and her husband, King Leopold, also learned of their location, and they were forced back into hiding in order to save themselves."

A wave of *boo*s washes over the crowd, and the empress allows it.

"I assure you that I am doing everything in my power, both as your empress and as my daughter's mother, to ensure that she and King Leopold are able to come out of hiding and reclaim their thrones soon. It is my greatest wish to see Temarin ruled by its rightful king and queen. But while that day is not upon us yet, I bring more joyous news from Friv—Princess Daphne has married Prince Bairre and is now Princess of Friv, cementing the alliance between our countries for generations to come."

More cheers at that, and Daphne knows where this is heading. She glances at Bairre, who is watching the empress with the same reluctantly rapt attention Daphne feels herself. "Whatever she says, don't stop smiling," she warns him.

"What?" he asks, turning to her with a puzzled frown, but Daphne doesn't have time to answer him because the empress is speaking again.

"And I'm *so* thrilled that the newlyweds have decided to pay Bessemia a visit," she says, gesturing toward the carriage Daphne, Bairre, and Cliona are in. On her cue, a footman opens the carriage door as the crowd erupts into cheers and applause again. This time the sound is deafening.

Bairre steps out first, but rather than letting the footman move forward to help Daphne down, Bairre turns to her, extending his hand, which Daphne takes, and after a second the bemused footman steps back. Daphne knows it wasn't a calculated move on Bairre's part, that in Friv there is no rigid protocol about carriage etiquette, but Daphne doesn't think she could have choreographed it any better if she'd tried. Because while the crowd might have expected Bessemia's least-favorite princess—not as beautiful or bold as Beatriz, not as sweet or kind as Sophronia—to smile and wave alongside the second-choice husband everyone knows neither she nor her mother selected for her, a bastard Frivian prince likely as wild and uncouth as his country is known to be, what they are seeing instead as Bairre takes hold of Daphne's hand is a love story.

No, Daphne may not be their favorite among her sisters, a fact that she has been keenly aware of for as long as she can remember, but if there's one thing she's learned from her mother, it is how to spin a narrative, and everyone loves a love story. Bairre moves to release her hand when her feet are firmly on the ground, but she holds fast to him, lacing her fingers with his as they walk up the marble steps toward her mother, the crowd cheering around them. If Bairre is surprised by the gesture, he recovers quickly, keeping their hands clasped even as they reach the top, coming to stand in front of the empress.

Cliona has stepped out of the carriage behind them, but she hangs back alongside the empress's entourage and the handful of attendants that accompanied them from Friv.

Daphne and Bairre have to release each other's hands to turn and face the cheering crowd, but then Daphne reaches for his hand again and Bairre catches on to what she's doing, lifting their joined hands to his lips and brushing a kiss over her knuckles, which causes the crowd to go even wilder than they did for the empress herself.

"Kiss her!" someone shouts, a cheer picked up by the rest of the crowd. Daphne summons a blush to her cheeks and makes a show of biting her lip and glancing back at her mother, as if for permission, though really she wants to see her mother's expression. The empress gives nothing away, a broad smile spread over her face, but that in and of itself is a tell to Daphne, who knows every one of her mother's different smiles better than anyone. This, she knows, is her annoyed smile, and while it used to sow anxiety and dread in Daphne, now it feels like a triumph.

The empress inclines her head in acquiescence, and Daphne's smile widens. She turns back to Bairre, who looks uncertain.

"Come on," she whispers without moving her lips. "Make it good."

Bairre smiles at the challenge and bends his head toward her, but Daphne meets him halfway, rising onto the tips of her toes. The kiss is briefer and more chaste than others they've shared, but the crowd doesn't care. They grow so loud Daphne can't hear anything else, not even her own thoughts or the quickened beating of her heart.

As soon as they reach the palace's entry hall, the empress's smile—still her annoyed one, Daphne notes—falls away, replaced by pursed lips as her eyes dart between Daphne and Bairre. Daphne prepares herself for the lash of her mother's ire now that they don't have the protection of an audience, but the verbal blow never comes.

"I'll send the physician to your rooms to attend you," she says.

"Which rooms are we staying in?" Daphne asks her.

The empress tilts her head to one side as if Daphne's question confuses her. "You'll be in your old rooms, Daphne," she says slowly. "I thought you would prefer it, no? You have such memories there, after all, and it's your home."

If the empress expects Daphne to argue about that, she'll be disappointed. Daphne *would* prefer to return to the old rooms she shared with her sisters. Staying anywhere else in the palace would feel unnatural. But she also can't imagine Bairre in those rooms—she could sooner picture the sun rising in the night sky. Still, she doesn't want to be separated from him with her mother so close. Logically, she knows her mother can't directly strike out at either of them while they're in the palace, but she also knows better than to underestimate her mother.

She decides not to ask for clarification and instead presume what she wants to hear—another trick she picked up from her mother.

"Oh, I would. That's very considerate of you, Mama. Wait until you see them," she says, turning to Bairre, keeping her voice bright. "Mama had the mantel in the sitting room commissioned to commemorate mine and my sisters' birth constellations—"

"Oh no, my dove," the empress cuts in, just as Daphne suspected she would. "I assumed Bairre would be more comfortable in the guest wing. Your rooms were designed for young girls, after all, and even if he doesn't mind all the pink and frills, I daresay he'll find the furniture uncomfortably small."

That strikes Daphne as a flimsy excuse. While the most recent renovation of the rooms happened when Daphne and her sisters were fourteen, she knows the beds are large enough for entire families, and the sofas and chairs scattered throughout, while constructed to appear dainty, are as big and sturdy as any other furnishings she's seen in the palace.

She's tempted to let it be and concede this choice to her mother. Perhaps a few weeks ago she would have been all too eager to accept her mother's orders without question, but now she is keenly aware that everything between them is a battle and that every bit of ground she cedes will cost her twice over in the looming war.

And even more, she is aware of the power she herself wields. The girl she was when she left Bessemia was little more than her mother's shadow, but that girl is gone.

She gives her smile a sharp edge. "Oh no, I *must* stay with my husband, Mama," she replies. "Imagine what people would say!" Though Daphne is sure that after her and Bairre's show outside, gossip about their marriage is precisely what the empress hopes to accomplish. "And I'm sure the furniture in my old rooms is perfectly fine for him—why, Beatriz, Sophronia, and I managed to pile onto all the chairs and sofas together plenty of times, and if they can hold the three of us, I'm sure Bairre will have no complaints. Isn't that right?" she asks, looking at Bairre.

Bairre clears his throat. "I'm sure it is," he says, offering the empress a smile of his own. "And I have no qualms about pink or ruffles, I promise."

The empress's mouth tightens and Daphne can see the calculation behind her eyes, weighing the advantages and disadvantages of pushing back. After a moment, she gives a single nod.

"Very well," she says, her voice coming out pinched.

"Wonderful, thank you, Mama. I look forward to seeing the physician—that journey was absolute torture." She turns toward the stairs that lead to the hall where her rooms are, Bairre at her side, but she pauses and wheels to the guard standing at attention by the front door. "Oh, and when Lady Cliona arrives, will you send her up to my rooms as well? She can take Beatriz's or Sophronia's old room," she adds to her mother, whose mouth purses again.

"Daphne, at that I must draw the line," she says. "Lady Cliona can stay in the guest wing, with the other guests."

"Oh, I know she should," Daphne says with a sigh. "But Lady Cliona is still so newly grieving her poor father, Mama. I can't stand the idea of leaving her alone. She must be surrounded by friends during this trying time."

If Daphne and her mother were alone—or even just with Bairre—Daphne knows her mother would refuse her, likely with a particularly cutting if true comment about how Cliona doesn't consider Daphne a friend, but while only the guards can hear their conversation, they are still an audience, so the empress is forced to perform.

"That is very kind of you, Daphne," she says, and Daphne is sure she's the only one who hears how terse the compliment is. "I'm sure in this single instance, your sisters would be happy to lend their rooms to Lady Cliona."

Daphne thanks her before continuing up the stairs. It

was a small battle, she knows, but she is still walking away triumphant.

Daphne's small victory against her mother is short-lived. As soon as her guards open the door to her old apartments and she steps into the sitting room, she's bombarded by the ghosts of her sisters. She sees Sophronia curled up in the armchair near the bay window, her legs pulled up against her chest, gown wrinkling, with an open book propped against her knee. She sees Beatriz pacing in front of the fireplace, gesturing wildly with her hands as she rants or raves about something or other, so overflowing with emotion that she can't sit still. She sees the three of them in the ball gowns they wore to their sixteenth-birthday party, piled together on the sofa, drinking stolen champagne from stolen glasses. She remembers Sophronia's toast, the words imprinted in her memory.

*To seventeen.* Sophronia's voice whispers through Daphne's mind as if her sister is in the room with her now. *Sixteen is when we have to say goodbye. By seventeen, we'll be back here again. Together.*

Daphne had no reason to believe that that wasn't an inevitable fact then. Now, it's an impossibility.

She senses Bairre watching her, feeling very much like a caged, feral cat as she makes her way around the room, pausing when she reaches the cream damask rug in front of the sofa. There, barely visible unless one knows to look for it, is the hazy halo of the champagne Daphne spilled that night.

Bairre clears his throat, interrupting her thoughts and bringing her back to the present.

"The fireplace is remarkable," he says, and it takes Daphne a moment to remember her comment downstairs, about how he must see the fireplace, particularly the white marble inlaid with gold to represent Daphne's, Beatriz's, and Sophronia's birth constellations. It was a ploy, a way to drive the conversation with her mother where she needed it to go, but she follows Bairre's gaze to the fireplace now and nods.

"It is," she says, stepping closer to it and reaching her fingers out to trace the Sisters Three at the center. She's always been able to see herself and her sisters represented there, in the shape of those stars. "What stars were you born under?" she asks him.

"I didn't know for most of my life," he admits. "Not until my mother approached me and told me who she was."

Bairre was left outside the Frivian castle as a newborn, Daphne remembers, with a note stating his name and little else, certainly no mention of his birth chart. But of course Aurelia would know exactly what stars her son was born under, even if she had to crawl outdoors midlabor to see them.

He counts them off on his fingers. "The Tilting Hourglass." For patience. "The Whispering Wind." For intuition. "The Hero's Sword." For bravery. "And the Empyrea's Staff."

Daphne purses her lips at the last one. "For magic?" she asks.

He nods. "That was the most interesting one to my mother as well," he admits with an embarrassed smile. "She thought it meant I was destined to be an empyrea. She had a lot of questions for me at thirteen, though my answers must have disappointed her. Like every child, I tried to wish on stars, just to see if it worked. And since she told me about the Empyrea's Staff, I've kept trying. Every so often, I still try, but nothing ever happens. Each time I'm not sure whether I should be disappointed or relieved."

Daphne thinks of Beatriz—an empyrea, though she still can't quite believe it. Her magic is killing her, Pasquale said.

"Relieved, I think," she tells him.

Before he can respond, there's a sharp knock at the door.

"Cliona, probably," Daphne says, crossing to the door. No doubt Cliona will be annoyed at having to share rooms with Daphne, but Daphne doesn't care. Let her add it to the tab of her anger against Daphne—at least Daphne knows her mother can't reach Cliona so easily here.

But when Daphne opens the door, it isn't Cliona on the other side. Instead, it's Mother Ippoline.

Daphne blinks several times, certain she's imagining the imposing older woman, who has never said so much as a word to Daphne during her mother's council meetings or when Daphne and her sisters did any charity work with her Sororia.

"Mother Ippoline," she says, trying to hide her confusion with a polite smile. She glances at the guards standing on either side of her door, and one gives an apologetic shrug. Daphne can't quite blame them for not turning Mother Ippoline away. Even if they aren't devout, Mother Ippoline is an impressive force, rivaling even the empress herself in some ways. Daphne thinks quickly. Mother Ippoline is, after all, on her mother's council, which means Daphne doesn't trust her. "My mother said she was sending someone to heal me, but I confess I'd hoped she meant my body and not my soul."

Mother Ippoline's eyes narrow. "Impudent," she chides. Daphne doesn't think that word has ever been applied to her before—Beatriz, certainly, but never Daphne. But instead of feeling chastened, she's almost flattered. Behind her, she hears Bairre laugh, though he turns it into a cough. "I suppose that must be your husband."

Daphne steps back, making quick introductions, but she is acutely aware of the guards' attention, and that every word of this encounter will doubtless find its way to her mother's ear before the day is done.

"Would you like to come in, Mother?" Daphne asks, though loath as she is to give the guards a show, she also doesn't want to let one of her mother's council members into her rooms. She's relieved when Mother Ippoline purses her lips, eyes darting between Daphne and Bairre.

"I would not," she says curtly. "But I should like to see both of you at the Sororia come nightfall."

Daphne frowns. She's never been to the Sororia before and has no interest in remedying that fact. "Whatever for?" she asks.

"Your marriage rites were performed in Friv," Mother Ippoline says, speaking slowly as if to a child. It grates on Daphne, but she manages to keep hold of her smile. "You are now in Bessemia."

"Are you saying our marriage isn't valid here?" Bairre asks from over her shoulder. "Surely another wedding isn't necessary."

"Not another wedding, no," Mother Ippoline says. "But I should like to bless you in the light of the Bessemian stars all the same, to leave no doubt as to the validity of your union."

Daphne hesitates, the invitation making her uneasy, though curiosity nags at her to accept. She knows there must be more that Mother Ippoline isn't saying—she just isn't sure she wants to hear it.

"Princess Beatriz and Prince Pasquale did it during their visit," Mother Ippoline says. "Though I suppose that isn't the strongest of endorsements, considering the tragedy that union became."

As far as Mother Ippoline and the rest of the country knows, Pasquale is dead and a traitor, and Beatriz is marrying his cousin, King Nicolo. A tragedy indeed, Daphne supposes. All the same, she finds herself eager to trace her sister's steps, to learn what she learned while she was here. The Sororia is as good a place to start as any.

She glances at Bairre, who nods as if reading her mind, before looking back at Mother Ippoline with a smile. "Very well, then," she says. "We look forward to it."

# Daphne

The afternoon passes in a blur. The physician Daphne's mother sent arrives, and when Daphne tells him the only lingering symptom of her fall in Friv is some muscle aches, he withdraws a vial of stardust from his leather medical case. Rather than giving it to her to use herself, as she's always done in the past, the physician makes the wish. Her muscles scream with a brief burst of pain before going quiet, all traces of achiness gone.

"Thank you," she says to him, but when she asks for more stardust in case the pain returns later, he shakes his head with an apologetic smile and no further explanation as he packs up his case and leaves. Daphne doesn't require an explanation, though.

"My mother's orders, I expect," she tells Bairre, who has watched the exchange quietly from a chair by the window. "Though whether it was her plan to begin with or retaliation for arguing with her downstairs, I can't say."

"Surely you can find stardust easily regardless," Bairre says. "There must be merchants happy to sell it to you."

Daphne isn't sure. "A few years ago, Sophie tore her favorite gown, but my mother said it was a just punishment for her clumsiness. The royal seamstress refused to mend it on her orders. Beatriz tried to take it to one of the seamstresses in Hapantoile, but they all refused to mend the gown. Beatriz said she even tried to buy thread in the same color as the gown so she could fix it herself—and what a disaster that would have been, given Beatriz's impatience—but they wouldn't even sell her that. Eventually, Sophronia had no choice but to throw the gown out." She remembers how sad her sister was, how she touched the delicate blush silk reverently before she handed the dress to a maid to discard. And the lesson did nothing to remedy Sophronia's clumsiness.

Not a lesson, Daphne corrects herself, seeing that memory through new eyes. It was simply a cruelty.

"Perhaps I can convince someone to sell it to me," Bairre says, though that, too, Daphne doubts. But she knows that having stardust on hand could be a welcome boon if the empress has her backed against a wall.

"Cliona may have better luck," Daphne says before frowning. "Where is she? I'd have thought she'd have arrived by now."

Bairre frowns, glancing behind him at the window, the sky outside darkening to dusk. "I don't know," he admits. "But surely she'll be here when we return from the Sororia."

Night has just fallen when Daphne and Bairre arrive at the Sororia in a carriage. Daphne was unsure whether they would be allowed to leave the palace, but when she told her guards of her intentions, they made sure that a carriage was waiting in front of the palace for them. Two of the guards followed the carriage on horseback, so Daphne knows she is in no way free from her mother's reach, but it's still more freedom than she expected.

She supposes she's meant to feel grateful for the trust, that she's meant to soften toward the empress. That if the empress isn't treating her like a threat, perhaps Daphne shouldn't view her as one either.

If that was the empress's goal, though, she's failed. Mother Ippoline greets them at the front door with same pursed lips and mirthless eyes she seems always to wear, and before Daphne can attempt to order the guards to remain outside, Mother Ippoline beats her to it.

"I'll not allow weapons inside the Sororia," she tells them. "But you are welcome to do your duty here and ensure that no threats breach our walls."

The guards exchange a look, but there is no arguing with her. If they offer to lay down their weapons, they'll expose their true purpose in following Daphne—not to protect her but to watch her.

Perhaps, Daphne thinks as she and Bairre follow Mother Ippoline into the Sororia, Daphne's reading of her was flawed. But she isn't ready to trust her quite yet, so she continues to play the fool.

"Where will we receive the stars' blessing, Mother?" she asks, glancing around the hallway Mother Ippoline leads them down, lit by golden sconces and lined with paintings of ancient saints martyring themselves in ways as creative as they are gruesome.

Mother Ippoline scoffs. "I have yet to treat you like a simpleton, Princess," she says without glancing back at them.

"And I would appreciate it if you granted me the same courtesy. Your sister certainly did."

At the mention of Beatriz, Daphne's heart gives a kick. She felt Beatriz's presence in the palace, but they spent most of their lives together in those halls. Now, though, she's struck by the knowledge that her sister walked these corridors, that she spoke to Mother Ippoline and likely had the same reservations Daphne herself feels about the woman's loyalty.

"My sister is nicer than I am," she says.

"Is she?" Mother Ippoline says, turning left down a smaller hallway, Daphne and Bairre at her heels. "I always heard you were the most charming."

Daphne has heard that too. Her mother always said that Daphne could convince a snake to eat its own tail. Still . . . "Nice and charming have little to do with one another. Charm is an arsenal. Sometimes niceness holds a weapon within it, but even then it's a facade put up to serve a point."

Mother Ippoline considers this. "And yet you feel no need to put up that facade with me?" she asks, sounding almost amused. "Should I be offended?"

"Flattered, I think," Bairre says. "It means she doesn't think you'd be fooled by it."

Daphne glances sideways at Bairre, surprised at the frank appraisal, though she can't argue with it.

"Then I'm flattered," Mother Ippoline says, her voice warmer than Daphne has ever heard it in the lifetime she's known the woman. She stops in front of a polished oak door with a cut-crystal doorknob and knocks three times. After a hesitation, a woman's voice shouts for them to come in. Mother Ippoline pushes the door open and gestures them into a large, well-lit sitting room warmed by a fire in the hearth. Two dozen women are seated—some clustered on the sofas and chairs but many sitting on the rug itself, the skirts of their dresses settled around them like flower petals.

It's the dresses themselves that surprise Daphne. Half, she would guess, are the gray dresses worn by Mother Ippoline and the sisters who live in the Sororia, but the other half are brighter in color and bolder in cut, showing off as much skin as the sisters are careful to hide.

"Princess Daphne, Prince Bairre," Mother Ippoline says, nodding toward the lone woman standing. She's maybe a decade younger than Mother Ippoline, with dark brown hair threaded with gray that hangs loose around her shoulders. The dress she wears is loose and light, but Daphne can tell even at a glance that it was expensive, made from silk embroidered with gold that is shimmery and almost sheer in the firelight. The woman is looking at Daphne with appraising eyes and a slight smile to her full, painted mouth. "May I introduce my sister, Elodia," Mother Ippoline says. "I believe you have mutual friends."

Daphne looks at the woman uncertainly for a moment. Mother Ippoline called her *sister,* but Daphne doesn't think she meant it in the way that all the women who call the Sororia home are *sisters*. There's a resemblance in their eyes, she thinks, and though she can't see Mother Ippoline's hair beneath her wimple, she wonders if it's the same shade of brown—with a bit more gray threaded in, perhaps.

Still, Daphne is wary. "What friends might those be?" she asks, aware of the attention of the other women in the room weighing on her skin.

Elodia smiles, as if Daphne's mistrust is endearing. "I'm the madam of the Crimson Petal," she says. "Does that ring any bells?"

It does, and judging by the way Bairre straightens, he recognizes the name too. "Violie," Daphne says.

"My daughter," another of the women in the bold dresses says, this one younger and blond and the very image of Violie, the more Daphne looks at her. "And we recently hosted some other friends of yours at the Crimson Petal for a night before they went on their way."

Leopold, Pasquale, and Ambrose, Daphne knows. She glances around the room, looking at the Sisters in their habits and the women she now realizes are courtesans in their bright gowns. She doesn't think she could have imagined a less likely group to gather, but she can wager a guess at what, exactly, has brought them together.

"I take it the empress doesn't know about this?" she says, glancing at Mother Ippoline with raised eyebrows.

Mother Ippoline's smile is pointed. "*An* empress does," she says with a shrug before nodding toward the woman seated at the center of the sofa, dressed in the habit of a Sister but with what Daphne immediately recognizes as the bearing of royalty. "Sister Heloise, though she was formerly known as Empress Seline of Bessemia."

Daphne's thoughts fog over. There is only one living Empress of Bessemia as far as she knows. But then . . . she doesn't know everything where her mother is concerned, does she? Strangely, Bairre doesn't look half as surprised as she feels.

"Your Majesty," he says, bowing his head before pausing. "Is that still the correct address?"

"No, but I appreciate it all the same," the woman—Sister Heloise now—says, her eyes on Daphne. "Stars above, you truly are the very image of your mother."

It isn't the first time Daphne's heard that. Once, she considered it a compliment. But the way Sister Heloise says it certainly doesn't sound like a compliment.

Sister Heloise continues. "Your sister—Beatriz—didn't know who I was, and it seems you don't either."

Bairre glances sideways at her, brows raised. "Empress Seline was the wife of Emperor Aristede," he explains. "The first wife."

Pieces slide into place in Daphne's mind. But . . .

"Let me guess—you, too, believed I was dead?" Sister Heloise asks. "I'm sure I would have been if I hadn't recognized a losing battle when I saw one. Your mother was a strong adversary, and one who played by no one's rules but her own. I knew that it was only a matter of time before she or my husband got rid of me, and there are only two ways for an empress to vacate her role. I chose the one that let me keep my life."

Daphne looks at the woman, an empress erased from history. Ripped out at the seams without so much as a stray thread left behind. And all this time, she's been living in the shadow of the palace. Daphne isn't sure whether she finds the woman's story to be a tragedy or a triumph.

"I told Princess Beatriz to make the same choice," Sister Heloise continues. "To run while she still could."

Daphne laughs—she can't help it; the thought of Beatriz ever running from a fight is every bit as unimaginable as her wearing the habit of a Sister.

"Yes, Princess Beatriz laughed too," Sister Heloise says. "I thought her a brave fool, but then I began to hear things, rumors that made their way even inside the Sororia walls, stirring a feeling that I haven't felt in quite some time. Hope."

"What rumors?" Daphne asks.

"Your sister healed one of my girls," Elodia says, motioning to Violie's mother. "A woman she never met. And she did it by pulling magic from a star."

"I saw it happen during my nightly prayers," Mother Ippoline says. "I cursed Princess Beatriz at the time for a foolish novice empyrea, learning her gift at the expense of our sky."

"You knew what she was?" Bairre asks.

"Nigellus told me soon after he realized himself, but I had my own suspicions long before. I thought the stars had a strange sense of humor in choosing her—after all, empyreas must be cautious above all else, and Princess Beatriz has never been that. But then I saw the constellation she pulled a star from—the Glittering Diamond—reappear in the sky a couple of nights later, and I realized a new star had risen in the place of the one your sister took down. The constellation was as whole as it has ever been in my lifetime."

"Violie and her friends confirmed it during their stay at the Crimson Petal," Elodia says. "That Beatriz can not only pull stars from the sky, but create new ones."

"She could," Daphne confirms. "But our mother knew it too—at least that Beatriz was an empyrea—and she found a way to bind her power. I tried to use . . ." She trails off. The wish bracelet will be too difficult to explain, and she feels like a fool for wasting the wish in the first place. "Well, I tried to break the bind from here, but it didn't work."

Mother Ippoline's brow furrows. "Are you certain about that?" she asks.

"Of course I am," Daphne says. "That was two days ago now. If it had worked, Beatriz would be here, or at least would have gotten word to me."

At that, a murmur ripples through the room, women turning to one another and speaking in low voices, but Daphne catches a few phrases. *She hasn't heard. No one told her. How could she miss it?*

Uncertainty settles over her skin and she turns to Mother Ippoline, who smiles.

"Last night, a starshower fell over Cellaria—over Vallon, specifically," she says. "It was a thing to behold, even at a great distance—we could see it from our windows. You didn't see it?"

Daphne shakes her head. They'd been traveling, holed up in a carriage farther north. But her mother was more irritated than usual this morning, and she was quick to give in to Daphne's insistence over the room arrangements—a small battle, Daphne thought, but her mother had bigger ones to fight, it seemed.

"What does it mean?" she asks, not quite daring to hope that it means what she thinks.

"It'll be some time before word of what happened makes

its way from Vallon to Hapantoile, but I don't believe it's a coincidence that the starshower happened on the night of what was meant to be Beatriz's wedding to King Nicolo."

Daphne's breath stutters. She can see it so clearly—Beatriz waiting until the wedding to use her magic, and causing quite the spectacle when she did. Beatriz always had a flair for the dramatic. A laugh forces its way past her lips.

"Beatriz did it," she says. "Beatriz summoned a starshower. To *Cellaria*."

"That is our theory as well," Elodia says. "And if it holds true, I assume Beatriz will be coming back to Bessemia as soon as she's able."

"Yes," Daphne agrees, remembering her last words to Beatriz, urging her to meet her in Hapantoile so they could fight their mother together.

"And what's your plan for when she does?"

At that, Daphne's joy dims slightly. Do they have a plan? She feels like the entirety of her plan so far has been to stay alive, to keep Bairre and Cliona alive. It's been all she *could* do. But with Beatriz here, they'll be able to do so much more. Instead of constantly defending themselves, they'll be able to actually attack.

"It's a work in progress," she says, her thoughts already turning. If Beatriz has the power of the stars on her side, what can't she do? Still, the empress bound her powers once, she can do it again. Which will mean they need a backup plan. And a backup to that plan as well, knowing the empress.

"You'll have our help in whatever it may be," Mother

Ippoline says, gesturing to the room and to the women gathered, Sisters and courtesans together, united in a common goal.

Daphne smiles. In her mother's wildest dreams, she couldn't imagine what's coming for her.

# Beatriz

Beatriz wakes to moonlight streaming through her window, her bones feeling like they've been replaced with lead—so heavy she can't move more than to open her eyes and blink around the room. The headache that erupts when she does is so painful that for a brief, startling moment she finds herself hoping death takes her, if only to spare her from it. She closes her eyes again and tries to think past the pain, to remember the circumstances that led her here.

Fragments of the night before piece together—the wedding-turned-coup-turned-miracle, the wish that she thought for sure would kill her but appears not to have after all.

Despite her earlier desperate thought, she's glad it didn't. She has so much more to do before she leaves this world, and the stars will have to drag her, kicking and screaming, if they hope to take her sooner than that.

"It'll pass soon." A voice cuts through her thoughts, and without thinking, she opens her eyes, the pain that follows warring with confusion as she takes in the strange woman standing at the foot of her bed, with a wild mass of dark brown hair and silver eyes that glitter in the moonlight.

Instantly, Beatriz is on edge, her wariness only slightly

lessened by the knowledge that if this woman wanted her dead, she could have killed her while she slept and been done with it.

But she is still a star-touched woman in a land where until very recently that trait alone would have been enough to see her imprisoned or dead.

"Who are you?" Beatriz asks, her voice coming out on a rasp.

The woman's mouth curves into something that might be considered a smile, though there is little warmth in it. "My name is Aurelia," she says. "It seems a wonder that we haven't yet met, given how much I know about you."

*Aurelia.* Beatriz knows that name, but it takes her a moment to remember where she heard it—or rather, where she saw it. In the letter she found in Nigellus's laboratory, the one telling him that Beatriz was a mistake he needed to fix and assuring him she would do the same with Daphne. Aurelia is the name of the empyrea from Friv.

"Give me one reason I shouldn't scream for help," she says.

If Aurelia is surprised at her reaction, she doesn't show it. Instead, she holds up a hand, showing a vial of stardust. "Because it wouldn't be worth the headache screaming would cost you," she tells her. "And because whatever pain you're feeling now, I can lessen."

It's a more compelling argument than Beatriz is keen to admit. Still . . . "How do I know it isn't poison?" she asks. When Aurelia's eyebrows arch, Beatriz manages a small smile, relieved that the woman in front of her doesn't know everything Beatriz does. "You told Nigellus to kill me, more or less."

"Ah," Aurelia says, understanding lighting her eyes. "Yes, well, you seem to be doing a good enough job of that on your own." She pauses, tilting her head and regarding Beatriz with mild curiosity. "Did you kill him?"

Beatriz isn't fooled by her casual tone, but she's too exhausted to lie.

"Yes," she says. "He was trying to take my magic and it was the only way to stop him. I don't regret it."

Aurelia looks at Beatriz like she doesn't quite believe her, but after a second, she nods. "He was a pompous fool, but there are few of us empyreas in the world and for all his faults I did consider him a friend."

Silence follows before Beatriz breaks it. "If you're expecting an apology from me, you won't get one," she says. "Though I am increasingly tempted to scream, headache or no."

Aurelia huffs out something that sounds like a laugh. "If I sought to kill you, Princess, I'd have smothered you with a pillow while you slept," she said. "And I've no use for an apology—I'd have killed him too in your position."

Beatriz eyes the stardust in Aurelia's hand for a moment before inclining her head in a nod of assent. "But," she says when Aurelia steps toward her, uncorking the vial, "I make the wish myself."

"Of course," Aurelia says, holding the vial out to her.

Beatriz tries to lift her arms and fails, her muscles too weak even for that, but Aurelia lifts her hand for her, her skin cool against Beatriz's. Beatriz begrudgingly accepts her help in pouring the stardust on the back of her hand; then she closes her eyes and wishes.

"I wish I felt as strong and healthy as I usually do," she says.

She sucks in a deep breath as the pain in her body and head flares, briefly, before fading. It doesn't disappear completely, but it's muted and manageable. She has no trouble pulling her hand from Aurelia's, though she doubts she'll be able to do anything more strenuous than a walk about the room anytime soon.

"Good enough," she says, sitting up straighter in her bed. Someone, at some point, changed her out of her wedding gown and into a nightgown, she realizes with some discomfort, though she knows she has bigger issues at present. "Now, what do you want?" she asks Aurelia.

"You caused a starshower in Cellaria last night," Aurelia tells her, as if Beatriz could somehow forget the wish that led her to be bedbound in the first place. "The first one in several centuries."

"Five, to be exact," Beatriz says. "I don't require a history lesson."

"You require patience," Aurelia replies tersely.

It's hardly the first time Beatriz has heard that, but she closes her mouth and indicates that Aurelia should continue.

"I did believe you and your sisters were abominations," Aurelia admits. "An experiment fueled by Nigellus's curiosity and hubris that would destroy us all, just as has been prophesized for centuries." She pauses. "Eight, to be exact," she adds, echoing Beatriz's earlier glibness. "But I was wrong."

Beatriz is quiet for a moment, turning over not just Aurelia's words but what she leaves unspoken. Aurelia couldn't have arrived in Cellaria so quickly after the starshower unless she was already nearby, and Beatriz feels certain that her reason for coming here in the first place had to do with Beatriz. If Aurelia had found her way into Beatriz's bedchamber two nights before, when she was deep in a drugged sleep before her wedding, Beatriz suspects Aurelia would have indeed smothered her with a pillow.

Nigellus's betrayal still stings, and Beatriz isn't inclined to repeat the mistakes she made with him, but she also knows that it's best to keep her enemies close. And, as loath as Beatriz is to admit it, she still doesn't understand her power or exactly how it's killing her. With Nigellus dead, Aurelia very well may be the only empyrea who can help her understand her magic and its limits.

"What do you think I am, then?" she asks Aurelia. "If not an abomination."

Aurelia tilts her head to one side, as if considering the question carefully. "A star," she says finally.

Beatriz laughs—she can't help it. "You're joking."

But Aurelia doesn't laugh. "How foolish have we have all been, Princess, to believe something as powerful as a star could be destroyed by human hands? But it wasn't until I *saw* you summon the starshower, saw what it did to you in turn, that I truly understood the nature of our power. We empyreas don't destroy stars when we wish upon them—we give them new life, turn them into thread and sew them into our world and our lives, every bit as magical as they were when they hung in the sky."

Beatriz tries to follow Aurelia's thoughts. It is easy to think of her wish for the starshower in those terms, and even to reframe her wish for Violie's mother to heal as a way of sewing magic into the world. Less so, however, when she recalls the wish she inadvertently made for Nicolo to kiss her. And what's more . . .

"I don't see what that has to do with me," Beatriz says.

Aurelia smiles. "Don't you?" she asks. "You know that Nigellus pulled a star from the sky to create you and each of your sisters. If those stars weren't, in fact, destroyed, where could they have gone but inside you?"

Beatriz stares at her, speechless. Not because what Aurelia is saying doesn't make sense, but because it does. Because she's seen proof of it with her own eyes.

"The Lonely Heart," Beatriz says softly, more to herself than Aurelia. "After Sophronia died, a star I hadn't seen in the constellation before appeared. When I asked Nigellus about it, he was surprised—he said it was the star he'd pulled down to create Sophronia."

"She returned to her rightful place," Aurelia says. "Just as you yourself are returning, a little bit at a time."

Beatriz shakes her head.

"I'm afraid you've lost me," she says.

"I believe that each time you wish on a star, each time you pull one down, a part of the star within you returns to the sky to replace it. And each time, the star that Nigellus placed in you upon your birth dims a little more, grows a little weaker, killing the human parts of you in the process."

"I suppose that would be a reassurance if I weren't so fond of my human parts," Beatriz says. "And Daphne is a star as well?"

"Yes," Aurelia says. "Even if she doesn't wield magic the

way you do, when her time in this world is done, she, too, will return to the sky, just as Sophronia did."

There's comfort in that, at least, Beatriz thinks. She has no understanding of what it means to be a star, of how much of their human minds and memories will follow them to the sky, but there is a future where she, Daphne, and Sophronia will be together again.

But much as she misses Sophronia, Beatriz doesn't want that future to come anytime soon.

"What is it you want from me?" she asks Aurelia. "To use magic, to abstain from it?"

Aurelia looks at her for a long moment. "I wish for you to understand the consequences of your actions," she says. "I know enough of your story to know that right now, you're far more concerned with your mother than my prophecies or theories."

"My mother poses a very real threat," Beatriz says. "To me, to my sister, to all of Vesteria. Whatever words you believe the stars whispered in your ear don't."

Beatriz expects this will rankle Aurelia, but she simply shrugs.

"Not yet," Aurelia says. "And hopefully, that remains the case. But the war between you and your mother is not a war for the stars to fight on your behalf."

"Oh, they told you that, did they?" Beatriz asks.

"They didn't have to. I learned the hard way about the cost we incur by involving the stars in our wars, Princess. The thread we sew with when we wish our wishes can sometimes become a noose. I tried it once, used magic to place a man I believed to be a worthy king on Friv's throne, to stop centuries of war from dividing my homeland and drenching it in blood; I laced his legacy with magic I believed him worthy of. I asked too much from the stars, so they returned the favor. They took my magic and demanded my son as well."

"You have no magic?" Beatriz asks before she can register the mention of the son.

"I still have my prophecies," Aurelia says. "But while I haven't attempted to pull a star down from the sky since the night I made Bartholomew king, I know that power is gone from me."

Beatriz knows what she means by that—she remembers how different she felt when her own magic was bound, how she could no longer feel the pull of the stars.

"No one else knows," Aurelia adds. "Bartholomew wouldn't have named me his empyrea if he did."

"What of your son?" Beatriz asks.

Aurelia is quiet for a moment, a flash of pain crossing her face. "There is a prophecy I told your sister once, but I only told her part of it."

"Daphne?" Beatriz assumes. Aurelia nods.

"I told her that the stars had been repeating the same thing to me, that they'd been all but screaming it. The blood of stars and majesty spilled."

The words pool in Beatriz's stomach like oil. "Sophronia," she says.

"Yes," Aurelia says. "And, also, no. As I said, it wasn't the whole prophecy. The whole of it is this:

> *The blood of stars and majesty, distilled*
> *In the veins of a champion, who will lead us to light*
> *Or doom us to darkness, an unending blight.*
> *Choices made and prophecies fulfilled when*
> *The blood of stars and majesty, spilled."*

Beatriz's unease grows with each word Aurelia speaks. Not Sophronia. She understands why Aurelia seems sure that it's her, but she isn't eager to concede anything to prophecies. After all, Beatriz herself made one up just recently, to name Gisella Queen of Cellaria. She swallows.

"Perhaps you aren't giving Daphne enough credit," she says. "Or Prince Bairre, for that matter—I've heard he's star-touched as well."

At the mention of Bairre, Aurelia narrows her eyes, and Beatriz recalls what she was saying about the prophecy, how she tried to fulfill it herself—presumably by trying to create a child born of stars and majesty. The stars, Aurelia could handle herself, and if she made Bartholomew king, it stands to reason she knew him well.

"Bairre is your son," Beatriz says, recalling the few details she knows of Bairre's birth. He was found abandoned on the steps of the Frivian castle not long after Bartholomew was crowned king, after a hasty marriage and the birth of an heir to solidify Bartholomew's claim to the throne.

Aurelia hesitates for a moment before she shakes her head. She leans forward, dark brown hair obscuring her face. "No," she says after a moment. "Though I've led him to believe as much, for his sake as well as mine. Bairre's mother was Queen Darina; Bairre was born two weeks after my son, though he was big for his age, and my boy was small. They looked so similar, both the very image of their father, both star-touched—I suppose Bartholomew was eager for an heir to solidify his reign and used stardust to achieve it. I remember how they looked when I laid them down beside each other in the royal bassinet—they could have been twins."

Beatriz hears what Aurelia doesn't quite say. "You took the prince—the real Cillian—and left the bastard in his place," she says.

Aurelia nods. "I had no desire to raise a baby that wasn't mine," she says. "But I kept him for a few months, called him by my true son's name, cared for him. And when he'd grown enough that I was confident no one would confuse him with his half brother, I left him in his bassinet on the steps of the palace. I thought . . . I suppose I thought it was a small kindness, to keep him close with his mother, even if I couldn't remain close to my own son. Though from what he—Bairre, as he's now known—told me, Darina spared him no love or kindness. A tragedy for both of them, I suppose."

"A tragedy you inflicted," Beatriz points out. "Because you wanted your blood to run through the veins of the star's champion."

"And I paid for it," Aurelia says, her voice rough. "By then, my magic was gone and I thought my price paid, but they weren't satisfied with that, so they took him too, my boy. I watched from afar as the stars drained him of life before he reached seventeen. The stars calling back the piece of them I stole for the sake of my ambition."

"Did he have magic?" Beatriz asks.

Aurelia shakes her head. "No, as it turns out. But the sky called him home all the same. And if you expect me to have some reason for why they took him while you and your sister still live, I don't have an answer for you. Making sense of the stars' motives is a fool's game, as I've long since learned."

Aurelia looks pitiable now, mouth twisted and eyes red with unshed tears, but Beatriz has no pity for her. "It must have been terrible for you," she says coolly. "To watch all of your schemes and plots for him die with his body."

Aurelia's glare is so sharp Beatriz can almost feel it, but she doesn't heed it.

"You and my mother are exactly the same," Beatriz says. "But at least my mother's plan was a smart one, built on more than a hallucinated interpretation of the stars' words. Instead you threw your son's life away for nothing at all. And if you expect any sympathy from me for it, you'll be waiting a very long time."

"I made mistakes, yes," Aurelia says. "But I don't need sympathy from you—I need you to learn the lesson I couldn't. Because even if you have a star in you, you're more human than not, and as humans, we serve the stars. They don't serve us. And should you forget that, they will remind you by taking everything you love, whether you're one of them or not."

From what Aurelia has just told her, Beatriz doubts that she bore her son any love at all, but she understands the warning all the same. It doesn't necessarily mean that she believes the warning, or that she can promise to heed it, but she does understand it.

"Fine," she says, smoothing her hands over the duvet covering the lower half of her body. "But my mother poses a very imminent, very real threat, and the last I heard, my sister was with her in Bessemia, ready to go to war with her alone if need be. I don't intend to let her do that, so magic or no, I'm leaving for Bessemia tomorrow morning, as early as possible. I can't stop you from joining me, but you would be far more welcome if you had enough stardust to hasten our journey."

Aurelia opens her mouth—no doubt not quite done with her omens and warnings—but Beatriz has heard enough. She reaches for the velvet rope hanging beside her bed. "You can leave now, of your own accord, or you can explain yourself to Cellaria's new queen, which I personally wouldn't recommend."

For a moment, Aurelia looks like she wants to call Beatriz's bluff, but when Beatriz gives the rope a sharp tug, she inclines her head with a small smile. "Until tomorrow, then, Princess," she says.

By the time the servant Beatriz rings for alerts Cellaria's new queen to her recovery, Beatriz has managed to drag herself out to the sitting room sofa—a feat that would have been impossible before the stardust Aurelia gave her but is still difficult. By tomorrow, though, she should be back to her full strength. She'll need to be, because lingering any longer in Cellaria won't be an option. Daphne told Beatriz to meet her in Bessemia, and Beatriz doesn't intend to keep her waiting.

When the door opens, Pasquale enters first, just ahead of Gisella, now officially crowned with a gleaming gold-and-ruby crown, Nicolo trailing just behind, his own blond hair now unadorned, and Ambrose rounding out the group.

"Not that I'm unhappy to see all of you . . . well, *half* of you, but there's no need to swarm me all at once," Beatriz says, but when Pasquale reaches out for her, she takes his hand and pulls him to sit beside her. Ambrose sits down on Pasquale's other side, but Gisella and Nicolo remain standing.

"I do hope you'll forgive me for remaining seated, but I just don't think I could manage a curtsy at the moment," she says to Gisella, who fights a smile—seeing through the fib Beatriz didn't truly bother to hide. She could rise, if she really wanted to, and could likely even manage a decent curtsy. *If* she wanted to.

"Are you feeling all right?" Pasquale asks. "You *look* better than before."

"I do feel better," Beatriz says carefully, setting her teacup down on the low table in front of the sofa. "Though I have Aurelia to thank for that—the Frivian empyrea. She appeared in my room just as I woke and offered me stardust to heal quicker," she adds before glancing at Gisella. "I missed an official proclamation, but I assume in admitting that I didn't just confess to a crime?"

"Merchants have been bringing in vials of the stuff since dawn," Gisella tells her. "I've tried it myself now—it got rid of the peskiest pimple that was haunting me for weeks." She reaches up to touch the side of her nose, as if in memory of the spot.

"If Aurelia is the Frivian empyrea," Ambrose says, frowning, "what's she doing here?"

Beatriz recounts her conversation with Aurelia; she feels Pasquale tense beside her.

"You don't trust her," he says.

"Of course not," Beatriz says, taking another sip of her tea. "But I'm also not fool enough to refuse any help she might give. In the fight against my mother, we need every weapon we can find, and while she doesn't have magic, I believe she might still be a weapon we can use." She sets her teacup down and turns to Gisella. "Which brings us to the next matter we need to discuss," she says.

Gisella seems to know where the conversation is going. "You made me queen, and I'm grateful for that," she says slowly. "But I can't have my first act as queen be to throw our army into a war that has nothing to do with Cellaria."

"I thought your first act was legalizing stardust," Beatriz says, unbothered.

"You know what I mean," Gisella says.

Nicolo clears his throat. He's been largely quiet since his public dethroning, reminding Beatriz of a dog with its tail between its legs, but now he speaks up. "Under other circumstances, I'd agree with you," he tells his sister. "But while you may be queen, Gigi, Beatriz is currently the most beloved person in Cellaria. You can't doubt that they would gladly go to war for her after what she's done for us. An army is a small price to pay for a miracle we've been waiting on for five centuries."

Gisella doesn't respond.

"She doesn't doubt it," Beatriz infers. "But that is,

precisely, what scares her. That despite the crown on her head, her subjects still prefer me to her."

"What *scares* me," Gisella snaps, her tone giving away how close Beatriz is to the truth, "is the very likely scenario where you lose and we lose with you. Your proclamation and prophecy were a nice touch, Beatriz, but I'm not about to trigger the trap you so cleverly wove in. Leading my people into a losing war would be many people's idea of betraying Cellaria, especially when the empress brings her own army to our borders, demanding vengeance. My reign wouldn't last the moon's cycle."

Beatriz winces, realizing that Gisella is right, but before she can summon a protest, Nicolo jumps in again.

"Do you believe it will last any longer if you refuse help to Cellaria's savior? The voice of the stars? The girl who brought magic to Cellaria again?" Nicolo asks.

"You know she isn't going to marry you, right?" Gisella snaps at her twin. "Save your flattery for a cause that hasn't already died a dozen painful deaths."

Nicolo's face flushes and Beatriz feels her own face warm, but Nicolo doesn't stand down. "You know as well as I do that the streets of Vallon are saying all of that and more," he says. "And by the week's end, so will the rest of Cellaria. Should she fail—should she die—while you refuse aid, who do you think the people of Cellaria will blame?"

Gisella's mouth snaps shut and she glowers at him.

"Not that I don't appreciate the support, Nicolo," Beatriz cuts in. "But since we're spinning hypothetical situations, I'd like to posit one where I don't die *or* fail. As you said, Gisella, you are a new queen—the first queen in Cellaria's history. You'll need allies outside your court as well. You may wish to hedge your bets, but you're still betting. And if Daphne and I do triumph over our mother, are you sure you want to make enemies of us?"

Gisella doesn't speak for a moment, but her face betrays the thoughts racing through her mind, frustrating her when they don't present a choice she likes.

"No one said being queen would be easy, Gigi," Beatriz says, allowing a taunt to slip into her voice. "I doubt it will be the last impossible choice you have to make, but in the end it's simple. Which enemy would you rather have? My mother, or me?"

Gisella considers that. "I'll loan you ten thousand soldiers," she says finally, shaking her head.

"How many are ready to ride at dawn?" Beatriz asks.

Gisella falters, unsure of the answer to that, but Nicolo steps in.

"Cellarian soldiers are always ready for war—King Cesare made sure of it," he says. "We can spare five thousand from the battalion based in Vallon, plus send word to two more battalions in the mountains that will be ready to join you as you pass."

Gisella purses her lips. "Take ten thousand and one," she says. "Nicolo will join as well."

Nicolo turns to his sister, bewildered. "I have no experience with war."

"You're good at bossing people around," she points out. "And you've always had a head for strategy. Besides, you asked for exile—consider this the start of it."

"Is this a punishment?" he asks her, sounding more hurt than surprised.

"It's an opportunity," Gisella says, her voice softening. "To decide who you want to be without me or anyone telling you."

"Despite the fact that you're *telling* me to be a soldier?" he asks.

"Consider it a choice, if you like, since we're all making difficult ones, apparently," she says, shrugging. "I won't force you, but either way—you can't stay in Cellaria. You know that as well as I do."

Nicolo looks at his sister for a long moment before turning toward Beatriz. "Then we leave at dawn," he says.

# Violie

Violie wakes to soft sunlight filtering through white linen curtains, but even that hazy brightness makes her groan and roll away from it. The bed she's in is soft, she realizes, so different from the hard, blood-soaked ground she remembers lying on. The events filter back to her—the certainty she was dying, how she felt the life leaving her body as surely as she felt Leopold's hand in hers, the desperation clawing at her chest, begging the stars to let her live. The stars that were falling over Cellaria—at Beatriz's command, she imagines.

She remembers Sophronia's voice whispering through her mind, granting her wish for life but warning she would soon yearn for death.

The pain that hit when the falling star crashed into her chest was unlike anything Violie had felt before—so intense she wanted to tear her own flesh from her bones in an effort to make it stop—but never once had she yearned for death. Which wasn't, of course, to say that she wouldn't yet.

Violie struggles to sit up, blinking heavy eyes as she looks around the room, taking in the clean white bedsheets, the plush four-poster bed, the thick wool rug covering most of the stone floor. *Where am I?* Her first thought is the inn, but if so this isn't the room she and Leopold stayed in before—it's bigger, with a larger bed and finer furnishings.

A room fit for a king, she realizes, just as the doorknob twists open and Leopold appears in the frame. When he sees her awake and sitting up, he sighs, the tension in his shoulders disappearing along with his breath.

"How are you feeling?" he asks.

Violie tries to smile, but even that hurts. "Like I got hit by a falling star," she says. "What happened?"

One side of Leopold's mouth lifts into a smile. "You got hit by a falling star," he says dryly.

"That, I remember," she says, shaking her head. "It's what happened before that, with the baron's army, and what I assume must have happened since that I'm unclear on."

"Right," Leopold says, coming into the room and closing the door behind him. He sits at the foot of her bed, close enough that she could reach out and touch him if she wanted to.

And she does want to, she realizes, a warm ache blossoming in her chest as her realization from the battlefield comes back to her. *I love him.*

"Apart from your being recognized, the rest of our plan went off without issue—with half the village armed, we took the occupying soldiers by surprise and overwhelmed them, taking their weapons and using them to arm the other half of the village," he says. "Freeing the girls from the granary was easy with that power, but that was when Janellia found us. She was distraught, but she managed to relay what you'd told her, that the baron was my uncle." Leopold lets out a low curse, shaking his head. "I should have seen it earlier—he was always a bitter, angry man, but I never thought he'd have it in him to amass such power."

"With you and your brothers gone, there was a power vacuum," Violie says. "And so he allied himself with the empress to take advantage of that."

"He allied himself with the empress long before that," Leopold says, reaching into his pocket and pulling out the heavy chain the baron wore, the one with Sophronia's wedding ring hanging from it like a charm. Violie's stomach sinks at the sight of it, at the thought of the baron taking it from Sophronia's lifeless body. "He admitted as much when I questioned him after the battle, and his men filled in what he didn't say. It would seem he was in the employ of the empress at least as long as you were."

Violie wishes she could summon surprise, but she can't. She knows better than most just how wide and deep the empress's network of spies goes. How much of the baron's drinking and gambling was real, she wonders, and how much of it was an act to keep anyone from suspecting there was more to him?

"And his army?" Violie asks. "Bessemian or Temarinian?"

"Temarinian," Leopold says. "Paid soldiers with alliance to his coin, mostly, but many others who swore allegiance to him because they had no other option and it seemed, at the very least, preferable to follow the orders of a countryman than one of the invaders. It was the only way they could take care of their families, and when I arrived with the villagers, almost all of them bent the knee right away."

"How many?" Violie asks.

Leopold shrugs. "The battalion was five hundred men," he says. "A little over four hundred changed their loyalty to me as soon as it became an option."

And they could change it back just as quickly, Violie knows, but when she says as much to Leopold, he shrugs again.

"And how many of them are asking themselves the same questions about my loyalty? They have every right to worry that as soon as I'm on the throne again, I'll go back to being the same useless king I was before," he points out. Violie opens her mouth to protest but shuts it quickly again. It's a fair point, but that doesn't mean she likes it. Leopold must see this, because he smiles softly. "Rebuilding Temarin won't be easy, Vi. For any of us. But if they're willing to help me do it, who am I to stop them? None of us are the worst decisions we've made."

*None of us are the worst decisions we've made.*

Leopold's words echo in the silence that follows them, digging their way into the pit of her stomach like seeds. She hopes one day they'll take root and she might actually believe them.

"And now?" she asks. "How long has it been since the battle?"

"Two days," Leopold says. "Long enough that everyone has celebrated, rested, and departed."

"Departed?" Violie asks. "Where?"

"Twenty-five volunteers riding south, twenty-five riding north, and fifty riding west," Leopold says. "Spreading stories and gathering support, just as you suggested. They'll stop where they can, tell anyone they meet what happened here, incite more rebellions in the villages and towns against the Bessemians occupying them."

He can't quite keep the excitement from his voice, and when he looks at her with nervous eyes, she realizes he's waiting to hear what she thinks of the plan.

"I think it's brilliant, Leo," she says softly. "With a little luck, you'll be marching into the Kavelle palace again before the last frost melts in spring."

Leopold's smile falters slightly. "You mean *we*," he says. "*We'll* be marching into the Kavelle palace."

When Violie doesn't respond, Leopold leans toward her, taking hold of her hands again. Violie tries to ignore the feeling of his skin against hers, warm and comforting and right.

"Vi, I can't do this without you," he says.

"Of course you can, Leo," she replies, squeezing his hands. "The last few days have proved that beyond any doubt. You don't need me."

Leopold hesitates a moment. "That doesn't mean I don't want you," he says quietly.

Violie bites her lip. She wants him, too. She wants to be at his side when he reclaims the palace, when he takes his throne, when the crown is placed on his head once more, this time earned and not just inherited. She wants to see him become the king she knows he can be.

But he doesn't need her. Daphne and Beatriz do.

"A starshower fell in Cellaria, Leo," she says. "You and I can both guess what that means—Beatriz has her magic back. If causing that starshower didn't kill her, she's on her way to Hapantoile as we speak, and she and Daphne will need all the help they can get to defeat the empress. That's a fight I need to see through to the end."

Leopold considers this, but Violie notes that he doesn't seem particularly surprised by the declaration.

"Even if I do manage to drive every Bessemian soldier out of Temarin, if the empress triumphs, my victory will be short-lived," he says quietly. "And I don't think Temarin could rise again from the ruin she will make of it."

"I won't let that happen," Violie promises him.

"And I believe you," Leopold says. "But it's my fight too. And I intend to see it through."

Violie shakes her head. "You're needed here, with your people," she says.

"My people do need me," Leopold agrees. "But the empress is a rot on all of Vesteria, and I can keep scrubbing my parts of it, or we can cut her out at the heart. The former is a temporary solution, and I won't sit idly by while someone else does the latter."

Violie understands that, but still . . .

"It won't do," she says softly. "For Temarin to see their king fleeing again."

"Not fleeing," Leopold corrects. "Marching. For Temarin, and with anyone else who wishes to join the fight. Does that include you, Violie?" he asks.

Violie looks at him, letting her eyes trace the sharp lines of his face, noting the ferocity that's taken up residence in his dark brown eyes. "Always," she tells him.

He smiles, relief clear in his expression, and Violie realizes he truly didn't believe that she would say yes. As if she wouldn't go to war on the stars themselves if Leopold were fighting beside her.

"You need rest," he says. "We'll leave tomorrow. Maybe the day after."

Violie shakes her head, though even that small motion pains her. "I'm fine," she lies, mustering a smile far brighter than how she feels. "We'll leave today. Get word to whatever troops remain—as soon as I get some food and have a quick bath, I'll be ready for war."

It's a lie, and one that Leopold sees right through, though after a moment of hesitation, he nods. "Then we'll leave today," he says.

# Daphne

Daphne wakes later in the morning than she usually does—nearly ten o'clock according to the marble clock standing in the corner of her room—but Bairre is still asleep beside her, so she doesn't feel too lazy. They were out late the night before, their conversation with the courtesans and Sisters at the Sororia going on until nearly three in the morning. They filled one another in on the gaps in their knowledge with Elodia and Violie's mother, Avalise, recounting their visit from Violie, Leopold, Pasquale, and Ambrose.

Daphne was annoyed to hear that the group had split in two when they left the Crimson Petal, with Violie and Leopold going to Temarin instead of accompanying Pasquale and Ambrose to Cellaria, which had been the plan. Still, she felt a grudging respect for Leopold for returning to his country to act like the king he'd never truly been when he sat on its throne. She doubted he would be able to uproot her mother's army in such a short time, but at the very least he might cause enough of a distraction to draw her mother's focus to Temarin.

Sister Heloise also told them about the passageway in the

empress's chambers that Beatriz used to escape the palace, though given how poorly that escape attempt ended, Daphne suspects her mother is having it monitored. Still, as Empress Seline, Sister Heloise lived in the palace for more than two decades—longer than Daphne and even longer than her mother—so Daphne asked her to sketch out all of the passages she remembered, in case one of them could be used.

The others also had bits and scraps of intelligence they'd gathered simply by going through their days overlooked, information Daphne knows she never could have had access to, no matter how charming or cunning she might be. The courtesans and Sisters have access to places and people Daphne doesn't.

A courtesan named Blanche recounted how one of the empress's council members, the Duke of Allevue, had barged into the home of Bessemia's royal treasurer, Madame Renoire, one night, demanding to speak with her. Blanche, who had been hired by Madame Renoire for the evening, had made herself scarce at the interruption, but she hadn't gone far and heard every word of their quarrel.

Apparently the duke took issue with Madame Renoire's limiting the amount he and others who worked for the empress were entitled to take from the treasury each month, but Madame Renoire insisted it was on the empress's orders.

"He got angry at that," Blanche recounted. "Asked what the empress was hoarding money for—said it wasn't like we were at war."

*Yet,* Daphne thought, but she knows her mother has been preparing for war on two fronts—with Cellaria and Friv. But the conversation told her that even the empress's closest advisors don't know the extent of her plans, and that they likely wouldn't approve if they did. Daphne can use that.

Sister Alessandria overheard something of interest while attending the star blessing of an infant born to the Earl and Countess of Grisvale—distant cousins of Daphne's on her father's side, who made a short-lived and half-formed play for the throne in the days following the emperor's death. Daphne only knows this because the empress often used them as an example of her generosity—rather than executing or exiling them, she accepted their oaths of fealty and demoted them from their former roles as duke and duchess. A punishment, to be sure, but also a reminder of how much worse she could do if she set her mind to it.

The earl and countess apparently forgot that lesson. With an heir finally born and their family line established for another generation, they apparently made some unwise comments at the star blessing, going so far as to boast to friends that their infant son could one day sit on the Bessemian throne, since the empress had, in the earl's words, *sold her daughters abroad.*

Daphne knows her cousins well enough not to be too surprised by their boasting, but what surprises her more is the fact that word of it didn't quickly make its way to the empress's ear. If it had, the empress would have made a public example of them and perhaps taken it out on their son as well, but Daphne recalls seeing them in the crowd when she and Bairre arrived.

"My mother is losing her grip on her court," Daphne told Bairre during the carriage ride home. "And I would wager her impromptu journey to Friv didn't help matters.

They can see that her attention is shifting past Bessemia's borders, even if they don't understand why."

"It's a weakness," Bairre surmised.

A weakness Daphne can exploit with the right weapon.

She turns the information over in her mind for a few moments as she lies in bed, her mind and body stirring awake, but it does no good. She needs coffee if she's to have any hope of making sense of court machinations and her mother's plots. She leaves Bairre to sleep and takes her silk dressing gown from the hook by her door, pulling it over her nightgown and tying the sash before stepping out of her bedroom and into the sitting room.

At the first sight of red hair in the room she spent so much time with her sisters in, her mind immediately assumes the woman with her back to her is Beatriz, but only for an instant. Cliona's hair is a brighter red than Beatriz's, and she's a full head shorter, her body less curved and more wiry. Daphne isn't disappointed to see Cliona, but she does feel instantly on guard.

"Good morning," Daphne says, brushing past her to the wheeled cart a maid left beside the fireplace, with an etched brass pot of what Daphne presumes is coffee and several bone china cups, with a plate of madeleines beside them.

Sophronia was always picky about madeleines, Daphne remembers, eyeing the tiny shell-shaped cakes as she pours herself a cup of coffee. She would always examine them for the size of the hump and wrinkle her nose if she found them too flat. Daphne blinks quickly, as if she can disperse memories of Sophronia so easily, and takes her cup of coffee, turning back to Cliona, who is watching her with the same wariness Daphne herself feels.

"You were out late," Cliona says.

Daphne wavers, torn about how much to tell her. Cliona has an annoying habit of seeing through Daphne's lies as easily as Daphne sees through hers, so hiding the truth from her now won't do Daphne any favors in earning back Cliona's trust, but on the other hand, Daphne feels uncertain about how much she *should* trust Cliona. She knows her mother had a reason for driving a wedge between them with Lord Panlington's murder, and then there's the fact that Cliona herself was missing for a significant portion of yesterday, not arriving at their apartments until after Daphne and Bairre had already left.

Cliona knows no one in Bessemia. Where could she have spent all those hours?

Daphne decides to proceed with caution, telling her only as much of the truth as she needs to.

"Mother Ippoline asked Bairre and me to come to the Sororia she runs—something about ensuring that our wedding is valid in Bessemia," she says, waving a dismissive hand. "I don't fully understand it, but there seemed little harm in it."

"Oh," Cliona says, brow furrowing.

"And you?" Daphne asks, careful to keep her tone casual. "You were out all day yesterday. I thought for sure you would be tired from the journey."

"I thought to get my bearings in town," Cliona says with a shrug. "The only other time I left Friv was to fetch you, and I didn't see much more of Bessemia than the woods and an inn on that journey. Hapantoile is . . . bigger than I expected."

Daphne laughs. "Yes," she says. "The first time you took me to Wallfrost Street, it was not what I was expecting."

"Mrs. Nattermore might face stiff competition here," Cliona says.

"Oh, I don't know about that. I doubt any of the dressmakers here keep gunpowder and rifles in their basements."

"As far as you know," Cliona replies with a smile.

Daphne laughs again, the sound seeming more genuine this time. This feels more natural, she thinks, realizing how much she's missed her friend. It's a temporary truce, she knows this. The wounds Daphne inflicted on Cliona won't heal so quickly, but they will heal. Daphne will do everything she can to ensure that.

"I miss Friv already, truth be told," she admits to Cliona as she makes her way to the sofa and sits.

"Do you?" Cliona asks, looking at her skeptically. "I must say, you fit so well here. It suits you."

"It did," Daphne says, sipping her coffee. "When I first got to Friv, I'd have given my right arm—maybe my left and both legs as well—to come back here, but . . . Friv grew on me. The place and the people."

She hopes Cliona hears what she doesn't quite say, but if she does, she doesn't acknowledge it. Instead, she clears her throat, looking away from Daphne.

"I'm getting better at lying, apparently," she says.

Daphne frowns, sitting up straighter and setting her coffee cup down on the low table in front of her. "What do you mean?"

"I did some exploring in Hapantoile yesterday, it's true, but not before your mother requested my presence in her study. Though *request* seems like a mild word."

Daphne, who has been on the receiving end of a countless number of her mother's *requests,* understands that all too well.

"What did she want?" Daphne asks.

"For me to keep a close watch on you," Cliona tells her. "To inform her of what you did, who you saw, if anything suspicious arose."

Daphne isn't surprised. She wonders if her mother's protest about Cliona staying here was a ruse—a way to convince Daphne that it was her choice when really it was what her mother wanted all along.

"You don't seem bothered," Cliona says.

Daphne shrugs. "My mother has spies everywhere, Cliona," she says. "I would have been surprised—and a little bit offended on your behalf—if she hadn't enlisted you. You can tell her about the Sororia—my guards overheard Mother Ippoline inviting Bairre and me there, so your confirming it would earn some trust from her without giving her more information than she has already."

"And the truth of what happened at the Sororia?" Cliona asks.

Daphne opens her mouth but quickly closes it again. She considers Cliona carefully for a moment.

"I'll tell you if you ask me to," she tells Cliona. "But that would mean giving you a secret to keep from my mother—a burden you may not want."

"I'm not afraid of her," Cliona scoffs.

Daphne laughs. "You're not a fool, Cliona," she replies. "Of course you're afraid of her—so am I. You might have managed to lie to me, but she's far less easily fooled, and if she senses a lie, she will pry it out of you—and I don't mean that figuratively."

Cliona swallows, her face paling slightly, but she considers her next words carefully. "Is it something I need to know?" she asks.

"Not yet," Daphne tells her.

"Is it good or bad?"

"Good, I think. Hopeful, at any rate."

Cliona nods, lips pursed. "When I need to know, tell me," she says.

Daphne smiles. "I will," she promises. "But in the meantime, I'm sure we'll have plenty of fun dreaming up fake stories for you to tell my mother about all my illicit plots and meetings."

When Bairre wakes up half an hour later, Daphne and Cliona are on their second cups of coffee, the plate of madeleines devoured between them—Sophronia might have found fault with them, but Daphne's far less discerning palate didn't. When the door opens, she and Cliona are engulfed in giggles at the idea of Cliona reporting to the empress that Daphne spent the day enlisting courtiers to join her in forming a choir to perform door-to-door in the palace each week, singing hymns.

"Not that I'm not happy to see the two of you getting along," Bairre grumbles, still half asleep as he makes his way to the coffeepot and pours the last dregs of coffee into the remaining cup. His chestnut hair sticks up at all angles, as Daphne's learned it often does in the mornings. "But must you be so loud?"

"Yes," Daphne tells him, causing another peal of giggles from Cliona. "Ring the bell for more coffee while you're up, will you? We've much to discuss and I'm supposed to join my mother for lunch at noon."

By the time afternoon approaches and Daphne leaves her rooms to join her mother for tea, she feels lighter than she has in days—weeks, maybe. It's hope, she realizes. Not just that she, Beatriz, and their friends will be able to stand against the empress, but hope for a future she never dared imagine before. She can't quite let herself envision what that future might look like, but she knows it will be hers.

Daphne enters her mother's sitting room, greeting the guards who hold the door open for her with a smile. Daphne is no stranger to her mother's apartments, but as soon as she steps inside, she can't help but feel like a child again. Perhaps it's the sheer size of the rooms that make up the empress's apartments—a bedroom, three sitting rooms, two dining rooms, a library, a study, and a separate bathing chamber. Daphne is surprised her mother's maids don't regularly get lost inside them.

Perhaps it's also the unchanging nature of the rooms that brings Daphne back to childhood so quickly. While her mother's wardrobe, hairstyle, and beauty practices change with the trends that affect the rest of the court, her rooms are static. The blue velvet sofa in the living room has been there for as long as Daphne can remember. The walls are covered in the same cream-and-gold-leaf wallpaper as they always have been. Even the small baubles scattered throughout the room—the candlesticks and glass bird figurines and painted vases—seem to have always been part of the room.

The door to the lesser of the two dining rooms is ajar, and Daphne glimpses someone moving inside—her mother, she would imagine, since the list of those permitted within the empress's rooms is very short. She steels herself and approaches, pushing the door open and immediately stopping short.

It isn't her mother waiting for her, but a maid—a young woman who looks to be in her early twenties. It shouldn't be unusual, given the size of the empress's chambers, to find a maid at work, but this maid isn't working. She's also, at least to Daphne's knowledge, not employed by the empress at all, but by King Bartholomew in Friv.

The maid isn't in uniform, but her dress is a simple gray cotton, her mouse-brown hair pulled back in a low bun. Her face is plain, neither beautiful nor ugly but simply unremarkable. Daphne knows that this woman worked in her household in Friv, that she tidied Daphne's bedchamber and pressed her wrinkled clothes. Daphne must have seen her every day for months. But while she's always been good at remembering the names of everyone who crosses her path, this woman's name slips through her mind like smoke.

It isn't an accident, Daphne realizes. Any good spy knows how to be overlooked and forgotten, and her mother would only hire the best spies to work for her.

Daphne recovers herself quickly and summons a bright smile that she hopes hide all trace of unease.

"Oh, hello," she says, deciding to pretend she knew the woman's identity all along, or at the very least suspected it. "I'm surprised my mother recalled you back to Bessemia—surely there are things to keep eyes on in Friv?"

Uncertainty flashes in the woman's eyes. "Her Majesty's plans aren't for me to question, Your Highness," she says. Even her voice is easy to ignore—little more than a mumble, with no scrutable accent or dialect.

"Of course not," Daphne says. "I don't suppose you told me your real name in Friv," she says, as if the thought has only just occurred to her and she didn't simply forget the woman's name. "What should I call you now?"

The woman opens her mouth to reply, but before she can, Daphne feels someone at her back, and the scent of roses leaves no doubt it's her mother this time. Daphne turns to her with a smile.

"Hello, Mama," she says. "I was just getting properly acquainted with your spy."

"Clever, isn't she?" the empress says with a smile of her own, directed not at Daphne but at the young woman curtsying. "I found Adilla at an orphanage in the country some years ago. They were ready to throw her onto the streets after she broke into the directress's private liquor stash for the . . . fifth time?"

"Sixth," Adilla murmurs, looking quite pleased with herself. Daphne can't blame her—she remembers all too well what it felt like to be the subject of her mother's pride.

"And only fourteen, too," the empress says. "Why,

Daphne, when you were fourteen you were still struggling with anything more than a basic lockpicking, weren't you? And even that you were quite noisy with. Adilla was undetectable, even when the directress enlisted the help of staff members to stay close to watch for the thief."

Daphne knows what her mother is doing, but that doesn't make it sting any less. She hides her bruised ego with a laugh.

"Clever indeed," she says. "Though I was just saying that I was surprised you brought Adilla back from Friv."

"Why should you be?" the empress asks, brushing past Daphne to take a seat at the small round table big enough to fit four chairs, though it is only set for three. Adilla is staying, Daphne realizes as she follows her mother to the table and takes one of the empty seats, leaving the third for Adilla. "My business in Friv is done, and I certainly won't waste her talents by keeping her languishing there, with little to do but watch snow melt. I'm sure she'll find the weather preferable in the Silvan Isles."

Daphne pours herself a cup of coffee, belatedly realizing her mother was hoping for a response to that, but the Silvan Isles don't mean much to Daphne. She can point them out on a map, but that's about it.

"I'm sure she will," Daphne says. She looks up to find her mother and Adilla watching her. Looking for some sign, but Daphne can't think of what it is.

"I received word from some less-than-credible sources that Prince Gideon and Prince Reid were seen on a ship from Friv bound toward one of the islands there," her mother said.

Daphne doesn't lose her smile, though now she understands what her mother was looking for. "They might well have," she says, shrugging. "As I told you, I wasn't trusted with that information."

It's true. For all Daphne knows, Gideon and Reid are in the Silvan Isles. She's grateful Violie insisted on keeping their location from Daphne, even if she was annoyed about it at the time.

"I don't see why you wouldn't send Adilla to Cellaria, though," Daphne says thoughtfully. "Beatriz's wedding was meant to be two days ago, and now that she's Queen of Cellaria, I'm sure you'll want to move quickly."

"All in good time," the empress says. If she does know about the starshower Beatriz caused—and Daphne has to imagine she'd have heard about it by now—she gives no indication, and Daphne doesn't want to tip her hand and show that *she* knows about it.

"Have you heard from her?" Daphne asks, taking one of the small finger sandwiches from the tall, tiered platter. "She must know our plans have changed by now?"

The empress doesn't speak, but she and Adilla exchange a look that irritates Daphne as much as it unnerves her. Adilla knows more of her mother's plans than a spy should—more than Daphne does, it seems. After all, the information the empress shared with Daphne about relinquishing her plans for Friv and Cellaria was all lies, but Daphne would wager there is more truth in what she shared with Adilla.

"Beatriz knows precisely what she needs to," the empress says finally before adding, almost as an afterthought, "I heard you and Bairre visited the Sororia last night."

Daphne rolls her eyes. "Mother Ippoline insisted on it, and you know how difficult it is to refuse her. And the ceremony to bless our marriage took ages—she was insistent on waiting for the Lovers' Hands to pass over Bessemia before she performed it, and they didn't appear until after midnight."

"Mother Ippoline is very devoted to traditions," the empress says with a shrug, but Daphne can feel her skepticism lingering. "What did you do for those hours while you waited?"

Daphne considers the question, knowing that any denial or deflection will only heighten her mother's suspicions, so instead she decides to lean into them. "Oh, Bairre and I wandered the Sororia for some time—it is quite a beautiful place at night, with the stars overhead. And the Sisters were performing their nightly rituals. A few of them have truly beautiful singing voices, you know, and fascinating stories."

The empress takes the bait, eyes glinting in the afternoon light pouring through the window. "And were there any Sisters in particular you found interesting?" The empress's voice is still light as she reaches for a tea sandwich of her own, but Daphne knows she's thinking about Sister Heloise, her suspicions shifted from Daphne's reasons for being in the Sororia to the former empress and what she might have told Daphne when their paths crossed.

Daphne could throw Sister Heloise to her mother to placate her—a target for her suspicions and ire that will distract her from Daphne for a time. A few months ago, Daphne suspects, she might have done just that, considered Sister Heloise a worthy sacrifice if it meant keeping herself safe. There would be a risk that Sister Heloise would tell her mother the truth about Daphne's visit to the Sororia, but it would be a small one. Sister Heloise would know that the true explanation wouldn't save her, only hurt Mother Ippoline and others she cares for, and in all likelihood, the empress wouldn't give her a chance to explain anything at all before having her killed.

It would be so easy.

"Oh, there was one who was fascinating," Daphne says, making a show of frowning like she's searching her memory for a moment before it comes to her. She's aware of her mother's growing impatience, but just before she reaches her breaking point, Daphne snaps her fingers. "Sister Geraldine," she says, naming a young Sister who was present the night before. "I believe she's their newest recruit, but she seems to be a breath of fresh air in the Sororia. Really, Mama, Mother Ippoline is getting old—perhaps it's time for her to retire and pass her wimple on to a new disciple."

The empress watches her for a moment, searching for tells Daphne is careful not to give. Finally she sighs. "Mother Ippoline has served the Sororia well for decades now. You're merely put out with her for ordering you around, but you know better than to let your anger control you, Daphne. Emperors and kings and even princes have the luxury of being controlled by their tempers—we do not."

Daphne hides her relief with a scowl before demurring. "Of course, Mama."

# Beatriz

It isn't that Beatriz is ungrateful for the soldiers Gisella loaned her, and she knows that she and Daphne will have a better chance of defeating their mother if they have an army at their back, but five thousand people naturally ride much more slowly than Beatriz would on her own, or even with just Pasquale and Ambrose.

Aurelia met them when they left Vallon with two dozen vials of stardust—not enough to speed their journey by much when divided by more than five thousand, but she uses them on the road instead, wishing for it to be swiftly traveled and shorter than it appears. She has to redo the process every hour or so, and Beatriz is skeptical of the effectiveness of the wish, but by the time they break for lunch, she's surprised when Nicolo informs her that they're approaching the Kellian Forest—they're much farther along than Beatriz thought they would get in six hours' time.

Beatriz and Nicolo dismount from their horses at the head of their party, the road behind them filled with soldiers as far as her eye can see who are doing the same. Pasquale is close enough to give her a questioning look, eyes darting between Nicolo and Beatriz, which Beatriz ignores. Pasquale isn't one to hold a grudge, not even against the person who stole his throne and sent him to be locked away in a Fraternia that was worse than most prisons. But he's slower to forgive Nicolo's conspiring with Gisella and the empress to have Beatriz kidnapped, and even Beatriz still doesn't know what to make of him now. She can't deny, though, that since losing his throne and nearly his life and being exiled by his twin sister, Nicolo is lighter in spirit than she's seen him since they first met. His sister challenged him to figure out who he was, and it seems to be a challenge he's eager to meet.

She wonders if she'll like the man he decides to be, but she doesn't let her thoughts take her too far down that path. Daphne always said Beatriz was a shameless harlot, but she refuses to be a foolish one.

Nicolo continues as Pasquale and Ambrose unpack lunch rations from their saddlebags. "At this rate, we'll be crossing into Bessemia before sundown with another five thousand soldiers meeting us near the border. Which raises an issue."

Beatriz glances at him with arched eyebrows. "You mean the message it will send when I lead an army of ten thousand foreign troops into Bessemia with no warning?"

"The message being *war*," Nicolo agrees.

"It isn't as if I can hide them," she points out.

Nicolo pauses, looking at her with appraising eyes that make her feel vaguely uncomfortable, like her coat has suddenly turned a size too small. "Couldn't you?" he asks. "If we waited until nightfall?"

Beatriz doesn't answer at first, caught on how to get around explaining the toll magic takes on her, the toll Aurelia believes is killing the human part of her each time she uses it. She's still trying to wrap her mind around that revelation herself, and she isn't keen on sharing it with anyone else. She hasn't even told Pasquale about it yet. She also doesn't want Nicolo to know that magic is killing her. It's bad enough that Pasquale does, that he looks at her with wary judgment every time she mentions using it. Even when she summoned the starshower—saving both their lives in the process—he urged her not to. And there is also a part of her that dreads having Nicolo view her as weak.

"You're new to magic still," she tells him instead, twisting her mouth into a patronizing smile. "But it isn't as simple as it seems, and the mechanics of obscuring more than ten thousand people and horses from view is a lot to ask, even of the stars."

He seems to accept that easily enough, but he holds fast to the point. "Then every village and city between Cellaria's border and Hapantoile will know you're bringing war to your mother's doorstep," he says. "They'll send riders to warn her. We can try to stop them, but it means making enemies of the Bessemian people, of *your* people. Do you want that?"

Beatriz doesn't. Of course the army is a threat, but not one intended against civilians, only her mother. She knows he's right, though—the Bessemian people are loyal to the empress, and they'll view a threat against her as a threat against them. They don't know who she truly is or what she's done, let alone what she plans to do, so of course they'll see Beatriz as the enemy.

She looks back at Nicolo. "Let me see your map," she says.

As he pulls it from the pocket of his cloak and unrolls

it, spreading the parchment over the ground and crouching down beside it, Beatriz beckons Pasquale and Ambrose over, and the four of them huddle around the map.

Nicolo picks up a twig and points the tip at a place just south of the Kellian Forest. "We're here."

The map was made in Cellaria, so not all the towns and cities of Bessemia are marked. Beatriz studied plenty of her own maps growing up, though, and while her mother never took her and her sister on her tours outside Hapantoile, she knows that if they continue straight on to the capital, they'll pass close enough to one of Bessemia's other major cities, Hilac. She takes the twig from Nicolo and points out the approximate location, a plan taking shape in her mind.

"These will be the first Bessemians who see us coming," Beatriz says. "Once we're past them, we'll have the cover of the Nemaria Woods to better hide us. There are smaller villages and towns that might see our approach, but they won't have the resources Hilac does. If they send a rider or two, we'll be able to intercept them easily. But with Hilac, we'll have one chance to change the narrative my mother has spent seventeen years building. We'll have to ride ahead to show them that we come in peace—that *I* come in peace, as a princess of Bessemia, not an enemy to be feared."

Pasquale's gaze snaps to hers, an uneasy understanding lighting his eyes.

"You and I will go to Hilac, Pas," she says. "I'll talk to the people there before they see our army approaching. I'll convince them we mean no harm."

"It's too risky," Nicolo says. "We should send scouts to

try to find another way to reach Hapantoile undetected. It'll mean waiting a few days—"

"No," Beatriz interrupts. "We don't have *a few days*." What she means to say is that Daphne doesn't have a few days, but Pasquale hears the words anyway.

"Your mother knows your weaknesses, Beatriz," he says slowly. "And she knows that impatience is chief among them. I know you're anxious to reach Hapantoile and Daphne, but you won't be doing her any favors by playing directly into what your mother expects from you."

Beatriz knows he's right.

"And my impression of Daphne, brief as it may have been, wasn't that of someone content to toil away, waiting for rescue," Ambrose adds. "Would she urge you to rush on her account?"

Beatriz knows the answer to that is a resounding *no*. If Daphne were here, she would recommend caution.

But Beatriz knows that another day of strategizing won't solve the impossible problem of sneaking ten thousand soldiers across Bessemia without drawing notice. Another *week* of planning wouldn't accomplish that. She takes a moment to weigh the possibilities, the best-case scenarios and the worst. Perhaps it isn't a level of meticulous planning Daphne would be proud of, but those few minutes are more than Beatriz usually spares, and they allow for something Beatriz didn't expect: confidence. She *knows* her plan is the best at hand, flawed as it might be.

"We need to lean into the theatricality of it. Give them a show," she says, looking to Pasquale. "Young lovers torn apart by a bitter crone is an age-old story for a reason."

"Your mother's hardly a crone," Ambrose points out with a laugh. "What is she, thirty-five?"

"Then we'll spin a story that will make them forget that," Beatriz says, glancing at Pasquale, who gives her a lopsided smile that she can't help but return. Stars, she's missed having him on her team.

With just Beatriz, Pasquale, and five guards, they ride more quickly than they were able to with the army, crossing over into Bessemia while the sun hangs low, grazing the peaks of the Alder Mountains to the west. By the time they reach the farms that sit on the outer edge of Hilac, twilight has just fallen and the farmers are heading in from their fields. Beatriz feels them watching their approach with wary eyes. She can't blame them—the skirmishes that cropped up on the border during King Cesare's reign likely left a mark here.

Silas—who Beatriz determined to be the loudest of their guards—notes their audience as well and does exactly as she instructed him.

"All hail Princess Beatriz of Bessemia!" he shouts, loudly enough that Beatriz half expects they'll hear him across the entire town, but he repeats the shout every few minutes as they draw nearer to Hilac's center, by which point townspeople are pouring out of the houses and shops to watch them pass.

All the while, Beatriz keeps a smile on her face and ensures that it looks natural. She waves at the people she passes, just as she always saw her mother do when she greeted the public. There are few things Beatriz admires about the empress, but she can't deny her gift for working a crowd, and that is a gift Beatriz herself needs now.

"Your Highness," a man says, his voice booming enough to cut through the din of voices. The crowd seems to part around him, and Beatriz pulls her horse to a stop, the others following her lead. The man, who is in his sixties with salt-and-pepper hair and a well-tailored if plain suit, bows to her, but she doesn't miss the confusion and wariness in his expression. "To what do we owe the honor of your visit?"

Beatriz widens her smile. "What is your name, sir?" she asks him.

"Isadore Kerring, Your Highness," he says with another bow. "I'm the Duke of Ogden's secretary."

"Ah, is the duke in town?" she asks, tilting her head. "I haven't seen him since his daughter's wedding, but I heard he since became a grandfather and I would be pleased to offer him felicitations in person."

If Isadore Kerring had doubts about her identity, that seems to settle them. He shakes his head. "Not at present, Your Highness. He's in Hapantoile."

Of course he is. The nobles spend little time in the domains they're responsible for, often passing the running of them on to hired help in the form of stewards and secretaries and bookkeepers. Most prefer Hapantoile and the glamour of court life.

"A shame," Beatriz says. "Though I suppose that means we must rely upon your hospitality, Mr. Kerring. My husband and I are on our way to Hapantoile and hoped to stay the night. Is there a public house you recommend?"

"The Gilded Lily would welcome you, Your Highness!" someone in the crowd shouts out.

"No, the Fallen Star has better wine and softer beds!" someone else adds.

"Princess Beatriz," Mr. Kerring begins, looking uncomfortable. "Please, I'm sure the duke would insist you avail yourself of his manor just outside of town—the maids can have it ready for you in a short time—"

"Oh, that's really unnecessary, Mr. Kerring," Beatriz assures him. "Not with such an excellent selection of public houses already open and available." She glances at Pasquale. "I believe we should eat our supper at the Gilded Lily and book rooms at the Fallen Star," she says, loudly enough for the crowd to hear—the last thing she wants is to offend one of the innkeepers. Pasquale inclines his head in agreement. As they rode, she warned him that the people of Hilac would likely have a poor opinion of Cellaria following the recent clashes between their countries at the nearby border, and he agreed to let her lead the conversation.

Hilac isn't a large town, but still she'd guess there are about a hundred people on the streets around her, with more figures appearing in the windows of the buildings nearby. "I'm so grateful for your hospitality," she says to them.

"And I would like to thank you all with a beverage of your choice from one of the public houses."

The offer sends a cheer through the crowd, and Pasquale gives her an impressed smile. Getting people to hear her out in exchange for a drink is the easy part, though. The real challenge lies ahead.

The Gilded Lily is decently sized but not nearly large enough for the crowd that is already queueing outside its doors by the time Beatriz and Pasquale arrive, dismounting from their horses and passing the reins to one of the guards.

"Two of you can stay outside the doors," Pasquale tells him and the other four guards, keeping his voice low. "But we need the other three to wait on the perimeter of the town, keeping watch for anyone who might make an attempt to reach Hapantoile before we do."

Beatriz knows the order is practical. No matter how persuasive she is, the chances of every single person in Hilac believing her are small. She keeps hold of her smile and she and Pasquale make their way into the Gilded Lily, past the crowd waiting for entry, who shout her name as she goes.

The interior of the public house is warm and cozy, with a large fire burning in the main room and a long banquet table with benches that Beatriz estimates would seat around fifty people.

"Not to worry, Princess Beatriz," Mr. Kerring says, coming in from another room that Beatriz would guess is the kitchen. "I've spoken to the innkeeper and he's assured me the crowd will be kept out until you depart."

"That isn't necessary, Mr. Kerring," Beatriz says. "I offered to pay for their drinks in large part because I wished to get to know the people of Hilac, and I wished for them to know me. Please tell the innkeeper to seat as many patrons as he has the space for."

Mr. Kerring's nervous eyes dart to the table, then back

to Beatriz. "You wish the people to . . . join your table, Your Highness?"

"I would like nothing more," Beatriz says.

Mr. Kerring looks like he might be ill. "When your empress mother visited us last, she stayed at the duke's residence. Surely you and Prince Pasquale would be more comfortable there as well?" he says, an obvious plea for her to do the same.

Beatriz would wager that the appearance her mother put in here in town was kept short and the townspeople kept distant. She might have given a speech to express her affection for the people, but the words were prewritten, by someone else's hand, and spoken to a crowd en masse. Beatriz's way is different, but that will make her words harder to ignore.

"I confess, I have a fondness for a good meal at a public house, Mr. Kerring," she tells him. "And getting to speak with the local population is a bonus. If you don't feel comfortable relaying my wishes to the innkeeper, I'll gladly do so myself."

Though Beatriz keeps her voice pleasant, she sees the flicker of fear in Mr. Kerring's eyes and finds it gratifying. He gives another jerky bow and starts to turn back to the kitchens, but Pasquale's voice stops him.

"Lord," he says.

"I . . . I'm sorry?" Mr. Kerring says, glancing back in confusion.

"It's quite all right," Pasquale says. "We travel more quickly than gossip, it seems, but I've relinquished my crown and title, so *Lord Pasquale* will be more than suitable."

More bewildered than ever, Mr. Kerring nods and scurries off to the kitchen.

Pasquale must feel Beatriz's eyes on him, because he turns to her and shrugs. "What? You pointed out they'd be less inclined to trust me—and by extension, you—because of past dealings with Cellaria when my father ruled. I thought to distance myself from him further. I'd have just asked him to call me *Pasquale,* but I thought that might actually give the man a heart attack."

Beatriz isn't sure he's wrong about that.

Ten minutes later, Beatriz is seated in an armchair the innkeeper dragged to the head of the banquet table despite her protests, with Pasquale in a matching chair at the other end. The first fifty or so people in the queue outside have been let in, taking seats around the table while the innkeeper's wife fills their glasses with wine, ale, or a nonalcoholic blackberry cider that Beatriz herself elects—she'll have to give this speech several times tonight and she needs to keep her wits about her.

Beatriz exchanges a few minutes of small talk with the people closest to her—a blacksmith and his wife on one side, a seamstress and a butcher on her other—before she gets to her feet and lifts her glass.

"I'm grateful for the hospitality you've shown my husband and me today—but I'm sure you're wondering why we're traveling to Hapantoile." She feels the attention of the room, of even the innkeeper, his wife, and the cook peeking out from the kitchen to watch.

On her way here, she considered how best to win the townspeople over, how to spin the story just right, what to leave out, what to include, but in the end she's decided to tell them the truth, even the parts of it that aren't flattering to her.

So she tells them about the training she and her sisters underwent growing up, how they always knew they would marry the princes they were betrothed to, but that the marriages were a means to an end in the empress's plans. She leaves out Pasquale's attraction to men and his relationship with Ambrose—that isn't her story to tell—but she does talk about her magic, how the discovery thrilled and terrified her. This close to the border, the people must have seen the starshower over Cellaria. They must have wondered what it meant.

She tells them about Sophronia, about how kind her sister was, though she suspects everyone in Bessemia knows of Sophronia's kindness, even if they never met her. She tells them about her bravery, too, how Sophronia was the first of them to defy their mother's plans, how her last words to Beatriz and Daphne were that she loved them all the way to the stars. She lets the people feel the loss of Sophronia, feel the pain that still lances through Beatriz when she talks about her.

"My mother is as responsible for Sophronia's death as if she'd operated the guillotine herself," Beatriz says, ensuring that despite the soft tone of her voice, every last one of the fifty people at her table hears her clearly. "And once she succeeded in that, she turned her attention to Daphne and me, going so far as to drug me and send me back to Cellaria, to marry the new king there, though as you can see, my husband still lived. You saw the starshower I brought down on

Cellaria two nights ago—a miracle, people say, though it is difficult for me to see anything miraculous with one sister dead and the other in my mother's clutches in Hapantoile. That is why I petitioned the newly crowned Queen of Cellaria for her help in saving Princess Daphne and making my mother pay for her crimes. Together, we are going to Hapantoile with an army at our backs and the stars lighting our path to save Daphne and all of Vesteria from my mother."

She lets the words sink in, though she suspects that if Daphne could hear Beatriz talk about her like a helpless damsel in a tower she would have quite a few protests. But Beatriz knows it's an effective ploy. She sees the tension ripple through the crowd, the disbelief giving way to fury in their eyes.

Finally, someone speaks—a woman at the center of the table, not much older than Beatriz, with coils of blond hair pinned atop her head and pensive blue eyes. "What are you asking of us, Your Highness?"

Beatriz understands the wariness in her voice—wariness she sees reflected in the faces of nearly everyone at the table. She might have a lot to lose by standing against her mother, but she has everything to gain as well. The people of Hilac and Bessemia at large stand to gain nothing if the empress is out of power. But if her mother triumphs, she will seek out every person in Vesteria who helped Beatriz and Daphne and punish them for it.

Yes, these people are right to be wary.

"Nothing," Beatriz tells the woman. "My mother is a dangerous enemy—no one knows that better than I do—and I know that our efforts against her may fail. If they do,

I won't have you suffer the consequences. All I ask is that when our army passes by tomorrow, you don't see them—stay inside your city, behind its high walls. Do not venture out as you normally might. Because if no one sees them, no one will be obligated to send a warning to Hapantoile."

"And if your efforts don't fail, Your Highness?" the woman presses.

For a moment, Beatriz is confused. "I'm sorry?" she asks.

"If everything you've told us is true, Princess, it makes Empress Margaraux a terrible mother, but it does not make her a bad empress. Our taxes are lower than they were under your father's reign, the trade routes negotiated with the rest of Vesteria have caused the economy to flourish, and with the exception of some clashes with rogue Cellarians near the border, war hasn't touched us while she's been in power."

Beatriz opens her mouth to answer but quickly shuts it again when she realizes she has no rebuttal. She knew that her mother was popular with the Bessemian people, but she attributed that to charisma and all of her mother's many masks. Beatriz sat through countless council meetings that bored her to tears while her mother and her advisors discussed tax codes and treaties, but she hadn't truly considered that her mother was well liked as empress at least in large part because she was *good* at it.

"You aren't wrong," she tells the woman after a moment. "My mother has been a good empress to you and I'm glad she has been, but do you believe that your taxes won't rise when she declares war on the rest of Vesteria? When she has to rebuild three countries she destroyed in order to conquer? Do you expect that in seizing Friv, Temarin, and Cellaria when they are at their weakest you won't be facing war on all fronts for the rest of your lives and the lives of your children and their children?

"I've lived among Cellarians for much of the past few months, and I guarantee that even if she manages to take Cellaria, she won't hold it easily. You believe the Cellarian skirmishes on your borders have been bad in the past, but they'll only get worse. And as for trade—will you be able to purchase wheat from Temarin when war razes their fields? Furs from Friv when all their hunters are forced to turn their weapons against invaders? And do you believe Cellaria will be able to purchase anything from you when their own economy is left in shambles?"

The woman has no answer to that, but Beatriz doesn't expect one. She looks over the table, meeting the eyes of anyone brave enough to look back at her. "My mother has been a good empress, yes," she says slowly. "But only because it has served her interests. Only because the support of the people of Bessemia allowed her to keep power when most of my father's court turned against her. But make no mistake—when she rules over all of Vesteria, she'll no longer need your support to keep her in power. So ask yourself this—if she has no loyalty to her own daughters, to children she carried in her womb and raised for sixteen years—why do you believe she would hold any loyalty toward you?"

Beatriz feels the discomfort in the room and she knows her words have landed with many of the people listening.

"And you would?" the same woman asks.

Though Beatriz feels her irritation with the woman start

up, she knows it isn't fair. It's a question the rest of the room is thinking, surely, but this woman is the only one bold enough to ask it.

"What is your name?" Beatriz asks.

The woman lifts her chin. "Brielle," she says.

"Brielle," Beatriz repeats. "I confess that my sister and I haven't had the opportunity to discuss who would rule in our mother's place." That, Beatriz realizes as soon as the words leave her mouth, followed by uncertain glances and silence, is a misstep. She hurries to correct it. "But both of us are loyal to Bessemia."

"So you say, but did you not go along with your mother's plots until you realized they would affect *you* personally?" Brielle asks.

Now Brielle really is irritating Beatriz, though she suspects that's because there is an uncomfortable amount of truth in her words.

"If I might interject," Pasquale says from the other end of the table, the first words he's spoken since they sat down. "I've been lucky enough to meet both remaining princesses of Bessemia, and as someone who saw from quite close what a terrible ruler looked like, I would like to tell you about the loyalty that Beatriz and Daphne have exhibited these past months.

"I've heard it said that Princess Daphne is the most like the empress, and I believe that is true in many ways. She's every bit as cunning and intelligent as her mother, but while Daphne doesn't bestow her loyalty lightly, when she does it is unfaltering. When Sophronia's maid fled the siege in Temarin after Sophronia was executed and sought help from Daphne in Friv, Daphne provided it. Even when Queen Eugenia sought to have the girl executed for treason, Daphne stood by her, believing the story of a servant over that of a queen."

That, Beatriz knows, is *not* what happened in Friv, but she can't help but marvel at how well Pasquale spins the story, keeping it close enough to what happened while changing the details that will raise more questions than they answer. And she knows that the crux of what he's saying is true—Daphne *did* believe Violie's word over Eugenia's in the end, and few people in her position would have done the same. She sees that story ripple through the captive audience as well, all of them far closer in station to a servant than a queen themselves.

"And Beatriz," Pasquale continues, lifting his glass of blackberry cider to her in a toast. "As someone lucky enough to have Beatriz's loyalty, I can tell dozens of stories of times she has demonstrated it, even when it has cost her dearly. She freed a jailed friend who was falsely arrested by my father. She saved me from being imprisoned in a Fraternia against my will after my cousin usurped my throne. And even now, when most people facing the threat she does from her mother would run as far from Bessemia as they could, here she stands—marching to confront an empress who has tried to kill her twice before, to save not just her sister but all of you as well, whether you recognize the danger you are in or not."

He pauses, his gaze sweeping the table, and lifts his glass into the air. "Bessemia would be blessed to have either one of them on her throne," he says. "So let us toast now to the future empress of Bessemia, whoever she will be. To the future empress."

For a painfully long moment, no one moves. Then Brielle lifts her glass. "To the future empress," she says.

Her words break the spell of silence hanging over the rest of the table, and one by one, everyone else raises their glasses. Including, Beatriz notes, Mr. Kerring.

"To the future empress."

# Violie

While Violie willed her aching body out of bed, Leopold spoke to the soldiers still gathered in the village where the fight with the baron had taken place two days before—soldiers whose numbers had doubled overnight as word spread to the surrounding towns and villages and those willing to fight for Leopold and Temarin arrived with whatever weapons and armor they could scrounge together. In the end, seven hundred of them agreed to march on Bessemia, while two hundred elected to remain in Temarin to continue the fight against the empress's invasion on home soil.

Up to the moment they departed, just before noon, more recruits were arriving, some all too happy to remount their horses and join Leopold's battalion—Leopold even had to turn some of the younger ones away, making a rule that only those sixteen and older can fight, though there is no rule restricting the gender of soldiers.

Unsurprisingly, Daisy and Hester—the girls who vandalized and robbed the armory—are eager to join the battalion; their stalwart siblings, Helena, Louis, and Sam, are decreed too young and stay behind with their parents, though not before Leopold softens their exclusion by naming them sworn protectors of the village and knighting them in front of everyone.

Even as they make their way east, toward the Bessemian border, people are drawn to his ranks like magnets—shouts of *Stars protect King Leopold!* coming from the crowds that gather to watch him pass. More decide to join him on the spot, mounting their horses or following on foot, taken up by the euphoric hope Leopold instills.

Violie wishes Sophronia could be here to see him like this, fully and truly himself as he speaks openly with any soldier who brings their horse beside his, waving to the people who cheer his name but keeping his focus steadfast on the road ahead.

She can't help but remember the speech he and Sophronia gave to the people of Kavelle, the one that ended in a riot. Violie knows that Ansel instigated the riot, used the chaos as a chance to make himself a hero and rescue Prince Gideon, but all he did was strike a match. Even without Ansel's influence, that speech would have failed. Yes, Leopold's words were heartfelt, his sympathy genuine, but he couldn't fathom how deep the damage he'd caused his country went, didn't understand then that he couldn't simply declare problems solved and damage erased.

Now Leopold doesn't stop to give speeches, though many of the people they pass ask him for one. Yes, he has a gift for pretty words, but now he lets his actions speak more loudly. Besides, if he kept stopping for speeches, they would move much more slowly, and they both know that time is of the essence if they want to reach Hapantoile to lend their help to Daphne and Beatriz.

They don't stop until long after sundown, when the horses are exhausted and they've all reached a level of hunger that won't be sated by bites of dried meat and hardtack eaten while they ride, but when they dismount, Violie looks at her map and realizes they've covered more ground than she thought, placing them right on the border between Temarin and Bessemia. If they can continue at this pace for another day, they should reach Hapantoile by the late afternoon.

Violie finds herself sitting alone while the rest of the battalion clusters into groups around small campfires, holding skewers of meat, bowls of stew, and cups of ale or water. The mood at the camp is jovial and almost giddy, the sense of camaraderie thick in the air. Leopold is a part of all of it, moving from group to group and toasting with the soldiers, clapping them on the back with a smile and a joke at the ready for some, a solemn word for others. He tells stories and listens to tales with the same enthusiasm.

Violie envies him his ease with people, but as she sits alone with her bowl of soup, she finds she pities him for it too. The skill he has of that boundless energy for others is as remarkable to her as it is exhausting, but then—that's part of what makes him such a good king, just as her propensity for her own company is part of what makes her an excellent spy. She needs no one, can be seen by no one, and can move through the world with no ties or connections to give her away.

If not for the impossible circumstances that brought them together, their paths would never have entangled, she thinks. They might have crossed, brushing past each other in a brief moment that left no mark, but that would have been the end. She would have seen a privileged, golden, untouchable king and he . . . well, he wouldn't have seen her at all.

She certainly never would have fallen in love with him, and as she shovels another spoonful of stew into her mouth, not caring that it's hot enough to scald her tongue, she can't decide whether she envies the version of her in that alternate circumstance or pities her.

"Mind if I join you?"

Violie looks up from her stew to find Leopold standing over her, his own bowl in hand. He nods toward the log she's sitting on, the one big enough to seat two.

She nods, shuffling over to give him space, and he sits down beside her. She thought she'd given him enough room to sit comfortably, but his leg is still pressed against hers, the connection between them feeling like an anchor.

"Why are you sitting alone?" he asks her.

Violie gives him a half smile. "You're the hero king, Leo," she points out. "Let them come to know you—it doesn't matter who I am."

He shakes his head. "I've answered plenty of questions about you tonight—Daisy and Hester in particular were full of them. I think they might idolize you."

Violie looks across the camp, finding Daisy and Hester sitting together on the far side of the clearing, deep in conversation, but when they feel her watching, they greet her with a smile and wave, which she returns. They're only a year or so younger than her, but it seems an eternity.

"I'm a curiosity," Violie tells him. "The girl hit by a falling star, saved by a miracle from above."

"That isn't what made you send Janellia from the tavern even though it put you in greater danger," he points out. "It isn't what made you tell me and everyone else that I should let you die to save Temarin."

A flush works its way to her cheeks. "You made the right decision, you know," she tells him. "And even if you had tried to save me, the baron never would have kept his promise. All it would have done is delay the inevitable and doom you and all of Temarin, too."

"I know," Leopold says, his voice going quiet. "But that doesn't mean that it wasn't the most difficult decision I've ever made, that I didn't make it knowing it would haunt me for the rest of my life."

Violie looks up to find him watching her, his expression intent. Of course, she thinks, just as his inability to save Sophronia haunts him. She's glad she won't be another ghost lingering over his shoulder.

"I'm fine," she says, as much to assure herself as him. "I'm alive."

*Dying is less painful than living,* Sophronia's voice said when she was on the verge of death, desperate for a miracle.

Violie knows that's true, as surely as she knows that she could die tomorrow, when they reach Hapantoile. She could die at the empress's hands, due to her own stupidity, fall sick of some lethal illness, or any number of other ways. She could just simply not wake up tomorrow. And if her last brush with death taught her anything, it's that the pain isn't what makes dying so terrible—it's the regrets.

"What is it?" Leopold asks, his brow furrowing.

Violie braces herself, looking at him and letting the camp around them fall away.

"I love you," she tells him, saying the words plainly, even as they feel like they're dragged kicking and screaming out of her. He opens his mouth to answer, but she doesn't give him a chance, plowing forward. "You don't need to say it back, I know it's less than ideal and of course there's Sophronia and I understand that you're still mourning her, that you likely always will be, but when I was dying in that field, all I could think was that there were so many things I hadn't done, so many things I'd left unsaid, and that . . . that was chief among them. So I had to say it, and I'm sorry."

The words come out in a rush, but the more she says, the more confused Leopold looks, and in the silence that follows, Violie becomes certain she's made a grave error, that when Sophronia's voice promised that she might soon yearn for death, this is exactly what she meant, because suddenly she wants nothing more than for another star to fall from the sky and hit her, this time killing her instead of bringing her back to life so she doesn't have to sit in this discomfort, this shame, this mortification.

She opens her mouth—to say what, she doesn't know—but before she can say a word, Leopold's lips seal over hers, stealing whatever rambling words she might have cobbled together. He kisses her with a soft hunger, his hand coming to cradle her cheek, and Violie is so absorbed in the feel of his lips and the taste of his tongue that she doesn't notice the cheers from the camp around them until Leopold pulls back, his cheeks surely as red as her own.

"I love you, too, Vi," he says, quietly enough that she knows she's the only one who hears. "It's different from the way I loved Sophie, but no less real, and I think . . ." He trails off for a moment. "I think it's what she wanted when she sent me to you, for us to find each other, grow with each other, and I think wherever she is, she's happy for us now."

# Beatriz

Beatriz and Pasquale stay the night at the Fallen Star, rising with the sun to see the first wave of Cellarian troops approaching from the south. When they meet them, they fall in with Ambrose and Nicolo, leading the way north, toward Hapantoile.

Two dozen riders fan out, scouting for any lone rider who might be heading toward the capital as well, to warn the empress of their approach, but they send no sign that they've intercepted anyone, which makes it all the more surprising when a rider approaches from the west as if the stars themselves are chasing him, heading straight for Nicolo. Beatriz watches, unease growing, as they speak quickly for a moment before Nicolo leads his horse toward hers, falling into step beside her.

"He spotted someone?" Beatriz asks, frowning. The riders were under orders to capture first and question after, but if the messenger managed to escape . . .

"A few hundred someones, though of course he couldn't get an accurate count," Nicolo says, tension clear in his voice.

Beatriz's stomach sinks lower. Had word managed to

reach her mother even before they set foot in Temarin? She knows her mother has spies everywhere—someone in the Cellarian court could have sent word to her even before they'd left the palace. Gisella could have . . . no, she stops that thought before it takes root. It's easy for her to direct her mistrust at Gisella, and while Beatriz knows that Gisella is more than capable of betraying her again, it serves her no purpose to do so now, secure on her throne, with thousands of her own troops at Beatriz's back.

But *someone* sent a warning.

"They're coming from the west," Nicolo continues, and Beatriz pulls her horse to a stop.

"The west?" she echoes.

It's possible her mother would send an army to meet them, but if she did, why would she send them around the Nemaria Woods? It would only delay them and put them out in the open, without the shelter the woods provide. It wouldn't make sense. Unless . . .

"Could they be coming from Temarin?" Pasquale asks from her other side. "Leopold was set on retaking his throne there. Perhaps—"

"I highly doubt he could have done that in the space of a week," Beatriz says. "It's far more likely my mother pulled some of her own troops out temporarily to consolidate her power here."

"What would you have us do, then?" Nicolo asks her. "The scout said we outnumbered them ten to one, easily. If we attack now, before they reach your mother, we save ourselves the trouble of meeting them under less advantageous circumstances."

He's right—the odds will never be better than they are right now, and if her mother does know she's coming, it means they've already lost the element of surprise. They might as well make the most of the advantages they do have. Still, she doesn't like the idea of attacking Bessemian soldiers who are following her mother's orders without knowing to what end. She managed to win over the people of Hilac—perhaps she can do the same with the soldiers, though she knows there's more risk with soldiers than civilians. "I'll lead half our troops ahead, through the woods to cut off their approach, while the rest close in from behind to ensure that no one gets away. Before we attack, I'd like to speak with whatever general is leading them."

A small tent is pitched on the southeast edge of the Nemaria Woods while a messenger rides to the approaching battalion to invite their general to meet with Beatriz, and while they wait, Beatriz paces, a goblet of Cellarian wine in hand, though she barely takes a sip.

She's so close to Hapantoile, she can almost taste the air there. If she got on her horse now and rode at a gallop, she could be at the city gates in two hours. She could be face to face with her sister an hour after that. The last thing she wants to be doing is standing in a tent waiting to negotiate and flatter one of her mother's generals into joining her or to fight a battle that, while she knows she'll win it, will still cost valuable time.

But if Daphne were here, she'd be the first to caution Beatriz against letting her impatience get the best of her, so she forces herself to breathe and takes another sip of wine before turning her gaze to where Pasquale and Ambrose sit on brocade floor cushions, each holding their own goblet.

"They're taking too long," she tells them. "If they were open to meeting with me, they'd have arrived already."

"It's been twenty minutes," Ambrose points out, which can't possibly be right—Beatriz is sure she's been here an hour at least, but when he holds out his pocket watch, Beatriz takes it from him, surprised to see that he's right. Only twenty minutes.

"I really do think it's Leopold," Pasquale says.

Beatriz doesn't want to puncture his hope, but she knows that hope will die soon enough regardless of what she says. It was foolish of Leopold to return to Temarin, and even more foolish of Violie to join him, because she certainly should have known better. If, by some miracle, the two of them are still alive, they won't be leading an army—they'll be fleeing from one.

"If you're right," Beatriz tells Pasquale instead, "I'll owe you a box of Renauld's finest chocolates when this is all over."

Pasquale smiles, his gaze flicking behind her briefly. "Be sure you don't forget the violet cremes—they're my favorite."

Beatriz blinks, momentarily confused, before she turns to find Violie and Leopold standing in the tent's entrance, both looking the worse for wear, but alive and here. Beatriz can't do more than stare at them, shocked silent.

"Well," Violie prompts, and despite the dryness in her voice, Beatriz hears her relief. "We were summoned by Saint Beatriz, but surely that can't be you. If you're a saint, I'm a unicorn."

Beatriz can't help but snort out a laugh. "It isn't my choice of title, but it seems to have stuck."

"It was bound to happen after she summoned a star-shower to Cellaria," Ambrose interjects.

"That *was* you," Leopold says with a grin. "You saved Violie's life."

"She did not *save* my *life*," Violie protests, then hesitates. "Though your timing was fortuitous."

Beatriz smiles, stowing that knowledge away for later, when she might be more inclined to gloat about it.

"And you?" she asks, looking between them. "Pas and Ambrose said you were determined to reclaim your throne."

Leopold's face reddens. "I'm determined to liberate Temarin from the mess I'm at least partially responsible for," he amends. He quickly tells them what has transpired since he and Violie separated from Ambrose and Pasquale, and when he finishes, Beatriz can't deny she's impressed. The boy standing in front of her isn't the same one she crossed paths with at that inn in Temarin, with shadowed eyes, shattered illusions, and a broken heart.

"Then our aims are aligned," she tells him and Violie. "I take it our destination is the same as well?"

"Hapantoile," Violie says, nodding. "Our army may be dwarfed by yours, but we'll fight together."

"Agreed," Beatriz says. "But Daphne is in the palace now, with my mother, and when she realizes Hapantoile's under siege, she'll kill Daphne and burn the city to the ground before she surrenders."

Violie considers this. "Then the five of us proceed to Hapantoile alone, disguised," she says. "Our armies stay in the woods, which should serve to hide them for a short while, and we get to Daphne and make a plan that will dethrone the empress while keeping everyone else safe."

Beatriz purses her lips. "I do enjoy a good disguise," she admits thoughtfully. "But we'll need to find somewhere willing to host us—somewhere we're sure the empress has no reach."

Violie exchanges a look with everyone else, and Beatriz feels left out of the loop.

"What is it?" she asks them.

"The Crimson Petal," Violie says.

The brothel where Violie's mother works and lives, Beatriz remembers—the same one Ambrose and Pasquale have received aid from in the past. She nods.

"Then we'll leave as soon as you two are able," she says.

Violie and Leopold exchange a look. "We're able now," Violie says.

Beatriz smiles. "Then we leave now," she says. *Hold on a little longer, Daph,* she thinks. *I'm almost there.*

# Daphne

"Are we boring you, my dove?"

Daphne straightens, blinking around the council chamber, at her mother sitting at the head of the large oak table. Despite the casual tone of her voice and the term of endearment tacked onto the end, the empress's dark brown eyes feel like a knife's tip pressed to her skin. The others at the table look at her too—Madame Renoir, General Urden, the Duke of Allevue, and Mother Ippoline—the last of whose gaze is particularly loaded.

Daphne spent the bulk of last night with her at the Sororia again, this time borrowing some of Cliona's clothes and sneaking out alone through a servants' entrance, leaving Bairre and Cliona to cover for her if the need arose. Daphne was surprised to get the summons from Mother Ippoline after supper, assuming they would wait for Beatriz before planning further, but Mother Ippoline greeted her with a thick stack of ledgers that Blanche, the courtesan Madame Renoir regularly employed, had managed to take from her office.

It led to a long night of reading through the numbers and running her own calculations with help from Mother

Ippoline before Daphne understood exactly what she was looking at—the Duke of Allevue had been right to be upset about the cut to his allowance. From what Daphne could tell, that was the least of the issues Madame Renoir had obscured with clever accounting and unchecked power.

But now Daphne, who's accrued no more than six hours' sleep over the last two days, is struggling not to nod off during the council meeting her mother invited her to sit in on—one she should be paying close attention to.

"Not at all," Daphne says, cutting her mother an embarrassed smile. "I'm afraid my injury is still affecting me."

"Really?" her mother asks, brows rising. "My physician assured me you were the very picture of health."

"Yes, I've tried to inform my body of that diagnosis, but I'm afraid it has a mind of its own," Daphne says, realizing only when General Urden fails to hide his burst of laughter with a cough and earns a glare from the empress that her tone was more wry than she intended.

Her mother looks at her, red lacquered mouth pursed in bemusement. "Perhaps you are in need of a nap, my dove," she says, her voice coated in concern that rings fake. "You sound far more like your sister than yourself, and you know how many times I had to eject her from council meetings for her behavior. I'd hate to have to do the same to you."

Her mother isn't wrong, Daphne thinks. Beatriz was the only one who ever talked back to their mother, while Daphne and Sophronia were always careful to mind their words and tones. Sophronia because she feared the snap of the empress's temper, Daphne because she feared her disappointment.

Now, though, the empress isn't disappointed in Daphne,

she's suspicious, which is far worse, so Daphne forces her exhaustion to the back of her mind and reaches for the cup of coffee a servant brought at the start of the meeting, though the half cup left has since cooled. She sips it anyway.

"I'm fine," she assures her mother. "And it is important for me to be here, isn't it? If I'm to run a country of my own one day?"

It's a challenge only her mother hears. While the empress promised Daphne she would inherit the Bessemian throne, she hasn't gone so far as to name her heir publicly. She won't, Daphne knows, the promise she made worth less than dust, but they are still dancing their dance, trying not to trip over the lies they've told each other.

"Of course it is," the empress replies smoothly. "But your health is of paramount importance. You won't be able to run a country if you're dead."

The words are casual enough, sounding to everyone else at the table like a figure of speech. Only Daphne—and perhaps Mother Ippoline—hears the threat.

"We'll have detailed notes sent to your rooms," the empress adds. "It will be like you were here the entire time. Rest, my dove," she says, reaching across the table to take hold of Daphne's hand, squeezing it. Daphne stares at her mother's hand around hers, the elegant fingers with their manicured nails, the gold rings that decorate them, a fraction warmer than her mother's skin. She wants to recoil from the touch, but there is a part of her still lurking deep, deep within that wants to lean into it, to revel in the small show of affection, no matter how much of a performance it might be.

She gives herself a mental shake and gently withdraws

her hand from her mother's grip, getting to her feet. "Yes, thank you, Mama. I believe I should get some rest."

Daphne steps into her rooms, leaving the guards to stand outside the door, exhaustion shrouding her thoughts and weighing down her movements. She should go to sleep early tonight, she thinks, even if it means missing dinner. The world won't fall apart in the next few hours at least. She reaches up to cover a yawn as she walks toward the door to her bedroom, walking past Beatriz perched on the sofa with a teacup balanced on her knee. Daphne mumbles a hello, her hand on the doorknob, and freezes.

Ever since she returned to Hapantoile, she's seen her sisters everywhere. Their ghosts haunt these rooms in particular, where they spent the bulk of their lives together. Of course her tired mind has summoned Beatriz now—so real she even catches that inexplicable scent of ambergris that always clung to Beatriz even before she bought her first bottle of perfume.

She'll just be disappointed if she turns around, she thinks. When all she sees is an empty sofa. She shouldn't even look, just step into her room and fall asleep and hope that in her dreams, she finds Beatriz and Sophronia.

"Daphne."

Daphne's breath hitches, and in the space of a single blink, she turns, flinging herself blindly toward the sofa and the very solid, very real Beatriz sitting there, not caring when she knocks the cup Beatriz is holding to the floor, spilling brown tea on the white rug.

Beatriz's arms come around her, holding her tight, and she presses her face to Daphne's neck, tears damp against Daphne's skin, but then Daphne is crying too.

"You shouldn't be here," she whispers, conscious of the guards so close, just outside the door. "Foolish, impulsive, idiotic," she chides, even as she hugs Beatriz tighter with each word.

"I missed you, too," Beatriz whispers back. "I couldn't stand to be away a moment longer. And I'm not afraid of her."

Daphne pulls back just enough to see her sister's face—so different from the last time she saw her, stepping into a Cellarian carriage in the Nemaria Woods, dressed in that dramatic red Cellarian gown, face laden with cosmetics. She looks as tired as Daphne feels, and in need of a good long bath. Her red hair is in a simple braid down her back, coming loose from the ribbon holding it, and her simple wool dress is fraying in places. *But she's here,* Daphne thinks. *She's alive.*

"You've never been afraid of her," Daphne says. "Which is *foolish.*"

One corner of Beatriz's mouth lifts in a smile, and she presses her palm to Daphne's cheek. "Fine, then," she says. "I'll be brave and foolish; you be cautious and conniving. She won't stand a chance against the two of us."

Something between a laugh and a sob saws out of Daphne's chest. "I have so much to tell you," she says.

"And I you," Beatriz replies. "I sent your husband to find mine at the Crimson Petal and said I would bring you along as soon as you got back."

Daphne shakes her head. "Mama is having me watched,"

she says. "I believe I got away without being followed yesterday, but I'm not sure enough of that to risk your life, Triz."

"Let her have you followed," Beatriz says, shrugging. "We have an army hiding in the woods outside Hapantoile, awaiting our orders. The time for hiding and sneaking and subterfuge is done. It's time to show her exactly who she raised us to be."

Daphne looks at her sister, searching the face that is as familiar to her as her own even after months apart. *Who she raised us to be.* The words burrow into her chest, igniting something. She nods once.

"And make her regret it," Daphne adds.

# Beatriz

Sneaking out of the palace with Daphne, both dressed in the gray wool dresses the palace servants wear, Beatriz almost feels like no time at all has passed. How many times did they creep through the halls and hidden passageways to explore the streets of Hapantoile without their mother knowing? Of course, they always had Sophronia with them, and the lack of her now is stark—a ghost all its own. She doesn't have to ask Daphne if she feels it too. How could she not?

But they don't speak as they make their way through cramped passageways and quiet halls, not about Sophronia or anything else. It isn't until they step into the crisp air outside the palace, the newly risen full moon casting the city in silver light, that Beatriz speaks.

"I wish Sophie were here," she says.

Daphne glances sideways at her as they wind through the paved streets of the city.

"I find myself thinking that at least once every day," she says. "Usually more."

"I've started to . . . not forget her face, exactly, but it's getting hazier in my memory," Beatriz says, even as shame claws at her for admitting it. Daphne doesn't say anything for a moment as they pass through the bustling crowds of people leaving work.

"I have too," she says finally. "But when I saw you again, I remembered that you have the same smile—not *that* one," she hastens to add when Beatriz shoots her a smile. "Your real smile—the one that always seems to take you by surprise."

Beatriz drops her smile. She supposes Daphne is right—that smile is the one she practiced in her vanity mirror growing up and honed with the courtesans she trained with to appear flirtatious and guileless while also highlighting the dimple in her left cheek just so. She isn't sure what, exactly, her real smile looks like, but she resolves to find out.

"You have the same eyes," Beatriz says after a moment. "Not just the color—we all have that—but the shape, and the brows."

Daphne doesn't speak for a moment, just follows as Beatriz leads them through the busy streets to the Crimson Petal, where she's never been.

"I spoke with her," Daphne says finally. "In Friv, we had a ceremony for Prince Cillian under the aurora borealis—a Frivian tradition."

"I've heard of it," Beatriz says softly, curiosity warring with more jealousy than she's willing to admit to. The curiosity wins out. "What did she say?"

"She sent you her love," Daphne says, her voice straining. "And she told me I needed to be brave now."

"That was what convinced you about Mama?" Beatriz asks, irritation prickling at her. It doesn't matter how much Beatriz has missed her sister over the last few months, no one annoys her quite as well as Daphne. "Not me, not Violie, not Leopold—"

"No," Daphne says, shaking her head. "Yes, but no. Sophie told me that I already knew the truth, deep down. That I had to be brave enough to see it, to act on it. I was . . . afraid of what it would mean if you were telling the truth. We built our lives on lies, Beatriz. I was terrified of what would be left when they crumbled."

"And what was left?" Beatriz asks.

Daphne smiles, and Beatriz realizes that in sixteen years of constant company, she's never seen Daphne smile like that, soft and sharp all at once.

"Only when I let the lies crumble could I see what I was truly made of. I used to think of myself as a poison, brewed and distilled by Mama to wield as a weapon. But she's the one poisoning our hearts, poisoning all of Vesteria through us. I won't be her poison, Beatriz. I intend to be the antidote."

Beatriz glances at her sister, noting the firm set of her jaw and the steel in her silver eyes.

"You're terrifying, you know that, right?" Beatriz asks as they approach the town house that serves as the Crimson Petal.

"I do," Daphne says pertly.

"And I am immensely glad that we're on the same side," Beatriz adds, reaching for the brass knocker in the shape of a rose.

"That makes two of us," Daphne says before suddenly hitting Beatriz's arm—hard.

"Ow!" Beatriz exclaims, grasping her arm. "What was that for?"

"Oh! When were you going to tell me you were an *empyrea*? A sainted one, too, by the sound of it!" she snaps. "That certainly would have been helpful to know."

"Would you have believed me?" Beatriz scowls.

Daphne considers this. "Likely not," she admits. "But that should make defeating Mama much easier—you didn't have to wait for me to do it, you know. Much as I'd enjoy having a hand in it, it would probably be simpler for you to just . . ." Daphne trails off, gesturing to the sky above.

"Oh," Beatriz says, swallowing. "About that."

She's interrupted by the door creaking open, revealing not Elodia or one of the courtesans Beatriz met earlier but Violie, still in a traveling gown with a smudge of dirt on her cheek. She smiles when she sees them, relief flooding her tired face.

"Beatriz found you," Violie says, ushering them in before the three of them exchange quick embraces in the foyer. "I thought she might be too recognizable in the palace, but she insisted she knew it better than I did."

"Which I do," Beatriz says before wrinkling her nose. "Couldn't you be bothered to bathe while I was gone?"

"I was hardly twiddling my thumbs," Violie retorts. "Besides, surely you can agree there are bigger things to worry about at present."

"I most certainly do *not* agree," Beatriz says, earning a giggle from Daphne. She'd forgotten about Daphne's giggles—so rare and so at odds with her personality—and the sound seeps through her like liquid warmth.

"Take a moment to bathe," Daphne tells Violie. "I'm

afraid we won't be able to concentrate on anything else until you do. The smell is quite strong."

Violie glances between them, glowering. "I already hate dealing with both of you together," she says without any real malice. She turns and starts upstairs. "Their Royal Highnesses are here, and they've ordered me to the bath!" she shouts down the hall as she goes.

"Leopold needs one as well!" shouts back a woman's voice. Seconds later, Leopold strides down the hall toward them, a sheepish smile on his lips.

"Daphne, good to see you're alive," he says, inclining his head toward each of them in turn.

"You too, Leo," Daphne replies. "Would it be too much to ask if you brought assistance with you?"

Leopold shrugs. "Around eight hundred men," he admits. "Which seemed impressive until we saw the troops following Saint Beatriz."

Beatriz glowers at him. "If any one of you calls me *Saint Beatriz* again, I'll show you just how unsaintly I can be," she says.

He laughs at her teasing. "Of course, if I could pull stars down from the sky, I might have managed an extra nine thousand as well," he says.

"Go bathe," Daphne tells him. "I won't hug you until you do—I fear Violie already left her odor on me." She sniffs at the shoulder of her dress and wrinkles her nose.

Leopold shakes his head but does as she says, darting up the stairs after Violie.

"There's something between them," Daphne says to Beatriz as they start down the hallway Leopold came from.

Beatriz stops short, staring at her sister in horror. "You're joking," she hisses, starting to walk again only when Daphne gives her arm a tug.

"I don't know if they've acted on it, but it's very obvious."

Beatriz opens her mouth to ask what Sophronia would think about that but quickly closes it again when she realizes she knows the answer.

"Sophie would be happy," Daphne says, as if reading her mind. "She cared for them both very much—when we spoke she had words for them, too."

Beatriz suspects her sister is right, but still. "It's very soon," she says.

Daphne shrugs. "Life is short," she says. "And none of us are guaranteed tomorrow. Sophronia, wherever she is, knows that better than anyone."

Beatriz looks at her, unable to hide her surprise. "I'm not sure who you are or what you've done with my sister, but Daphne would never spout such romantic nonsense."

Daphne lets out a low laugh. "Yes, well . . ." She trails off, cheeks turning pink. She doesn't need to finish the thought, though. As soon as they reach the room at the end of the hall—a kitchen with a large oak table, Pasquale, Ambrose, Elodia, Avalise, and Bairre gathered around it—Beatriz sees the way Bairre's eyes go right to Daphne, the way Daphne's entire body seems to soften slightly, like a weight has been lifted from her shoulders. A look passes between them that Beatriz can't read, but it sends an unexpected needle of jealousy through her. She and Daphne, along with Sophronia, have always been able to communicate like that, with a mere look. Seeing Daphne share a similar bond with someone else, a stranger to Beatriz, is disconcerting, though the feeling is quickly drowned out by something warmer.

The Daphne she's spent the last half hour with is altogether different from the Daphne she said goodbye to in the Nemaria Woods. She knows her sister well enough to know that no one can change Daphne but herself, but Beatriz likes the person Daphne has become, and Bairre is part of the story of how she got here—a story Beatriz wants to hear sometime.

"Welcome to the Crimson Petal, Princess," Elodia says to Daphne. They've already met, Beatriz realizes when no introductions are made.

"Thank you," Daphne says as she and Beatriz find a space around the table, the two of them shoulder to shoulder. "I was just asking my sister why she couldn't use her magic to defeat our mother, but I got the distinct feeling I wasn't going to like her answer."

"The magic is killing her," Pasquale supplies. "A little more every time she uses it."

Beatriz feels Daphne stiffen beside her.

"I'm fine," Beatriz assures her. "But he's right, it does . . . affect me. Badly. And it takes me longer to recover each time it does. Aurelia also made mention of a prophecy that makes her think that my using magic to affect human matters like this could lead to the stars going dark, which sounded like nonsense to me, but—"

"It isn't nonsense," Bairre interjects, brow furrowing as he leans across the table. "My mother has her faults, I know that, but her prophecies come true without exception."

Beatriz is surprised at his outburst, but she recalls what Aurelia told her about Bairre—a secret that isn't hers to share with him.

"Be that as it may," she says, shaking her head, "if it comes down to it, I would rather place the fate of the world in the care of the stars than my mother. Thus far, they've proven far more trustworthy."

"Still," Daphne says, "we aren't going to risk your life unless we have to."

*There's* the pragmatic sister Beatriz remembers. She's relieved to see that she's still there, beneath the newfound softness.

"We have nearly eleven thousand troops all together to the south, in the Nemaria Woods," Pasquale says. "We can take the city by force and your mother will have no choice but to surrender."

Beatriz and Daphne both let out an identical snort.

"She won't," Beatriz says. "We know about the tunnel from her bedroom, but I'd wager there are more. If we attack Hapantoile with enough power to intimidate her, she'll run long before she surrenders."

"And besides," Daphne adds, "I'm not keen on using the people of Hapantoile or the troops you and Leopold have kindly sent us as fodder in this fight. That's what she wants—to turn the countries of Vesteria against one another, to sow chaos and distrust and make it easier for her to conquer them. If we manage to win against her only for Bessemia, Temarin, and Cellaria to find themselves at war again, we still lose."

Pasquale frowns, but after a moment, he nods.

"What then?" he asks.

"The fight is with my mother and my mother alone," Daphne says. "Your troops are in the Nemaria Woods?" she asks Beatriz.

Beatriz nods. "Awaiting our word."

"Keep them there," Daphne says. "I'll return to the palace tonight and find a way to lure her there tomorrow. It will be an ambush, over quickly. She'll never see it coming."

"Pity, that," Beatriz says dryly. "Though you can't return to the palace. It's dangerous. You already said you thought she suspected you—"

"She does, but she can't act on it," Daphne says. "She needs me killed on Frivian soil, by Frivian hands. While I'm in Bessemia, I'm safe."

"Are we forgetting the fact that she had me drugged and dragged back to Cellaria?" Beatriz asks.

"No, but she knows better than to try to poison me," Daphne says with a sly smile. "I would never fall for it."

"Are you blaming me for getting poisoned?" Beatriz asks her, incredulous, though she knows Daphne might be right. Daphne knows poisons—how to brew them and how to detect them. She likely *wouldn't* have gotten herself poisoned.

"I'm saying that Mama knows our weaknesses," Daphne says. "Poison isn't mine."

"You aren't invulnerable," Bairre points out, his voice low and firm.

"No," Daphne agrees with a sigh. "But I know the risks. As do we all. This is one I'm willing to take."

Beatriz opens her mouth, ready to argue—it isn't necessary for Daphne to put herself in that sort of danger, there are other ways to get at the empress, she didn't come all this way to see her sister again just to lose her—but before any of those words make it past her lips, she closes her mouth again and swallows them down.

"There's no arguing with Daphne when she's made up her mind," she says to Bairre.

"No, though I can't say I don't enjoy it when you make a valiant effort," Daphne says. "I can get Mama into the Nemaria Woods tomorrow, and I know exactly how to go about it."

Beatriz frowns. "How?" she asks. "She'll sniff out a lie right away."

Daphne smiles. "That's why I intend to tell her the truth."

# Daphne

Leaving Beatriz to return to the palace feels impossible, but as midnight approaches, Daphne forces herself to do it. As they say their goodbyes on the stoop of the Crimson Petal—Bairre in the foyer, saying goodbye to the others—Beatriz presses a glass vial into Daphne's hand. Stardust, Daphne realizes when she looks down at it, the fine powder glittering in the moonlight.

"Bairre mentioned that Mama was making it difficult to acquire stardust of your own," Beatriz says.

Daphne nods her thanks and moves to tuck the vial into the pocket of her cloak, but Beatriz stays her hand.

"It's the stardust from when I pulled the star down in Cellaria to cause the starshower," she explains. "Aurelia says that stardust created by empyreas using magic is stronger than any that falls naturally, and she believes stardust created by me might be more powerful still."

Daphne can't resist rolling her eyes. "Yes, I feel truly lucky to be blessed by your special saintly stardust, Beatriz," she says, though there's no real barb in the words and Beatriz laughs. The laugh, Daphne notes, is a little too strained at the edges for her liking.

"Jealous, Daph?" Beatriz asks.

Daphne looks at her for a moment, her own smile slipping. She recalls how she felt when she broke the lock on Beatriz's magic when they were connected, how the magic flooded her briefly—beautiful, yes, but painful, too. Pasquale's words come back to her: *The magic is killing her.*

"No," she tells Beatriz softly. "Not at all, though I would still take the burden from you if I could."

Beatriz closes Daphne's fingers around the vial, squeezing her hand tightly. "I don't have to tell you to use it carefully," Beatriz says. "I'd wager you had plenty of opportunities to use your wish bracelet before you did, but you held back."

Daphne can't deny that. But when the moments came when her life was at risk, her thoughts weren't on a bracelet around her wrist. And besides, she always managed just fine without magic. But she knows that is exactly the sort of attitude Beatriz is getting at now.

"Don't be a hero, Daphne," Beatriz tells her. "Survive. No matter what."

A year ago, Daphne would have laughed off the command—of course she would survive. Of course Beatriz would survive—how silly to think otherwise. But a year ago she'd have thought the same of Sophronia, that none of them could leave this world without the others. Now she knows different. Promising anything is just foolish sentimentality.

Still . . .

"I will," she promises Beatriz. "And you as well—Sophronia already martyred herself. If you go and do it too, it will make me look bad by comparison."

Beatriz exhales a brief laugh before crushing Daphne to her again, each hugging the other tightly.

"I promise," she says. And though Daphne knows neither of them has any business making those sorts of promises, the words soothe her all the same.

"My father used to tell Cillian and me stories about battle," Bairre says to Daphne as soon as they're safely back in their rooms. They used the maze of servants' passages to reach an empty parlor down the hall, where they crawled through the window and climbed along the eaves to avoid being seen. It's the window that opens to Cliona's room, but there's no sign of her—a fact that unnerves Daphne. "He described how it felt to sneak into enemy camps under the cover of night. This reminds me of that."

"We've been in an enemy camp for days," Daphne reminds him, frowning at the empty bed, the linens still unrumpled and pillows perfectly fluffed. "Where could Cliona be at this hour?" she asks.

Bairre frowns, glancing at the bed before starting toward the door that leads to the sitting room. "Perhaps she couldn't sleep?" he says, as much to himself as to her. "She's always kept strange hours, even in Friv."

"I suppose it's difficult to plot a rebellion under the king's nose during daylight hours," Daphne says, following him.

The sitting room is empty too, but Bairre picks up a piece of parchment from the low table in front of the sofa, holding it out for Daphne to see. She recognizes Cliona's handwriting and steps closer to him so she can read the note.

> B+D, I was summoned to deal with some things. Don't worry.
>
> C

Daphne blinks at the brief note, half expecting more words to appear. "Is that all?" she asks.

"What more could she say?" Bairre points out. "If someone else found it before we did, it couldn't say anything more."

Daphne knows he's right, but she still takes the letter from Bairre and turns it over as if something else might be written on the back. Nothing is, but Daphne does notice a smudge of ink in the bottom corner, like someone dragged their thumb over it while the ink was still wet. She carries the letter toward the warm glow of the hearth, dropping to her knees to get a better look in the firelight.

"It's an *M*," she says, tilting it so Bairre can see. He crouches down beside her, peering over her shoulder.

"For Margaraux," Bairre says.

"I'd wager just about anything she's with my mother—that's the summons."

The clarification doesn't make her feel any better.

"Cliona can handle herself," Bairre says, placing a hand on her shoulder.

"I know," Daphne says. But even if that's true, it doesn't prevent Daphne from wanting to track her down now to be sure of it. If she does that, though, it will only put Cliona in more danger.

Cliona is savvy and coolheaded, Daphne tells herself, and

if those qualities fail her, she also knows Cliona is armed even when she visits the privy. She wouldn't meet with Daphne's mother and not have a weapon or two close at hand.

The thought makes Daphne feel only marginally better.

"We're so close to the end now," she says, turning to Bairre. "And I feel like I'm holding my breath, waiting for it to fall apart."

"I know," Bairre says. He tightens his hold on her shoulder and pulls her toward him. Daphne softens, dropping her face into the crook of his neck and inhaling deeply. Even here he still smells like Friv to her, like cedar and spice and, inexplicably, snow.

*Like home,* she thinks.

She lifts her head and looks at him, his star-touched eyes searching hers, almost golden in the firelight.

"I love you," she tells him.

One corner of his mouth lifts in a smile. "You really are frightened," he says.

He isn't wrong. Daphne's body feels so tightly wound she can scarcely breathe. The future looms in front of them, a giant starless sky—no constellations to warn of what's to come—but it isn't only fear, it's hope, too.

When her mother is dead, Daphne's life will be entirely her own and she will be able to do what she wants with it. There will no fear of repercussions, no danger in her mother's disappointment or disapproval, no expectations from anyone.

"When this is over, I want to return to Friv," she tells him.

Surprise crosses his face. "You do?" he asks.

"I do," she says. "I know things are complicated there,

and there very well may not be a throne to sit upon, but I don't need one. I'm not even sure I want one."

"You do," Bairre says, shaking his head. "From the moment we met, you were very clear about that, Daphne. You were born to be a queen."

"I wasn't, though," Daphne says, a laugh breaking forth from her chest. "I was born to die. That's all. Everything else was always lies and illusions I was told were destined for me. But when this is over, Bairre, my life is entirely mine to do with what I wish. And what I wish is to strengthen Friv, however I can. With you, if you want me."

Bairre looks at her—a look she's seen before but not from him. It's the way a person looks just as she twists the dagger she buried in their chest. He closes his eyes and leans forward, resting his forehead against hers.

"I always want you," he says, his voice hoarse. "Always. However much of you I can get, in whatever way you wish to give it to me. I love you, too, Daphne. I ache with how much."

Daphne bites her lip, running her hands over his shoulders and down his arms, enjoying the feel of him beneath the soft cotton of his shirt—the tension of his muscles, the scattering of goose bumps when her fingertips reach the bare skin of his forearms.

"I ache with it too," she admits quietly. "But I never want to stop."

He kisses her then, his mouth stealing her breath and her fear and breathing something else into her instead, something that burns through her veins like fire. It isn't the way they kissed on the steps of the palace, a performance for an audience who wanted to witness a fairy tale. It isn't even the way they've kissed before, behind closed doors, passionate, yes, but held back by duty and fear.

There is no holding back now, no secrets left between them, and any shadow of fear for what tomorrow will bring outshone by the glow of a future beyond that, a future they can share. Daphne's fingers tangle in his hair, holding him as close as she can—still not close enough. His hands burn even through the thick wool of the servant's dress she wears. It suddenly feels too hot—too tight against her skin. She slides her fingers from his hair and reaches behind her, for the row of buttons that begin at her neck, not breaking the kiss as she begins to slip them from their holes, one at a time.

*There are too many,* she thinks with mounting frustration, but then Bairre's fingers are there too, helping her, pushing the dress off her shoulders and down her arms, freeing her to the air and his gaze.

He pulls back just enough to look at her, still in her chemise, though she's aware of how thin the silk is, baring far more than it hides. His gaze slides over her skin, raising a trail of goose bumps everywhere it touches.

"Stars, you're beautiful," he says on an exhale, the words barely more than breath.

A flush heats her cheeks, but she can't deny that she *feels* beautiful when he looks at her like that.

"I want to see you, too," she tells him, tugging at the hem of his shirt, which he obligingly pulls over his head a little too quickly, the cuffs catching on his hands and leaving him tangled. They both laugh as she helps him, undoing the links holding the cuffs together and pulling the shirt the rest of the way off.

Her eyes drink him in, the smooth planes of his chest, the dusting of chestnut hair, the ripple of his abdomen as she touches him, smoothing her hands over his skin. She never wants to stop touching him, but when she reaches the waist of his trousers, his hands come to halt her exploration.

*Did I do something wrong?* she thinks. She didn't have Beatriz's training with courtesans—she has no idea what she's doing or even what she should want, only that she wants him, but if he doesn't feel the same way . . .

"Daphne," he says, his voice low, barely more than a rasp. "We don't . . ." He trails off, swallowing. "I want this. I want you. But I don't want you to do this out of fear for tomorrow."

Daphne looks up at him, her confusion and embarrassment morphing into amusement.

"Bairre," she tells him. "Fear isn't why I want you. Fear is what's stopped me from acting earlier, and I don't intend to waste another day letting fear win."

He lets out a shaky exhale. "I've never . . ." He trails off again, looking uncomfortable. A slow smile works its way over Daphne's face.

"Neither have I," she says. "We can figure it out together."

He lets out a laugh and then he's kissing her again, getting to his feet and pulling her up with him. They stumble toward her bedroom, kicking off their shoes and stockings on the way. Bairre's trousers follow as they close the door, then Daphne pulls her chemise over her head and tosses it aside. Both of them stand naked in the light of the stars pouring through the open window, looking at each other with lust-drunk eyes.

They didn't choose each other, she thinks. Not even when they said their vows and became husband and wife. That choice was made by their parents, for reasons that had nothing to do with them. If Cillian hadn't gotten sick and died, would she be standing here with him? Would she have spared more than a glance at the prince's surly bastard brother? Would she have found the strength to turn against her mother and plot against her under her own roof?

Daphne doesn't know the answer to that. Perhaps she never will. But she knows that even if it was the stars and her mother that led her here, with Bairre, this choice is hers. *Theirs.*

She reaches for him just as he reaches for her and they fall together, tumbling onto her bed in a tangle of kisses and limbs and laughter, the feeling of his body pressed against hers more intoxicating than an entire bottle of champagne. They choose each other with every kiss, touch, and stroke, pleasure building slowly until it crests, shattering through both of them, and they're left satiated and drained, dragged into a deep sleep still wrapped in each other's arms.

# Violie

Just as the stars are fading from the sky under the threat of the rising sun, Violie, Leopold, Pasquale, and Beatriz depart from the Crimson Petal. Ambrose is staying there to await Daphne's signal, at which point he'll saddle a horse and ride to meet them in the Nemaria Woods.

Hapantoile is only just beginning to yawn awake, with candles flickering to life in windows as they pass by with the earliest of risers, but the streets themselves are empty apart from the four of them.

Violie herself still feels half asleep, her eyes bleary and thoughts soft-edged. She barely registers when Leopold brushes the back of his hand against hers until he does it a second time and she realizes it wasn't an accident. She looks up at him, eyebrows raised to find him watching her with a furrowed brow.

"What is it?" she asks, keeping her voice low so that Beatriz and Pasquale, walking just ahead of them, don't hear. It isn't that she wants to keep secrets from them, but the attachment between her and Leopold is so new, and involving his dead wife's volatile sister would likely crush whatever fragile thing is growing between them. And Violie doesn't *want* to crush it. The very idea of it makes her feel unmoored.

"We're being followed," he whispers back.

Violie tenses, resisting the urge to look around her.

"You're sure?" she asks, though she knows the answer to that and the look he gives her confirms it. He's sure.

"Two sets of footsteps behind us—keeping their distance, for now."

Relief washes over Violie. Two sets of footsteps are an easy threat to face, if they're a threat at all.

"Townspeople getting an early start on the day, perhaps?" she asks, but Leopold shakes his head.

"The sound of their boots, the rhythm . . . it's regimented. Military or guards is my guess."

Still, two guards can be dealt with between the four of them.

She quickens her pace enough to catch up with Beatriz and Pasquale, Leopold beside her, and they relay Leopold's suspicions. Before Violie can get more than a few words in, Beatriz is reaching for the dagger at her hip, withdrawing it from its sheath. Violie, Leopold, and Pasquale hasten to draw their own weapons. The sound of swords slipping from sheaths echoes around them in every direction—more than just two, Violie realizes, a sickening dread taking root. Leopold realizes it too, his face paling in the predawn light.

"It's an ambush," Beatriz hisses. "Scatter and run—meet in the woods. *Go.*"

Violie doesn't need to be told twice. She runs east, down a narrow alleyway, relieved when Leopold falls into step with her. He's still a stranger to Hapantoile, but Violie knows these streets as well as she knows the sound of her name.

"Two of them went that way!" a sharp voice shouts, and the thud of boots against pavement sounds behind them.

"Stay close to me," she tells Leopold, taking a sharp right out of the alleyway onto a wide road—mercifully empty but exposed. Another alleyway leads past the rear entrances of the butcher's and baker's—the baker is unlocking the door as they run past him, and he lets out a string of curses, loud enough to draw attention.

Violie rounds another corner, and a grim smile tugs at her lips when she catches sight of a large wooden cart piled with empty apple crates parked beside a single-story house.

"Come on," she tells Leopold, running toward it.

"What are you—" he starts, but breaks off when Violie sheaths her sword and climbs onto the cart, then onto the precarious pile of apple crates. Standing on the tallest one, she can just grab the ledge of the house's roof, pulling herself up onto it. Leopold is right behind her, hoisting himself onto the roof mere seconds before the guards turn down the alley, thundering past the apple cart without thinking to look up.

When they're gone, Violie lets out a breath, the adrenaline pumping through her fading and leaving worry in its wake. She looks at Leopold.

"Beatriz and Pasquale . . . ," she begins.

She sees her own fears play out on Leopold's face before he seals them away behind a tight smile. "They'll be fine," he says.

The dread pooled in her stomach spreads. "They were

following us, Leo," she says. "They were ready. They knew where we were—my mother—"

He grabs hold of her hand, squeezing it tight. "Vi," he says, his voice low. "We can't go back, you know that. They'll be watching for us and you won't be doing your mother or Elodia or Ambrose any favors by returning. As soon as we're able, we'll go back, I swear it, but we can't without an army."

Violie wants to scream at him, to tell him she doesn't care what happens to her, she just needs to keep her mother safe, but she swallows the words down. She forces herself to breathe, letting the cold hand of panic clenching at her heart loosen enough for her to see that he's right—she can't help her mother right now. She looks around them, at the stretch of tile roofs, glinting in the light of the rising sun.

"They'll have guards at all the gates searching for us too," she tells him. "Inspecting anyone entering or leaving."

"Is there another way out?" he asks.

Violie wracks her brain, searching her memories of running around Hapantoile. "No," she says. "But if we can get word to the troops . . ."

"The Sororia," Leopold says. "Your mother said the Sororia was on our side. Surely the guards at the gate would let a Sister pass unchecked."

Violie doesn't think—she grabs Leopold's face and kisses him quickly on the lips, leaving him surprised but smiling slightly.

"This way," she tells him, scrambling to her feet. "But tread lightly—the last thing we need is to alarm the sleeping townspeople."

# Beatriz

Beatriz blinks awake, the darkness that greets her no different from the darkness behind her eyelids, but she feels cold stone beneath her and coarse rope against her wrists, binding her arms to a large, smooth pillar. Marble, she thinks. She blinks a few more times, her eyes adjusting a little more with each blink until she can see vague shapes. More pillars supporting a high arch that stretches farther than Beatriz can see. Long marble boxes covered with slabs line the far side of the space, and though she can't see it from her current position, she knows those slabs are carved with names and dates and carefully chosen constellations, all inlaid with gold. She knows that one of them bears her father's name, and another bears the name of his father before him.

As a child, she leapt from one tomb to another, wooden practice sword in hand while Daphne gave chase, Beatriz laughing, Daphne's brow furrowed deeply in concentration even then, when the stakes were so low. She and Sophronia carried candles to read the names of each emperor who ruled Bessemia, reciting stories about them, some from the history books they read and some made up entirely. Beatriz would tell ghost stories to fit the atmosphere, making Sophronia shudder and shriek with terror and glee.

They're in the catacombs beneath the palace, where the rulers of Bessemia have been buried since the dawn of the empire—not the public memorials erected for them in temples across the country, but their true resting place, where they're safe from grave robbers and vandals. Deep in the bones of the palace where no one can reach them—where few even know they lie.

Movement catches Beatriz's eye and she turns her head, her eyes adjusting just enough that she can make out a figure bound to the pillar beside hers, five feet away.

"Pasquale," she hisses—because it has to be Pasquale. The last thing she remembers is making a wrong turn and ending up in an alley with a dead end, six guards closing in on them.

"I expect my mother wants a word," she called out to them, with more bravado than she felt. "I'll come peacefully if you let my husband go."

"Those aren't our orders, Your Highness," one of the guards said, but before Beatriz could ruminate any more on that, something small flew toward them, piercing her throat like the sting of a wasp. After that she remembers nothing.

A poisoned dart, she realizes now, the faint echo of its sting still pulsing in her neck.

"Pasquale," she whispers again when he gives no response. If it isn't Pasquale here with her, if the guard meant that their orders had been to kill him—

"We aren't dead, I take it," Pasquale groans out.

Relief floods Beatriz, but it's short-lived.

"Not yet," she tells him. "But I can't imagine my mother had us brought to the royal catacombs for tea."

"Is that where we are?" he asks.

Beatriz nods before remembering he can't see her. "Yes, this is where we used to do much of our training—as far from the prying eyes of court as we could be. We played here too, even when we weren't supposed to. It wasn't difficult to sneak in once you knew the way."

"I don't suppose you know the way out?" he asks.

"I do, but I'm assuming you're bound too, and I'd wager my mother took precautions to keep us here. Locked doors. Guards standing outside them."

Pasquale is quiet for a moment as he absorbs that. "Thoroughly trapped, then," he says.

"Afraid so," she agrees. "Violie knows the streets of Bessemia better than I do, though—she and Leopold might have gotten free and gone for help."

"And what about—" he starts, but Beatriz interrupts him.

"Shh," she hushes. She knows he was about to ask about Daphne—likely still asleep half a dozen floors above them. But while the dark makes it seem like they're alone, Beatriz knows better than to assume as much. Darkness can hide many things, she knows, an eavesdropper among them. "Careful what you say," she warns him.

Pasquale seems to catch her meaning, falling quiet for a moment. "But there is hope," he says carefully.

Beatriz smiles, the feel of it sharp. "I'll have hope until I take my last breath, Pas," she says.

"Not much longer, then," a voice calls out from behind them.

Beatriz tries to twist enough to see around the pillar she's bound to, barely making out the faint glow of a lantern approaching them.

It isn't a voice she recognizes, and as the woman comes closer, she doesn't look familiar either—not much older than Beatriz, with a plain face, plain brown hair pulled back in a severe bun. Plain black leggings with a white tunic and a cloak thrown over the top. But as she steps closer, Beatriz realizes she isn't alone. The woman holds a chain, pulling a second figure along, stumbling in the dark he's unaccustomed to.

"Ambrose!" Pasquale shouts, recognizing him at the same time Beatriz does.

"Pas?" Ambrose asks, looking around in the dark in the direction Pasquale's voice came from.

"Who are you?" Beatriz demands of the woman, who smiles.

"I've gone by many names over the years, but Adilla will do," she says.

The name also catches nothing in Beatriz's memory. "Whatever it is my mother promised you," Beatriz tells her, "it's a lie."

"Everyone lies," Adilla tells her, giving a smile laced with pity that sours Beatriz's stomach. "When you accept that, the truth is worthless. But the empress pays me well and doesn't wish me dead, so if you hope to sway my loyalty I fear it will be a losing battle."

"What do you want, then?" Beatriz asks.

"I brought you a friend," Adilla says, gesturing to Ambrose. She leads him to the pillar on the other side of Pasquale, tying his arms around it and securing his wrists with rope just as Beatriz's and Pasquale's are. Beatriz watches her fingers tie the knot, lit by the lantern she sets beside her while she works. The knot is familiar—one Beatriz herself had to practice. Impossible to untie without the use of her hands.

"And now what?" Beatriz asks when Adilla stands up, lifting her lantern with her.

Adilla shrugs. "I don't know more than I need to," she says, not sounding bothered by that fact. "But the fun won't start until your other friends arrive."

With that, she turns and walks off the same way she came in, humming to herself as she goes, the glow of her lantern getting smaller and smaller before disappearing entirely.

# Daphne

The sharp edge of a blade against her neck wakes Daphne, and she blinks up into the early-morning light to see Cliona looming over her, dagger in hand and expression empty and cold.

"Cliona—" she starts, but Cliona lifts her finger to her lips and presses the blade harder against Daphne's skin, the threat clear. Cliona cuts her gaze to Bairre, still sleeping beside her.

"You're going to get out of bed and come with me," Cliona whispers to Daphne. "I have orders to kill him if he makes trouble. Don't let him make trouble."

Daphne swallows, even as the movement presses the blade harder against her throat. She understands what Cliona is saying, the unspoken plea. Under normal circumstances, Daphne wouldn't be inclined to take requests from someone trying to kidnap her, but in this her and Cliona's goals are aligned.

She glances at the duvet covering her from the shoulders down.

"Will you allow me the dignity of getting dressed first?"

she asks Cliona mildly. "Or does my mother wish for me to parade down the halls naked?"

A flicker of surprise crosses Cliona's face as she glances at Daphne's body beneath the bedclothes, and Bairre next to her. Just as quickly, it's gone, smoothing away into that cold emptiness once more. She removes the dagger and gives a quick nod.

"Dress quickly," she whispers. "And quietly. And don't even think about taking a weapon with you."

"Wouldn't dream of it," Daphne says, though they both know that's a lie.

"You have one minute."

Cliona turns her back, her fingers flexing around the hilt of her dagger.

Daphne hurries across the room, dressing without much thought, her mind consumed with trying to understand what is happening and why—Cliona has betrayed her. She shouldn't be surprised by that, but it hurts all the same. What did the empress offer her? Whatever it is, Cliona must know it's a lie, that as soon as Daphne is dead and the empress has won, she'll kill Cliona, too.

"Ten seconds," Cliona says just as Daphne is pulling on her cloak. In the pocket, she finds the vial of stardust Beatriz gave her the night before. She's about to shove it into her bodice when Cliona's voice stops her.

"Don't," Cliona says.

Daphne grits her teeth. "Bairre will need it if he hopes to get back to Friv alive," she tells Cliona.

Cliona hesitates, glancing at Bairre's sleeping form. After a second, she nods. "Then leave it for him," she says.

Daphne does, walking toward Bairre's bedside table and setting the stardust there.

"Happy?" Cliona whispers.

"Not particularly, no," Daphne whispers back, and that's when she sees it—the flicker of movement behind Bairre's eyes. Not asleep, Daphne realizes, but pretending. She needs to get Cliona out of the room before she realizes it too. Daphne holds her hands up to Cliona. "Would you like to search me for weapons?" she asks.

"Not at the moment," Cliona says after a second of consideration. She grabs Daphne by the elbow and leads her out of the room. Daphne chances one last look over her shoulder, her eyes meeting Bairre's; he gives her a small nod just as the door closes between them. He'll get help from Beatriz and the others, she knows, and that hope buoys her against the growing dread in her belly.

"Where are you taking me?" Daphne asks as Cliona leads her out of the sitting room and into the hall, where five guards wait, not just her usual two. Without a word, they fall into formation around Daphne and Cliona, not to guard them, Daphne realizes, but to obscure the dagger Cliona holds to her back from the sight of anyone they pass.

Cliona glances sideways at her, face unreadable before she turns her attention forward once more. "To Beatriz," she says, the words lifting Daphne's heart and shattering it all at once.

Daphne feels numb as Cliona and the guards force her down flights and flights of stairs. To the catacombs, some part of her realizes, unsurprised. She's tempted to try to speak to Cliona again, to reason with her, but she holds her tongue. The guards know what they're doing—they must have some inkling of where they're taking Daphne and to what end. Cliona won't change her mind in front of them. She can't. But as they walk, Daphne's mind turns over how they got here, what their mother is planning, and how they can get out of it.

Bairre knows what happened to her—he'll get help somehow, from someone. But if the empress already has Beatriz, who else does she have? Is there anyone left to help them? Or is this the end for her? Is this how she loses?

They approach the large iron door at the bottom of the last flight of stairs, flanked by two guards, who move aside at their approach, one of them pulling the door open and the other handing Cliona a lantern to hold with her empty hand. From there, Daphne and Cliona enter the catacombs alone, the darkness making it difficult to see anything past the ring of light surrounding them.

"Daphne?" a voice calls out—Beatriz, she knows, her heart clenching.

"It's me," she calls back, trying not to betray the fear coursing through her.

Beatriz lets out a string of curses in both Bessemian and Cellarian as they draw closer. Daphne takes in the hazy sight of her Beatriz, Pasquale, and Ambrose bound to marble pillars—none looking injured, she notices with some relief, but incapacitated all the same.

"Cliona?" Pasquale says. "What are you doing?"

Cliona doesn't look at him as she guides Daphne to the pillar on Beatriz's other side, pushing her to sit down and pulling a coil of rope from the pocket of her cloak.

"What I must," Cliona says coldly as she binds Daphne's hands behind her, just like the other three.

Daphne looks up at her onetime friend. "Cliona, whatever she promised you, whatever she threatened—"

"Don't," Cliona snaps, the venom in her voice surprising Daphne. "You have precious little life left—don't waste your words on me."

With that, Cliona turns and leaves again, taking the light with her.

When she's gone, Daphne lets out a long exhale.

"Constrictor knot?" she asks Beatriz, tugging at her wrists experimentally.

"Afraid so," Beatriz says. "It's the same one Adilla used on Ambrose, and I expect whoever tied up Pasquale and me used it too, by the feel of it."

"Adilla?" Daphne asks, raising her eyebrows. "I should have known she was a part of this. She's a bundle of sunshine, isn't she."

"A delight," Beatriz agrees. "And very adept at tying knots—unlike your friend."

Daphne turns her head toward her. "What do you mean?" she asks.

Beatriz drops her voice to a whisper. "I suspect that if you twist your wrists with a good deal of pressure, should you not dislocate your shoulder in the process, you might be able to slip free."

Daphne's fingers grab at the knot, feeling as much of it as she can and trying to summon an image of what it looks like. Beatriz is right—if Cliona meant to tie a constrictor knot, she made a mistake.

"A simple error, if one doesn't have much practice," Beatriz says, but Daphne hears the question in her voice. Was it an error? Or did Cliona purposefully mistie her bindings?

Daphne doesn't know the answer, and she isn't going to place all her hope in someone else when being wrong means death.

"What are you waiting for?" Beatriz asks. "Break your bindings and get us out of here."

But Daphne doesn't move; her mind is a whirl of possible ways out of the catacombs, yet nothing comes to her.

"Where are Violie and Leopold?" she asks.

Beatriz looks at her, confusion clear even in the dark. "We split up when we were attacked on our way out of the city—we think they got away. Ambrose said the guards were looking for them when they raided the Crimson Petal."

"They came about an hour after Beatriz, Ambrose, Violie, and Leopold left," Ambrose says. "They brought me here, but they took the women somewhere else."

"Alive?" Daphne asks.

"I believe so," he says. "But I can't be sure."

Daphne is sure, though. If her mother wanted the courtesans dead for helping them, she'd have had them killed in their beds, a message sent loud and clear. If she's keeping them alive, there's a reason for it.

"Daphne, what are you thinking?" Beatriz asks.

"I'm thinking that we wanted to face Mama ourselves," she tells Beatriz, relaxing her arms and easing tension from the knot binding them—for now. "And she's been kind enough to give us that chance."

Beatriz looks at her for a moment. "Do you have a plan you'd like to share?" she asks.

Daphne doesn't reply for a moment as Cliona's words come back to her from what feels like a lifetime ago. *Sooner or later, Daphne, you're going to have to trust someone.* Easier said than done, in Daphne's experience. She's always worked alone—even when it came to her sisters, she always felt separate. But she isn't alone in this. *They* aren't alone in this. She thinks about Bairre, imagines him sneaking out of the palace the same way they did last night, going for help. She thinks about Violie, the most persistent person Daphne has ever met, as determined to see the empress defeated as Daphne and Beatriz are. She thinks about Leopold, how Sophronia once called him brave and Daphne didn't understand it. He is brave, though, and he's out there somewhere, ready to fight with them. She thinks about the courtesans and the Sisters, risking their lives for a fight that has little to do with them, working together despite the different paths their lives have taken. She even thinks about Cliona, how each of them has betrayed the other in different ways, how perhaps Cliona *did* fool her— but she doesn't think so. In her gut, she knows who Cliona is, and she trusts her.

"Mama raised us to stand alone," she tells Beatriz, a

thread of steel winding through her voice. "But we aren't alone, Triz. My plan is to trust that, and to be ready to act when the time comes."

She can hear Beatriz gritting her teeth. "That isn't a plan. It's a prayer," she says.

"You're the saint," Daphne volleys back. "If anyone can work with a prayer, it's you."

# Violie

It takes the better part of an hour of climbing across Hapantoile's rooftops before Violie and Leopold reach the Sororia, its buttresses and steeples stretching higher than any other building in Hapantoile, apart from the palace itself. They make it from the roof of a residential building three stories tall, down to the carriage house pressed between it and the Sororia, but there, they pause, crouching low behind the peak of the carriage house's sloped roof.

Two guards stand outside the Sororia's main entrance, dressed in the empress's colors. Violie would wager there are more at the back entrance, and she doubts they've come to protect the Sisters within. First the Crimson Petal, now this. The empress knew all along, she realizes. She let Daphne plot against her, let her gather allies, waiting and watching until Beatriz arrived and she made her move.

Daphne was bait—something Violie knows better than to ever say to Daphne's face, should she see her again.

"What now?" Leopold whispers to her.

Violie thinks. The guards aren't looking their way—their attention focused on the street in front of the building—and the carriage house is close enough to the second floor of the

Sororia that they can crawl through one of the windows. It's only a question of who they'll find on the other side of the window.

"Bairre," Leopold says suddenly, jerking her out of her thoughts. She's confused until she follows Leopold's gaze and notices the Frivian prince crouched behind the carriage house, eyeing the guards, though when he hears his name, he looks up, eyes widening when he sees them. Violie beckons him up and Bairre looks around, confused, before seeing a low fence to the side of the carriage house. He uses that to climb to the top of a gabled window, then leverages himself up to the roof, crouching beside them.

"What are you doing here?" he hisses. "Where's your army?"

"Where's your wife?" Violie volleys back, regretting it when his mouth tightens and he looks away, jaw clenched. Quickly, they catch one another up.

"You don't know where they took Daphne?" Violie asks.

"No, and you haven't seen Beatriz?"

"No," Leopold admits.

"I would bet good money they're in the same place," Violie says, glancing at the palace looming in the distance.

"There's no use barging in without assistance," Bairre says. "I was hoping the Sisters could get a message to you and Beatriz, assuming you were with your armies."

"It would seem the Sisters are preoccupied," Violie says. She tries to think strategically. The guards won't see the Sisters as a threat, but they would want to keep watch over them all the same, which means they'll sequester them in the same place. When she says as much to Bairre, his eyes spark.

"The chapel," he says. "That'll be the largest room. It's on the ground floor, with a glass roof to see the stars through."

An idea takes shape in Violie's mind, and she shares it quickly. When she finishes, both Bairre and Leopold look at her like she's gone mad. Maybe she has.

"Unless either of you has a better idea, we're doing it," she says.

Neither of them speaks for a moment, instead exchanging a look.

"Fine," Leopold says with a grave nod. "I suppose it would be a waste of breath to tell you not to do anything reckless."

"It would," Violie says. "Now give me a boost through the window before we're seen."

Violie lands on the floor of a Sisters' dormitory on silent feet. Crouching below the window, she looks around. Empty, as she suspected. She stands and goes straight to the small, plain wardrobe near the door, opening it and finding three habits hanging neatly. She wastes no time, pulling a dark blue tunic over the dress she's already wearing and securing a wimple so that her hair is covered before adding the headpiece. Then she picks up the glass vase on the end table, holds it high above her head, and smashes it against the wood floor, sending water and cut flowers everywhere.

A shout goes up from somewhere in the Sororia, and Violie hastens to hide—or rather, to pretend to hide. She crouches behind the wardrobe and summons frightened tears that manifest just as the door to the room opens and heavy boots approach.

The guard finds her immediately, grabbing her by the arm and dragging her to stand, ignoring her dramatic sob of pain when he does.

"You said you searched this room, Ren," the guard holding her snaps at a second, who stands in the doorway, looking around in bewilderment.

"I thought I did, sir, but they do all look the same."

"Fool," the first guard says. "Take Peter and search again—thoroughly this time."

"Yes, sir," the guard says, backing out of the room. When the first guard drags Violie down the hall, she sees the second guard, Peter, speaking with a third guard before they set off in the opposite direction, opening a door and slipping inside. *That's two down,* she thinks as she snivels and cries and begs the guard for mercy.

"Enough," he bites out. "If you can't keep quiet I'll gag you."

Violie pretends to be cowed by the threat, but really she's paying attention to the halls he pulls her down. No guards here, she notes, but after going down one flight of stairs and around a corner, he opens a large oak door and shoves her inside, into the chapel Bairre described. A large space with a vaulted ceiling made of glass. The dozen pews are filled, Sisters clustered together, not speaking. Some, Violie notices, have their hands bound. Others are gagged, like the guard gripping her arm threatened to do to her. But when her eyes catch her mother's, she realizes it isn't only Sisters gathered, but the courtesans of the Crimson Petal, too.

Relief slices through her at the sight of her mother, alive, but she knows that relief will be temporary if she can't free them.

The guard shoves her into a pew on the other side of the chapel from her mother, beside an elderly sister who glares at the guard and bares her teeth around the gag in her mouth, but the guard ignores her, walking to the front of the chapel to speak with a guard there. In addition to the man who brought her here, there are eight other guards in the chapel.

"Two guards are searching upstairs," she whispers without moving her mouth to the gagged Sister beside her. "How many others have you seen inside?"

The Sister straightens beside Violie, and without looking at her, she grabs hold of Violie's hand, hidden from the guards' view by the pew in front of them, and traces a circle on Violie's palm.

"Zero," Violie infers. "So eleven guards total."

The Sister squeezes her hand, which Violie takes as assent.

Eleven guards, plus two at the front doors, presumably two at the back. Fifteen total. Fifteen armed guards against . . . forty unarmed women, she counts quickly. Add Violie, Leopold, and Bairre into the equation, all three of them with weapons of some kind, and the odds seem to be in their favor.

There's a loud thud from above and everyone in the chapel looks up to see Leopold land on the glass ceiling in a crouch, peering down at them and lifting his hand in a mocking wave.

Violie gives a scream, as if terrified, and the Sister beside her follows her lead. The rest of the room follows, letting out terrified shrieks and pointing.

"What are you waiting for?" the guard who dragged Violie in shouts to his men—the leader, she presumes. He points to a cluster of five guards standing near the altar. "You lot, stay here and watch them!" he shouts. "The rest of you, seize him—dead or alive."

The head guard leads the men out of the chapel, leaving only five guards—none of whom looks particularly pleased to have been relegated to nannying duty.

Above them, Leopold runs off, but as soon as he's disappeared, a gunshot goes off in the other direction—coming from the rear entrance, Violie knows, and quickly followed by a second.

Bairre has killed both guards there.

The remaining five men exchange panicked looks before one of them draws his sword, making his way down the aisle. "Stay and cower with the women if you want!" he shouts over his shoulder. "I'm going to fight."

Three of the men follow, leaving one behind.

"Surely you can manage a bunch of Sisters and courtesans well enough, Thomas!" one of the guards shouts at him. "Use the pistol if you have to—we don't need to keep them all alive."

It isn't lost on Violie that Thomas is the youngest of the guards, and nervous. He looks around at the chapel and gives a quick nod, keeping his hand on his pistol.

After the four guards go, leaving only Thomas, Violie screams, doubling over and grabbing at her stomach, though really she's grabbing the dagger hidden beneath her tunic.

"Ow, please, I'm hurt!" she shouts, looking at the guard with wide, tear-filled eyes.

After a brief hesitation, the guard comes toward her, his pistol hanging at his side.

"Sister, are you al—"

Violie doesn't give him a chance to finish the sentence. As soon as he's close enough to reach, she lunges up, embedding the dagger in his stomach.

The guard gasps more than screams as he crumples to the ground at her feet. "Hurry!" she shouts to the stunned women watching her. "There is no time to waste—the rest will be back soon. Untie anyone bound, and anything that can be used as a weapon, take with you."

No one hesitates. Violie helps ungag the woman beside her, who looks at her with thoughtful eyes. "I do hope you've thought this through, child," she says.

Violie doesn't answer, instead crouching down to pry the pistol from the dead guard's hand, holding it and her dagger up to the woman. "Do you have a preference, Sister?" she asks.

"Mother," the woman corrects, eyes darting between the weapons. "Mother Ippoline. And I'll take the dagger."

Violie passes it to her, hilt first. "Be careful with it—it's my favorite," she says.

"Violie!"

Violie turns to find herself in her mother's arms, held tightly to her chest. "You foolish, brave girl," her mother chides, punctuating each word with a kiss to Violie's face. "What in the name of the stars were you thinking?"

"She was thinking to save our lives, Avalise," Mother

Ippoline says. "Though that *does* answer my next question about who, exactly, you are."

"We can have more thorough introductions later," Violie says. "Prince Bairre and King Leopold caused those distractions, and I'm not keen on leaving them to defend themselves alone against fourteen guards."

Half the women choose to stay in the chapel to defend against any returning guards rather than attack, but by the time Violie leads the remaining women and their makeshift weapons—mostly heavy brass candlesticks and pointed tapestry rods—down the halls of the Sororia, it's to find that Bairre and Leopold have managed the bulk of the work.

They fight back to back in the Sororia's entryway, only five guards still standing. Four pistols lie on the floor, bullets spent, Violie assumes, and now they fight with swords instead.

Violie lifts her pistol, taking out three of the guards farthest from Leopold and Bairre with three successive shots, and while the final two are distracted by the shots, Leopold and Bairre take their advantage, dispatching them both.

In the quiet aftermath, Violie's eyes search Leopold for wounds and she feels him do the same to her, but neither of them is hurt, to her relief. He comes toward her, not noticing the movement of one of the guards at his feet—the head guard, she realizes belatedly, just as his hand grabs the hilt of his sword.

"Leo!" Violie shouts just as the guard strikes, arching

upward in a desperate burst of power, sword aimed at Leopold's chest.

Leopold only just manages to jump back, out of reach of the blade's arc, and the guard falls to the floor again with an anguished cry.

Bairre steps forward, sword poised to finish the man off, but Violie holds up a hand.

"Wait," she says, and Bairre pauses, the tip of his blade at the man's chest, just where his heart is. "He seemed to be the leader. I doubt Margaraux told him much, but he may know something."

Bairre looks down at him. There's a smear of blood on his cheek, she notes, though it doesn't seem to be his. The look on Bairre's face is cold, the set of his mouth hard.

"Well?" he asks the man. "This morning my wife was forced from our bed and taken somewhere against her will. Where?"

The guard glares up at Bairre, matching the coldness in his expression, but it shatters the second Bairre leans on his sword, pressing it into the guard's chest, millimeter by millimeter.

The guard screams. "The catacombs!" he shouts. "The empress had them taken to the catacombs!"

Bairre eases up, looking at Violie, who gives a nod.

"I've been there—twice, both at the empress's command. They're far underground."

"Which means Beatriz won't be able to seek assistance from the stars, even if she does live until nightfall," Mother Ippoline says.

Violie closes her eyes. Beatriz's magic was supposed to be their fail-safe, but even that isn't an option. And the only way to the catacombs is through the palace. She doubts they'll be able to waltz in, especially if the empress has put out an alert for the guards to find them.

Someone clears their throat, drawing attention to the front door, left open to the morning sun. Aurelia stands there, hands clasped in front of her and her ermine cloak draped over her shoulders.

"Nightfall isn't necessary," she says, her impassive eyes sweeping across the room, lingering a moment on Bairre.

"Mother?" Bairre asks, bewildered.

"How can Beatriz wish on a star when no stars are out?" Leopold asks.

"One star is," Aurelia says.

"The sun," Mother Ippoline whispers. "Surely, you can't mean . . ."

"It has long been prophesized that one day the stars would go dark," Aurelia says. "And I have since come to be sure that Beatriz would cause it. The sun is what gives all other stars their light—should she wish upon it, the stars would in fact go dark."

"And kill us all in the process," Violie says, shaking her head.

"Should another empyrea attempt it, yes," Aurelia says. "But Beatriz's magic will create it again. From what I've observed of her powers, we would be in darkness for a day, perhaps two. An unpleasant time, to be sure, but no. It wouldn't kill us."

"Would it kill Beatriz?" Violie asks.

Aurelia hesitates. "I suspect so," she says. "Though only the stars can say for certain."

"Then no," Leopold says. "We'll find another way."

But Violie suspects there isn't one. And if she's right, the least they can do is give Beatriz the choice.

"The catacombs are far belowground," she says, looking around. "How could we get sunlight in?"

Bairre reaches into his pocket, pulling out a vial of stardust. "Beatriz gave this to Daphne yesterday—it's from the wish she made for the starshower, and she said it was more powerful than any other stardust. Could that get sunlight into the catacombs?" he asks Aurelia.

"I believe so, yes," Aurelia says. "But we would need to know exactly where they are."

"That," one of the Sisters says, stepping forward from the group, "I might be able to help with."

"Empress Seline," Bairre murmurs to Violie, who looks at the woman with surprise.

She didn't know Empress Seline still lived, let alone that she was so close, but she doesn't have time to dwell on that. If anyone will know the inner workings of the palace, it's the woman who once ruled over it.

"What did you have in mind, Your Majesty?" Violie asks.

# Daphne

The next time someone approaches, lantern aglow, Daphne knows it's her mother before she can see her face—she knows the cadence of her steps, feels the whisper of her presence like a chill against her skin.

The empress doesn't come alone—as she draws nearer, Daphne sees Adilla on one side of her, Cliona on the other, each girl holding a lantern of her own. Daphne searches Cliona's face—cast in high relief in the flickering light of her lantern—but finds no hint there of her true intentions. A thread of doubt winds through her. If she trusts Cliona and is proven wrong, it isn't only she who will suffer for it. Can she really risk so many lives by placing her trust in Cliona?

"No hello for your mother, Beatriz?" the empress asks, coming to stand before them, between Beatriz and Daphne. She sets her lantern on the stone floor at her feet.

"Hello, Mother," Beatriz says, her voice unbothered, but Daphne hears the fear and anger deep beneath the surface. The empress hears it too and smiles.

"I do wish you'd done your duty in Cellaria, darling," the empress tells her. "For your own sake, you understand. I didn't wish for it to come to this, but you've left me no choice."

Beatriz smiles. "You know me, Mama. I simply *must* be difficult. And it simply wouldn't do to die on Cellarian ground."

The empress lets out a hard laugh. "Nigellus told you that, did he?" she asks. "I won't pretend to be surprised. For one with so much power, he was a weak man. As it happens, though, I'm not concerned with the conditions of your deaths."

She reaches into the pocket of her cloak and withdraws two velvet pouches, cinched with gold rope. She empties one just in front of Beatriz's outstretched legs, then empties the second in front of Daphne.

Soil, Daphne realizes, understanding dawning. She understands why Cliona is here, why her mother didn't simply have Pasquale and Ambrose killed. Because she needs them to do what she can't.

"Why not do this in the first place?" Daphne asks her mother. "You could have hired assassins and imported soil and finished us off as infants, if you'd wanted to."

"Is that what you believe me capable of?" the empress says, looking at Daphne with cold eyes. "I raised you, trained you, ensured that you had the very best that your lives could offer you. I acted as a mother to you for sixteen years. Without me and my wishes, none of you would ever have taken a single breath. I gave you your lives."

"And then you washed your hands of us and told yourself that whatever happened to us wasn't your fault," Daphne says. "Did you truly believe that? Or did you only care that no one else thought it was your fault? Sophronia—"

"Sophronia's death was quick and merciful, which was

more than she deserved after betraying me as she did," the empress snaps. "It's more than either of you deserves too, but luckily for you I will be kind."

*Kind.* Not a word Daphne would ever have used to describe her mother, even before understanding what she was capable of.

"So you'll have me killed by a friend who betrayed me?" she asks, cutting her gaze to Cliona, who flinches slightly.

"Under duress, I assure you," the empress says before glancing at Pasquale and Ambrose. "I assume neither of you will willingly kill Beatriz?"

Pasquale laughs. "Never," he bites out.

"Not even to save him?" the empress asks, gesturing to Ambrose.

Pasquale hesitates, but after looking at Ambrose, he shakes his head. "Neither of us is walking out of here alive, no matter what you promise."

"The danger of breaking so many promises, Mama," Beatriz taunts.

"Perhaps," the empress says. "But *your* deaths certainly don't need to be quick or merciful. Which of you will break first, I wonder? To save yourselves or each other from one more moment of agonizing pain?"

Neither Ambrose nor Pasquale answers her.

"You're a monster," Beatriz tells her.

"It's hardly the first time I've heard that, Beatriz," the empress says, shrugging. "I'm afraid it's long since lost its sting. But I'm growing tired of talking." She moves toward Ambrose and Pasquale, intending to begin torturing them. Intending to kill Beatriz first.

"Then begin," Daphne says, drawing her mother's attention. "Begin with me."

The empress looks at her, brows raised in surprise. "Very well, then," she says. "If you insist. Be a good girl and stretch out your legs, will you? That's it, on the Frivian soil."

Daphne feels the dirt underneath her legs, cool against her skin, and then she looks away from her mother and toward Cliona, who approaches with slow, measured steps. Cliona keeps her gaze down, as if she can't bear to look Daphne in the eye as she kills her. She draws her dagger and holds it pointed toward Daphne, ready to strike.

Panic sets into Daphne, flooding her body and drowning out any thought or hope. Cliona isn't looking at her because she's consumed with guilt, because Daphne miscalculated, because Cliona is going to betray her after all and bury that dagger in Daphne's chest.

But then Cliona's eyes snap to hers and something uncoils in Daphne's chest. She twists her wrists, feeling the rope grow taut like a pulled thread. And then she's up on her feet, grabbing the second dagger that Cliona holds toward her, hilt first, and lunging toward her mother, who stumbles back in surprise, throwing her hands up in a paltry defense against cold, sharp steel.

Daphne knows half a dozen places she could strike, but she goes for the chest, the tip of her dagger piercing the skin above her mother's heart without hesitation—until she hears the scream she knows right away is Cliona's, and it constricts around her heart like a snake.

She looks away from her mother's frightened face to see Cliona on the ground, clutching her stomach, crimson staining her gown as Adilla stands over her with a dagger in hand.

The half second of distraction is all her mother needs. She drives the heel of her hand upward and Daphne hears the bones of her nose crack half an instant before pain blinds her and sends her stumbling half a step backward, her grip on the dagger loosening as it drops to the ground with a clang that echoes through the catacombs.

"Daphne!" Beatriz screams. "Behind—"

But it's too late for Beatriz's warning. Adilla grabs Daphne by the elbows, wrenching her arms behind her back and pinning her there, her grip too strong to break free from. Daphne tries all of her tricks from combat training—stomping at Adilla's feet, rearing her head to try to break her nose, throwing her entire body back to catch Adilla off-balance and topple her to the ground. None of it works. Adilla seems to anticipate every move she makes and evade them with ease. But Daphne keeps trying, until she catches sight of her mother, walking toward Cliona, sprawled on the ground and holding her wound.

"Get away from her!" Daphne shouts, but her mother pays her no mind. She picks up Cliona's dropped dagger and crouches beside her.

"It didn't have to come to this," she says with a sigh. Then she takes Cliona's left hand in hers and uses the dagger to cut it off in one clean movement.

# Violie

Empress Seline leads Violie, Leopold, and Bairre to the graveyard outside the Sororia, a maze of tombstones and crypts, many trampled by ivy and cracked by time, but others shiny and new, the dates etched in recently.

"When the castle was built, the emperor and empress at the time had a disagreement," Empress Seline tells them. "The empress was common-born and wanted to be buried with her family, while the emperor understood the need to secure their tombs where they could never be desecrated or robbed. As a compromise, he arranged for the royal crypt to be below the graveyard, connected by a tunnel to the rest of the palace. At this very moment," she says, stopping and looking back at Violie, Leopold, and Bairre, "your friends are below our feet. Deep below our feet, admittedly, but should you dig straight down, I have no doubt you would reach them."

Bairre nods, looking at the vial of stardust in his hands.

"You have to phrase it carefully," Leopold says. "If the catacombs collapse altogether, they're all dead."

"How much sunlight will Beatriz need?" Violie asks Aurelia.

"A single beam should do," Aurelia says. "But will she know it for what it is?"

"She will if I can tell her," Violie says. "Do you have any more stardust—specifically from Friv? If so, I can speak with her."

Aurelia purses her lips. "I don't, only what I gathered in Cellaria," she admits, and Violie feels herself deflate. "But," Aurelia adds, "we have no way of knowing how strong Cellarian stardust is. And given that the stardust will have a personal tie to Beatriz, it might just be enough to work."

Violie smiles. "Then what are we waiting for?" she asks.

# Daphne

*This is it,* Daphne thinks, watching her mother's impassive face as she comes toward her, holding Cliona's severed hand with a dagger aimed at her. *This is how it ends. But stars damn me if I don't fight until the last.* Contrary to what her mother said earlier, she will not die a good girl. She will die a warrior.

She throws herself back against Adilla, driving her boots into her mother's stomach and using the leverage to propel Adilla backward, her head slamming against the marble pillar Daphne was bound to with a crack. Adilla has no choice but to release Daphne's arms, and Daphne wastes no time, snatching a dagger from the ground and stabbing Adilla with it, just where her neck meets her shoulder.

Daphne doesn't pause to watch her die, trusting her work and her aim, instead coming toward Beatriz and slicing through the ropes binding her hands. She tosses the dagger, still dripping with Adilla's blood, to Beatriz, hilt first, and her sister catches it without looking, scrambling to her feet, attention focused on their mother, doubled over and catching her breath.

Daphne grabs Adilla's dagger from its scabbard and

comes to stand beside her sister, both of them facing their mother, still holding the severed hand and the dagger.

The empress straightens to stand, her chest heaving as she looks between Beatriz and Daphne, both approaching her now, armed and unyielding.

"My doves," the empress says slowly, a soft smile curling at her lips. "Surely we can discuss this. I know I raised you to be sensible creatures."

"You raised us to be lambs, blindly awaiting slaughter," Daphne tells her, taking a step forward, then another, Beatriz matching her every move. "Your mistake was in telling us we were lions often enough that we believed it."

"I underestimated you, yes," the empress says, her voice a soothing coo. "But all the more reason for us to work together now, to rule over Vesteria together. I can give you power, more power than you could ever hope for without me."

"I don't want power," Daphne tells her mother.

The empress laughs. "Liar," she bites out. "I know you, Daphne. I know your heart better than you ever could. You're like me—you always have been."

Daphne has thought the same. Once, it felt like a compliment, then it felt like an insult. Now, though, it is simply a fact. She shares a good many traits with her mother—but she isn't her, and that is a choice she has made, one she will always make.

"You," Daphne tells her mother, "are nothing. What power do you think you'll wield when you're dead? What legacy have you left behind? The world will forget you, but I will forget you first. After today, you will never cross my mind again, do you understand?"

Hate shines in the empress's eyes, but Daphne is strangely relieved to see it. After all, it's *real*. Here, in the end, she sees beneath her mother's many masks, at the pain and ugliness and hate that have shaped her.

"I'm not like you," Daphne says, more to herself than her mother. And then she charges at her without hesitation, burying her dagger in her mother's chest, piercing her heart. Daphne watches, centimeters away, as the light leaves her mother's dark brown eyes, the tension sapping from her body as she collapses against Daphne, and Daphne releases her to the ground. Dead.

It's only then that Daphne feels the cold steel, piercing her stomach, the pain a quiet throb, dulled by shock and adrenaline. She looks down and sees the silver hilt of the empress's dagger protruding from her stomach.

"Daphne!" Beatriz screams, reaching her just as Daphne collapses, darkness swarming her vision.

# Beatriz

Beatriz clutches Daphne to her chest, the weight bringing her to her knees. She lays Daphne down gently, trying to focus past her panic, on the dagger sticking out of Daphne's stomach.

"Don't remove it," Cliona says through gritted teeth from a few feet away. She's managed to sit upright, the bloody stump of her wrist wrapped up in the skirt of her gown. She's pale, sweat covering her face in a glassy sheen, but she's alive.

"I know," Beatriz snaps. "Can you untie them?" She nods toward Pasquale and Ambrose.

"Don't worry about us," Pasquale says. "Get help for Daphne."

"From whom?" Beatriz asks. She's sure the guards will be quick to switch sides now that the empress has fallen, but Beatriz knows her sister won't survive the journey upstairs. She looks down at Daphne's slack face, touching her hand to her sister's cheek.

*She can't die*, Beatriz thinks. *Not after all of this. If she does, what is the point of winning? Of saving a world without Daphne in it?*

Cliona moves to crouch beside her, Daphne between them. She examines the wound with a shrewd eye, but when she doesn't speak, Beatriz knows exactly what she sees.

"It's fatal," she says. "Isn't it?"

"Yes," Cliona says, her own voice tight with tears. "Yes, it's fatal."

*It isn't fair,* Beatriz thinks. *None of this is fair.*

"Beatriz," a voice whispers through her mind. Violie.

"Not now," Beatriz snaps.

"Just listen—whatever you're doing, we're coming."

"Too late, unless you have a miracle."

"We do," Violie says.

Beatriz tightens her grip on her sister, holding her tight as Violie tells her the plan they're enacting, giving Beatriz a choice, though Violie doesn't realize the true choice she's giving.

She doesn't need to use magic to destroy her mother—Daphne took care of that. But she can use magic to save Daphne, wishing on the sun to heal her. If she does that, it will cost her the last of her humanity. If she saves her sister, she will die. She knows this deep in her bones.

Looking down at Daphne's face, her expression slack, her chest rising and falling in shallow breaths, Beatriz realizes it isn't a choice at all.

"Do it," she says through gritted teeth.

# Violie

"Beatriz said to do it," Violie tells the others.

Bairre gives a nod, unstoppering the stardust and pouring it out on the back of his hand. It looks like any other stardust Violie has seen before, but she supposes Aurelia knows better than she does about what it can and can't do.

"I wish a hole drilled through the ground, large enough to shine a beam of sunlight on Beatriz without the ground collapsing," he says.

It happens immediately, the ground between them falling away as if through a tiny sinkhole, creating a narrow tunnel, just large enough for Violie to fit through should she be inclined to try it, which she isn't.

"Did it work?" Leopold asks, peering down into the hole.

"I don't know," Violie says before a commotion in the streets outside the graveyard catches her attention. "But I'm sure we'll know soon enough—one of our armies seems to have arrived."

# Beatriz

A beam of sunlight hits Beatriz, bathing her face in warm, golden light.

"What in the name of the stars . . . ," Cliona says, but Beatriz ignores her. She tilts her head toward the light, closing her eyes and feeling it the same way she feels the stars. But it isn't the same, she thinks. The sun doesn't make her blood dance, it doesn't fill her with a giddy energy that tugs at her, begging her to use its magic.

Yet she feels its magic all the same, now that she's searching for it. She feels the thrum of its power echo through her, its warmth enfolding her in its arms. She smooths Daphne's black hair away from her pale face and smiles as tears spill down her cheeks.

"I wish—" she begins, her voice clear and strong.

"Beatriz, no!" Pasquale shouts, fighting against the ropes that still bind him, but Beatriz ignores him. He'll forgive her for this, she hopes. One day.

"I wish my sister's wounds were healed," she says. Then she leans down to kiss Daphne's cool forehead as she reaches to pull the dagger from her stomach.

The air ripples around them, the ray of sunlight flickering

and going dark, leaving only the glow of the three lanterns. Daphne's body tenses in Beatriz's arms as she gasps, bolting upright to sit and looking around with wide silver eyes. Daphne's hands fly to her stomach, feeling for a wound Beatriz knows isn't there.

In the dim light, Beatriz watches as understanding sparks in Daphne's eyes, as her mouth forms a small O and she looks at Beatriz with a mix of awe and horror and fury.

"Beatriz, what did you *do*?" she demands.

A familiar pain stabs through Beatriz's head, sharper than ever before, and Beatriz can feel the energy spill from her body like blood from a wound. The world spins around her, but she focuses on Daphne, even as darkness edges her vision.

"I love you all the way to the stars, Daph," she says, and then she allows the darkness to drag her under.

Sophronia stands before Beatriz, surrounded by the inky black of a starless midnight sky. In some ways, she looks just as Beatriz remembers her, but this Sophronia stands taller, smiles more brightly, and shimmers like she bathed in stardust.

"Sophie," Beatriz breathes, reaching for her and seeing her own hands shimmer with the same incandescence. Sophronia steps into her embrace, holding her tight. Sophronia's body fits against hers, just as it always has, and she even smells the way Beatriz remembers—warm sugar and roses.

"Is this death?" she asks against Sophronia's shoulder. If it is, it's a far better fate than what she envisioned.

"Yes and no," Sophronia says, stepping back to look at

her. "Nigellus pulled us from the stars, Beatriz, and to the stars we must return. You pulled down the sun."

Beatriz remembers that—the beam of light shining down on her face, going dark after she made her wish. "But Daphne survived. She must be furious with me."

"She is," Sophronia assures her with a small smile. "The stars aren't pleased either, though they admire your brazenness."

Beatriz knows she should apologize, but she can't. Daphne is alive, so she has no regrets.

"Aurelia said a piece of me returned to the stars each time I used magic," she says to Sophronia. "That the stars being reborn was actually pieces of me replacing them."

"She was right," Sophronia says. "But to replace the sun itself . . . no piece of you would suffice. In order for a new sun to rise in its place, it requires all of you."

Beatriz suspected this. She knew exactly what it would cost her when she made her wish, and being here, seeing Sophronia again, holding her . . . it's more than she could have hoped for. And yet.

"You aren't ready," Sophronia says, silver eyes searching her face.

"Were you?" Beatriz replies.

Sophronia considers it. "I believe so, yes," she says softly. "Which isn't to say I wouldn't have liked more time. More time with you and Daphne. To grow more with Leopold. To meet new people and try new things and see more of the world. I would have loved all of that. But I'm happy here, watching you and watching the world, seeing things grow from the seeds I planted during my life."

"You planted a lot of seeds," Beatriz says, thinking about how much Leopold changed after marrying Sophronia, and even more after her death. Violie as well. Even defeating the empress—it couldn't have been done without Sophronia's influence months ago. Her seeds were still growing.

"You've planted some of your own," Sophronia tells her. But when Beatriz doesn't answer, she smiles. "But not enough."

Beatriz shakes her head. "Perhaps it never feels like enough," she says.

Sophronia tilts her head. "What would you do?" she asks Beatriz. "With more time?"

Beatriz laughs at the question. "What wouldn't I do?" she asks. "Travel the world, spend more time with Daphne and Pasquale and Ambrose. Ensure that Gisella stays in line. Perhaps kiss Nicolo a few more times."

"Really?" Sophronia asks with a snort.

"Why not?" Beatriz asks with a laugh. "The kissing was quite fun before all that came after it. I wouldn't mind doing it again. But then, I'd likely kiss other people too. Whoever I wanted to, if I had the time. And I would want to make certain that Bessemia is all right, of course. Daphne will be a great empress, I have no doubt, but I'd help her as much as I could—make sure she and Bairre have time for themselves."

"Anything else?" Sophronia asks.

Beatriz looks at her. "I would just do what I wanted—become who I want to be. Isn't that what anyone wants from life?"

Sophronia smiles. "That," she says to Beatriz, inclining her head, "that sums it up well. I did what I wanted and became who I wanted to be and in the end, I was ready to go. But you aren't."

Beatriz's throat tightens, but she forces a smile. "All the same," she says, "here I am, and the sun needs to be reborn."

"It does," Sophronia says slowly, her brow furrowing in deep thought, the way it always used to when she was trying to decipher a particularly challenging code. "But perhaps . . . I could be the sun."

Beatriz watches her mind work—always a fascinating thing to behold. "Can you . . . do that?"

Sophronia nods. "For a little while, yes. It's a star, after all, like any other. But it isn't my place. The sky will call you home someday."

"A little while?" Beatriz asks. "Is that days? Weeks?"

If so, perhaps it would be better to go now, to die with just the taste of life on her lips, before she can take a bite and know all that she will be missing.

Sophronia shrugs. "Oh, I think I can manage to hold it long enough to see you wrinkled and gray. Seven decades. Maybe eight. Nine would be a challenge, but I do enjoy a challenge."

"That's a little while?" Beatriz asks, surprised.

Sophronia laughs, the sound buzzing through Beatriz like champagne bubbles.

"We're stars, Beatriz," she says. "Ninety years is nothing when we have eternity. I'll wait for you, and for Daphne. And I expect you both to arrive with a lifetime's worth of stories when your time comes."

"Sophie . . . ," Beatriz says, reaching out for her sister and taking her face in her hands. "You sacrificed yourself once. I can't ask you to do so again now."

"Sacrifice," Sophronia says, shaking her head and leaning into Beatriz's touch. "I consider it a gift, Triz. After all, how many girls get a chance to be the sun?"

Beatriz laughs. "Well, when you put it like that," she says. "I miss you so much. Daphne does too."

"I know," Sophronia says. "Give her my love and tell her how proud I am of her. And . . . if I could ask you one favor . . ."

"Anything, Sophie," Beatriz says.

Sophronia hesitates. "Tell Leo and Violie that I want them to be happy, that I'm happy they've found each other. That it would hurt me if they let my ghost stand between them."

"I will," Beatriz tells her, then hesitates. "Is it not a bit soon, though?" she asks.

Sophronia shakes her head. "A human lifetime may pass in a blink for us, Triz, but it's all they get. And I won't begrudge them a single moment." Sophronia reaches up to take hold of Beatriz's wrists, easing her hands away from Sophronia's face.

"Go now," she tells Beatriz. "We both have work to do."

Beatriz wants to protest—wants to stay here with Sophronia forever—but it isn't goodbye. They'll see each other again, even if it isn't for ninety years.

"I love you all the way to the stars," Beatriz tells her.

"I love you all the way to the stars," Sophronia echoes.

# Daphne

When the sun disappeared from the sky, chaos ensued, naturally. It didn't help matters that it happened not long before Hapantoile was invaded by not one but two foreign armies, though instead of laying siege to the capital, the Cellarian and Temarinian soldiers aided the panicking Bessemians, helping light lanterns to line the streets and ensuring that each home had enough firewood to last.

Daphne didn't see any of this, but Violie told her about it later, after she led Bairre and Leopold to the catacombs in time to find Daphne holding Beatriz's body, sobbing uncontrollably no matter how Pasquale, Ambrose, and Cliona tried to pull her away.

"She isn't dead," Daphne kept saying, her voice growing more and more hysterical. Some pragmatic part of her believed she was in denial, but a larger part knew it to be true. And when Bairre crouched down beside her and reached for Beatriz, he confirmed it.

"Her pulse is weak," he said. "And her heartbeat is barely there, but she isn't dead."

*Not yet* had been left unspoken, but together, he and

Pasquale carried Beatriz's body out of the catacombs and into the palace, where guards, servants, and courtiers watched them pass in stunned silence.

"Your Highness?" someone asked, the crowd parting to reveal the Duke of Allevue. It took Daphne a moment to realize he was referring to her. "No one can find your mother—people are panicking. The sun—"

"My mother is dead," Daphne told him, her voice sharp. "And if she weren't, the sun would be the least of our problems. It will be temporary, I've been assured. Light candles and have any extras sent into Hapantoile for those who can't afford them. The same goes for firewood."

"D . . . Dead, Your Highness?" he asks, eyes wide.

"Yes," Daphne says. She can't elaborate further, so she leaves it at that. "We also have need of a physician and as much stardust as is available," she adds. She isn't sure either can help Beatriz now, but there is also the matter of Cliona's hand to see to. Cliona, for her part, doesn't complain, merely holding the stump of her arm, haphazardly bandaged with a strip of fabric she tore from her skirt, as she follows Daphne and the others to their chambers.

"Yes, Your Highness," the Duke of Allevue says as she passes him. "I mean . . . Your Majesty."

Daphne barely hears his correction, but she hears the words that come next, spoken by the crowd en masse.

"Long live Empress Daphne."

The words echo in Daphne's mind as they make their way to the rooms. Once, being *Empress Daphne* was her wildest dream—one she would have given everything to see come true. Now it fits poorly, chafing at her skin and making her desperate to tear it off.

She takes hold of her sister's limp hand and squeezes it. *Please be all right, Triz,* she thinks.

Daphne stays at Beatriz's bedside all day and all night—only knowing the difference between the two by watching the grandfather clock that stands in the corner. She keeps hold of Beatriz's hand, her fingers on her sister's pulse. The faint thrum is steady—not strengthening or weakening—but with every breath Beatriz takes, Daphne is filled with fear that this will be the moment it stops altogether.

The physician has nothing helpful to say about her state, having no idea what caused it or what to expect, but he sews up Cliona's arm and the gash in her stomach, using stardust to ensure that both wounds will heal without infection.

Daphne's friends stay with her in groups, but no one knows what to say. Daphne is grateful for their silence—there is nothing she wants to hear, after all, apart from the sound of Beatriz's voice.

She remembers climbing into bed beside Beatriz, and she must doze off sometime after three o'clock in the morning, because suddenly, she feels fingers combing through her hair. She blinks her eyes open to find Beatriz watching her, silver eyes bright in the darkness.

For a moment, neither of them moves or speaks, and then Daphne is holding her sister tight, Beatriz holding her back.

"You're alive," Daphne murmurs.

"It seems so," Beatriz says. "Sophronia sends her love."

Daphne pulls back to look at her. "What are you talking about?" she asks.

Beatriz opens her mouth, then closes it again. She peers past Daphne—to the grandfather clock. "It's morning," she says. "There's no time to explain—wake the others. No one will want to miss this."

Daphne grows more and more annoyed at Beatriz as they climb the spiral staircase that leads to the palace's tallest tower, Leopold, Violie, Bairre, Pasquale, Cliona, and Ambrose behind them. Every time she asks her sister what she's doing, she's met with silence, but she's too curious to turn back now.

When they reach the top of the tower, the cold air kisses their skin, the sky still dark though it's well past dawn. It's the first time Daphne has truly seen it, the effect of Beatriz's pulling down the sun, but it takes her breath away. It isn't only the darkness itself, but the absence of any light at all. No moon visible. No stars. Just infinite black as far as the eye can see.

"So this is what it feels like to see the stars go dark," she says to Bairre.

"It isn't the end of the world, though," he says. "And my mother assures me it's temporary—"

"It is," Beatriz interrupts. "Any minute now . . ."

Daphne frowns. "What do you mean?" she asks.

"It was supposed to be me," Beatriz explains, keeping her eyes on the sky. "The stars I've taken from the sky before, some part of me replaced them, just like Sophronia's star in the Lonely Heart reappeared after she died. But the sun would have required all of me to rebirth—that's why it killed me. Or tried to. But Sophronia took my place."

Daphne frowns. "That's unbelievable," she tells her sister.

"All the same," Beatriz says with a shrug.

It's then that Daphne sees the light—a pinprick of gold against the black sky, a single star. Before her eyes it swells and grows, bathing the sky in pale pinks and blues and lavenders of sunrise, almost blinding in its brightness.

"It's Sophie," Beatriz says, bracing her hands on the ledge of the window and leaning out, offering up her face to the sun's light.

Disbelief still gnaws at Daphne, but she follows Beatriz's lead, leaning out into the light of the new sun, letting it caress her skin. A sob bursts from her lips, and she reaches up to cover her mouth.

"Sophie," she whispers. Because it *is*. She would know her sister's touch anywhere, and she feels the glow of her presence.

The others feel it too, and when Daphne looks around, she sees them staring at the sun with rapt eyes—even Bairre, Pasquale, Cliona, and Ambrose, who never met Sophronia, are entranced at the sight of it, the feel of it.

"Sophronia's the sun," Leopold says slowly.

"Until the day I die, yes," Beatriz says. "But that won't be for some time yet."

Beatriz catches hold of Daphne's hand, and Daphne squeezes it. "She's beautiful," Daphne says. It hurts to look directly at her, but Daphne can't help trying.

From their vantage point, they can see the townspeople pouring out of their homes, courtiers coming to stand in the palace courtyard, all looking up at the sun, pointing and cheering.

"She's perfect," Beatriz adds.

Perhaps it's Daphne's imagination, but she could swear the sun shines brighter now than it ever has before.

# Beatriz

Bessemia mourns its empress, and Daphne and Beatriz play along, dressing in black and arranging a spectacular funeral fit for an empress, a final act as the dutiful daughters, and one they play well. The story they spin is that Adilla murdered her—an unknown girl with unknown motives that may never come to light, but it's a good thing Daphne and Beatriz were there to subdue her before she could hurt anyone else.

The sun disappearing for a day is a harder event to explain, but the title of *saint* that has followed Beatriz from Cellaria helps matters, and when she tells a group of courtiers and palace servants that the stars turned dark after protecting her and Daphne from Adilla, they believe it easily enough.

But there are other questions that are more difficult to answer.

After the funeral, as Daphne, Beatriz, and Violie walk back to the palace together, Daphne brings up the one that's been plaguing her the most.

"Why must I be empress?" she asks them.

Both Beatriz and Violie stare at her. "Are you being forced?" Beatriz asks.

"It feels that way," Daphne admits. "It felt like it was just . . . decided. I suppose when it looked like you would die, I was the only option, but now . . ."

"Do you not . . . want to be empress?" Violie asks.

"Not particularly," Daphne says. "Not anymore. I want to return to Friv."

Beatriz laughs, earning a glare from Daphne. "I'm sorry, but if I'd told you last year you'd be saying that, you would have pummeled me."

"All the same," Daphne says, shaking her head. "I love Bessemia—truly I do—but they deserve better than an empress who feels yoked to the throne."

"Forgive me for saying so," Violie says carefully. "But I don't believe Friv will want you—or anyone—as queen."

"Oh, I know that," Daphne says. "But I do think there's much to figure out there, and it's a diplomatic knot I would very much enjoy untangling."

"With Bairre," Beatriz says, fighting a grin. "Your fingers grazing every so often, just so."

Daphne blushes. "He is my husband," she says.

"He doesn't have to be," Beatriz points out. "Now that Mama is gone—"

"I *will* throttle you if you say another word about that," Daphne says. "I chose Bairre, and he chose me, and Mama has nothing to do with it."

"Fine, then," Beatriz says, lifting her hands. "You want to frolic through Friv with Bairre."

"I don't *frolic*." Daphne scowls.

"Have you told him what Aurelia told me? About his true parentage?" Beatriz asks her.

Daphne shakes her head. "It isn't my story to tell. But I *will* be having a word with Aurelia to convince her to tell him. He deserves to know, and so does Queen Darina. Though I don't think Bairre will ever call her *Mother* after the way she's treated him his whole life."

Beatriz knows that's the right decision, but she's sure it isn't easy for Daphne to keep a secret from her husband, and she feels guilty for sharing the information in the first place; still, she doubts Aurelia would have told Bairre on her own.

"So you don't want to rule Bessemia," Beatriz says, and when Daphne shakes her head, Beatriz glances at Violie. "And you?" she asks. "We could keep up the pretense of you being Sophronia—we could say you were disfigured in a fire and when we healed your face with stardust, you looked different."

Violie laughs, shaking her head. "No offense to Sophronia, but I'm very much looking forward to being called the name my mother gave me again."

"Still," Beatriz says, almost hopefully, "you wouldn't be the first commoner empress of Bessemia, and you'd certainly be an improvement on the last one."

"Flattered as I am by that high praise, I'll have to pass," Violie says.

"Planning on running back with Leopold to Temarin?" Daphne asks. "I'm sure you'd make a fine queen there, too."

Violie opens her mouth, but she closes it again, considering her words carefully before speaking. "Perhaps one day," she says. "But there's a lot to do in Temarin just as Violie.

And you?" she asks Beatriz. "Are you anxious to return to Cellaria?"

"Stars, no." Beatriz snorts. "Even if I didn't believe Gisella would have me assassinated if I tried."

"What will you do, then?" Daphne asks her.

Beatriz doesn't know how to answer. She told Sophronia about all the things she wanted to do, but now that she's here among the living with a wide future in front of her, she doesn't know where to begin.

"You'd make a good empress," Daphne tells her.

"Mama would roll in her grave at the thought of it." Beatriz laughs, shaking her head.

"All the more reason, then," Daphne says. "Empress Beatriz . . . it does have a nice ring to it."

Beatriz can't pretend she doesn't agree, but . . .

"I want to see the world," she tells Daphne. "I want to be able to go to taverns and dance all night. I want to flirt outrageously and kiss more boys than I can count. I don't want a stuffy life, stuck in the palace presiding over council meetings and courting favor at tea parties."

Daphne considers that for a moment. "Friv gets very cold in winter," she says. "I wouldn't mind being in Bessemia for part of the year, helping you rule. Ruling in your stead, should you wish to leave for a while."

"And as much as I love Temarin, Bessemia is my home," Violie adds. "And my mother would never leave, so I'll have to come here to visit part of the year. Should you need any assistance."

"You can't be serious," Beatriz says, looking between them.

"And why not?" Daphne asks. "Being empress is a big job

for one person. You shouldn't have to shoulder the burden yourself."

Beatriz frowns. "I just . . . never thought I would be empress."

"I never thought I would want to live in Friv," Daphne points out.

"I never thought I would fall in love with a king," Violie adds.

"And," Daphne says, waving an arm at the cloudless bright blue sky, and the sun shining down on them, "I don't think anyone ever thought our sister would be the *sun*. But here we are."

When Beatriz doesn't respond, Violie nudges her with her elbow. "Well? Shall we call you Empress Beatriz?"

The more they say it, the more Beatriz likes the sound of it. And she did promise Sophronia she would make the most of her life—how many seeds can she sow as empress?

"Empress Beatriz it is," she says.

# Acknowledgments

I started writing the Castles in Their Bones series in 2018, and finishing Daphne, Beatriz, and Sophronia's story is bittersweet. Working on these books has been challenging in more ways than I expected, but those challenges have been so rewarding, and I'm incredibly grateful for everyone who has given their support, kindness, and hard work to make this series as magical as it is.

Thank you to my agent, John Cusick, for seeing this series through from that first fevered email about an idea I'd had about triplet princess bride spies to the finished series. I am, as ever, grateful for your unwavering support and all the gems that have come from our brainstorming sessions over the years.

Thank you to Krista Marino, my fearless editor, for always helping me dial things up a notch (or five) and giving me the tools and guidance to tell the best story I can. Working with you has made me a better writer, and I'm so grateful to you for that.

Thank you to everyone else at Delacorte Press and Random House Children's Books but especially Lydia Gregovic, Beverly Horowitz, Barbara Marcus, Jillian Vandall,

Lili Feinberg, Jenn Inzetta, Jen Valero, Tricia Previte, Shameiza Ally, Colleen Fellingham, and Tamar Schwartz.

Thank you to my family, as always, for being my rock: my dad, David; my stepmom, Denise; my brother, Jerry; my sister-in-law, Jill. Thank you to my New York family, Jefrey Pollock, Deborah Brown, Jesse, and Isaac.

Thank you to the friends and loved ones who have kept me sane while toiling away on this book: Cara and Alex Schaeffer (and Gwenevere too!), Chris Bridge, Sasha Alsberg, Alwyn Hamilton, Julie Scheurl, Nina Douglas, Katie Webber Tsang and Kevin Tsang, Elizabeth Eulberg, and Kat Dunn. I know I'm forgetting at least one person, so if it's you, I owe you a drink.

And I'd be remiss not to thank my dogs, for all the cuddles and brainstorm walks, without which these books would not be possible.

Finally, thank YOU. For picking up this book and taking Daphne, Beatriz, Sophronia, and all their friends (and enemies) into your heart. It means more to me than I can find the words to express.

# About the Author

Laura Sebastian grew up in South Florida and attended Savannah College of Art and Design. She now lives and writes in London, England, with her two dogs, Neville and Circe. Laura is the author of the *New York Times* bestselling Ash Princess series—*Ash Princess, Lady Smoke,* and *Ember Queen*—and the Castles in Their Bones series—*Castles in Their Bones, Stardust in Their Veins,* and *Poison in Their Hearts*—as well as *Half Sick of Shadows,* her first novel for adults, and *Into the Glades,* for middle-grade readers.

laurasebastianwrites.com